MW01673449

by Rong Rong
作者：融　融
English Editor: Emili Hart
英文编辑：菲颖

SUSU 素素

Memory of a Foreign Student
一个女留学生的回忆

Candle Light Printing LLC
美国烛光出版社

Dedicated to: Sage and Aila: My two granddaughters that bring me great joy.

此书献给我深爱的小孙女Sage和Alia。

"Susu", an international marriage novel published in Beijing, China more than two decades ago, has unexpectedly delighted many girls and women. Many young girls cherish a desire to marry, thus, I have the motivation to republish this novel in English and Chinese with minor corrections and edits.

Thanks to Emili Hart, a young college student who edited the English version.

长篇小说《素素的美国恋情》2001年由中国青年出版社出版，第一版销售一空。之后在美国由发行量数一数二的中文报纸《星岛日报》连载，尤其得到憧憬婚姻的女孩和女士们的喜爱。二十三年后，作者做了少许修改，以双语重版此书。

感谢年轻的大学生菲颖成为此书的英文编辑。

Prologue

The university bustled with vigor as countless students made their way down the boulevard. The summer air was unbearably hot—so hot that it would have been enough to light a match.

It was on this sweltering hot day that I decided to pay a visit to the Registrar's Office. The sun beat down on the three-story building in front of me ominously, making the bricks glisten in the light. It was almost as if the sun had dried up everyone's sweat. Despite sweating myself, I felt no relief from the heat. Instead, I felt like I was suffering from a high fever.

I came from mainland China ten years ago. Even so, I had yet to adapt to the customary air conditioning that was found in every indoor building. As such, when I stepped into the Registrar's Office, I shivered from the sudden drop in temperature. I caught a glimpse of some old newspapers piled up on a chair across the room and felt the urge to wrap myself up in them for warmth. I didn't have the nerve to, though, opting to wrap my arms around my chest to keep myself warm instead.

I took some time to acknowledge the fat woman who received me. From how tight her knitted blouse was, I assumed that she probably had some kind of metabolic disorder. Her upper body looked like undulating mounds from the side. I presumed that she must be eating something because she kept chewing something as she typed away on her computer keyboard.

After I filled out all of the required forms, the fat lady turned to me. "You came late," she told me. "It's highly unlikely that anyone will share a dorm room with you. If you live alone, you'll be required to pay a much higher expense."

At the time, my listening skills in English were very poor. Thinking that she was going to assign me to a "higher" floor, I agreed.

While we were talking, a burst of hot wind came through the door. In rushed a beautiful girl, full-set with a slender figure and blonde hair. Her charming appearance reminded me of a movie star. Her straight blonde hair seemed gilded, I noted, as it glittered under the light. Her eyes were large and looked reminiscent of the grey-blue water of lakes. She was set with well-groomed eyebrows that resembled two small brushes, long and black, finished with a slightly upturned nose and a set of pearly white teeth. Her face was expressive as she talked. She introduced herself as Lisa before apologizing profusely for coming late, explaining that she had some family matters to attend to. She had a sunny demeanor even as she apologized, her eyes smiling

引子

那年夏天，大学的林荫道上，走着不同肤色的学生。空气又干又烫，好像划一根火柴就会着火一般。

我就是在那个时候去报到的。太阳把那栋三层楼的红砖房晒得冒油发亮。阳光好像把人们身上的汗水都吸干一样，我热得流不出汗，发烧一样地难受。

我从中国大陆来，十年前，对于空调和室内外的冷热差异非常不适应。走进注册办公室，我冷得一阵阵哆嗦。对面的椅子上有一摊被丢弃的报纸，我真想一把拽过来裹在身上。可我不敢去拿，只能自己抱住双肩力求暖和一点。

接待我的是一位新陈代谢出了问题的胖女人。她的绿色针织上衣绷得很紧，侧看，好像连绵起伏的山丘模型。她的嘴里一直在吃东西，一边对着计算机打字，一边咀嚼不停。在我填完了所有的表格以后，她对我说，你来晚了，没有人和你合租一个宿舍，费用比原来要高出许多。我当时的英文听力很差，以为安排我住在高楼上。没听懂，居然回答了OK。正说着，外面卷进来一阵热风，一个金发，秀丽，身材苗条的姑娘闪了进来。她的整个形像就像电影演员，金头发像涂了腊似的，又直又亮。眼睛大得好像灰蓝色的湖水一样透明。她的眼睫毛像两把小刷子，又长又黑。鼻尖翘翘的，一口雪白的牙齿，一说话就是满脸的表情。她自报名字：莉莎。一再抱歉地说，因为家里什么事情，来晚了。她的脸上总是挂着笑容，

as she continued.

As Lisa was explaining her situation, the fat woman was still talking to me. "You could rent a room off-campus. It's cheaper, but it may take some time to find one," she advised. She glanced at Lisa. "You could also share a room with her if you want…"

"I hope someone can share a room with me," Lisa broke in. "I don't have much money."

I understood the term "no money". "Same here," I interjected.

The fat woman turned back to me with an incredulous expression. "Are you kidding? You wanted to rent a room alone, and now you say you have no money? Did you come from Japan or Taiwan or something?"

In response to her outburst, I tried to explain myself. I told her that when I paid the tuition, I only had two hundred dollars left in my pocket. I ended up seeking out illegal work to keep myself together. I then turned to ask the fat woman how much I should pay for the housing.

"All of the information is in the brochure. Did you read it?" She asked sternly.

I paused. Since I have to use the English-Chinese dictionary to read the brochure, how could I even read everything in it? I fell silent, mute like a dummy.

Beside me, Lisa gasped. "Nine hundred fifty?" She blurted out.

Her words became slurred in my brain as I suddenly felt weak. My face turned white and my eyes blacked out. I could barely make out Lisa's words as she cried out that I was suffering from heatstroke.

Lisa dashed out of the room and quickly returned, bringing in an ice bag from who knows where. She placed it on my forehead gingerly before saying, "I don't think it'll be suitable for her to live alone. May I share a room with her?" She asked the fat lady who was helping us.

The fat lady rolled her eyes, revealing the whites of her eyes. "Only if she agrees," she says bluntly, referring to me.

When I heard that Lisa wanted to be my roommate, I was elated. Despite my dizzy, weak, and feverish state, I immediately grabbed Lisa's hands as if I had just found my savior. "Yes, yes, yes," I repeated several times, responding with an agreement.

Nine hundred fifty cut in half is four hundred seventy-five per person, I thought to myself. Back then, one dollar was equal to seven yuan, which is the basic unit of Chinese currency. That was still a large sum of money to me, albeit much better than nine hundred fifty.

Upon my response, Lisa held my hands back tightly and shook them warmly. "Thank you! Thank you…" She thanked me repeatedly.

From that moment, we became not only roommates but also friends, to my surprise and happiness.

即便在说“对不起”的时候，眼睛也带着笑意。

她进来的时候，胖女人正在给我解释：你可以自己到校外租房子，价格低一点，但是需要一些时间，等等。她瞟了莉莎一眼，说，如果你想和她分租的话……。

莉莎马上接话说，我希望有人和我合租，我没有很多钱。我听懂了“没有钱”。我说，我也是。她说，你开玩笑吗？一人独住一个套间，还说没有钱？你从日本来还是台湾？我吓了一跳。付了学费，我口袋里只剩了二百美金。我的生活费还要靠打黑工去赚呢！我转身问那个胖女人：宿舍究竟要付多少钱？她说，都在文件里，你没有看到吗？那时我看文件要查英汉字典，哪能看得那么仔细？我哑巴吃黄连，无话可说。莉莎接口说，九百五。我脸色一白，眼睛一黑，昏过去了。

莉莎大喊：她中暑了！

她飞奔出去，不知道从哪里搞来了一个冰袋，敷在我的前额。一边说，我认为她不适合一个人独住，让我分租那个套间，可以吗？

胖女人翻出了两个白眼珠，说道，如果她允许你……。

我其实没有真的昏过去，是头晕，身上很烫，必须合上眼睛。一听到莉莎要和我一起租房，我马上拉住了她的手，像找到了救兵一样，YES，YES，说了好几遍。心里想，这九百五，现在削掉了一半，变成了四百七十五，刚来的时候，一美金等于七元人民币，对于我来说，那是多么大一个数目啊！

莉莎握紧了我的手，摇了又摇，“谢谢！谢谢！”，说个不停。我们就从那时候开始，歪打正着地做了朋友。

Chapter 1

Lisa had a car, so we ended up traveling to the dorm together. Once we had arrived, I helped her move her belongings piecemeal into the building and took a moment to examine my new surroundings.

The dorm was classy—similar to the hotels in my country—with thick walls and wide corridors. As Lisa and I walked down the hall, I noticed a public laundry room, a pay phone, a soft drink vending machine, and an elevator, which we used to get to our room on the second floor.

I followed Lisa down the corridor until we made it to room 205. "Here we are," she remarked, opening the door swiftly.

Upon entering the room, we were immediately met with a soft carpet under our feet. The living room in front of us was furnished with a comfortable-looking sofa and a coffee table. The bathroom already had towel racks and a linen closet. There were two bedrooms, both of which included a double-sized bed, a closet, a desk, and a shared balcony that overlooked countless pine trees and lush green lawns. I was overwhelmed. I didn't realize how much better it would be compared to my home in mainland China.

Lisa quickly disappeared into her room, busy with her things. Unable to offer my help, I walked into my room, still bewildered by the lavishness of the dorm. This was the room that I rented for almost five hundred dollars a month! That was equivalent to three thousand yuan a month, or one hundred yuan a day! Back in China, I couldn't even afford to spend one hundred yuan a month on food. How much did I even make in a year?

The more I thought about it, the more I felt like this dorm was a luxury for me and that I shouldn't live in such a place. I started to feel sick from thinking of the days when I would work laboriously in the countryside.

I tried calming myself down by laying on the bed. It was too soft. My body sank into the mattress uncomfortably, as I had hurt my back while working in the countryside. The longer I lay there, the more uncomfortable I felt, but I was too tired to acknowledge it, letting my body relax into the mattress further until I fell asleep.

When I woke up, I was covered with a thin blanket. Glancing outside, I noticed that the streetlight outside had already lit up. I groggily dragged myself up and turned on the light, still feeling as though I was in a dream.

Upon turning on my light, I heard a light knock on my balcony door. It was Lisa. She carefully walked into my room through the glass door on the

第一章

莉莎有车，载我去看了宿舍。我帮助她，把车里零零散散的行李搬了进去。

这个宿舍真是高级。就像国内的酒店一样，墙很厚实，走廊很宽。一路走过去，我看到了公共洗衣房，投币电话，饮料自动售货机。我们住在二楼，有电梯。莉莎手里拿着钥匙，到了205室，她说，这就是了。我们一进门，就踩上了软绵绵的地毯。客厅里有沙发和咖啡桌子。厕所里，有毛巾架和壁橱。两个卧房，合用一个长阳台。外面是高大的松柏和绿色的草坪。每个房间里都有一张双人床，有壁橱，还有写字台。天啊，比我在中国的家不知道要好多少倍！

莉莎进了自己的房，不停地忙碌。我插不上手，就进了另一房间。这就是我花将近五百美金租来的房子呵！三千多人民币一个月，一百多元一天呵！我在中国的时候，一个月都吃不了一百块钱！我一年的工资有多少？我越想越觉得奢侈，觉得自己不应该住在这种地方。我不由地想起了以前在农村的岁月，心里很不好受。

我往床上一躺，床太软，身体陷了进去。我的背在农村干活时受过伤，不能睡席梦思。我越躺越觉得不对劲。我就这样睡着了。

当我醒过来的时候，外面已经亮起了路灯。我的身上盖着一条薄薄的毯子。我打开灯，好像仍旧在梦里一般。这是在什么地方？

莉莎正在阳台上，看见灯亮了，就来敲门。她从阳台那个玻璃门进来，问我感觉如何？我拢了拢散在脸庞的乱发，看着身上的毯子感激地说：好多了，谢谢你！

balcony and asked me how I was feeling.

As I straightened out my disheveled hair, I glanced down at the blanket that I was using. Lisa must have put it on me while I was sleeping. "I feel much better now," I told her gratefully. "Thank you!"

"That's good," Lisa replied. "By the way, where's your luggage?" She asked.

"At my friend's house," I answered. "I'll call them to bring it over."

"I can drive you there instead," Lisa proposed. "But do you want supper first?"

Upon Lisa's mention of food, I realized that I was admittedly a bit hungry. However, to save money, I declined. "I'm not hungry," I told her. "Did you have supper yet, Lisa?"

"I did," Lisa answered. "In that case, let's go get your luggage. I have a date tonight!"

A date? 'We have already spent so much money,' I thought to myself. If we goof around instead of studying hard, how could we expect to have a hopeful future?

My train of thought paused here. I suddenly felt like I was getting old. Back in China, those words were said by our elders; maybe it was because the burden of life was on them. Young people never knew such sorrows. When we face our responsibilities, however, our hearts grow old, our words resemble those of our elders, and we become old ourselves, too. At this moment, I realized that Lisa's tuition was probably paid by her parents.

As Lisa drove me to my friend's house, I felt my hunger growing. My friend's house was a long distance from the university, located on the other side of the mountain. When we arrived, my body felt drained from hunger. I recalled the times when at home, even leftover foods were a delicacy. The memory brought on a sudden wave of homesickness as I realized how far away from home I was. Even worse was the fact that I was alone, which meant that I had to take care of everything by myself. The revelation made me feel even more lost and lonely.

The friends who kept my luggage were a couple who were also students. Their aunt in China was a mutual friend of my mother. They were kind enough to pick me up from the airport and receive me into their home for several days, even though my relationship with them was cordial at best. I recalled going out to town with them to learn some things about American culture and food while I was coping with the jet lag from my flight. As a show of appreciation, my mother had bought expensive gifts for them, including a pair of gold rings and some traditional Chinese tonics, neither of which they needed. They must prefer cash, I thought to myself.

To save money on rent, my friends decided to live far away from the university. They had an old car, which they used to get to class. Gas money cost less than the extra rent they would have paid had they lived closer to the school, although it meant that they had to sacrifice a lot of time to get there in the first place. They couldn't exchange time for money, so they didn't particularly care for the gifts.

The husband of the couple had gone to work at a restaurant. His wife asked us if we had supper, and I responded that we had. Fortunately for me,

她说，你的行李在哪里？

都在朋友的家里。我说，我打电话请他们送来。

莉莎说，我开车送你吧，要不要先吃晚饭？

我其实是有点饿了。但是，为了省钱，我说，我不饿，你吃了吗？

莉莎已经在学校的餐厅了吃了饭。她说，那么我们就走吧！我晚上还有约会呢！

约会？我心里想，花了那么多钱，不好好读书，三心二意的，怎么会有出息？想到这里，我觉得自己好像老了许多。这些话，在中国的时候，都是长辈们说的。可能是因为负担在他们身上吧！年轻人不识愁滋味。现在，当我们面对自己的责任时，心也老了，话也老了，人也老了。我估计莉莎的学费是家长负担的。

朋友家住在很远的山背面。我们开到那里时，我已经饿得有点发慌了，身体好像被掏空了似的。这个时候，我真想家呵！没有家，什么都要靠自己，令人心寒！想起在家的日子里，哪怕剩饭剩菜都是美味佳肴！

朋友是一对大学生夫妇，他们在国内的姨妈是我母亲朋友的朋友。那么老远拉过来的关系，他们还是接受了我。到机场接我，临时让我住了几天，解决时差的不适，同时，带我去了解了一些美国的食品消费。母亲买了很贵重的礼物：一对金戒指和一些中药补品送他们，其实并不是他们需要的。他们一定更喜欢现金。这对夫妇为了省房钱，住得离学校很远。但是，他们有一辆破车，算下来汽油费比房钱便宜。这些便宜中，不包括多花费的时间，但是，在时间不能换钱的时候，他们也就不在乎了。

朋友到餐馆打工去了。他的太太问我们吃了没有？我说，吃了。幸亏莉莎听不懂中国话，否则，我的谎言一眼就会被识穿。我们把两个沉重的箱子装上车，告别了他们就走了。

回来的路上，路过一家出售隔夜面包的商店，我想请莉莎停一停，进去买一个面包。中国学生一到这儿，都打听买便宜货的消

Lisa didn't understand Chinese; otherwise, she would have known that I was lying. We quickly loaded my two heavy suitcases in the car before saying goodbye to my friend. Then, Lisa and I began our drive back to the university.

On our way back, we passed a store that sold bread. When Chinese students arrived here, the first thing they did was see which stores had the best deals and bargains for food. It was this particular store that had the cheapest bread, hotdogs, eggs, and ripe fruits in stock. I wanted to ask Lisa to make a stop here so I could buy some bread, but I bit my tongue both out of respect for her date later and to save face. I didn't want to look cheap in the eyes of Americans.

Once we arrived back at the dorm, I gave Lisa five dollars for gas money. She took it apathetically. 'Maybe she believed that I came from a wealthy family,' I thought. That couldn't be further than the truth, though. I can't even afford to buy a bicycle, let alone a car!

Lisa then went out for her date while I stayed in my room to sort out my belongings. I put my everyday underwear into the big drawer and my toiletries in the cabinet in the bathroom. While sorting through my makeup box, I found a bag of Chinese plum candies. Maybe it was from someone in my family who knew that I loved sweet-and-sour candies, or maybe it was someone who thought that it was something that I could give to my American friends. I couldn't recall.

Although I meant to unpack my two largest suitcases after putting my toiletries away, I was too hungry to stop myself from tearing open the bag, stripping two of the candies, and stuffing them into my mouth. As soon as I started eating them, the doorbell rang with a high-pitched "ding-dong".

I figured that it was Lisa returning home for something. Expecting her, I went and opened the door. To my surprise, Lisa wasn't at the door; instead, standing in front of me was a white man wearing a faded yellow shirt and a pair of sunglasses, looking like a skunk from a movie scene. Upon seeing him, I was so startled that I almost passed out for the second time that day, so I opted to lean on the doorframe for support while greeting him.

The man asked me something, but I couldn't understand what he was saying. He asked me if Miss so-and-so was here.

"No," I responded.

The man then asked me where she had gone.

"No," I repeated.

He continued to ask me questions, and my answer to all of them was a resounding "no". Maybe my pronunciation wasn't very clear since I was speaking with a couple of candies in my mouth. Regardless, the man seemed to understand me. He thanked me politely and left.

As soon as the man left, the high-volume speakers on the lower floor began to blast off. The bass of the speakers made the floor under my feet tremble as if there was an earthquake. Suddenly, a group of men and women came into the building, making such a loud racket that I thought the whole dorm might crumble down.

I couldn't believe how such a great commotion could take place in such a beautiful building. It was at this moment that I told myself that I wanted

息。最便宜的食品都在这家商店出售。面包和热狗，鸡蛋和熟透了的水果。但是，我想到莉莎晚上有约会，不要耽搁她的时间，更为了面子，不想让美国人瞧不起，没有让她停车。回到宿舍，我还给了她五美金，作为汽油费。

她竟然也心安理得地拿走了。我心里想，可能莉莎真是认为我很有钱呢！实际上别说汽车我连自行车也买不起呀！

莉莎外出约会了，我在宿舍里整理箱子。我把一些必须用的内衣放进了大抽屉，把牙刷牙膏等日用品取出来，准备放到厕所装饰橱里去。突然我在化妆品的盒子里发现了一袋中国的话梅糖。可能是家里什么人知道我爱吃这种酸中带甜的硬糖，也可能是谁，认为这种糖有中国特色，可以当礼物在美国送人？反正，在带来的两个中国最大号的箱子里，究竟装了些什么，自己并不很清楚。我正饿得不行，马上撕开糖袋，连剥了两粒，一把塞进嘴里。正在这时，“叮当”一声，门铃响了。

我以为是莉莎回来了，完全没有戒心地开了门。结果，站在门口的是一个白人男子，晚上还戴着太阳眼镜，流里流气的，就像电影里的坏人一样。我吓得差点儿昏过去，只觉得眼前一阵发黑，扶靠在门框上。那个男人问我的话，我都听不懂，或者说，简直进不了我的耳朵。他问我，某某小姐在吗？我答：No。他说，她去了哪里？我说，No。所有的问题，我都回答No。可能是因为嘴里含着两颗话梅糖的关系，这个No字不很清晰，给了这个男子想像的余地。他好像都听懂了似的，很有礼貌地谢了谢我，走了。

这个男人刚走，楼下的高音喇叭响了起来，脚下的地板好像地震一样，抖了又抖，随着，就是男女吵架的嘶叫声，好像要把整栋楼都掀翻了一样。这么漂亮的一栋建筑，里面怎么这样乌烟瘴气？就是从那个时候开始，我作出了离开这个鬼地方的决定。我心里想，四百七十五美金，还要受这个洋罪！我不给吓死也要被逼疯，还不如以前下乡时住的芦苇茅屋安全。我真想大哭一场，发泄一下上当受骗的冤屈。

to leave this hellish place. I paid four hundred and seventy-five dollars, yet I got this kind of suffering in return. If I wasn't already scared to death, then I would have gone crazy. It would be safer to live in a thatched hut instead of this diabolic place. I desperately wanted to have a good cry and vent out all of my sufferings, feeling as though I was cheated out of my money.

To my surprise, Lisa returned to our dorm room early. Upon seeing my suffering expression, she stared at me for a long while. I felt embarrassed under her gaze and gave her a wry smile.

"Susu," Lisa spoke quietly. "You look more beautiful at night than during the daytime. Your body language is full of the charm of an Oriental woman," she finished, leaning back on the sofa with one hand on her cheek as if imitating my posture. Her eyebrows and eyelids drooped as she did so, and I couldn't help but laugh.

"Your date ended so soon?" I asked.

Lisa sighed. "I waited for over half an hour and my date didn't show up," she replied. "Forget about it. Let's go have a good time by ourselves."

"How?" I asked.

"Don't you hear the party downstairs?" Lisa answered playfully. "We can drink, dance, make new friends…"

'Oh, so she wants to get me into trouble,' I thought to myself. I wasn't in the mood for that. "I'm tired," I responded. "Why don't you go yourself?"

"Oh, come on," Lisa fussed. "You took an afternoon nap today. You should go out and relax! Don't be shy," she encouraged. "We're all new here. Don't miss your chance to get familiar with the people on campus." She took my hands and led me out of the door.

I had no choice but to follow her, wobbling out of the room.

莉莎回来了。她见我满脸委屈的样子，微笑着注视了我好久。我被她看得不好意思，只好以苦笑来应付。莉莎说，素素，你到了晚上比白天更漂亮。你的肢体语言多么带有东方女性的魅力。说着，她靠在沙发上，一手托腮，垂下眉毛和眼睛，就像演戏一样，学我的样子。我忍不住笑了起来。

我说，你的约会已经结束了？这么快呵？

她说，我等了他半个多小时，没有来。算了，我们自己玩。

我问，玩什么呀？

她说，楼下不是在开PARTY吗？喝酒，跳舞，交结新朋友……。

我心里想，她是要拖我下水呢！我哪有心思玩呵？便说，我累了，你自己去吧！

她说，你刚才睡了午觉，应该出去放松放松。不要怕陌生，大家都是新来的，通过Party，相互介绍认识，这么好的机会，不能错过呵！说着就拉着我的手往外走。

我无可奈何，跌跌撞撞跟着她出了门。

Chapter 2

Lisa led me down the crowded hallway downstairs, where people were eagerly twisting their bodies to the beat of the music blaring through the speakers. Long tables were placed by the windows, stocked with various refreshments such as biscuits, buns, drinks, beers, fruits, and practically anything else you could think of.

Lisa handed some money to a dark-skinned student and turned to me with that same cheery smile that she seemed to always wear. "It's on me," she said. "Have a good time."

As Lisa focused her attention elsewhere, I couldn't help but notice how underdressed I was for the party. I was only wearing a striped black-and-white tight-knitted vest, plain jean shorts, and a pair of casual flip-flops. Lisa was also dressed casually for her date, wearing a simple black dress that outlined her graceful angel-like figure.

All eyes turned to Lisa like searchlights as soon as she began to dance in the crowd. Taking advantage of the fact that nobody was looking at me, I began to stuff my empty stomach. I first ate a slice of cake and washed it down with a glass of orange juice. Then, I moved towards the watermelon, savoring the sweetness of each bite.

While eating, I watched Lisa dance in the crowd, sometimes dancing with boys and other times dancing on her own. Her movements were so elegant; her body formed various curving lines as she danced, all of her limbs swaying with unbelievable coordination and grace. Not long later, though, she disappeared further into the crowd until disappearing from my line of sight.

I was in high spirits, continuing to enjoy the refreshments that were so meticulously lined up along the tables. Someone asked me to dance and I accepted their request, dancing with them before retiring back to the refreshment tables for some more orange juice. I was not shy to talk to strangers when they approached me, sometimes nodding at their words or exchanging a few polite words with them.

As I continued to chat with the people around me, a young man approached me. He introduced himself as a new philosophy professor at this school. Since I was taking a philosophy class this semester, I continued to talk with him. He seemed to be well-versed in Chinese culture and even had some knowledge about Laocius, Chuancius, Confucius, Mencius, and other Chinese philosophers. Though I did my best to listen to him, I wasn't able to pick

第二章

楼下，乐声大作，走廊上都是人，有的扭动身体，有的尽兴喝酒。靠窗边，摆着一张张长桌子，上面都是吃的东西，饼干啦，小面包啦，饮料啦，啤酒啦，还有水果等等。

莉莎给了一个黑人学生几张钞票，满脸笑容地回头对我说，我请客，你好好玩。

我庆幸自己没有作什么打扮，上面穿一件黑白条紧身针织背心，下面穿一条牛仔西式短裤，脚上是夹趾拖鞋。莉莎虽然也穿得随便，但是，毕竟是为约会准备的行装，一件黑色的简易连衣裙，把她优美的体形勾画得如仙女一般。莉莎一进人群就跳起舞来，吸引了许多探照灯一般的目光。我呢，趁机把肚子填包了，一边吃甜饼，一边喝桔子水，还吃了许多西瓜，这里的西瓜真甜！

开始的时候，我还能看到莉莎。有时候，她和男人跳，有时候，她独自一人跳。她的舞姿很美，四肢和身体组成弯弯曲曲的线条，过渡和结合得天衣无缝。后来，她在我的视野里消失了。

我吃饱了喝足了，精神饱满。有人请我跳舞，我就跳一会儿。然后退到窗边去喝桔子水。我也敢于和陌生人打个招呼，点点头，聊几句。聊天的时候，有一个男人，自我介绍是这个学校的哲学老师，年纪很轻，才来工作。我正好也选了哲学课。我们就聊了起来。他好像对中国蛮了解的，老庄孔孟的，也能说不少。我只听他说，没有全部听进去。但是，我记住了他的姓名。不知道是因为他可能成为我的老师，我对他重视了一些，还是因为别的我不知道的

up everything that he said. However, I made an effort to remember his name: Charlie Thomson. Since there was a possibility that he would be my future professor, I made sure to pay some special attention to him.

As our conversation died down a little, Charlie invited me to dance, to which I accepted. His hand made its way down my lower back, gently leading me away from the tables to dance. I followed him in time to the music, turning and moving my body to his lead. Compared to other couples at the party we were rather civil and almost professional, keeping a comfortable distance between each other as we danced. Charlie was a head taller than me, I noticed; in fact, my nose was on the same level as his upper chest. I couldn't help but smell the cologne he had put on, and I had to admit that it was quite a nice fragrance.

Then, someone else asked me to dance, to which I accepted once more. After that, I drank some more orange juice. Charlie stood aside the whole time, no longer asking me to dance with him; however, he didn't ask anyone else to dance either. He was simply observing the crowd, watching people as they mingled with each other.

I didn't know how much time had passed until Lisa returned, wiping sweat from her brow gracefully as her lips positioned themselves into a pout. She seemed angry.

"I found him," Lisa seethed through gritted teeth.

"Who?" I asked.

"David," she replied harshly.

Before I could ask who this 'David' person was, Lisa nudged me and told me to look towards my left. There, I saw a man and a woman kissing.

He seemed familiar. Wasn't he the man who had knocked on my door? I began to study him and noticed that he was wearing a faded yellow T-shirt—the same one that the man from earlier was wearing. This guy was the one who knocked on my door earlier!

Before I could bring it up, Lisa began to complain with tears in her eyes. Apparently, David was supposed to be her date tonight, but instead, he was here—partying with another girl instead!

My thoughts quickly jumbled up into a giant mess. Lisa's date, that skunk of a man who knocked on my door, and this man kissing the woman before my eyes—they were all the same person! What kind of logical sense did that make? Who knew that this date that Lisa missed would end up in the beginning of another love story?

Lisa's complaints started to fade. Heartbroken, she understandably went back to her room by herself, leaving me behind. I stayed in the hallway, right at the edge of the party's center. When Lisa left, I suddenly had an urge to go further into the crowd and take a look.

I don't remember what I was thinking at that time. Maybe the exciting atmosphere of the party made me curious about what was lying further inside, or maybe Lisa's dating riddle gave me a spike of adrenaline. Who knows—maybe I had just eaten too much sugar (I later learned that sugar is a stimulant). Regardless of what it was, I was bold enough to push into the crowd as a result of my curiosity.

原因，我知道他叫查里．汤姆斯。查里邀请我跳舞，他的手搭在我的腰上，随着音乐，我配合他，转身，弯腰，和他一起向前后退，跳了好几分钟。但是，我们都很文雅，不像其他人那样粘在一起。

他比我高一个头，我的鼻子正对着他敞开的胸口，他是喷了香水的，气味不错。

后来我被别的男学生邀请去跳舞，跳完了，我再喝桔子水。查里一直站在旁边，没有再来邀请我。但是，他也没有邀请别人跳舞，此刻的他，在我的眼睛里，如同一个旁观者，凑凑热闹而已。

不知过了多少时候，莉莎一边擦汗，一边走到我身边，嘴巴翘得老高，生气地说，我找到他了。

我说，谁呵？

戴维德。她答道。

我正想问谁是戴维德，莉莎拉拉我的手，示意我朝左前方看。那里正有一对男女抱在一起亲吻。

哎哟，那个男人不就是刚才来敲门的人吗？他穿的鹅黄体恤，一眼让我认出来了。我还没有来得及说，莉莎眼泪汪汪地抱怨起来。原来戴维德就是今天要约会的男朋友。他在这里出现了。

我的脑子一下子混乱了起来。莉莎的男朋友，那个流里流气的男人，眼前和女人亲嘴的男人，原来就是一个人！这里面是怎样的逻辑关系呵！又有谁知道这场错过的约会不会不引出一场美好的爱情故事？

莉莎伤心极了，顾不上我，独自回房去了。

我一直在走廊上玩，在PARTY的外围，莉莎走后，我突然萌生了一种要进去看看的欲望。我当时究竟是如何想的，现在都不记得了。我是被环境吸引过去的，也可能是因为莉莎留下了那个谜，也可能是吃了太多的糖份（很久以后，我才知道糖是一种兴奋剂）。我胆大无穷，好像探险一样地走了进去。

Despite the flashing of the colorful lights above me, it felt dark. Some people were scattered all over the floor, looking as though they were buried alive in a pit from some cheap horror movie. Others were either standing up straight, aimlessly staring at the ceiling, or lying down together in heaps of bodies. However, they all shared one similarity—they all seemed like they were losing their minds in some way or another. Some were as drunk as a sow and others were acting as crazy as a rabbit.

I continued to push my way towards the living room despite the countless bodies that littered the floor under me, but I didn't stop. Someone beckoned for me to come over, and another person wanted to shake hands with me. I just ignored them, too intent on reaching the living room to acknowledge them.

Suddenly, I felt myself slip into the arms of a stranger carelessly. I didn't have time to react before someone held my waist from behind and put me over their shoulder like a sack of rice. I let out a cry as I felt myself getting carried away—ignoring the shouts and whistles that followed—but this didn't deter the person from hurrying out of the room at all.

"Fool. You're a foolish girl," the person carrying me mumbled, and I immediately recognized the voice along with the smell of a rather familiar cologne. It was at this moment that I realized who was holding me.

Charlie.

Though my arm ached from his tight grasp, I wordlessly let him carry me until I realized that he had dropped me, ungracefully landing on the lawn of my dorm building.

In a fit of anger, I quickly got on my feet and instinctively dusted the dirt off my clothes. I wanted to call him—Charlie—names, but my English was so poor that I didn't know any curse words. I wanted to strike him, but something held me back, so I glared at him as coldly as I could instead. If looks could kill, then he would be dead. This was the most confident I had felt ever since I had come to America, I thought. I had every reason to think that I was in the right here. Even though Charlie might become my teacher, I wanted to teach him a lesson instead—a lesson about basic human respect.

As I calmed myself down, I took note of Charlie's rather pitiful state. He was gasping, wiping sweat off his brow with the back side of his hand desperately, completely and utterly speechless during that moment. However, his eyes showed honesty and tenderness as he looked at me. He was hardly afraid of my glare; if anything, he seemed to be welcoming me as he held my gaze. It was as if I was fire and he was water; he somehow quenched my fit of anger.

Feeling my anger start to fade entirely, I found myself rather amused at the whole situation instead. I started to laugh, and soon enough, Charlie found himself laughing quite loudly as well. We laughed until we were doubling over and holding our stomachs, and I felt the gravity of my stress float away for that brief moment.

That summer night was cool. The breeze glided over the trees' canopy and gently, almost affectionately, ruffled my hair. With a smile still wide on my face, I raised my head to look at the sapphire sky above me. The stars and

很暗，微弱的灯光五颜六色。到处都是人，包括地上，像电影里的“活人坑”一样，一条条躯体，有的弯曲，有的笔直，有的面朝天，有的叠在一起。坐着的，立着的，躺着的，都好像失去了理智，或者烂醉如泥，或者疯狂如魔。我从客厅进去，几乎无插足之地，但是，我没有停止。几次踉跄，差点儿被绊倒，我还是没有停。有人向我打招呼，有人想拉我的手。我都不在乎。突然，一个不小心，我跌入一个陌生人的怀抱。我居然没有反抗。正在这时，有人从背后拦腰抱住了我，把我扛在肩上，像米袋一样，扛起了就朝外走。我因吃惊而大叫一声，众人跟着起哄。但是，我马上听到了一个熟悉的声音：傻瓜，你是傻瓜丫头。我还闻到了熟悉的香味，我已经知道了扛我的是谁。我的腹部压在他的右面肩膀上，左手臂被他捏得生疼。我居然驯服地让他把我扛着走了好长一段路，直到宿舍大楼外面，被扔了下来，屁股坐在了草坪上。

我一骨碌爬起来，本能地拍掉身上的泥土，心里有一股说不出的怒火。我想骂他，没有足够的语言。我想谢他，觉得太便宜。我瞪圆了眼睛，盯着他看，像利剑一样直刺他的眼睛。我觉得这是我来美国十几天以来最有自信的时刻，我觉得自己有一肚子的道理，应该好好地教训一下这个能成为我老师的美国人。

他喘着粗气，用手背抹去额头上的汗水，一时无言。但是，他的眼睛是真诚的，眼光是温柔的，他迎接着我的目光，好像在欢迎我一样。他是不怕利剑的，他是喜欢利剑的，如果我是一盆火，那么，他就是一盆水，他把我的怒气全部浇灭了。我忍不住“咯咯”地笑起来。他也朗声大笑。

我们俩就这样相隔三四步远的距离，面对面地大笑。

夏天的夜晚清凉清凉，微风从树叶间滑过来，撩起了我的头发。我昂首遥望蓝宝石一样的天空，只觉得满天的星星都在笑，月芽儿也在笑。这一切，多么熟悉，多么美丽！突然间，我仿佛回

moon seemed to be smiling down on me, too. All of it just felt so familiar and so beautiful! For the first time since I had arrived in America, I felt truly content, feeling as though I was back in my hometown under this dazzling diamond sky.

To keep these special emotions to myself, I refrained from telling Charlie about it. I giddily wished him a good night and returned to my dorm room, eager to tell Lisa the whole story—only to find that she had shut herself in her room. Perhaps she was trying to sleep after what had happened with her date.

Since I was better at writing in English than I was at speaking it, I decided that I should write down what had happened in my diary. Perhaps I could even use this experience to write an essay on what I saw in America!

It didn't really matter what I chose to do, though. All I knew was that I absolutely had to write it down. Once I did, I would remember it. After all, today was my first day at an American college and the mark of the beginning of my life in a foreign land; what better day to start record-keeping my experiences? It was a perfect start.

I couldn't believe how happy I was feeling. Hours earlier in the daytime, I felt as though I was sick, overwhelmed by the new environment and lack of money in my pocket, but now my heart was engulfed with a feeling of gratitude. I was grateful to my first American friend, Lisa, and my second American friend, Charlie. Although our interactions were short and simple, both friendships felt as though an artist's brush had made its way onto my life's canvas and painted beautiful bright colors onto it.

Despite being my same self without much money in my pocket, I was no longer afraid of what would happen in the near future. I wasn't worried about where my breakfast tomorrow would come from and I wasn't even worried about next month's rent. All of these things suddenly felt manageable in my head. For the first time, I believed that I had the ability to find a job. I was confident that I could make my current bitter life into a sweet one. Maybe this change was a result of my varying moods, but I didn't really care.

I quickly wrote down all of my thoughts down on a piece of paper. I wasn't sure where all of my English vocabulary came from, but I couldn't help but feel impressed as I reread my work. I was so intoxicated with my writing that it felt like I was drinking wine.

Maybe I was still affected by jetlag, I thought, turning my head to look outside briefly. As the sun approached the horizon at the breaking point of dawn, I was overcome with drowsiness and tumbled down onto the floor, completely asleep.

到了家乡一样。为了保住这份美好的感受，我什么话都没有对查里说，扭身跑回了宿舍。我急着想把故事告诉莉莎，可是她已经关门进入了梦乡。我想，自己的口语本来就不好，要说也未必能说清楚和说准确，不如把事情都写出来，作为日记？回家作业？美国见闻？都可以。无论如何，我必须把它写出来，只要写到了纸上，就有了记录，有了保存的价值。这是我在美国大学的第一天，也是我异乡生活的开端。真是一个好开端啊！

我想到白天的时候，我像病人一样，像一个落魄的穷光蛋，可是，现在我多么快乐！原来我下定了决心要从这里搬出去，现在，我心里充满了感激。我感激我的第一个美国朋友莉莎，第二个美国朋友查里。虽然只有几分钟几小时的接触，但是，友谊就像一支彩笔，给我的生活涂上了亮丽的颜色。同样的我，口袋里没有几个铜板，我变得不再害怕。同样的我，不知道明天的早饭在哪里，但是，我不再操心。我的脑子一下子变得好使唤了。我相信自己有能力找到工作，相信自己能把苦日子过得甜甜蜜蜜。所以这一切，不都因为一份不同的心情？

我写了一张又一张，我不知道哪里涌出来那么多的英文词汇？我写一段，念一段，自我陶醉着，像呷美酒一般……。

可能还是时差在作怪，到了天边出现了一抹亮光的时候，我感到了困意，倒地而睡。

Chapter 3

When I woke up the next day, it was already noon.

Lisa was nowhere to be seen, the room feeling a little suffocating as a result.

I quickly took a shower, put on some makeup, and went out to the college library to find today's newspaper. I flipped through the paper until I saw a page listed with various contacts, copying down all of the phone numbers of those who were in need of housekeepers or babysitters.

Once I finished, I made my way to the nearest payphone and dialed each of the numbers one-by-one. Someone needed a nurse for an elderly person suffering from paralysis, but I didn't have a nursing license. Another person needed a janitor and a gardener, but I didn't have the experience for either. So far, all of the calls were made in vain. Some families needed a babysitter, but when I called, they had either already hired someone or wanted to meet for an interview. Other families didn't want to hire a student since they needed a full-time employee who would be willing to cook and clean their home as well.

I was now at the last number and I felt discouraged. I thought that if this one failed, then I would need to go to a restaurant and become a dishwasher. One of my friends had mentioned that their restaurant needed a dishwasher, but he was worried that I wouldn't be able to handle the exhausting work. Shaking off those thoughts, I sighed and dialed the last number in without a shred of expectation.

After a few rings, a woman greeted the phone calmly. I took my time to introduce myself, deliberately avoiding the possibility of bringing up the job too quickly. I was afraid that I would lose the chance at the job if I got to the point too directly.

Once the woman seemed satisfied with my introduction, I decided to bring up the main subject. "I just read your ad in the newspaper," I said. "How old is your child?"

"Less than two," the woman replied. Her voice was quiet and she sounded as though she was chatting while sitting comfortably on a lavish sofa in a nice, air-conditioned room.

"Can she say 'Papa' and 'Mama' now?" I asked.

"Yes, she's beginning to say a few words."

I decided to carefully probe on. "She can walk, can't she?"

第三章

第二天，我醒来的时候，已经是中午。莉莎不知道去了哪里？房间里有点闷热。我赶紧洗了澡，梳妆一番，出了门。我先到学校的图书馆找到当天的报纸，把广告中当地人需要家庭服务的电话抄了下来。然后到公用电话处，一一给对方挂电话。有的是瘫痪老人需要护理，我没有护理执照，白打了。有的是打扫卫生，有的是花园工作。我没有经验，也不行。有几家寻找看顾孩子的，电话过去，有的要约时间面谈，有的已经找到人了，有的不要学生，是全天工作，包括做饭，清洁卫生。我有些泄气。只剩下最后一家了。心想，如果再不行的话，只能到餐馆去洗碗了。我的老乡朋友曾经提到，他们的餐馆需要一个洗碗工，但是，他担心我经不住那样的劳累。

电话接通以后，是一个女人的声音。我没有马上谈工作的事情。怕谈，怕丢失了最后的机会。自报姓名以后，我说，刚看到你们在报纸上的广告。你的孩子多大了呵？

不到两岁。她答道，话音沉稳。那种声音就像在有空调的房间里，舒适地坐在沙发里聊天一般。

我说，开口叫爸爸，妈妈了吧！

是呵，是呵，她说，开始呀呀学讲话了呢！

我说，学走路了，是不是？

她说，对，对，摇摇摆摆地走呢！

几句对话，让我感觉到她很坦诚，对我毫无戒心。于是，我便轻松地无顾忌地介绍起自己来了。我说，我特别喜欢孩子，以前修

"Yes, she can wobble now," the woman responded.

Judging from the conversation, I felt like this woman was very frank and direct. With this in mind, I began to tell her about myself and my background without hesitation.

"I really love children," I explained. "I took a few courses in child education. I can play piano, draw and fold paper toys, but I'm still single—I mean, I'm not married. Would you be worried if I took care of your child?"

"Doesn't matter, doesn't matter." Her response was so quick and direct that it almost caught me off guard. "I'm at home most of the time."

"I see," I responded. "I'm a college student," I continued on. "I don't have much time for work."

"I would only need you to be here for only three to four hours a day," the woman assured me.

"That's good," I said. I paused briefly, contemplating whether or not I should bring up the subject of pay, but the woman brought it up before I could.

"Generally, we pay four dollars per hour," she explained. "But I'll give you four and a half dollars. What do you think?"

"I don't care about money," I replied without hesitation. "I love children, so it's up to you."

The woman paused for a moment, seeming to contemplate my answer. "…Five dollars," she told me, the same direct tone lacing her voice. "You're a student and you need the money."

I was touched. Five dollars an hour meant fifteen to twenty dollars a day, which was just the right amount to cover my rent. I replied to the woman's offer happily, but she didn't hear my answer and asked if I was still there. "I'm still here," I replied. "Thank you. You are very kind and understanding," I told her.

During this time, I didn't know if a professional in child education or child care should have a higher pay. However, I only took a few courses in such subjects; I wasn't studying it as a profession. Five dollars per hour was higher than the pay for the dishwasher position at the restaurant, so I was satisfied regardless.

At my response, the woman over the phone laughed. "In that case, why don't you come this afternoon?"

I told her that I had no car and asked her to tell me the best public transportation route to take in order to get there. She gave me her home address, which I quickly jotted down. However, I wasn't familiar with the area, so I took a mental note to buy a map later.

Just as I was finishing writing her address, the woman sighed. "It takes a lot of time to ride on public transportation. It's better if I come to pick you up," she decided. "Where do you live?"

"I'm at the university library right now. I can wait for you outside," I explained. I then gave the woman a brief physical description of myself, telling her that I was Chinese and was wearing a white T-shirt and a black miniskirt.

"Well, you speak English very well," the woman praised me. "We'll meet

过幼儿教育的课程，我会弹钢琴，画画，折纸玩具，但是，我是单身，没有结过婚，让我带孩子，你放心吗？

没关系，没关系。她接话很快，没有片刻的犹豫，说完再补了一句，有我在家呢！

我说，我在大学读书，恐怕没有许多时间。

她说，每天只需要三到四小时。

我说，这最好了。心里想，应该谈价钱了。不料她已经说了出来。

她说，我们原来的开价是每小时四元，我给你四块半，你觉得如何？

我说，我不在乎钱的，就是喜欢孩子，随便你啦。

她停了停，说，五元吧，你是学生，需要钱用的。

我听了心里一阵感动，十五二十元一天，不正好付了我的房钱？那个太太没听到我的答复，哈罗，哈罗地招呼我。我答道，是的，我在这儿呢。你真理解人，我们做朋友吧！当时，我不知道幼儿教育专业人士带孩子，价格还可以高很多。不过，我只是选修了一些课，算不上专业人才，五元一小时，超过了餐馆里的洗碗工，我很满意了。

她在电话里笑了，说道，那么，你今天下午就来吧！

我说，可是我没有车，请告诉我坐公交车的路线。她说了他们家的地址。我一一记下，但是，两眼一摸黑，还得去买一份地图呢！

就在我作记录的时候，女人说，坐公交车很慢，还是我来接你吧！你在哪儿？

我说，我在大学的图书馆门口等你。我告诉她，我是中国人，穿白T恤衫，黑短裙。

她夸奖说，你的英语说得很好，我们半小时以后见。

终于在最后的机会里找到了一份轻松的工作，好像比赛赢了球一样，我在心里对自己说了声“好样的！”。我直奔电梯，想利用剩余的半个多小时，到图书馆的五楼找份中文报纸看看。来美国以后，我还真不知道世界上发生了什么事情呢！

in half an hour."

Once we exchanged our goodbyes and courtesies, I hung up and sighed in relief. I was thankfully able to get an easy job at the last chance. "Bravo!" I exclaimed to myself, pumping my fist into the air in victory. I ran straight to the elevator, wanting to use the half an hour of free time I had to go to the fifth floor of the library and read a Chinese newspaper. Ever since my arrival to America, I didn't have time to read any newspapers, so I really had no idea what was happening in the world.

The fifth floor of the library was extremely quiet. As I stepped out of the elevator, I noticed rows of tables near the windows for studying, each corresponding seat having been occupied already. Iron bookshelves lined the other side, resembling an army of iron that extended ridiculously long. I made my way to the shelf housing all of the international newspapers and took a copy of the "World Journal" published in North America.

Unexpectedly, I noticed Charlie sitting beside the newspaper shelf with a large pile of Chinese articles in front of him. I circled around him in light, fluttery steps, and quietly whispered to him: "Mr. Thomson, you are a sinophile."

Charlie was startled at my voice and raised his head. Upon seeing me, he smiled. "Ah, it's you, Susu," he said.

"What wenjian are you reading?" I asked.

Charlie frowned. "What does wenjian mean?"

"It means 'document.'"

"Ah," he nodded in understanding. "I'm reading articles on Chinese history. What are you doing here?"

I shrugged indifferently. "I'm just trying to get familiar with the environment."

Charlie shifted a little towards the windows and motioned for me to sit down. I followed his lead and sat next to him.

"I have to leave soon," I told him quietly. "Someone's coming to pick me up."

"To pick you up?" He seemed surprised but quickly gathered himself with a sheepish cough. "Well, may I ask you out for dinner tonight?"

I hesitated a little at his words, but figured that having dinner with him might explain his behavior last night. "Okay," I accepted. "But... Will you pick me up, or will you send someone else to pick me up? I don't have a car," I explained.

Charlie paused, seeming to be thinking about something serious. I looked into his eyes, trying to guess what he might be thinking. His blue eyes wavered, seeming to change color in the light. His eyes felt secretive, as if he were trying to hide something.

He took a deep breath and smiled at me, seeming to have calmed himself down. "Where should I pick you up?"

I took out the piece of paper that had my future employer's address scribbled about and showed it to him.

"Wow," Charlie sucked in a breath. "This is the richest region in the city!"

I only blinked at his words. It was?

图书馆里安静极了。靠窗的一边是书桌，一张挨着一张，几乎坐无虚席。另一边是书架，一望无际的样子，简直像一支钢铁的军队。我从报架上取了份北美《世界日报》，沿着窗边一路走去，寻找空余的位子。想不到，居然发现了查里也坐在那里，他的面前放着一大堆中文资料。我蹑手蹑脚地绕到他的身后，用中文轻轻地说，汤姆斯先生，原来你是中国通。

查里大吃一惊，猛抬头，看见我，马上转为笑容，说道，是你呵，素素。

我说，你在看什么文件呵？

他皱眉问道，文件是什么意思？

我改口说英文，他答道，噢，中国历史。你呢？

我漫不经心地说，玩玩。熟悉一下环境。

他往窗边挪了挪，请我坐下。我说，马上有人来接我，我得走了。

他自言自语地说，接你？但是，马上回过神来，问道，今天晚上，我能请你吃饭吗？

我稍微犹豫了一下。老实说，我对他昨晚的举动，并不理解。也许，我可以在吃饭的时候，测一下他的目的。

我说，好呵。你来接我，还是请别人送我？我没有车。

他没有马上回答。我看他的眼神，好像在想很严肃的事情。他的蓝眼睛不停地转动着，变换出不同的光彩，像暗藏着密码似的。然后，他深呼吸一下，转入了平静。他问我，到哪里接你？

我就把口袋里的便条拿出来，给他看地址。

哇，他一边抄，一边说，这是城里最富裕的地区。好，我七点准时到。和查里告别以后，我隐隐觉得有点饿了。心里想，从昨天到今天，我没有化一分钱给自己买食品。现在，找到了带孩子的工作，应该好好招待自己。但是，一看表，只剩下了五分钟，没有时间了。我去了厕所，喝了几口自来水，赶快下楼，到门口等候。

一眨眼的功夫，一辆白色的面包车停在图书馆门口，车门打开，下来一个非常窈窕的女子。她的头发剪得特别短，几乎像男人的发式一样，上身穿重磅丝绸的浅灰色针织无袖衫和配套的短裙，

“Good, I’ll come at seven sharp,” Charlie continued. “I’ll see you then, Susu.”

After saying goodbye to Charlie, I realized that I was somewhat hungry. Now that I had found myself a job, I thought that it might be good to get myself a good treat. I glanced down at my watch to see if I had enough time to do so, but sure enough, the woman who would soon become my employer was due to arrive in five minutes— certainly not enough time to eat. I quickly went to the bathroom, drank some tap water, and hurried down the stairs to wait at the door of the library.

Quickly after, a white minivan stopped at the door of the library. A good-figured woman with a pixie cut stepped out of the vehicle gracefully, wearing a light gray sleeveless blouse and a matching miniskirt. She was wearing a bright shade of red lipstick and her eyes were covered with a pair of expensive-looking sunglasses. I noted how compelling the red and black colors were together.

The woman came up to me with a smile, her red lips glittering in the sun. I saw my face reflected in her black sunglasses as I looked up at her, smiling back in greeting.

“Anna,” the woman introduced herself, shaking my hand lightly. Her voice was slightly hoarse, reminding me of an alto singer from a pop song.

“Hello, Anna,” I greeted. “I’m Susu.”

She led me to the minivan and opened the door for me. Once we were both in the vehicle, Anna turned to the backseat. “Kristeen, this is Susu.”

After fastening my seatbelt, I turned to the backseat to see an adorable little girl—the child I assumed I would be taking care of. She was like a living doll, with curly hair, round eyes, and a naïve smile. She was tucked into the child safety seat, her smooth hands and feet barely peaking out from beneath the safety buckles. This child was so cute that I felt like a flower was blooming in my heart. “Hi, Sweetheart. My God, how are you so lovely?” I gently cooed to her, the words slipping out of my mouth.

I couldn’t fight the smile that came onto my face as I forgot all vehicle safety rules and climbed into the backseat to sit next to Kristeene. I played the ‘finger game’ with her, sometimes bending my fingers and other times putting the fingertips of my hands against each other. I let her touch my nose and said “nose” every time she did so. Then, Kristeen would touch my eyes, mouth, hair, and ears, and I would repeatedly say those words to help her learn as well. She was not a shy child; in fact, every time I said some word, her laughter rang out like a brass bell and her little feet and hands would move happily in the seat.

When we reached the house, Anna climbed out and untied Kristeen’s seatbelt.

“I can take her, if you’d like,” I offered.

Anna let me carry Kristeen out of the child safety seat and smiled. “She likes you so much,” Anna told me. “I’m jealous.”

“But you’re her mom,” I replied. “The happiest one. Who could replace you?”

Anna let out a small laugh. “Do you think we look alike?” She asked me,

整个的脸好像被口红和太阳眼镜霸占着，红黑相争。她看到我，笑着走过来，唇上的红色在太阳下闪闪发亮，我的脸印在她的眼镜里。

安娜。她很轻地握了握我的手，作自我介绍。她的声音有点沙哑，像唱流行歌曲的女中音。

你好，安娜。这是素素。

上车吧，她说，里面凉快一些。

我跟在她后面，她给我开了车门，等我上了车，才走到车的那一边，把驾驶员的座位往前一推，对后座说道：这是素素，柯丽丝。

我正在插安全带。听她这么一说，马上朝后面看。嘿，小宝贝也来了呀！老天爷，你为什么那么可爱？我情不自禁地乱说一气。看着这个活生生的洋娃娃，我的心里真是乐开了花。瞧她那卷曲的头发，滚圆的眼睛，天真的笑容，被绑在儿童坐椅上的安全带底下，手脚白嫩光滑，时不时还吐出那粉红的小舌尖儿。我喜形于色，忘乎所以，越过障碍，爬到了后排，坐到柯丽丝的旁边。我和她玩手指游戏，一会儿弯弯勾，一会儿顶指尖，我让她点我的鼻子，我就说Nose，点我的耳朵，我说一声Ear，点我的眼睛，嘴巴，头发，我不断重复着这些单词的发音。柯丽丝一点不怕陌生，我说一次，她就发出铜铃般的笑声，手舞足蹈，欢天喜地。

到家的时候，安娜下了车，解开柯丽丝的安全带。我说，我来抱她。安娜说，她那么喜欢你，真让我妒忌。我说，你是妈咪，最幸福了，谁敢和你比呵！

安娜说，你觉得我和她很像吗？一边取下了太阳眼镜。我一时语塞，答不上来。她们根本不像！安娜的脸干瘦干瘦，额骨颧骨都棱角分明，下巴也是尖尖的。但是，她的体形很匀称，走起路来，好像舞台上的模特儿一样，左右前后地摆来摆去，非常妩媚。

我说，不像妈妈像爸爸。我亲亲柯丽丝的脸蛋，一边说，柯丽丝集中了父母所有的优点，是不是？

安娜带我楼上楼下走了一遍。这是一栋三层楼的大洋房。底楼是公共场所：客厅，起居室，书房，办公室，厨房，厕所和化

taking off her sunglasses. I was speechless and couldn't find it in me to answer.

Their faces were not even similar. Unlike Kristeen's rounded features, Anna's face was thin and lean with high cheekbones and a sharp, angular jawline. Her features and symmetrical, lean figure reminded me of a model. She even walked like a runway model with the way she swung her hips so gracefully.

"Maybe not like mom," I admitted, "but like her dad." I kissed Kristeen on the cheek gently before continuing. "She got all the good genes from both parents, didn't she?" I remarked playfully.

After our short conversation, Anna gave me a tour of the house. It was a mansion with three stories, I noted. The first floor was made up of the living room, family room, study, office, bathroom, and vanity, but there was also a bedroom which I presumed to be for a maid. The second floor was home to four bedrooms and a couple of bathrooms. Anna led me inside the master bedroom, and I had to refrain from dropping my jaw at the sight. The master bedroom was absolutely luxurious, decorated with Italian-styled furniture and long, floral curtains. There was a sauna, double showers, and a huge bathtub in the bathroom as well.

Two of the other bedrooms on this floor had oriental-styled furniture—one with Chinese-style rosewood carvings and the other with Japanese-styled furniture. After briefly touring those rooms, Anna led me to Kristeene's bedroom, which resembled a children's playroom.

After the tour, I headed back downstairs to the living room with Kristeene in my arms. She was tired, rubbing her eyelids with the back of her hand while yawning continuously. I let her lean on my shoulder and quietly hummed a lullaby, gently patting her back in an effort to let her fall asleep. Minutes later, sure enough, she fell asleep, and I gently laid her down in her crib.

Anna was on the phone, so I took some time to admire how luxurious the living room was. A piano, leather sofas, and large, detailed vases decorated the room. An expensive-looking carpet was also set in the living room as well.

However, I couldn't ignore how hungry I felt while waiting for Anna. I was starving, feeling as though I was flooded over by a tide of hunger. I stood up and made my way to the kitchen, fingers and legs trembling as I weakly did so. As soon as I reached the refrigerator, I opened it and poured myself a glass of orange juice, gulping it down without any hesitation. Then, I went to the sink and splashed cold water on my face. Shamelessly, I returned to the refrigerator, looking for something to eat.

This refrigerator was as large as a closet with double doors, but it was mainly empty save for some beers and other drinks, neither of which I could have as a meal. I saw some fruits in a drawer of the fridge, but I didn't know where the fruit knife was. I couldn't eat them without peeling the fruits first. I then spotted some fruit yogurts, but I didn't like dairy, so I left them untouched.

Just as I was about to close the refrigerator doors, Anna came in. I felt embarrassed, not having an explanation for why I was looking in her fridge. I didn't even dare to meet her eyes.

Anna didn't seem to notice my embarrassment and simply pointed to a cabinet by the sink. "Kristeene's food is over here," she explained, opening the

妆间，还要一间卧室，我猜想是给佣人住的。二楼，有四个房间。主卧室非常豪华，窗帘又高又长，印有淡黄色的水仙花，意大利家具。厕所里，有桑拿房，双淋浴，和巨大的浴盆。健身房也设在二楼，里面有各种不同的运动器具。另外两个房间，其中一间的家具是日本式的，另一间是中国的红木雕刻。柯丽丝的房间靠在主卧室的旁边，完全像一个儿童乐园。

柯丽丝有点累了，用手背揉眼睛，不停地打呵欠。我让她趴在我的肩膀上，一边哼着小曲，轻轻地拍着她的背，在室内来回走动。不一会儿，她就睡着了。

我把柯丽丝放到了她的小床上，下楼找安娜。

楼下的客厅很大，有钢琴，有皮质沙发，有落地花瓶，还有非常珍贵的锦织地毯。安娜正在打电话。

我没事可干。等待中，突然觉得饿极了，好像被饥饿的潮水淹没一样，手指和双腿都颤抖了起来，浑身出冷汗。乘她还在电话上，我赶紧去了厨房，打开冰箱，不管三七二十一，倒了一杯桔子水，一口气喝了下去。我走到水池子旁边，不停地用冷水冲脸。我再打开冰箱，上上下下地找东西吃。那是一个像衣橱一样的双门冰箱，里面却空空如也，除了啤酒和饮料，能当饭吃的东西一样没有。冰箱的抽屉里有一些苹果，桃子，梨和葡萄，但是，我不知道水果刀放在哪里，不削皮，没法吃。我还找到了几罐水果酸奶，但是，我不喜欢吃乳制品。

正在这时，安娜进来了，我心里一阵紧张，不知道如何解释，不敢抬眼看她。

安娜说，柯丽丝的食品在这儿。她指着水池旁边的一个储藏柜，走过去，打开门，里面是一个小冰箱。

噢，在这儿。我说，她午睡醒来，吃什么好呢？

安娜取出一小瓶苹果酱，一片干酪。

我说，干酪让她自己拿着吃？我喂她苹果酱。

安娜说，素素，你真是内行呵。

我说，安娜，刚才我有点口渴，喝了一杯桔子水。你在电话上，不好意思打断你。

cabinet to reveal a small mini-fridge.

"Oh, I see!" I exclaimed, relieved at the cover that Anna had unknowingly provided me. "What will she eat after her nap?"

Anna answered me by taking out a small bottle of applesauce and a piece of cheese.

"Can she hold the cheese and eat it herself?" I asked. "I can feed her the applesauce."

Anna smiled. "You're an expert, Susu," she remarked.

I smiled at her compliment, but it soon faded as I caught eye of the empty glass that I had used to drink her orange juice out of earlier. "Anna, a moment ago I felt thirsty and drank a glass of orange juice," I confessed. "You were on the phone, so I didn't want to interrupt you."

"It doesn't matter," Anna laughed a little as she replied to me. "You can eat whatever you'd like. We just don't have very much in the refrigerator right now since we usually eat outside." She opened another cabinet and gestured for me to come over. "This is where all of our utensils are."

I thanked her gratefully, stopping myself from drooling as the thought of apples and peaches appeared in my mind. I couldn't show my hunger like this in front of Anna. I secretly hoped that she would leave me alone for a little while to take a nap or something so I could have some freedom to eat.

Surprisingly, just as I was thinking that, Anna started to get ready to leave. "I'll be going out for some business now," she told me. "When Kristeene is sleeping, you can do whatever you'd like. Once school starts, you can bring your homework, too."

I thanked her repeatedly for her kindness.

Anna paused for a moment before approaching me. "You can bring some close friends here an use the guest room on the third floor," she whispered to me. I could practically hear her smile under her breath.

I blushed down to my neck at her words. Judging from her mysterious and ethereal presence, she seemed to tell me that out of kindness, but I took it differently. The so-called 'close friend' must mean a boyfriend, right? I felt like I should explain to her that I didn't have a boyfriend. For some reason, though, I didn't say a word, staying rooted in place with a bright red face.

I watched Anna walk away until she disappeared from my sight. She seemed so close yet so distant sometimes. I felt like she was very unpredictable. I would later learn that she went out every afternoon only to return before seven P.M., so I wonder what she really does for 'business'. On my first day of work, though, I didn't even question it.

Once Anna left, I ate two peaches and my hunger was satisfied. However, the drowsiness came to trouble me once again. I went to Kristeen's bedroom and laid on the floor next to her crib, already exhausted. I soon fell asleep.

It was the jetlag again.

安娜笑着说，没关系，冰箱里的东西随便你吃。实在也没有食品，我们都在外面吃。她打开了另一扇橱门，拉开抽屉说，看这里，刀具和餐具都在。

我谢了谢，咽了一下口水，脑子了出现的都是苹果和桃子。但是，在安娜面前，我不能露馋相。我希望她也去睡个午觉什么的，给我一点自由。

正这么想着，安娜果然要走了。她说，我要出去办些事情。柯丽丝睡觉的时候，你做什么都行，开学以后把功课带来做吧！

我又谢了谢。

安娜走了几步，退回来，凑近我的耳朵小声说：来个熟悉的朋友也没有关系，你可以用三楼的客房。

不知怎么的，我的脸一下子红到了脖子。她那付神秘而得意的样子，看上去出于好心，到了我这里，完全变了味。所谓熟悉的朋友，无非是指男朋友。我应该向她解释，我没有男朋友。但是，不知道为什么，我一个字都没有说，反而面红耳赤，好像被她击中了要害一样。其实，我感到害羞的是后面一句：三楼的客房。这间客房，以后真的派了用处。我注视着她的背影和脚步，一直看到她消失。这个女人给我忽近忽远，捉摸不定的感觉。她走路的样子，就像挂在空中的乐谱，温柔婉约，自成风景。在以后的许多日子里，我几乎每天看着她在下午出去，七点以前回来。她究竟去干什么呢？第一天刚来，我根本没有想。

安娜离家后，我吃了两个桃子。饥饿解决了，困意又来干扰。我回到柯丽丝的睡房，躺在地上，不一会儿就睡着了。

哎，还是时差在作怪。

Chapter 4

At seven o'clock sharp, I noticed two figures making their way down the hallway.

Anna waved to me with a calm smile. "Look who's here, Susu," she gestured for me to come over. She seemed so calm, as if she was introducing Charlie to me even though I already knew him. It seemed like they were already familiar with each other. "Charlie's inviting you for dinner tonight," Anna continued.

I nodded and smiled at Charlie. "Thank you, Anna," I said. "I already gave Kristeene a bath."

"That's so helpful of you, Susu. Thank you," she said, holding my hands gratefully. Her eyes showed endearment and honesty as she gently placed something in my hand. I guessed that it was the money. Since Charlie was standing beside me, I didn't look and just put it in my bag.

After Charlie and Anna exchanged goodbyes and I hugged Kristeene and Anna respectively, Charlie and I left the house.

When I came to the house in the afternoon, I was too busy playing with Kristeene that I hadn't noticed the house's surroundings. Now that I saw it clearly, it resembled a castle; in fact, the property occupied at least a few acres. Anna had only given me a tour of part of the house—probably only the parts that their family normally used. Smaller buildings stood behind the main house's structure, but I didn't know what they were used for. Each building had little spires on the top, resembling the peaks of a mountain range. The building's white walls matched the tiles and yellow-tinted window frames of the rest of the structure. Outside, tall trees and flowers circled the large lawn in front of the house. A small brook meandered through the garden, a cute little white bridge built over it. The whole structure looked like it came straight from a fairytale.

The sun was beginning to set. I looked around myself, feeling as though the whole world was becoming hazy and mysterious. The golden afterglow of dusk was everywhere, painting itself on the surrounding flowers, trees, and blades of grass and stripping them of their own natural color. I glanced at Charlie, whose bronze face resembled that of a high-spirited warrior in an oil painting. I believed myself to also be high-spirited and red-faced at that moment.

After getting into the car, I asked Charlie, "do you think I should put on

第四章

安娜和查里像是约好了似的，两人同时出现在过道上。准七点钟。

安娜说，素素，瞧，谁来啦？她那满脸的笑容好像在迎接自己的朋友一样。我不知道他们在外面是否互相作了介绍，看上去很熟悉的样子。

今晚查里请你吃晚饭呢！安娜说。

我朝查里笑了笑，对安娜说，我给柯丽丝洗了澡。

安娜说，素素，你真好。谢谢，谢谢。她一边说，一边握住了我的手。我感到，她把东西塞到了我的手心里。她的眼神非常可亲诚恳。我猜那是钱，因为查里在场，我没有看，放进了包里。

我和柯丽丝和安娜分别拥抱，查里和安娜握手告别，我们走出了这幢房子。

下午进来的时候，我忙着和柯丽丝玩耍，根本没有注意房子的外形和周围的一切。现在，我才看清了，那是一座城堡，占着几亩地。安娜只带我参观了其中的一部份，可能就是平时经常使用的部份。主楼后面的那些建筑，不知道派什么用场。每栋房子都有教堂那样的尖顶，组合在一起，像群山峻岭一样。白墙棕瓦，米黄的窗框，和内部的窗帘非常相配。房子的周围花树围绕。房前有平坦的草坪，还有一条河流从中穿过，上面架着一座白色的小桥。

太阳已经沉下去了。我朝周围看看，只觉得整个世界变得朦胧神秘。金灿灿的霞光无处不在，花卉，树木和草地，都失去了本色，成了晚霞的俘虏。查里古铜色的脸像油画里的勇士一样，神采

some makeup before going to dinner?"

I already knew that the makeup that I had applied earlier that day had been washed off when I splashed cold water on my face. Even worse, when I had slept in Kristeene's room in the afternoon, my clothes had gotten wrinkled, so I was feeling a bit self-conscious.

"If you want to go back to your dorm, I can drive you there," Charlie replied simply.

I thought that it was unfair to Charlie to waste his time. I then remembered about the money that Anna had given me, fetching the twenty dollars out of my bag. 'Two peaches, a glass of orange juice, a nap, and twenty dollars—what good luck!' I though to myself.

With the money tucked neatly into my hand, I shook my head. "It's okay. I can buy some makeup when we come across a supermarket, and then I can do it in the car. We don't need to go back to the dorm." Charlie nodded and exited from the highway at my response.

Honestly, I wasn't really intending to buy any cosmetics, but I did need to buy a gift for Charlie. According to Chinese tradition, I couldn't let him give me a ride and dinner without anything to give in return!

As we pulled into the parking lot of the supermarket, I took note of how large it was. This was my first time visiting a supermarket in America, but I figured that it would be easy and quick to pick up a few things. However, upon entering, I was dumbfounded. I had no idea where to go to find the things that I needed. It felt as if I was lost in the vast corn fields back in the countryside in China.

The fact that Charlie was waiting for me in the car didn't help my anxiety at all. My legs quickly carried me right and left, here and there. I scurried through each aisle, desperate to find what I was looking for, and I finally stumbled upon a shelf with some glass bottles of all shapes and colors. I tried to look closely and read the label, but the words on all of the bottles were in foreign languages.

I didn't know what to do. I had learned that in a foreign land, I could always ask someone if I had any questions. However, in this maze of a supermarket, I wouldn't be able to get any help because no one was around to answer my questions in the first place.

All I knew was that I was looking for wine. "Wine, wine, wine," I repeated to myself quietly, as if hoping that it would hear my call. Eventually, I finally found the wine section, but I still didn't understand why there were so many different brand names for the same type of white or red wine. What was the difference? Plus, how was I supposed to choose one wine among all of the different brands and prices?

'I'll stop here,' I thought. I had yet to learn the basics of how to shop in an American supermarket. Would it be considered as too expensive or luxurious to buy wine during my first shopping spree?

Just as I was about to leave the supermarket, a friendly middle-aged store assistant behind me asked if I needed any help. My instinct was to decline, afraid that I wouldn't be able to say what brand and price I wanted for the wine. However, before I said anything, I noticed that the word "MANAGER"

奕奕，容光焕发。我相信自己也一定红光满面。

上了车，我对查里说，你觉得我是否应该梳妆打扮一下再去吃晚饭？我知道自己脸上的化妆已经全部被冷水洗掉，下午睡在地毯上，衣服又皱又脏。

查里说，如果你想回宿舍，我送你回去吧！

我想了一下，觉得很不妥。为了我而浪费查里的时间是不公平的。我偷偷地看了看安娜给我的钱，是二十元。我心里想，两个桃子，一杯桔子水，一个午觉，还拿二十美元，我真是交了好运呵！

我对查里说，算了，路过任何超级市场，我进去买一点化妆品，就在车里解决了，我们不回宿舍了。说句心里话，与其是去买化妆品，更是为了买一件送给查里的礼物。按照中国人的规矩，总不能白让人家开车，白吃人家的饭吧！

查里答应着，从高速公路上拐了下来。

这是我第一次走进美国的百货超市。原以为买两样东西很简单很快就能办完，想不到一走进去就傻了眼，好像看见的是乡下的一片玉米地，不知道应该到哪里去找东西。心里好着急，因为查里在外面等我。两条腿从东跑到西，再从西面倒回来，跑了一条又一条走廊。终于看到了陈列架上无数个玻璃瓶，各种形状各种颜色，凑近看，全部都是外国字，我被吓得不知所措。如果说在异国他乡，有什么不懂可以开口询问，那么，在超市里，有了嘴巴也得不到回答。

我找葡萄酒。葡萄酒，葡萄酒，一边自言自语，希望它们听见我在呼唤，同时，在排着长队的瓶子商标上的外国字上搜寻。好不容易找到了，却还是看不明白。为什么同样颜色的白酒和红酒，却有不同的名字？他们的区别在哪里？还有，不同的品牌和价格，我该如何选？算了，算了，心里想，超市购物应该从ABC学起，一上来就买酒是否太高级了一点？

我正准备退出去，身后来了一个中年男售货员，笑嘻嘻地问我要不要帮助？本来我想婉言拒绝的，因为怕自己根本就说不清楚哪个牌子哪种价格。我还没有说出口，看到了他衣服上贴着一个“经

was plastered above his name tag.

Maybe he could help me.

So, I made up a story. I told the manager that my 'boyfriend' had asked me for dinner and I wanted to give him a bottle of red wine as a gift.

"I just don't know what brand and what type he likes," I sighed, wrapping up my story. The manager was listening intently, so I continued on. "Could you help me? I have twenty dollars." To avoid answering any questions I might not understand, I decided to go on. "He's waiting for me in the car," I added. "I'm in a hurry."

The manager was happy to help, and with his guidance, I was able to buy a bottle of red wine, lipstick, and eyeliner.

By the time I had returned to the car, it was already dark.

"If you feel like going to a restaurant would be inconvenient, we can go to my place," Charlie offered, noticing my slightly frantic state. "I could make barbecue steak."

I was surprised and stayed silent for a moment. I could feel that he said those words in a burst of courage, and he did it without a shred of hesitation. "...Charlie, let's go to a coffee shop," I finally responded.

He answered with silence.

We drove on the highway for a while, going at such a speed to the extent that all of the cars passing us looked like moving streaks of light. I glanced at Charlie, unsure of where he was taking me, but I shrugged it off. I lit up a small lamp beside me and opened my makeup case, painting my lips red and tinting my cheeks a rosy red with the lipstick I bought. When I finished drawing my eyeliner, I studied myself in the mirror for a while, satisfied with my work. I wasn't putting on the makeup for myself, but rather for Charlie. I felt as though a man would feel embarrassed if his date didn't pay any attention to their looks in public. I turned towards Charlie, hoping that he was satisfied with my appearance.

Charlie didn't notice it at all. Instead, he focused all of his attention on driving. I went back to staring out the window, feeling as though the atmosphere had shifted. He seemed like he was thinking of other things. After all, why else wouldn't he even attempt to make some conversation?

Our headlights shone on exit sign upon exit sign. I lost count of how many signs we passed, and at this point, I wasn't even sure if he was driving with any destination in mind.

The car was completely quiet. The silence was suffocating to the point where I felt like I couldn't even breathe, and the dim lighting of the car wasn't helping. I looked over at Charlie again, only to see the outline of his side profile. Why was he acting so different from yesterday? My thoughts were quickly overridden by my hunger, though, and I immediately lost all interest in studying the psychological patterns of other people.

Instead, I let out a light, intentional cough to attract his attention.

"So, excuse me," I smiled at Charlie while speaking, hoping that he would catch onto my lively tone. "You must be hungry."

"Yes, I am," Charlie answered. "We'll exit here." His tone began to sound more confident—more like the way it sounded last night. "There's a well-

理”的牌子，上面还写着姓名。于是编了一个谎言，说道，我的男朋友请我吃晚饭，我想买瓶红葡萄酒送给他。我不知道他喜欢哪个牌子哪种类型，你能帮助我吗？我有二十块钱。为了避免回答自己不懂的问题，我补充道，他在车内等我，越快越好。

在超市经理的帮助下，我买了一瓶红葡萄酒和一条唇膏和一支眼线笔。

天已经黑了，回到车内，查里说，如果你觉得去饭店不方便的话，到我家去好吗？我来烤牛排。

我吃了一惊，没有回答。我能感觉到他说这些话是花了点勇气的，而且他的口气并不很坚定。

我说：查里，我们上咖啡店去坐坐吧！

他沉默不答。

他的车在公路上开了很久，车外闪进来一道道移动的光束。我不知道他要把我带到哪里去。我把化妆镜打开，旁边的小灯跟着亮了起来。我涂红了嘴唇，然后点一点在手心里，用手指涂匀，擦上双颊。我画完了眼线，对着镜子横看竖看，心里想，这化妆其实不是为了自己，而是为了查里。看在他作为一个男人的面上，如果女伴不注意容貌，在公共场所有失查里的身份。我朝查里看了看，希望他对我满意。

查里没有注意，集中精力在开车。但是，我觉得气氛有些奇怪，他好像在想别的事情。否则，为什么连应付性的谈话都没有？前方，一个接一个的出口牌被车灯照亮，一个接一个地闪了过去，汽车无目标地开着。沉闷，令人透不过气。关了化妆灯，车内很暗，我只看到他一个侧面的轮廓。昨晚的查里为什么和今天如此不一样？但是，我很饿了，懒得去琢磨别人的心理。我故意咳嗽了一声，把他的注意力吸引了过来。

我朝查里笑了笑，说道，你一定很饿了吧！

嗯，他说，我们就从这个出口下去。他的声调变得自信了一些。

那里有一家知名的意大利饭店。 他说。

known Italian restaurant there," he added.

Moments later, we linked arms and headed into the restaurant together. To a stranger, it didn't seem like we weren't well-acquainted with each other; rather, it looked as though we were in a relationship together.

The waiter, clad in a white uniform with a white towel draped over his left arm, led us to a table. He reminded me of one of the busboys of an ancient restaurant in Chinese history. The waiter said something to us that I didn't understand, and Charlie responded in English. Judging from his reply, I gathered that they were simply making some polite conversation.

I couldn't help but be amazed. So many people in America spoke a foreign language in America, but still had the talent and work ethic to open well-respected restaurants and businesses.

The waiter left and quickly returned with two glasses of ice water and menus. Charlie asked me what I liked, and I shrugged my shoulders in response. The words on the menu were basically hieroglyphs to me. All of the names for the noodles were written in Italian. Since my English was still so poor, how was I supposed to deal with a third language?"

With this in mind, I told Charlie, "Since you're taking me to dinner, Charlie, you can choose for me."

Charlie nodded and proceeded to ask me what kind of wine I'd like to drink. I was completely lost when it came to foreign wine, too, so I didn't know how to respond. I thought back to my hunt for wine in the supermarket, making a mental note to learn more about wine in America later so I could feel less idiotic about it.

Regardless, I quickly thought of a reply. "Well, Charlie, since you'll be driving, we'd best not drink wine," I stated casually. "Why don't we order first to get the noodles cooked? I'm so hungry that I think I'm going to faint soon," I joked, but I was still half-serious. I was really hungry.

Charlie smiled and shook his head. "I don't usually drink wine," he admitted. "I like to drink green tea."

'You like to drink green tea?' I thought to myself, pleasantly surprised. "Well," I started, pointing a finger at myself and giving Charlie a half-lidded smile, "as long as you have this Chinese friend, I'll keep you supplied with it. I brought a lot of Chinese green tea with me."

This conversation helped us relax a bit more. It was strange, I thought. Considering the fact that Charlie and I had laughed our hearts out together last night, I thought that we had lost all shyness and tension between us. In fact, if we had stayed on the lawn for one more hour that night, I couldn't imagine to what extent our relationship would have developed.

Today, however, it seemed like we were starting from the beginning all over again. Human beings really were strange, especially when it came to the relationship between a man and a woman. Once the heart is closed off, they become total strangers.

I continued to contemplate our relationship. Just a moment ago, Charlie had linked my arm with his as we came into the restaurant. Was that only a social habit to perform for other people? I couldn't tell. However, if we hadn't walked in with our arms tangled together, what difference would it have made

我们是挽着手臂进饭店的。在别人的眼里，我们不是一般的朋友。可是，在我们之间，绕着一个很大的谜。

男招待穿一身白色的衣服，左手臂上搭着一条白毛巾，有点像中国历史上跑堂的小伙计。年轻人热情说了一些我听不懂的话，查里用英文回答。从查里的答复中我得知都是一些客套话。意大利人真厉害，在美国的土地上说外国话，还能成为有名的饭店，令人刮目相看。招待转身而去，不一会儿给我们送来冰水和菜单。

查里问我喜欢吃什么，我耸耸肩，让他给我选。这种菜单，对我就像天书一样。各种面条的名字，都是意大利文的拼写和发音，我的英文还没有过关，哪里对付得了第三语言？我说，查里，你请客，我听你的。他问我喝什么酒？我对洋酒也是一窍不通，恰好刚才到超市去领略了一下酒市场，里面的品种令人眼花目眩。我想，这个领域还是晚一点踏进去吧，否则一定出洋相。

我说，查里，免了吧，你还要开车。心里想，赶快赶快，把定单送出去，把面条做出来，我饿极了，快要晕过去了。

查里应允道，挥手叫来了招待。

我说，平时很少喝酒。我喜欢喝绿茶。

喜欢喝绿茶？

对啊，你喜欢吗，查里？我指着自己的鼻尖，眯眼笑道，只要留着这个中国朋友，你的茶叶我包了。我带来了许多许多中国的绿茶。

我们之间的气氛从这个时候开始，松弛了一些。这个感觉只有自己领会。我想，昨天晚上，我们面对面地大笑，好像互相都失去了警戒。如果我们在草坪上多呆一个小时，不知道和查里的关系会发展到什么程度。今天，一切重新开始。人就是这么奇怪，特别在男人和女人之间，一旦关上了心灵的大门，就像陌生人一样。刚才他还是挽着我的手臂进来的，看上去，好像是出于一种形式，是做给别人看的。但是，剖开来看，我们挽手和别人又有什么关系？是不是双方都在找理由实现理智不允许的愿望？

招待先送来了面包，我学着查里的样子，涂上牛油，不管三七

on others? Were we both looking for some excuse to indulge in a seemingly forbidden desire?

My thoughts were interrupted when the waiter promptly returned with some bread. Charlie took a slice and buttered it and I imitated him, buttering my own slice before eating it and washing it down with a gulp of ice-cold water without considering my stomach's comfort.

Charlie smiled as he watched me eat. "You were hungry, too," he noted.

I nodded. "I was," I replied. "The bread just smells so good."

The waiter then returned with our second meal course: salad. This was my first time eating salad, and I had trouble swallowing it; the leaves reminded me of the tough texture of fruit rinds. However, I was able to eat it with some sips of ice water in between bites.

We hadn't finished our salad before the noodles came, but that wasn't a problem to me. My noodles were covered in some type of red sauce and a snow-white substance on a top. I hastily pushed the salad aside, ready to wolf down the noodles into my stomach, but I realized that I had no chopsticks to eat the noodles with. How could I eat these noodles without chopsticks?

As I contemplated this question, I glanced at Charlie, who only looked at me with a smile.

"Does it taste good?" He asked.

"Yes, it's good," I responded despite having no idea how to eat the noodles without chopsticks.

I cast a stealthy glance towards Charlie and watched him as he put his silver fork into the noodles and twirled it around. When a good amount of noodles wound up on his fork, he would then place it in his mouth and eat it. I followed his example and tried to do the same. When Charlie chewed, his mouth was shut tight and he didn't make a sound, so I was also careful to chew like he did in an effort to use proper etiquette. This dinner was starting to feel exhausting—on one hand, I was so hungry that I wanted to eat whatever we ordered, but on the other hand, I forced myself to imitate Charlie to the last detail.

All of this happened right before Charlie's eyes. He didn't know that I hadn't paid enough attention to him yesterday, being too busy with my studies to really care. Considering the extent of the relationship we had reached last night, his intention of asking me out for dinner today now seemed reasonable to me. However, the relaxed atmosphere we had created just moments ago became icy again while eating our noodles.

As we finished our dinner, Charlie suddenly called the waiter over and ordered a bottle of white wine. My heart sank for two reasons— one, if he drank now, how would he be able to drive later? — and two, I wondered if I had bought him the wrong type of wine. Clearly, he liked white wine, but that wasn't what I had gotten for him. Luckily, though, I hadn't given it to him yet.

Charlie asked for two glasses. He filled them both and handed one to me, raising his glass as he said in Chinese: "Susu, a toast for your arrival here!"

I was shocked when I heard him say those words in Chinese. I toasted my glass with his, raised the glass to my lips, and took a sip of the delicious wine. The taste lingered in my mouth, and I suddenly felt emotional, fighting

二十一，混着冰水送下去。

查里笑着说，你也饿了吧！

我说，这面包真香。

第二道是色拉。第一次学吃生菜，很难下咽，好像在吃水果皮一样。但是，我也混着冰水，把他们吞了下去。色拉还没有吃完，面条来了，上面覆盖着鲜红的番茄酱，酱上像下过雪一样，白茫茫的一片。我赶紧把色拉推向一旁，准备一口气把面条统统到入胃里。嘿，我暗自笑起来，没有筷子怎么吃？我朝查里看看，他问，味道还好吗？

我说，很好吃。心里想，我还不知道如何吃呢！

我偷偷地瞅了一眼查里，看到他把银叉插入面条，稍微挑一点起来，然后直竖叉尖，转几圈，当面条全部绕上去了，然后提起来，送到嘴里。我也照着做。查里咀嚼的时候，闭紧嘴巴，不出声音。我都照着做了，嚼得很小心，生怕咬着了自己的舌头。这顿晚餐，一方面，因为饥不择食，另一方面，强迫自己入乡随俗，我吃得很累很累。

这一切，都是在查里的眼皮底下发生的。他不知道我因为忙于学习而忽视了对他的注意力。这可能是他最不能理解的地方。按照昨天晚上我们之间的热度，他今天请我吃饭应该算是顺水推舟，但是，刚才稍微松弛了的关系，在吃饭的过程中又变得冰冷冰冷。

快吃完的时候，他突然把男招待叫来，要了一瓶白葡萄酒。我心里一沉，他要开车，怎么能喝酒？同时，我联想到自己买错了酒的类型。查里喜欢白葡萄酒，亏得还没有送给他。

查里要了两个高脚玻璃杯，斟满，递了一杯给我，说道：素素，为你洗尘。

我大吃一惊，因为他对我说了中文！

我和他碰了碰杯沿，然后移到唇边，呷了一口清醇的葡萄酒。含在口中的迟迟不肯往下走，眼睛里却涌出了泪水。那句中国话：素素，为你洗尘。我突然有一种想哭的感觉，多么想放声地大哭一场啊，在这陌生的地方！平时被压抑的情感，因为一句中国话，顿

the tears that threatened to fall down my cheeks as Charlie's words repeated in my mind.

I suddenly felt as though I wanted to cry. Not just any cry, though—I wanted to have a raw, unfiltered cry in this strange place that I felt so confused in. My emotions, usually suppressed, flooded like a tide just because of his words. I lowered my head, twirling the white napkin around my fingers. My tears began to dampen the cloth, each droplet spreading out in a wet circle.

I swallowed the wine and raised my eyes to meet the soft look in Charlie's eyes, which shone prettily with sympathy, protection, and understanding. He seemed to be waiting for me, waiting for my own eyes to meet his, and once they did, I melted completely. It reminded me of the party where I had met him when we were gazing at each other on the lawn. The only difference between then and now was that I was tearing up this time.

Charlie reached his hand to me, his muscular arm crossing over half of the table's surface. He opened his palm, gesturing for me to give him my hand. I did so, placing down my glass to hold out my hand. Charlie took my hand in his, gripping tightly. His warmth soothed the metaphorical pain that spread throughout my skin and bones, and I could feel his emotions through our hands. The interaction felt so strong, so magnetic—I could only describe it as electric.

Once we finished the wine, the wall between us crumbled. Charlie hadn't spoken a word, opting to watch me instead. He cocked his head to the side a little and smiled. With my mouth shut and tears trickling down my cheeks, I smiled back. He moved to my side and took a handkerchief out of his pocket. I presumed that he would use it to wipe away my tears, but instead, he just moved closer to me until his lips were just a feather's distance away from my cheeks. It was then I felt him kissing my tears away, moving up slowly to kiss my eyelids. I couldn't help but fall into his hold.

I suddenly felt shocked at what was happening. Oh, God—we had only known each other for the past two days, and we hadn't even spent five hours interacting. I didn't even know who he truly was—his hopes, his dreams, his aspirations—and he surely didn't know mine, either. Even so, however, I pushed these thoughts away. At this moment, nothing else mattered; this was meant to happen.

时，像潮水一样泛滥。我低下头，把白色的餐巾布绕在手指上，一边绕，一边看着大颗的泪珠落在白布上，化成一朵朵淡淡的水晕。

我咽下了那口酒，刚抬眼就遇到了查里柔软的目光。那双漂亮的蓝眼睛饱含着同情爱护和理解，一直在对面等着我。等着我迎上去，把我溶化掉。啊，我好像回到了聚会的夜晚，在草坪上，我们就是这样互相对视的，不同的是，这一回，我的眼睛湿淋淋。

查里伸过手来，健壮的手臂越过半个台面，伸到我的面前。他摊开了五指，好像在向我要什么东西。我放下了酒杯去接他。他把我的手捏在手心里，捏得很紧。他的体温就这样通过我的皮肤和骨头间的疼痛，传给了我。他的感觉就这样通过我的手告诉了我。他的感情就这样随着双手的接触溶进了我的感情。我们之间像接通了电源一样互相感应。

一瓶酒之后，我们中间的围墙彻底地崩溃了。查里始终一句话都没有说，只用眼睛看着我。他侧着头，微笑着。我也抿着嘴笑，一边流眼泪。他从口袋里拿出手绢，坐到我的旁边。他没有用手绢，没有给我擦眼泪。他一点一点地凑近我，吻我的眼泪，吻我的眼睛。我倒在他的怀里……。

老天爷，我们只认识了两天，加起来不满五个小时。我们互相都不知道对方是谁？从哪里来？要到哪里去？但是，此时此刻，好像一切都是多余的，都是不需要的，都是不在乎的，一切都是注定要发生的。

Chapter 5

The car ride back to my dorm was entirely silent. Charlie held my hand while driving, but didn't say anything. Honestly, had he offered for me to stay over at his home, I probably wouldn't have refused. However, it seemed as though we couldn't make up our minds about what we wanted to say. We were both roaming at the threshold of emotion and reason: one step over the threshold, one step back—and endless cycle of indecisiveness. The events that occurred in the restaurant seemed like a dream. Charlie was the hero who rescued the maiden that I was at that moment, but now, we found ourselves far from the roles we played at the restaurant.

I no longer had any desire to spend the night with him, and neither did Charlie. At this moment, we weren't even in a defined relationship, so how would spending the night with him make any sense?

My thoughts ceased to a halt when the car stopped in front of my dormitory.

"I had a very good time tonight," Charlie said with a warm smile on his face.

"Me, too," I replied to him, thanking him for the night out. Charlie opened the car door for me, and I got out, making sure to avoid standing too close to him.

Then, we parted. Similar to the first night when we had met, we just stamped it out.

Because of the jetlag, I had trouble sleeping for the night. I got up and took out my diary, thinking about Anna talking about her boyfriend. With a swish of my pen, I started writing: 'Just came to the foreign land. I hope to adapt to the environment and be accepted, and I hope I can live happily like the fish in ponds. I'm excited to make friends, but maybe I don't have any desire for a boyfriend or any friends of the opposite sex yet! Charlie's a good man… He's responsible, but most likely treats me well out of protection and sympathy! When a man and a woman like each other, it doesn't necessarily mean they'll fall in love… At least, Charlie and I won't. There's an obvious difference in both status and finances between us. Not the type of love that would work, I think…'

第五章

查里送我回来的时候，我们俩都出奇地沉默。他一边开车，一边握着我的手，但是，没有说话。如果这个时候，他开我到他的家里，我可能不会拒绝。但是，我们好像都在情感和理智的门口徘徊，跨一步就过去了，退一步又回来了。饭店里的亲热就像一个梦，一场戏，当英雄把美人救出来，落幕之后，我们都发现自己和角色有很远的距离。我没有和他有过夜的冲动。查里好像也没有。我们之间只在手拉手的水平。最后，车开到了宿舍的门口，他朝我笑笑说，过了一个很开心的夜晚。我谢了谢他，说道，很温暖。他为我开了车门，我出来的时候，居然不敢靠近他。我们就这样分手了，就像第一天晚上，刚刚把火烧起来，就把它踩灭了。

因为时差，我又是一宿未合眼。我想到安娜谈及的男朋友之事，我在日记中写道：乍来他乡，希望被环境接受和容纳，希望能够如鱼得水般地生活得愉快，所以，我期待朋友，期待友情。但是，恐怕不是对男朋友和恋人的渴望。查里是好人，是个负责任的男人。他待我，充其量是出于爱护和怜恋。男女相悦，未必要马上堕入爱河。至少我和查里没有。我们之间存在着明显地高低和强弱之区别，这不是我理解的爱情……。

在意大利饭店里我们喝酒拥吻以后，我很少见到查里。我的哲学老师是一个脱顶的老头。他穿得很邋遢，布衬衫从来不烫，就像他的脸差不多，都是皱纹。西短裤又肥又大，长过膝盖，好像是长裤剪去了一小截。他经常说一些令人吃惊的话，好像把人生看成一场游戏。而且，这个老头特别幽默，总是和学生开玩笑。有一次，他提早进教室，坐在讲坛后面。上课到一半的时候，他走到讲坛的

I paused. I hadn't seen much of Charlie lately, save for the time we drank wine in the Italian restaurant together. He wasn't my philosophy professor, either. In fact, my philosophy professor was a bald old man with wrinkled features who wore dirty clothes. His short pants were always very big and hunge just below his knees, which looked like someone had cut his trousers short. He always said something surprising or conventionally odd and seemed to view life as a game. However, the old man was humorous and always joked with his students. One time, he entered the classroom early and sat behind his desk. Once students started trickling in, he walked to the front of his desk and raised his forefinger. He paced to and fro while saying: "Now is the time you need to focus. No negligence! Attention! Everybody, pay attention!" A loud laughter echoed in the classroom, and I was sure that his bright red pants weren't helping the humor of the situation.

In fact, the big red pants seemed to cut my professor into two parts: the upper torso mimicked an old man while the lower torso mimicked a fashionable girl, two things that were not matching. Like the others, I was surprised—but when I realized his intention, I found that I could no longer laugh. He asked us to consider the question of why he decided to wear red pants and how his choice of attire affected our perception of him. That question was not only real, but it was also very serious. Now, I felt as though we (as the students) were the ones getting sneered at. I began to listen to his lectures intently and found that I quite enjoyed them, so I wouldn't need to ask to transfer to Charlie's class.

After class, I made my way back to my room. There was no private phone line in the dorm, so Anna came to fetch me for work and I returned home after seven o'clock.

Every morning, I drank a glass of milk and ate two pieces of bread. Sometimes, the cheapest bread cost only thirty-five cents, so I was able to save some money. For lunch, I ate two eggs and a bowl of rice. The cheap eggs were ninety-nine cents a dozen. I ate some fruit at Anna's house in the afternoon and had both milk and bread for supper.

In the evenings, I studied in my room. I went to the library only when I needed to find some information about something. Usually, though, I didn't go to the library. It was quite far from my dorm, and I was also afraid that I might bump into Charlie there. He and I were like two bundles of wet firewood; neither of us could burn easily, but if our bundles of fire were rubbed together, then a flame might be kindled. Maybe if the bundles of firewood had some distance apart, they would dry sooner. I would rather keep the firewood, so I chose to distance myself from him. Besides, Charlie was a professor who was clearly busy with his work, so I didn't want to bother him.

It was now a Friday evening. Anna drove me back to the dormitory, and she spoke much less this time. Because of it, I only played with Kristeene and

前面，举起了食指，一边走，一边说，现在是你们最需要集中思想的时候，不得有一点马虎。各位注意，集中注意力！整个教室哄堂大笑，因为我们发现他穿了一条鲜红颜色的裤子！

肥大的红裤子把他一截为二，上身陈旧苍老，下身如娇艳的大姑娘，很不协调。我跟着大家一起放声大笑，但是，当我领悟了他的意图之后，再也笑不出来了。他让我们思考红裤子背后的问题，那个问题不仅不好笑，而且是相当严肃的。我感到应该嘲笑的恰恰是自己。我的听力在他的课上进步很快。我很喜欢听他的课，没有要求换课到查里的班级。

宿舍里没有装私人电话，下了课，安娜就来接我，到七点以后才回来。

我每天早上喝一杯牛奶，吃两片白面包。面包便宜的时候，只要三毛五分钱一条。中午，我吃两个鸡蛋，一碗米饭。降价的鸡蛋九毛九分钱一打。下午在安娜那里吃水果。晚饭也是牛奶和面包。

我在宿舍里晚自修，除非必须查资料，才去图书馆。我尽量不去，一来，到图书馆要走一段路程，二是，怕在那里遇到查里。我和他就像两捆潮湿的木柴，不会马上烧起来，但是，碰到了，也有烧着的可能。也许离得远一些，反而干得快一些。我宁可留着木柴，等到该着火的时候，自然地干燥。再说查里是老师，开学以后一定很忙，也一定会结识许多新的女学生。我就不去打扰他了。

那是一个星期五的晚上，安娜送我回宿舍。路上，她的话明显减少。我只顾着和柯丽丝玩，也不去理会。车开到我的宿舍面前，安娜突然问我，素素，这个周末如何安排？

我说，没有安排呵。

她说，能不能帮我照看柯丽丝？

好呵，我说，你需要几个小时？

安娜说，在我们家过夜。

我楞了一下。从来没有想到去那么豪华的房子里“过夜”，这个邀请来得太突然，我不知道如何回答。

你要外出吗，安娜？我问。

thought of nothing else—until the car halted before my dormitory, that is.

Before I could say goodbye, Anna suddenly asked me, "Susu, do you have any plans for this weekend?"

"Not yet," I responded.

"Then can you help me out by looking after Kristeene?"

'That wouldn't be any trouble', I thought. "No problem. How many hours do you need?" I asked.

"You can stay in my house for the night."

I was dumbfounded. I had never even thought I would have the offer to stay a night in such a luxurious house. The invitation was so sudden that I was at a loss for words. "Will you be away for the whole night, Anna?" I asked curiously.

"No," Anna replied. "Guests will be there."

"Oh," I responded. Anna didn't say anything else, so I didn't ask anything more. At any rate, there would be hustle and bustle in her house, which wasn't a big deal anyway. I already loved the idea of staying in a house like that for the night. In fact, when I took a nap on the carpet of Kristeen's room every afternoon, a recurring thought often flashed across my mind: 'when will I be able to live in such a house?'

Was this the premonition, I wondered? If I could stay at Anna's house and keep working for her in the evenings, maybe I wouldn't need to live in the dorm in the future. Plus, twenty-four hours on duty would increase my income to one-hundred and twenty dollars per day. If I could work like this for two days, I would earn half of my monthly rent. I was exhilarated by the thought but kept my expression nonchalant.

As I was lost in thought, Anna handed me a check instead of the usually twenty dollars in cash. When I looked at it, I saw that she had paid me fifty dollars. I smiled. "Anna, does this include tomorrow's pay?" I inquired curiously.

"No, not at all," Anna responded, smiling back at me. "The extra money is for you to go out and have a good time this Friday evening. Then, you can come to my house on the weekend, okay?"

I thanked her repeatedly and put the check into my bag, waving Anna goodbye, but I still had a load of questions. Anna wanted to bribe me to spend this weekend in her house with double pay. Surely that meant that the guests were VIPs, so I couldn't help but wonder: who were they? What was going to happen? Did it have anything to do with Anna's frequent outings?

From the way she talked and all of the extra money, I knew that she relied on me heavily to look after Kristeene. Although I appreciated Anna's straightforward nature, I was mildly disgusted with her way of solving problems with money. Of course, when I accepted her fifty dollars, I gave her my promise. However, I didn't want to give her such an impression. I couldn't consent im-

不是，安娜说，家里有客人来。

噢，我答。她不说下去，我也不追问了。反正，他们家将会很热闹，我喜欢热闹的场面。

其实，每天下午，我午睡在柯丽丝房间的地毯上时，心里曾闪过这样的念头：哪一天，我能住在这样的房子里？我想，这是不是一个先兆，如果能够在他们家过夜的话，也许以后，我不需要再住宿舍？再说，二十四小时的值班，我的收入就有一百二十美金，如果干两天，就能付半个月的房钱。一百多元美金，对于我来说是多么重要啊！我激动得心快要跳出来了，但是，我不让她看出来。

安娜没有像往常一样，在我下车前给我二十元现金。她拿出了支票本，写完递给我，我看了看，是五十美金，便笑道，安娜，你把明天的钱也算进去了？心里却有点警觉起来。

Not At All，她说，这些多余的钱给你星期五晚上出去玩个够。周末就来我们家，好吗？

我谢了谢，把支票放入手袋，心里却存入了许多的问题。安娜想用加倍的价格买下我到他们家度周末的承诺，说明这些客人很重要。他们是谁？将发生什么事情？和安娜平时的外出有什么关系？从她的口气和多余的钱里，我知道她很需要我，好像不是一般的需要，而是非去不可。看着她坐立不安的样子，我同情她毫无城府直来直去的态度，但讨厌她用金钱来解决问题的方式。按照常规，我拿了五十元美金就等于答应了她。我不想给她那样的印象，我不能马上答应她。拖延时间可能增加我的价码，时间越长，价码越高。我要让安娜倒过来感激我。

我不知道自己为什么变得如此狡猾。大概是因为我有点儿看轻这个女人。帮她带孩子没有多久，我便掂出了这个女人的份量。她有很多钱，但是，并不懂得人生的艰辛。她每天迫不及待地等着我去他们家，就是为了自己能够脱身，到一个神秘的地方去。她的心好像并不在这个家里，可爱的柯丽丝也不能把她拴住。

安娜等不及了，说道，素素，要你放弃两天的休息，我很难开口。但是，……哎，我不知道应该如何向你解释。她的声音很

mediately, since delaying my answer would increase my pay. I wanted Anna to be grateful to me, not the other way around.

I'm not sure why I became so devious. Maybe it was because I looked down on this woman. Not long after I started babysitting Kristeene, I had already started to analyze this woman. She had a lot of money and didn't understand the difficulties of life. Every day, she eagerly waited for me to arrive so that she could leave her home and go off to some mysterious place. Her heart was not at her home. Even the lovely Kristeene couldn't get her to stay.

"Susu, I know I don't have the right to ask you to give up two days of rest for me, but—" Anna's voice went off, breaking me out of my thoughts as I turned to her. "Ah, I don't know how to explain it," she said, her tone sounding quite downhearted and depressed. She took off her sunglasses, revealing her glossy eyes.

"It's no problem," I finally said. "I would like you to tell me some details... Like what I should bring and what I should do while staying at your house."

Anna's posture immediately relaxed. It looked like a heavy burden had been lifted from her shoulders. Just during that moment, I could see her eyes starting to water while involuntarily turning back to look at Kristeene, her teary eyes drawing a curve of sorrow. It touched my heart.

All of a sudden, I realized that the guests coming to Anna's house this weekend may concern Kristeene. If I had kept silent for a few more minutes, Anna might have told me the whole story. Nonetheless, though, I wouldn't let her tell me. I was afraid that it might be a sad story. I feared that I would become weak before her if she vented her emotions.

Gently interrupting Anna's train of thoughts, I said softly, "Anna, you don't need to give me any explanation. I will come on the weekend. Where would you like me to stay?"

"...The third floor. Okay?" She replied quickly, caution lacing her voice.

When I heard Anna say "third floor", my heart tightened. Those two words were like a phantom that would haunt me sooner or later; I just didn't realize that it would come so soon. I had no time to think too much, instead turning to Anna once more. "You haven't told me what I need to bring yet."

"Oh, what do you need to bring?" Anna hummed in thought. "Maybe some changing clothes, but we have everything else you might need upstairs."

I nodded and got out of the car, waving Anna goodbye. Before I left, she called out to me: "Nine o'clock tomorrow morning. I'll pick you up here, okay?"

"Okay," I agreed. "See you tomorrow." Without turning back, I ran into the dormitory, too jumpy to wait for the elevator, opting to run up the stairs instead. My heart was filled with ecstasy. I just exchanged my twenty-four a day for more than a hundred dollars. Moreover, I now had food and board for free. It was nearly unthinkable for someone like me, who had just arrived in

沮丧，使得本来就低沉的声调变得更加沉闷。她把太阳眼镜摘了下来，我看到了她近乎哀求的目光。

没关系。我说，我需要你告诉我一些细节，住到你们家去，我应该带一些什么东西？做哪些事情？

安娜如释重负，原来挺得笔直的身体，一下子松驰了下来，往后一仰，倒在椅背上。就在那一瞬间，她的眼睛潮湿了。她回过头去看了看柯丽丝，泪光抛下一道悲凄的弧线，好像从我的心里穿过一样。我突然意识到，周末的客人可能和柯丽丝有关系。如果我再沉默几分钟，安娜说不定把故事和盘托出。但是，我没有让她说出来。我担心那是一个伤感的故事，害怕自己在感情面前变得软弱。我打断了安娜的思绪，温和地说，安娜，你不必给我任何解释，我来就是了。你让我住哪里？

三楼……好吗？她干脆地回答，后面补了了一个“好吗”，显示了她的小心翼翼。

我听到“三楼”两个字的时候，心头不由地抽了一抽。三楼好像是一个幽灵似的，迟早要找上我，没有想到这么快就来了，我也顾不上想太多，问道，你还是没有告诉我，需要带什么东西？

什么东西？安娜反问道，也许，替换衣服？楼上什么都有。

我下了车，安娜在我的背后说，明天早上九点，我来这儿接你，OK？

OK，明天见！我头也不回地飞奔进了宿舍楼。我没有上电梯，一个阶梯一个阶梯地踩上去。我的心中装满了快乐，双脚在楼梯上又蹦又跳，好像要把快乐抖出来和整栋楼分享。一百多美金换走我一天一夜二十四小时，有吃有住有休息，对于刚来美国的我来说，简直是不可想像的事情。

打开房门，莉莎正在厕所里使用吹风机，我说，劳驾，劳驾，让我用一用马桶。

莉莎关了机器，跨出厕所时丢了句话给我：看你像一阵风似地，从哪里回来？我才想起来，住进来以后，发生了那么多的事情，我都没有机会告诉她。

America.

When I opened the door to my room, I was immediately greeted by the noise of Lisa's hair drier coming from the bathroom. I knocked on the wall to let her know that I was there before opening my mouth to speak. "Can I use the bathroom for a minute? Please, please," I asked her frantically.

Lisa turned off the hair dryer, but cast a few words behind her as she stepped out of the bathroom. "Geez, you came flying in like a gust of wind. Where are you coming from?"

I gaped a little, realizing that I hadn't even had the chance to tell Lisa about everything that happened to me since moving in. "Hey, you don't come back every night either. Where are you going? How are your studies going?" I raised my voice to respond to her, hoping she would be able to hear me through the closed door.

"It's going well," Lisa shouted back, her voice slightly muffled by the hair dryer she continued to use in the living room.

"Where are you going tonight?"

"A party," she responded.

"Without an appointment?" 'Speaking of appointments,' I thought. 'I never got the chance to talk to her about that boyfriend of hers.'

"Nope, no appointment."

After washing my hands, I walked to the living room to talk to her. "Earlier, your boyfriend, David—is that his name?—had come to see you. I forgot to tell you," I admitted.

Pivoting around abruptly, Lisa turned off the hair dryer and faced me. "What? What did you say? He came to see me?"

"Yes, he came here just as you went out to meet him."

"Susu!" Lisa called out, her mouth forming a solid gape. She stood in front of the long mirror in the living room, completely dumbfounded by what I had told her. Taking quick and fractic steps, she began circling around the living room like a spinning top, her hands settled on her face in embarrassment.

Watching her made me dizzy, so I stepped forward to embrace her. "Lisa, stop! It's my fault. I forgot to tell you. You go find him and I'll apologize to him," I offered.

I held her hands and led her to the sofa, repeating what I had said. Lisa's face flushed and paled simultaneously, her hair looking as disheveled as messy straw. I realized that the situation was more serious than I had thought. "Lisa, can you go meet him tonight? I'll go with you to the party and I'll explain what happened to him," I said softly in an attempt to make amends.

Lisa shut her eyes and shook her head. "It's too late," she sighed. "He's already gone."

My arms went limp. Gone? Did she mean that he was… Dead?

I felt like my head was about to explode. My whole body collapsed on the

我放大了嗓音，对着门外的她说，你自己每天晚上不回来，你到哪里去了？读书还好吧？

好。她的声音拌着机器声一起从客厅里传过来。

今晚你上那儿去？

Party。

约会吗？我问，突然记起来她的那个男朋友。我洗完了手，马上跑过去告诉她。

没有约会。她说。

早先你的男朋友，戴维德，是不是他的名字？他来找过你，我忘了告诉你。

莉莎猛转身，关了机器，反问道，你说什么？他来找过我？

是呵，就是你出门去等他的时候，他来这儿找你。

素素！莉莎喊了一声，张大了嘴，说不出话来。她站在客厅的大镜子前面，整个人就像螺丝钉一样，踩着碎步，三百六十度地转着，双手捂着脸。

我看得头晕，上前抱住了她，说道，莉莎，停下来！是我的错，我忘了告诉你。你把他找来，我赔罪。

我把她按在沙发上，一边又一边地重复着上面的话。莉莎的脸一会儿红，一会儿白，刚刚吹干的头发像稻草一样乱七八糟。我感觉到事情比想像的要严重。但是，还是争取弥补自己的过错，说道：莉莎，今晚你能碰到他吗？我和你一起去Party，好吗？我给他解释。

莉莎闭着眼睛，不停地摇头，说，太晚了，他已经走了。

莉莎说“走（Gone）”了。我理解为“死（去世）”了。我的头“轰”地一声爆炸，整个身体瘫倒在莉莎的旁边，压着了她的一条腿。

你怎么啦？莉莎推推我，反问道。

我拉长了脸说，他死了？为什么去死呵？

莉莎给了我一拳，打在我的左肩膀上，哭笑不得地说，走了，不是死了。他离开这个城市了。

sofa beside Lisa, pressing on her leg.

"Susu… Are you okay?" Lisa asked slowly, gently tapping me.

"He… Died?" I asked, a horrified expression still on my face. "What was the cause of his death?"

Lisa gently hit me on my left shoulder with her fist. It seemed like she was at a loss as to whether to laugh or cry. "No, Susu," she said. "He left, not died. He left this town."

I sat up vigorously and pumped my fist in the air, relieved at her words. "You scared me!"

Lisa chuckled. "Yeah, he gave up a football scholarship at another college for me and enrolled in this college instead, but now…" She trailed off. "Well, anyway, we were classmates at the same high school." Pausing, she turned to me. "Hey, Susu, why didn't you mention it before?"

I took a moment to ponder my response. I wanted to tell her that I didn't know of your love life or relationship and that we didn't have a chance to see each other for long recently. Plus, misunderstandings between people were normal. To me, if a couple broke up because of a simple misunderstanding, then losing the relationship wasn't worth any regret. I didn't say any of this out loud, though. After all, it was still a rough patch in a love affair, which hurts the same nonetheless. I had some experiences like that. So, because this misunderstanding was partially my fault, I was willing to shoulder the burden of the blame.

"Well," I finally started. "As long as he is alive, there's some way to reach him. Do you have his phone number? And has he contacted you recently?"

"I have his phone number, but he hasn't contacted me at all," Lisa frowned.

"Give me his phone number and I'll call him to explain what happened."

Lisa's eyes widened in surprise at my words, remaining silent. I poured her a glass of icy water, and she drank it in quick gulps, telling me his phone number.

I thanked her and left the room, using the payphone in the hallway to call David. When he picked up, I introduced myself and asked if he still remembered me. He told me that he did.

"Good," I said. "I wanted to explain what happened the night you came to pick Lisa up. At that time, my English was so poor that I didn't understand what you were saying. It caused this current misunderstanding between you two," I explained. "That night," I continued, "Lisa waited for you for a long time, but it was in vain. She looked for you everywhere, afraid that something had happened to you."

David was silent for a moment, then responded. "We had an appointment that night. We agreed that she would wait for me in the dorm room."

"Yes, yes," I replied quickly. "She was waiting for you in the room. Then she told me to tell you that she would be back soon, but I didn't understand.

我“腾”地坐起来，打回莉莎一拳，说道：如果你把我吓死了，也是一条人命。

莉莎笑了，说，他是为了我而放弃了另一个大学足球队的奖学金，到这里来读书，我们是高中同学……。

素素，你为什么一字不提呢？

我想为自己做一点辩护：我哪里知道你们的恋爱关系？你也没有做关照呵。后来，我们俩根本互相不见面，哪有机会提及？再说，人与人之间出现误会，是很正常的事情。如果这点小误会能把相爱的人拆开，这种关系有什么值得留恋？但是，我没有说。毕竟，那是一场失败的恋爱，我也有过失恋的经历。如果因为我的过失，能减轻莉莎挫败的心理负担，我愿意背这个十字架。我说，只要他还活着，就有办法。你有他的电话吗？他走了以后，没有和你联系吗？

莉莎说，有电话，但是没有联系。

把电话号码给我，我来告诉他。

莉莎瞪大了眼睛看着我，半晌不说话。

我给莉莎倒了杯冰水。她一口气喝完，报出了电话号码。

我冲出房门，去打走廊上的公用电话。电话接通，正巧，戴维德在家。我介绍了自己的身份，问他还记不记得我。他说记得。我说，记得就好。那个时候，我的英语不行，你的话我都听不懂，造成了你们之间的误会。那天晚上，莉莎等了你很长时间，没有等到，她到处找你，以为你出了什么事情。

他说，那天我和莉莎说好了，叫她在宿舍里等我。

我说，是呵，是呵，她是在宿舍里等你，她让我转告如果有人来，请留下。她一会儿就回来的。但是，我没有听懂，是我的错，对不起，对不起。莉莎到今天还在想念你，你不能抽空来看看她吗？

正说到这里，莉莎懒洋洋地过来了。

电话那边说，她没有其他男朋友吗？

我说，你说到哪里去了？我们住一个宿舍，她天天晚上在家

It's my fault. I feel really sorry. Lisa is still thinking of you, even today. Could you squeeze a little time to come see her?"

Just as I said that, Lisa slowly walked over.

"Doesn't she have another boyfriend?" David asked accusingly.

"What a question!" I exclaimed. "No, she doesn't. We live in the same dorm room. She's in the room every night. She's heartbroken."

There was nothing but silence on the other end. I whispered to Lisa that he would come to see her, but she shook her head, clearly in disbelief. "Are you still there, David?" I asked into the phone.

"Yes, I am."

"Is there anything you'd like to say to Lisa? I can deliver your message to her for you," I offered.

No answer.

In a low voice, I told Lisa that David was thinking of her very much. Her eyes began to turn red from crying. Uncovering the phone, I said, "David, Lisa wants to speak with you." I forced the phone into Lisa's hand, but she only sobbed and couldn't utter a word.

I then took the phone from her hand, saying into the receiver, "David, did you hear that? She's sobbing so sadly. Come see her tomorrow, okay?"

David said that he would come tonight.

When I hung up, Lisa hugged me tightly and began jumping up and down. We bounced our way back to the dorm like a pair of rabbits.

I told Lisa what I had told David over the phone. Then, I paused. "Lisa," I added. "Please forgive me for not telling the truth. I know that you had dates with other boys, but I also know that you still love David. Now I've finished my task to pull you both back to your original spot. How it goes from here depends on you," I told her.

Teardrops were still on Lisa's eyelashes, but her mouth was wide with a smile. "That's okay," she said. "If I have problems later, I'll just say that I don't understand, like you."

I laughed. "Is David going to drive here?"

"Yes," Lisa responded, rummaging through her clothes. "He's about two and a half hours away."

At her words, I began to think of where I should go tonight. My mind drifted to Charlie.

里，很痛苦呵。

对方沉默了一会儿。我和莉莎咬耳朵说，他要来看你了。莉莎摇头不相信。

我对着电话说，戴维德，你在线上吗？

YES，我在。他说。

你有什么话要转告莉莎吗？对方仍旧不回答。

我悄声地对莉莎说，他说非常想念你。莉莎的眼睛马上红了。

戴维德，莉莎要和你说说话，好吗？我把话筒塞到了莉莎手里。莉莎抽泣着，说不出话来。

我把电话抢过来，说，戴维得，听到了吗，她好伤心呵，明天过来看看她，好吗？

戴维德说，今晚就过来。

挂了电话，莉莎扑上来抱着我乱跳。像两只小兔子一样，跳回了宿舍。我把和戴维德谈话的内容复述了一遍，我说，莉莎，请原谅我没有说实话。我知道你和其他男孩子约会，也知道你心里仍旧爱着戴维德。我的任务已经完成，把你们拉回到原来的地步，怎么走下去，全靠你自己。

莉莎的眼睫毛上还挂着泪珠，脸上绽开了笑容，对我说，以后出问题，就说没有听懂，像你一样。

我大笑，问莉莎，戴维德开车过来？

莉莎正在翻箱倒柜地寻找衣服，一边说，是的，大约两个半小时。

我想，今天晚上，我应该到哪里去呢？我想到了查里。

Chapter 6

I had finally decided what to do tonight.

I opened up my suitcase, picked out all kinds of tea cans, and stuffed them into a plastic bag. Then, I took a bath, put on some makeup, and wore a sexy dress that I had bought in China. It was a pretty beige color and tight-fitting, only suiting Oriental women with a good figure. I didn't dare to let my family see it since it was backless, so I had hidden it in my pillowcase. Up until now, I couldn't understand why I chose a dress of this style. My disposition would normally never allow myself to wear such a dress while walking down the street, but tonight, I decided that I would use it.

When Lisa saw me walking out of the bathroom, she immediately gaped. "Oh my gosh. Oh my gosh! You turned yourself into a demon," she guffawed. "Are you going to a banquet or something?"

"No," I replied. "I was just envious of you and David. I want to dress beautifully to console myself."

Lisa pursed her lips. "My gosh, you look so pretty. If only I were a man!"

"If you were a man, all of the students on campus would hate me," I remarked with a small grin.

Lisa walked over, noticing the tea cans I had stuffed in that plastic bag. "Hey, don't hide that from me. You're going to see someone with this gift, aren't you?"

"Yes, I want to see a friend... But I don't know where he is," I said.

"...You're lying."

"No, it's true!" I responded. "I don't know where he is. I want to find him."

Lisa paused, pondering for a moment. "Well, if he's one of the students on campus, I probably know them."

I was caught off-guard by the fact that she knew most of the people on campus already, but quickly brushed it off. "Do you know Professor Thomas? In the philosophy department?" I asked.

"Charlie Thomas?"

"Yes."

"Yeah, I know him," Lisa told me. "You want to see him?"

At first, I wanted to explain everything that had happened with Charlie. After second thought, though, I changed my mind. Had I explained every-

第六章

我打开箱子，把龙井，毛峰和碧螺春等各种精装成罐的茶叶找出来，装进了一个塑料马甲袋。我去洗了澡，化了妆，穿一件很性感的连衣裙。这件衣服是我在国内的华侨商店买的，因为背后是空的，我不敢让家里人知道，悄悄地把它藏在枕头套里面。我到现在都弄不清当时为什么要买这样的款式，按照我的习性，是绝对不敢穿着这样的衣服走上大街的。但是，今天晚上，我居然记着它，而且穿上了身。衣服是淡棕色的，只有细腰黑头发的东方女人才能穿出风韵来。

莉莎看到我从厕所里出来的时候，变色地喊着：我的老天爷，我的老天爷！你这个妖精，今天晚上要去赴宴吗？

NO，我说，我妒忌你和戴维德，想穿得漂亮一些安慰自己。

莉莎蹶起了嘴说，如果我是男人就好了。

我说，如果你成了男人，这校园里的哥哥弟弟都要恨死我了！

这时，莉莎发现了我放在地上的茶叶包，一个跨步跳到我的面前，说道，不要瞒我，你准备了礼物去见人呢！

我说，是呵，我想见一个朋友，但是，不知道他在哪里？

她说，谁像你这样编织谎言？

我说，真的，我不知道他在哪里？我要去寻找。

莉莎说，学校里的人吗？我大多认识。

我心里想，这个姑娘真是厉害，没几天已经像梳子一样把大学梳理了一遍，便问道，你认识哲学系的老师汤姆斯吗？

查里．汤姆斯？

嗯。

认识呵，你要见他吗？

嗯。

thing, it would seem like I had a guilty conscience. It wasn't like I wanted to have a relationship with Charlie, after all. I didn't have any such hope for that. I just wanted Lisa and her boyfriend to have the dorm room all to themselves for the night.

Lisa came out of her bedroom with a bag that had previously held a designer's dress. She transferred my tea cans into it, and I smiled at her intention. My initial plastic bag really looked out of place next to my pretty dress.

"Well, I've got to drive you there," Lisa said. "Professor Thomas lives pretty far. I don't know if he's at home or not right now, though."

"How do you know where he lives?" I asked.

"Oh, it's an open 'secret,'" she said. "I've attended his class several times. He always mingles with the students as if they're friends. He doesn't really act like a professor sometimes."

"Maybe he's gone to a party on the campus, then."

Lisa paused and turned to me, slightly intrigued by my words. "Are you planning to go to a party to find him?"

That was a tough question. I suddenly felt inexperienced and pitiful. Ever since classes had started, I passed each weekend in my dorm while reading and doing homework. I had never thought of having a "good time" for even a little while. However, there was a chance today. I even had some money from Anna, and I also wanted Lisa to have the dorm room to herself. I was wearing the pretty dress but didn't have anywhere to go. I felt disappointed. "I don't know. I… Don't know how to find him," I admitted.

"My dear Susu, it's okay," Lisa told me. "Let me help you," she said with confidence. "Now, listen to me. I have his home phone number. You can call him first. If he's not at home, I'll drive from party to party to look for him, okay?"

"But what if David comes while you're gone?"

"Don't worry. Go make a call first," Lisa urged. "We still have time before David arrives."

I dashed out of my room to make my way to the payphone once more. The line rang several times without any answer. I thought that I must wait until his answering machine began to work, but to no avail. It seemed like no one was going to pick up.

Just as I was about to hang up, someone picked up the phone. "Sorry, sorry. I was in the bath," the voice from the other line spoke. It was Charlie, and he didn't even ask who was calling him first.

I didn't say anything, opting to listen to his blabbering first. I thought that he must've been speaking to someone he had made an appointment to call him.

Charlie finally paused his rambling. "Oh, right. Who is this?" He asked.

Now I was in low spirits and didn't know whether or not I should answer him. I thought that if Charlie had another appointment, where else could I go? I was ready to hang up, but suddenly remembered the tea cans I had packed. I couldn't just give up—I wanted to give him those tea cans!

我本来想解释一下查里请我吃饭，我要送他礼物等等。但是，我改变了主意。为什么要解释呢？难道我真的心虚吗？真的想和查里有不同于一般朋友关系吗？我觉得不是。我是为了把宿舍让出来给莉莎和她的男朋友共度一个快乐的夜晚。莉莎从自己的房间里拿来了一个品牌的礼品袋，把我的茶叶罐头装进去。我明白她的好意，否则，塑料口袋和我的打扮一点儿也不相配。

莉莎说，我必须送你去，他住得挺远的，也不知道是否在家？

我说，你怎么知道他住在哪里？

她说，那是公开的秘密。我旁听了几次他的课，他什么都懂，和学生像朋友一样，没有老师的架子。

我说，也许今晚他出席在哪一个Party，校园里的？

你打算一个一个Party去找？莉莎反问我。

莉莎一下子就把我问倒了。我突然觉得自己很幼稚很可怜，开学以来，每一个周末我都是在宿舍里度过的，看书做功课，从来没有想到应该玩一玩。今天，机会来了，安娜给了我钱，宿舍要让给莉莎用，我穿上了漂亮的衣服，却没有去处，也没有伙伴。我好失落啊！对自己发了脾气，尖声地叫起来：我不知道。我不知道如何去找他？

亲爱的素素，请不要着急，让我来帮助你。莉莎说得很自信很耐心。这样吧，我这里有他家里的电话号码，你先打过去问一问。如果不在家，我开车陪你一个一个Party去找。

我说，那怎么行？戴维德来了，怎么办？

莉莎说，快去，打电话要紧。在戴维德来之前，我们还有一些时间。

我再次冲出房门去打走廊上的公用电话。铃响了很多次，没有人接。我想，等吧，等他的录音留话。铃响个不停，没有录音。算了，挂掉吧！正在这时，对方有人接起了电话，对着电话连声说，对不起，对不起，我刚刚洗完澡……。那是查里。他居然没有问一问我是谁？

我没有吭声，听他唠叨，心里想，是不是他在对一个约好了打电话的人说话？

终于，查里收住了，问道，你是谁？

我的情绪很低落，不知道应不应该回答他。心里想，如果查里已经有了约会，我还有什么地方可去？我不应该让他知道我打电话

"Charlie, it's me," I spoke slowly, my tone cautious and listless.

"Susu!" He exclaimed in surprise. "I wasn't expecting you to call me."

I felt slightly stunned at his words, pausing for a moment before responding. "I wanted to give you some green tea. Do you have time?"

"Yes, of course," he said. "I wanted to see you, too. You left your cosmetics and wine in my car. I'll return them to you now."

"Okay," I said. "See you then." I hung up and felt tears on my cheeks.

It was a Friday evening, so students were flocking to and fro in the corridor. I didn't go back to my dorm room immediately, instead standing behind the window with my back to the corridor, looking at the scenery from afar. Someone whistled at my bare back, but I didn't care. The sound of music came from afar, a sign of weekend partying. I gazed at the distant starry sky and recalled the first night that Charlie carried me on his shoulder as well as the time we hugged tightly after dinner. I remembered how nice it felt to have his body against mine. I regretted not making a move on him sooner, lest other girls would snatch him away from me.

I looked at the cement road through the window, hoping to see his car pull up at any minute. I didn't see his white Honda yet, so my heart felt jittery as I continued waiting for him.

I started daydreaming. As soon as Charlie would arrive, I would fly downstairs into his embrace. I fantasized that he would caress my hair and call out to me, saying "gosh, you fool of a girl!" with a smile on his lips. I would wait for him to kiss my eyes, ears, and lips. I felt like that half an hour I was waiting lasted longer than a day.

His car finally appeared in the parking lot. I watched him park his car, open the door, step out, and shut the door. Charlie came toward the dorm building. I felt like I should just fly downstairs and meet him at the building door like I had planned, but something was holding me back, and I wasn't sure why. I involuntarily turned toward my dorm room, but wasn't expecting Lisa to be right in front of me. I didn't know how long she had been standing there, but she scared me out of my wits.

"He's here," Lisa acknowledged.

"Let's go," I nodded and pulled Lisa back to our room.

"You're hiding something," Lisa noted cautiously. "If it's a secret, maybe you'll feel better talking about it," she said, handing me a tissue.

I took the tissue and gently patted my face dry from my tears. "Lisa," I started, "I don't have any secrets. I just feel lonely, especially tonight on a weekend. I feel like I've lost my spiritual balance."

Lisa paused, contemplating my words. "It's okay, Susu. Charlie is a good man and a worthy friend," she said gently. "I wish you well tonight."

I gave Lisa a hug and went into the bathroom to check on my makeup. "Since he's here, I should cheer up. Can't let him see my tears," I whispered to my reflection.

The doorbell rang shortly after. Lisa opened the door. Charlie came in, his car keys in one hand and my cosmetics and wine in the other. It looked

去找他。让他去赴约会吧，只当我没有找过他。我准备挂电话，突然，想起了那些茶叶，我本来不就是为了给他送茶叶去吗？

是我，查里。我说得很轻很慢，有气无力。

素素！他惊叫起来。素素，真没有想到你给我打电话！

我好像噎住了似的，顿了好久才说，我想给你送一些绿茶，今晚你有空吗？

有空，有空。他说，我正想去找你呢！你把化妆品和葡萄酒留在我车里了，我给你送去吧！

嗯，再见！我挂上了电话，发觉自己的脸上都是泪。

星期五，晚上，走廊上时不时有来往的学生。我没有马上回宿舍，背对着走廊，看窗外的风景。有人对我裸露的后背吹口哨，我没有在乎。远处隐隐约约传来了铿跄的鼓乐声，那是PARYT的信号。我望着遥远的星空，想起了第一天晚上查里把我扛在肩膀上，想起了那天吃晚饭，我们拥抱在一起，和他身贴身的感觉真美好。我有些后悔，为什么不能再跨前一步，把他抓住，不让他被别的女人抢了去？我的眼睛一直望着窗外，沿着那条通进来的水泥路，看到尽头。我哪里是在看风景？我等看他的车，那辆白色的丰田车，不见到他的车，我的心悬在半空。望眼欲穿，我像着了魔一样胡思乱想。我想着，查里一到，我就飞下楼去，和他抱在一起。我幻想着他揉摸我的头发，亲昵地叫我“傻姑娘”，我等着他来舔我的眼睛，耳朵和嘴唇……。我觉得这半个小时比一天还要长。

终于，他的车来了，开得那么慢，缓缓地驶进停车场。我看着他泊完车，开了车门，他出来了，把车门关上了。查里来了，朝宿舍楼走来了！我应该飞奔下去，我应该把他拦在宿舍的门口。我为什么不走？为什么还站在这里？为什么？为什么？没有答案。身体却不由自主地转了回去，面朝着宿舍的方向。未料到，莉莎站在我的背后，我不知道她站了多少时候，我被她吓了一跳。

他来了。莉莎说。

走吧。我点点头，拉着莉莎回了宿舍。莉沙说，原来你有秘密。说出来吧，你会好受一些。

我接过她递来的面纸，复盖在眼睛上吸收泪迹。我说，莉莎，我没有什么秘密，我有点孤独，尤其在周末的晚上，心里不太平衡。

她说，查里是个善良的男人，值得交朋友。祝你今晚快乐！

我给了她一个拥抱，进厕所补妆。对着镜子，我自言自语，开

like he was giving me a gift.

When I came out of the bathroom, Charlie's face seemed to light up. Since Lisa was here, though, he didn't praise my appearance or anything. It was like we were going back to the first time we had met. We didn't shake hands, hug each other, or even touch each other at all. I was half-expecting him to hold me in his arms this time, but he didn't.

To clear the silence, I began to speak. "Charlie, Lisa's boyfriend will come to see her tonight. Let's go out," I suggested, giving him the tea cans while he handed me a plastic bag with my belongings inside. I took out the wine, gave it to Lisa, and wished her a happy night.

We left the room, walking in the corridor in a single-file line. He stood on my left as we took the elevator down and walked to his car. When we arrived, Charlie opened the door for me and we quickly made our way down the highway. Neither one of us spoke.

The car sped like a beast, darting into the darkness recklessly. I didn't know where we were going. I felt like I was sitting on needles, not daring to even glance at him.

Several times on the road, I silently wished that he would stop somewhere remote so that we could be close. I had hoped that he would turn and say, "Susu, you look so beautiful tonight." I wished that I could have given him a charming smile and let him kiss me, but no such thing happened.

I didn't know how much time had passed. My enthusiasm began to fall, and I started to feel disappointed. It was like I was a beggar for emotions, and a poor beggar at that.

The car finally reached a halt in front of a bungalow. "Susu," Charlie finally spoke. "You wouldn't mind visiting my home, would you?"

I responded by saying that we had nowhere else to go.

He opened the car door for me and held out his hand to help me out. I gave him my hand like any polite lady should do during the occasion. We made our way to the house together before he pulled out his keys and opened the door, leading me to his living room.

Charlie gestured for me to sit on the long sofa and told me that he was going to boil some water in the kitchen. I obliged and took in the scenery of his home. His living room was rather petite. The long sofa faced the windows, which gave me a nice view of the scenery outside. There was a footpath behind his garden that was lined with all sorts of flora ranging from flowers and bushes to tall trees. Flower bulbs snaked among the bushes and trees, some high against the blossoms and some hiding low in the branches like naughty imps. The design was quite romantic, if I did say so myself.

I concentrated my attention back to Charlie's living room. There was a fireplace beside the sofa and a soft chair placed in front of it. A few magazines littered the coffee table, so I picked one up and began flipping through the pages. A couple moments later, Charlie came in with two cups of tea and sat down beside me.

He looked at me with a smile. "Thanks for your green tea."

心点，他来了，不要让他知道我流了眼泪。

门铃响了。莉莎开的门。查里一手拿着钥匙，一手拎着我的酒和化妆品，好像送礼物给我一样。

我从厕所所里出来的时候，查里的眼睛确实亮了一亮，但是，在莉莎的面前，他没有任何夸奖我的言词。我们又像上次一样，没有任何身体的接触，没有握手，更没有拥抱，这一回，我是期待着他来拥抱我的。他没有。

我说，查里，莉莎的男朋友老远地赶来看她，我们出去吧！我给他茶叶，他给了我沉甸甸的塑料袋。我取出葡萄酒，给了莉莎，祝她晚上快乐。

我们就这样离开了宿舍。我们在走廊上走，一前一后。我们进了电梯，他站在左面，我站在右面。我们走到他的车旁，他给我开了车门。我坐了进去，他上车。我们上了公路。两个人居然都没有说一句话。

车开得很快，像一头野兽似的，不顾一切地撕裂着黑暗。我不知道他向哪里开，更不知道要到哪里去。他的目光一直注视着前方，我连看他一眼都不敢看。如坐针毡！一路上，我几次想叫他停下来，停到一个什么荒野地方，让我们喘一口气。我盼望着他能够回头看我一眼，说一声，素素，今晚你好漂亮。我盼望自己能够妩媚地对他笑一笑，让他亲一亲。但是，我没有。什么都没有发生。

不知过了多少时候，我从情感的高峰上跌了下来，我开始失望，开始抱怨，开始反感。我觉得自己像一个情感乞讨者一样，非常可怜。

车停了。停在一栋平房前，他说，素素，你不介意到我家里去坐坐？

我说，没有别的地方可去了。

他给我开了车门，伸过手来接我一把。我按礼貌把手给了他。我从车门里出来。他关车门。我跟在他的后面。

我看着他拿出钥匙，开门，引我进客厅。

他请我在长沙发上坐下，说，我去厨房烧壶水。

我环视了一下周围，客厅并不大，一个长沙发对着宽敞的玻璃窗，可以观赏外面的风景。花园里有一条小径，

两旁有花卉和树丛，各色的灯泡穿插其间，有的高一些，和花朵交相辉映，有的躲在树丛里，好像调皮捣蛋的夜精灵。很别致很

I nodded and took the cup from his hand, placing it on the coffee table. Turning my head towards him, I smiled and asked, "What else do you want to say?"

"You are really beautiful."

I let out a small giggle, but immediately put my hand on my mouth.

"I want to kiss you," he said.

I hastily turned away from him and picked up my teacup. I blew at the tea leaves gently and took a sip.

"Don't go back tonight and stay here with me."

I put the cup back down and involuntarily leaned back on the sofa, closing my eyes as I did so. I had been waiting for him to say that for the whole evening. I had nowhere to go and had to stay here for the night anyway. My lonely soul needed some security and a cove of safety. My tense nerves needed to relax in the presence of his love. My skin was hungry, and my heart was dry. I needed a lover's shadow in my eyes. These were all things that I needed right now. "Charlie," I whispered, letting out a long breath that I didn't realize I was holding.

He moved closer to me, his warm hand reaching my back and gently touching my bare skin. I started breathing faster, so I had to open my mouth to get some air. Then, he licked my dry lips.

Charlie was just so gentle. Every move he made was full of emotion. He kissed me and pulled back slowly, mumbling to himself before turning his attention back to me. "The first time I saw you," he began, "I wanted to bring you here. I really wanted to kiss you that night, but I didn't," he went on. "I guess tonight's gonna make up for it."

He looked like he had more on his mind, so I just stayed quiet, staring into his eyes.

"The other night after dinner, you took off so fast," he whispered. "You owe me, you know? Did you even realize I was hitting up the library every day, hoping to see you? But you never showed up," he continued. "Why'd you never come to my class? Why were you avoiding me? Did you think I wouldn't catch on to how you felt?"

Charlie kept on kissing me, lightly praising me after each one. He said my eyes were full of wisdom, my nose was perfectly shaped, my neck was pretty, and my lips? Well, those were his favorite.. Same went for my skin, chest, legs, and feet. He was so locked in on my features that I think he almost forgot about the rest of me. If I were a pond, he'd have stirred up some intense waves.

That night, we slept together. My jetlag disappeared.

浪漫的设计，可是，我没有欣赏的心情。沙发的旁边是一个壁炉，壁炉前方有一个很低的软椅。咖啡桌上放着一些杂志。我顺手拿起一本杂志翻起来，查里端了两杯茶过来，坐在我的旁边。

他看着我，微笑着，说道，谢谢你的绿茶。

我接过茶杯，放在咖啡桌上，歪着头，对他笑了笑，问道，你还想说什么？

你真美。

我"扑哧"一声笑起来，用手捂住了嘴。

他说，我想亲亲你。

我赶忙转移视线，拿起茶杯，吹了吹浮在水面的茶叶，呷了一口。

今晚不要回去了，住在我这里。

放下茶杯，我不由自主地仰在沙发上，闭上了眼睛。整个儿的晚上，就在等着他说这句话。我没有地方可去，只有留在这里。我那孤独的灵魂需要一个归宿和安全的港湾，我那蹦紧的神经需要为爱情放松和舒展。我的皮肤是饥饿的，我的内心是干枯的，我的眼睛里需要有爱人的身影。这就是我要的呀！我长长地舒了一口气。

他就这样靠近了我，温暖的手从我的背后伸过去，贴在我的皮肤上，一点一点地移动。我的呼吸越来越急促，不得不张开嘴巴。我感到了他，他的舌头舔着我干燥的嘴唇。查里很耐心，很温柔，一举一动都包含着丰富的感情。他一边吻着我，一边喃喃自语。他说第一次见到你，就想把你带回家。那天没有吻你，今天要补上。他说，晚餐的那天，你溜得好快，今天要加倍地偿还。他说，天天到图书馆等你，你为什么不来？为什么不到我的班里来上课？你为什么要躲着我？你以为我不知道你的心思吗？

他吻到哪里都要赞美一番。他说我的眼睛很聪慧，我的鼻子很乖巧，我的脖子很秀美，我的嘴巴太玲胧，我的皮肤，我的胸部，我的腿，我的脚丫……。查里几乎到了忘我的地步，哪怕我是一潭死水，也能被他推出波浪，何况我是一泉活水？

那天晚上，我们俩一起呼呼入睡。我的时差从此消失得无影无踪。

Chapter 7

The following day, I rose earlier than Charlie, recalling the commitment I made to work at Anna's place. I moved stealthily, snagging a colossal T-shirt from Charlie's closet and pulling it over my head. It draped around me like an oversized sleepwear gown.

Heading to the kitchen, I set the kettle ablaze. Once it whistled its readiness, I tossed in a handful of dragon-well tea leaves and doused them with hot water. Next, I made my way to the bathroom for a bath. The cascade of water seemed to echo rather loudly, for midway through, Charlie rapped on the door, urgently seeking entry.

Behind the veil of the shower curtain, he raised his voice, addressing me. "Susu, did you sleep well last night?" he inquired. "And what's with the early rise?"

"I slept like a log, thanks," I replied. "I have to get back to the dorm. Someone's picking me up at nine."

Charlie flushed the toilet, and suddenly the bathwater surged to a scalding temperature. I yelped, shutting off the tap. At once, Charlie reappeared in the bathroom, yanking back the shower curtain and carrying me into the bedroom without hesitation.

"Let me go!" I shouted, resisting his antics. But Charlie paid no heed, depositing me onto the bed. Soap bubbles clung to him as well, but he nonchalantly peeled off his clothes and used them to pat himself dry.

I shielded my eyes and turned away, avoiding his gaze. He chuckled and playfully pulled the blanket away, exposing me in all my nakedness. Swiftly, I darted into the closet, sliding one door shut, only for Charlie to slide the other open. I scampered out, racing back into the bathroom, hastily locking the door. Suddenly, a loud yelp from outside pierced the air, as though something had tumbled onto him. I flung the door open, concerned, but it was a ruse.

Charlie swiftly entered the bathroom, and we ended up taking a bath together. We frolicked like carefree children, until he held me close, his voice a soft plea. "Just stay here with me, okay?"

"Charlie, I'm an international student," I began, "I want to study, get my degree, and besides, I need to earn my keep. I have to work."

Charlie seemed taken aback. "Oh, you work? What kind of work?" He

第七章

第二天，我醒得比查里早，因为心里记着要去安娜家里上班的事情。我蹑手蹑脚地爬起来，从查里的壁橱里拿来一件短袖的圆领汗衫，望头上一套，正好像睡袍似地把我大半个身体都遮住了。

我到厨房去，先烧了一壶水，倒了些龙井茶在茶缸里，泡上。然后，去厕所洗澡。可能是放水的声音太闹，在我洗到一半的时候，查里敲门进来小便。隔着浴帘，他问，素素，昨晚睡好了没有？为什么起得这么早？我说，睡得很好。我得回宿舍去，九点钟有人来接。

查里拉了一下抽水马桶的水箱，我的洗澡水突然烫了起来。我“哇哇”乱叫，赶快关掉水龙头。查里听见我的尖叫，不知道发生了什么事情，立刻返回来，撩起浴帘，抱起我就走。我先是慌乱后是挣扎，一边喊着：放下我！放下我！他扔我到了床上，自己的上身和短裤上都是肥皂泡沫和水迹，好像落汤鸡一般。他干脆脱了裤衩，揉成一团往身上擦。然后，一丝不挂地站在床边。我假装捂上眼睛，转过身去不看他。他笑着扑上来把盖在我身上的毯子全部掀掉，也让我赤身裸体。我赶快从床上滚下来，躲到了他的壁橱里。壁橱有两扇拉门，我拉上一扇，他拉开了另一扇。我从壁橱里逃出来，躲进了厕所，锁上门。忽然，他在外面“哎哟”叫了一声，好像被什么东西压着了似的。我赶紧开门，以为出了什么事情，想不到中了他的圈套。他“哈哈”大笑挤进浴室，抱起我一起洗澡。我们就像两个幸福的孩子在温暖的水雾中玩耍……。最后，他搂抱着我说，哪里都不要去，陪我，好吗？

我说，查里，我是留学生，我要读书，拿学位，还要赚钱养活自己。我是去打工的。

他说，你去打工？打什么工？你哪有时间打工？你的父母或者亲戚不资助你？那个有钱人家是你的什么人？不是你的亲戚

fired a barrage of questions. "How do you find time for it? Do your folks support you? What's your deal with that affluent family you stayed with?" The cascade of questions subsided as he finally exited the bath, wrapping himself in a large towel before changing into a T-shirt and trousers.

I quickly donned last night's dress and secured my hair with a white towel. "I don't have any family here," I answered. "I babysit for a wealthy family. The woman who hired me, Anna, is picking me up at the dorm."

Charlie frowned. "Susu, why didn't you tell me earlier?"

"Why would I need to tell you? I'm doing fine, aren't I?"

He scratched his head sheepishly. It seemed he wanted to say something, but no words emerged. I brushed it off, taking his hand and walking with him to the kitchen. I poured two cups of tea and settled down, sliding one cup towards him. He didn't take it, choosing instead to hold my hand, pulling me close.

Charlie untied the towel around my head and gently dried my hair. The towel grew damp from the moisture, but he continued, all in silence.

"You know," I broke the quiet, "it's pretty common for an international student to work. Weekends are prime time, too. I can earn more."

He raised one of my arms, his touch gentle. I watched as he closed his eyes, kissing my shoulder and trailing down to my fingertips.

His tenderness moved me deeply. I wanted to stay, to let go of concerns about tomorrow or the future. After all, when love wells up from the heart's depths, it's like a barrel of gunpowder. Lovers are willing to set it off and face whatever comes together. But I couldn't simply shrug off my responsibilities. I had to look after Kristeene today; I had promised Anna. How could I break that promise?

"While Kristeene naps, Anna said I can use the time as I please," I explained softly, hoping to ease his worries. "She even said I could invite a friend over."

"Really? Can I be that friend?"

I remained quiet, offering him a smile.

He smiled back and returned his focus downward. "I'm a fool, huh?" He chuckled, knowing it was a rhetorical question.

I laughed lightly before glancing at my watch. My eyes widened at the time. "I've gotta go," I told him. "I need to go back to the dorm, pack some clothes. I'll be staying at Anna's tonight."

Charlie instantly tensed. "What? You're staying the night?" He questioned. "Why do you have to sleep there?"

"She's paying me to stay overnight." I realized how my words might sound and a blush warmed my cheeks. "I mean, it's not like that, not at all," I quickly clarified.

"No, no, I get it," Charlie reassured. "I just don't get why she wants you to stay."

吗？……他问了我一连串的问题，一边用大毛巾上上下下地吸干身上的水珠，然后套上了体恤和短裤。我套了那件性感的连衣裙，头上裹了一条白毛巾，答道，我在美国举目无亲，我给有钱人家带孩子。今天早上，安娜要来宿舍接我。我是一个卖火柴的穷女孩。

他说，素素，你为什么不早告诉我？

我说，为什么要告诉你？我不是挺好的吗？

他抓了抓头发，想说什么，动了动嘴唇，没有声音。

我拉着他的手，一起去了厨房。我倒了两杯茶，坐下。我把一杯推到他的面前。他没有接茶杯，而是握住了我的手，把我拉到身边。他解开我头上的毛巾，把湿泸泸的头发夹在毛巾中，不停地搓。毛巾把水份和潮气都吸被纳进柔软的纤维，变厚变沉几乎能溢出水来。查里却像得了失语症一样，没有说一句话。

我开玩笑说，哲学家，留学生打工是很平常的事情，周末正是好机会，可以多赚一些钱。

他托起了我的一条手臂，横在他的面前，轻轻地抚摸我的皮肤，然后闭上了眼睛。他从我的肩膀开始亲吻，缓缓的移动，一直吻到手指。

他的一举一动都牵连着我的感情。我多么想留下来陪他啊，哪里都不去了！哪怕没有明天，没有前途，又有什么关系？爱到深处时，内心像火药桶一样，甘心情愿，同归于尽。但是，当我吃饼干的时候，我的胃把我拉回到现实之中。照顾柯丽丝是我的工作，我已经答应了安娜，怎么可以毁约？

我安慰他说，安娜倒是说过，在柯丽丝午睡的时候，我可以自由支配时间，包括请熟悉的朋友来玩。

他说，我可以去玩吗？

我故意不回答，抿着嘴对他笑。他也笑了，自言自语道，我是傻瓜。

我看了看手表，说道：我得走了，我要回宿舍拿衣服，今晚在安娜那里过夜。

你说什么？要在那里过夜？为什么要在那里过夜？查里的脸一下子绷得很紧。

我说，睡觉也给钱呵。说完，我的脸红了，心里怦怦乱跳，说道，你不会误解我吧！

他说，No，我不懂她为什么要留你过夜？

"Alright. Let's get going," I said. "I don't have time to head back to the dorm. I'll explain it all tomorrow, okay?"

He nodded. As we made our way to the door, I checked my watch again. It was already past eight. "Charlie, I need to call Anna and have her pick me up here," I admitted. "There's not enough time for me to return to the dorm."

Charlie agreed, saying it was the best plan. He held me close, nearly carrying me back into the living room as I veered off on another topic. "I need to grab some underwear at the supermarket," I mumbled, "otherwise I'll have nothing to change into." I then asked Charlie for his address and phoned Anna.

While I was on the call, Charlie disappeared. When he returned, he carried a silver gift box. "This is for you," he said, motioning for me to take it. "Open it."

I obliged, unwrapping the box with care. Inside was a set of ladies' loungewear. A blouse and skirt in mauve brocade with delicate rolled edges and knitted flowers adorning the fabric. I turned to him, surprise in my eyes. "Where did this come from?" I asked.

He chuckled. "I'm a magician. You don't believe me?"

"You're giving me a present that was meant for you?"

He just smiled. "Does it fit?"

I quickly checked the label on the collar and tilted my head in surprise. What a coincidence! The set was just my size. There was no way I could believe Charlie was a magician, but there was also no way he had time to go to the store and find something like this in two or three minutes. The only other possibility that crossed my mind was that Charlie might be seeing another girl who happened to be the same size as me. I didn't show any suspicion, though. I simply hugged him and thanked him for his kindness.

Anna arrived shortly after. Charlie opened the car door for me and kissed me right in front of her before letting me climb inside.

I thought it was a good thing that Anna knew I stayed over at Charlie's place. For one, it might add to her guilty conscience. And secondly, it might make her trust me more, since it gave more credibility to the idea that a girl like me living in her house wouldn't engage in any misbehavior.

My thoughts gradually faded as I took in my surroundings. Something felt off. I noticed that Kristeene wasn't here, and to make matters worse, Anna was completely silent. Usually, she'd be chatting non-stop by now. There wasn't even any music to fill the silence.

I decided to start a conversation, just for the sake of it. "Anna, where's Kristeene? Why didn't she come along?"

"Her dad's back," Anna's tone was sharp and cold.

"Oh, does her dad not come home often?"

"Yes," Anna responded. "He's in the international trade business. The man flies all over the world."

我说，我们走吧！我也不知道为什么，明天告诉你，好吗？

走到门口，我再看了看表，已经过了八点。我说，查里，我得给安娜打个电话，让她到这里来接我。时间来不及了。

查里是求之不得，他几乎欢呼一般地抱着我，回到了客厅。

我说，我只能顺路去超市买内衣了。我没有替换的衣服。

我要了查里的地址，给安娜打电话。

在我打电话的时候，查里不知道去了哪里。一会儿，他拿来了一个银色的礼品盒，说道，打开看看，给你。

我打开一看，里面是一套镂空钩花镶边的紫红稠缎女内衣裤和睡裙。我惊讶地说，这是怎么回事呵？

他笑着说，我是魔术师，你信不信？

我说，你把别人的礼物给了我？

他说，尺寸对不对？

我赶紧把领子后面的商标翻出来，一看，更惊讶，和我的尺寸居然一模一样！我怎么会相信查里是魔术师呢？二三分钟的时间里也不可能去商店买礼物。只有一个可能，查里的生活里有另外一个女人，一个和我个子差不多的女人。但是，我不露声色，给了他一个拥抱，谢了他的好意。

不一会儿，安娜来了。查里为我开了车门，当着安娜的面吻了我，才让我上车。我觉得挺好的，让安娜知道我在查里处过夜，一能增加她的内疚感，二使她对我放心，一个陌生的女孩子住到她家里去，不会有什么出格的行为。

一上车，我就觉得气氛不对。首先，柯丽丝没有来。第二，安娜一直沉默着，不像往常那样喋喋不休地说话，也不听音乐。

我没话找话说，安娜，柯丽丝呢？怎么没有来？

她父亲回来了。

噢，她的父亲不常回家吗？

嗯，他做国际贸易，全世界飞。

我们之间的谈话到此为止，一路无语。我想，如果安娜是柯丽丝的母亲，如果安娜和柯丽丝的父亲关系和睦，当丈夫好不容易回家一次，她应该很幸福。可是，安娜反而比平时更少了生气。我好像对安娜每天下午出去三个小时有了些许的同情和理解。我怀疑她是去会情人的，那三个小时一定是她一天中最开心的时光？我偷偷地瞟了她一眼，忽然觉得她一夜之间瘦了许多，她的脸，她的手，几乎只剩下了皮肤和骨头，而且多了许多皱纹。整个的她只能用形

Our conversation ended there, and the car was filled with silence. I thought Anna would be happy that her husband was back after so long, but she seemed to be in much lower spirits than usual. It was at this moment I gained some understanding for Anna's frequent outings. I suspected she went to meet her lover. That must be the highlight of her day.

I stole a glance at her and suddenly noticed how her appearance had changed. She seemed malnourished, having lost a lot of weight compared to the last time I'd seen her. She was like a walking skeleton. Had I simply not observed her closely before, or had she really changed so much overnight? I felt awful. Poor Anna! I wished I could share some of her pain. I silently promised myself to take good care of Kristeene over the weekend.

The car finally came to a stop, and we arrived at the immense castle that Anna and Kristeene called "home".

Three vehicles were already parked in front of the building. There was a luxurious black car, an antique car, and a sleek convertible. Upon entering the house, Anna led me directly to the third floor, swiftly avoiding the commotion downstairs. I hadn't seen any of these people before.

"Guests will arrive in the afternoon," Anna explained. "You have about two or three hours to familiarize yourself with everything on this floor. You can use the south-facing bedroom," she pointed to the room, and I nodded. "If any guests get too drunk tonight, they can sleep in the north-facing bedroom. Otherwise, that room will be vacant as well."

I nodded and followed her into the room I'd be staying in. This room was a bit larger than my dorm, but it had a mysterious aura that I wasn't quite accustomed to. Anna walked to the window and pulled the curtains open. Sunlight immediately filled the room.

Anna then pointed out the baby monitor on the nightstand, and after ensuring I was settled, she left. The baby monitor was about the size of a book. It had a switch and an antenna that looked like a pigtail, allowing me to listen in on any sound that came from Kristeene's room. Anna told me the device would let me check on Kristeene if she started crying, though she said it was unlikely, since Kristeene usually slept soundly at night.

I took some time to explore the third floor. There was a living room with a television and sofas, multiple bookshelves, and a skylight on the roof. The south-facing bedroom seemed to be the main room, with a bathroom attached inside. That was convenient, as there was another bathroom in the hallway for other guests to use. That meant if any inebriated guest ended up on this floor, they wouldn't share a bathroom with me.

Once Anna left, I slid open the closet door in my room. Inside were various sleeping gowns for both men and women, along with multiple pairs of soft-soled shoes and slippers. I then moved to the bathroom, which had a spacious vanity and a cabinet filled with an array of cosmetics, perfumes, hair products, and a hair dryer. It all made my eyes grow weary and my head spin.

销骨立来形容。难道是我以前观察得不够仔细，还是被安娜的悲凉情绪所传染，带上了“有色眼镜”？她怎么可能在一夜之间换了人样？安娜好可怜！我希望能为她分担一些痛苦。我想，周末这两天，我一定要尽心尽力，把孩子带好。

正想着，汽车开进了城堡的围墙。

大楼前已经停了三辆汽车，其中一辆黑色车非常豪华，设计得古色古香，是敞篷车。进了门，安娜引我直接上了三楼，我看到有不少人在楼下忙碌，这些人平时从来没有看见过。上楼梯的时候，我听到了男人的说话声，那是从二楼的主卧室传出来的。我好像听到了柯丽丝的笑声。到了三楼，安娜说，客人都要下午来，你有两三个小时熟悉一下这层楼的情况，朝南的睡房你用，朝北的那间，如果今晚有人喝醉的话，就住在那里。否则，是空的。她进了我的客房，我跟在后面。房间比宿舍的睡房大一点，里面暗暗的，有一种神秘的气氛。安娜走到窗旁，拉开了窗帘。霎那间，满屋子灿烂的阳光。安娜向我交待了睡房里一个特殊的传音器以后，就走了。那个机器像一本书大小，上面有个开关，还有一根小辫子一样的天线。能够“窃听”柯丽丝房间里的声音，她要求我晚上放在枕头旁，如果柯丽丝哭的话，要下楼观察一下。

我不停地点头，表示自己都记住了。

不过，她说，一般来说，她睡得很安静。

我的睡房是三楼的主卧室，内连着厕所和浴室，外面还有一个公用的浴室。也就是说，如果有酒鬼，也不和我共用一个厕所。三楼也有客厅，有电视机，长沙发和一排书柜。客厅的屋顶上有个玻璃天窗。

安娜走了以后，我打开睡房的壁橱，里面挂着各种式样的男女睡衣，地上整齐地排列着各种款式的软底鞋和拖鞋。厕所里有一个梳妆台，墙上一面巨大的镜子，吊橱里什么都有，化妆品，香水，电吹风，护发用品，等等，等等，令人眼花缭乱。另一个立地橱柜，挂着一件件厚实的毛巾浴衣，架子上叠着整齐的大小毛巾。所有的家具一尘不染，好像刚刚被人收拾干净。我稍微化妆了一番，在自己的头发和脖子上喷了一点香水。

我想休息一会儿，倒在睡床上，觉得这种席梦斯绷得很紧，没有陷下去的危机。以前我以为席梦思都是一样的，弹性不足柔软有余。想不到软床中也有不同的类型。我想，如果将来我在美国

A tall cabinet stood against the wall, holding some plush bathrobes and towels inside. I decided to put on a bit of makeup and sprayed some perfume on my hair and neck.

I stretched out on the bed for a moment's rest. The mattress was firm, a departure from what I was accustomed to. I used to think all mattresses were the same, without variations of softness and firmness. If I got married in America someday, I'd definitely invest in such a mattress.

Hold on, why was I suddenly thinking about marriage? And in America, of all places! My mind wandered, and I couldn't help but smile. Hypothetically, who would I marry? Charlie? No, who knew how many girlfriends he'd had. I'd just arrived in America; I couldn't rush into marriage so easily. I wanted to acquaint myself with this country first, to enjoy some freedom before settling down.

Recalling Charlie took me down memory lane to my first love. Back then, I believed we were destined for marriage, until I learned he'd chosen another girl as his wife. His parting words still lingered in my mind, urging me not to harbor hatred and dismissing marriage as a mere transaction.

I vehemently disagreed. I'd always seen marriage as a pinnacle of love, not a cold calculation of 'benefits'. In those days, I felt deceived. Yet now, his words held a new truth.

He had a point. Love between two souls need not be bound by marriage. And donning rings doesn't always signify genuine affection. Those who entwine love and marriage either deceive themselves or challenge an ideal. They're either naive or possess a rare wisdom, a truth I'd only recently grasped.

On one hand, the end of love isn't necessarily a tragedy. On the other, setbacks can stretch one's resilience and endurance, particularly when innocence is lost. After such a heart-wrenching experience, it's like a seal breaking, paving a highway to shared happiness.

I went through a few relationships after that, embracing whatever came my way and releasing it just as freely when it slipped through my fingers. Charlie, Anna, Lisa, David—none of them comprehended life quite like I did. It was as if my philosophy professor, the one with the distinctive red pants, was my kindred spirit.

I raised my gaze. The curtains framing the window were adorned with Oriental cherry blossoms, the furniture echoing in a delicate dance of pink petals, mirroring the vibrant clouds adorning the sky. It was a reflection of my own inner state.

I rose and approached the window, peering down at the garden below. A surge of spirited energy coursed through me.

Just then, Anna's call echoed from downstairs.

结婚，非得买这种席梦思不可。哎呀，我怎么想到结婚呢？还要在美国结婚？我不由地笑了，嫁给谁呢？查里？不，谁知道他究竟有多少女朋友？刚来美国，哪能轻易定终身？我还要好好看看这个国家，看到自由自在的时候再说。

我从查里想到自己的初恋。那是好几年前的事情了，可是一旦啓开记忆的大门，往事依旧历历在目。我以为自己会和他结婚的。在爱得难分难舍的时候，突然得知他娶了别人作老婆。我永远忘不了他和我最后的一次见面。他说，素素，不要恨我，婚姻是为了利益。

我一直以为婚姻是爱情的升华，怎么一下子变成了利益的结合？

他说，这个社会互相欺骗，你真的信了邪。

我一句话也说不出来，简直不知道是否应该活下去？我想了好长时间才想通了。他是对的。只图爱情的男女不需要婚姻，有婚姻的男女未必有爱情。相信有爱情的婚姻，不是欺骗自己就是挑战梦想，不是浅薄无知就是大智大慧。就在这虚无和真实的一线之间，多少人因为宁信其有，非信其无，赌博似地押上了青春和生命，结果输得两袖空空！

过了很久，有一天我突然想通了。失恋未必是一桩坏事情，挫折往往从反面来冶炼生命的弹性和韧度。尤其是失去贞操，痛定思痛以后，反而像打碎镣铐一样，开拓了两性相悦的自由路。后来，我有过不少男朋友，一夜情，几夜情，更长一些的情，我都拎得起，放得下。该来的时候展开双臂欢迎，该走的时候，决不哭哭啼啼。查里，安娜，莉莎，戴维德，他们都没有像我那样把人生看穿，只有那个穿红裤子的哲学教授，和我心灵相通。

窗框上垂挂的窗帘，印着东方的樱花，床单，床罩，枕头都和窗帘配套，粉红的樱花团团簇簇，如天上飘着的彩云，就像我今天的心情。

我走到窗旁，望着楼下的花园，居高临下，心旷神怡。正在这时，听见安娜在楼下叫我了。

Chapter 8

Anna's call drew me downstairs. When she caught sight of me, her face lit up. "Susu!" she exclaimed. "I have wonderful news: Kristeene can walk on her own now."

In near unison, we hurried to the master bedroom. Just then, Kristeene was toddling towards us, resembling a duckling taking quick, unsteady steps. She sported a white gauze dress, a tidy red bow perched on her head. Spotting me, she giggled and called out, "Si—Si!"

She pronounced "Su" as "Si". I couldn't help but break into a smile.

I circumvented Anna and lifted Kristeene into my arms, pressing my cheek to hers. "Kristeene, my sweet girl, you're walking and saying 'Susu,'" I cooed with affection. "I'm so proud of you!"

Setting Kristeene back down, I encouraged her, "One more time. You can do it, can't you?" Kristeene started to walk, and I followed along, crouching down and counting, "One, two, three, four..." I grinned as Kristeene echoed my words. It was like a playful march, our voices rising in unison. I was so engrossed in the game with Kristeene that I hardly noticed the others in the room until someone called my name. I stood up quickly.

I was still buzzing with excitement. I must have looked quite the sight: flushed cheeks, high spirits, and a beaming smile. "Yes?" I responded, turning to face a tall, refined man.

He rose from the sofa and extended his hand, which I shook. It was cool and smooth. "George Dickson," he introduced himself.

"Susu," I replied. "How are you, Mr. Dickson? You have an amazing daughter," I said cheerfully.

"Please, call me George," he said with grace. "I've heard that my daughter has taken a liking to you."

I chuckled at his words. "Yes, indeed. I'm a bit of a big kid myself, so we

第八章

我下楼去，安娜已经等在楼梯口。她说，素素，告诉你一个好消息，柯丽丝能自己走路了！

我们俩几乎是跑步奔向主卧室，安娜在前，我跟在后面。想不到，柯丽丝不需要圈圈椅的帮助，正独自迎面走来，像个小鸭子一样，摇摇摆摆，前挺后蹶地走着，脚步很碎很快，好像靠着速度来维持平衡，不至于跌倒。她穿一身白色的薄纱连衣裙，头上一个大红的蝴蝶结。她看到我，大声嚷嚷：素----素-----！

她把“素”说成了“嘻”，惹得我忍俊不禁。

我越过安娜，跑过去，一把抱住她，贴上她的圆脸蛋，亲昵地说，柯丽丝，我的宝贝，你能走路啦！你能叫素素啦！我真为你高兴！

我放下柯丽丝，说道，再来一遍。柯丽丝往回走，我蹲着弓步，伴在旁边，和她一起移动，一边数着数字：

One, Two, Three, Four……。我说一个数字，柯丽丝模仿我说一遍。我们就像军事训练那样，一边喊口令，一边换着步伐。我只顾着和柯丽丝玩，没有注意室内的人物，直到有人轻轻叫了我的名字，才站起身来。

我仍旧沉浸在兴奋之中，脸色一定很好看，红彤彤的，精神也很饱满，满脸笑容。我说了声“YES”，回身一看，一个高大文雅的男子从沙发上站起来，向前走了几步，伸出手来。他的手很冷很软。他自我介绍说，乔治. 笛克荪，柯丽丝的父亲。

你好，笛克荪先生。你有一个出色的女儿。我把长发甩向肩膀后面，兴致勃勃地说。

叫我乔治，他说。听说，我女儿很喜欢你。

是呵，我是大孩子，我们玩得很好。

get along splendidly."

"I haven't been home for two weeks," he marveled. "She's been making incredible progress."

"Kristeene is quite clever!" I responded with just as much enthusiasm. "She's eager to learn. Whenever I play the piano, she'll dance."

"Really?" George's eyes gleamed with interest, though he maintained his refined composure. I finally took in his attire: a gray-green dressing gown and supple leather slippers. His gaze never wavered from me, but oddly, I felt at ease under his scrutiny. Yet, I soon realized it was likely my backless dress that had captured his attention. I instinctively wrapped my arms around my back, attempting to shield myself.

As Kristeene held onto my skirt, I lowered my arms to embrace her. With a feigned calmness, I said, "Daddy's back. Why don't you call for 'Daddy'?"

Kristeene looked at George and reached out both her arms, a clear sign she wanted her daddy to pick her up. Anna stepped in and gently took the girl, saying, "Daddy's tired. Guests will arrive in the afternoon. Let Daddy rest." George coaxed, "Come on, Kristeene, come to daddy." However, Kristeene's joyful face had transformed, her nose and eyes now scrunching together, lips pursed. "Oh-ah!" she began to cry. This was the first time I had seen Kristeene in tears. She never shed a tear in my presence. Witnessing this discord between the husband and wife, causing the child to cry, a surge of anger coursed through me.

I suggested, "Kristeene, let's go outside, to the lawn, okay?" The child threw herself into my arms. I carried Kristeene out, forgetting to greet George and Anna. I couldn't endure the oppressive atmosphere in the master room for even a minute, with its stiff silence and false harmony. It brought to mind the novels and movies I'd encountered, portraying the secret intrigues among family members. Today, I witnessed it firsthand. When this "castle", complete with a small bridge and a clear brook, with the moon's shadow and the blooming flora, fell into the hands of people who felt nothing for each other, it was a true waste of beauty.

In her bathroom, I washed Kristeene's face and let her gaze at herself in the mirror. I encouraged her, "Kristeene, smile and say hi." Kristeene waved and cheerfully said "Hi!" into the mirror, her face lighting up with a smile. I fetched two towels and some toys, then carried Kristeene downstairs.

It was well past noon, and the servants bustled to and fro in the hallway.

他说，我两个星期没有回家，女儿的进步令我吃惊。

我说，柯丽丝聪明好学，我弹琴的时候，她还跳舞呢！

真的吗？他的眼睛里闪着喜悦的光芒，但是，依旧不失文质彬彬的风度。他穿一件灰绿色的长睡袍，黑色的软皮拖鞋，眼睛一直打量着我。我被看得很不自在。突然我意识到了是自己身上的性感连衣裙，招惹了他的注意，马上把双臂绕到□背去，遮住露裸的部份。这时，柯丽丝走到了我的脚边，拉我的裙子。我不得不腾出手来抱她，强作镇静地问道，爹地回来了，怎么不叫爹地？

柯丽丝朝乔治看看，伸出了双手，要乔治抱。安娜走上来把女孩接住，说道，爹地很累，下午有许多客人来，让爹地休息。乔治说，来，柯丽丝，爹地抱。柯丽丝朝乔治看看，本来一张快乐的脸，这时，眼睛鼻子都挤到了一起，嘴巴翘得老高，“哇”地一声哭了起来。这是我第一次看到柯丽丝哭泣。她在我的面前从来没有流过眼　泪。看到他们夫妻暗中作对，殃及孩子，我的心里涌起了一股无名之火。我说，柯丽丝，我们到外面去。去草坪，好吗？孩子一边哭一边朝我扑过来。

我抱着孩子往外走，竟然忘了给乔治和安娜打招呼。主卧室里那种压抑的气氛，僵硬的平静，假装的和气，我一分钟都不能容忍。我想到以前看的小说和电影，讲有钱人家的内部勾心斗角，今天也算亲眼目睹了一回。这个城堡，这栋大楼，小桥流水，花树月影，落在互相没有感情的人手里，真是白白浪费了。

我到柯丽丝的浴室里，给她洗了脸，逗她看镜子里的自己。我说，柯丽丝，笑笑，说“哈哎”。柯丽丝扬了扬手，对着镜子说“哈哎”，笑了起来。我拿了两条大毛巾和一些玩具，抱着柯丽丝下了楼。

这时，已经过了中午十二点，人们在走廊里来来往往地忙着，外面的草地上多了许多长桌子和长椅子，上面复盖白色的桌布。我把毛巾铺在有阳光的草地上，让柯丽丝自己玩。然后坐在一张有树荫的桌子旁，想着刚才的事情。

柯丽丝的父亲，一个做国际贸易的富人，如果仅仅凭几句对话和他的长相，是一点不令人讨厌的。他长得高大挺拔，温而文雅，举止不卑不亢，十分得体。但是，想到安娜突然之间像残花败柳一样，失去了生命的活力，我觉得这个男人非同寻常，好像有一肚子的坏水。究竟是他发现了安娜的秘密，要扼杀她的快乐？还是因为

Long tables with white tablecloths were set up on the lawn outside. I spread towels in the sunlight and let Kristeene play on them. Then, I sat at a shaded table, pondering the recent events.

Kristeene's father, a wealthy man in international trade, had left a favorable impression. Our conversation and his demeanor were both agreeable. He was tall, robust, refined, conducting himself appropriately. He neither exuded haughtiness nor displayed excessive humility. Yet, when Anna crossed my mind, wilting like a flower and losing her zest for life, I felt that this man was far from ordinary. Had he uncovered Anna's secret, quashing her happiness? Or did Anna harbor guilt, unable to face him? Or perhaps it was the weight of George's responsibilities that led to Anna's infidelity? I had no answers.

A rattan basket on the table held fresh bread and buns, covered with a blue-and-white striped napkin. The inviting aroma of freshly baked goods wafted up, making my mouth water. Glancing at my watch, I realized it was lunchtime, and my appetite surged.

Not far ahead, an elderly woman worked on a flower arrangement, placing blooms into a large vase. She wore a sky-blue dress with small floral prints, a matching broad-brimmed hat atop her head.

I called out, "May I have some bread from the table? I'm quite hungry."

She replied, "Go to the kitchen. There's a better lunch for the servants than just bread." She smiled at me, adding, "You must be Susu, I presume. I'm Betty. We all know you."

"Hello, Betty. How does everyone know me?"

"We live in the neighboring house and see you come every day to care for the child."

"So?" I joked, "I'm in the spotlight, while you're in the shadows. You can see me clearly, right?"

Now I understood that the small house attached to the "castle" was for the servants. How many were there? Cleaners? Gardeners? Those responsible for laundry? Quite a few, it seemed. But generally, no one did the cooking. Only when George returned home did someone inevitably attend to him.

Betty said, "We all like you. Kristeene likes you, too."

"That's true," I replied, "I like her as well." I noticed that Betty hadn't mentioned Anna.

I asked, "Betty, what's the occasion for today's gathering?"

"Birthday party. George turns fifty today."

"Is Mr. Dickson really fifty? He looks younger."

安娜心中有愧，做贼心虚抬不起头来？或者是因为乔治本身的责任造成安娜的不忠？我没有任何线索。

桌子上有一个大藤篮，里面放着许多面包，上面盖着一条蓝白方格子的餐巾布。面包刚刚出炉，散发着诱人的香味。我的食欲一下子被唤醒了，看看表，已经到了午餐的时间。瞬间，满嘴的口水不停地涌出来。

前方走来一个胖胖的老大妈，手臂上挽着一个大花篮。她穿了一件小碎花天蓝色的宽松连衣裙，头上带相同布料做成的宽边遮阳帽。

我大声问道：我可以吃一点桌上的面包吗？我饿了。

她说，到厨房去吧！那里有工作人员的午餐，比面包好多了。她朝我笑了笑，说道，你是素素吧，我是蓓蒂，我们都知道你。

蓓蒂，你好！你们为什么都知道我？

我们住在隔壁，看你每天来带孩子。

是吗？我开玩笑说，我在明处，你们在暗处，是不是？

这时，我才知道，主楼后面连体的房子是给佣人住的，那里面住了多少人？清洁工？花匠？洗衣烫衣？也不少吧。平时没有人做饭，但是，乔治回来住的话，一定有人服侍他。

蓓蒂说，我们都很喜欢你。柯丽丝也很喜欢你。

是的，我说，我也喜欢她。我注意到蓓蒂没有提及安娜。

我说，蓓蒂，今天是什么Party？

生日Party，乔治五十岁生日。

我说，笛克荪先生已经五十岁了吗？看上去他很年轻。

蓓蒂说，五十啦，眼睛一眨，他也五十啦。

我说，你在这里住很长时间了吗？

她说，二十多年了，他父母在世的时候，我就在这里了。

我说，那么说，你对他们家很了解。可是，他们家一张照片和画像都不挂，不知道为什么？

蓓蒂笑了，没有搭话。她在每张桌子的中央都放了一个大花瓶，精心地把篮子里面的花卉插进去，布置得像一个大型的扇面，五彩斑烂，生气盎然。她的笑容有点诡秘，好像在告诉我。她是知道内情的，不说而已。她给花瓶灌水，然后打开一把小花伞，插在花瓶里中央遮太阳。这是我第一次看到把伞罩在花瓶上。蓓蒂真聪明，否则的话，一个下午晒下来，鲜花都变成花干啦。

"Fifty," Betty affirmed, winking, "He's fifty now."

"How long have you lived here?"

"Over twenty years. I was here even when his parents were alive."

"So, you know their family quite well. But why aren't there any portraits or pictures on the walls?"

Betty smiled mysteriously, offering no response. She placed a vase on each table and meticulously arranged flowers in a fan shape, creating a lively burst of color. Her smile held an air of secrecy, as if she possessed inside information but had no intention of divulging it. She filled the vase with water, then inserted a colorful miniature umbrella to shield the flowers from the sun. It was the first time I'd seen an umbrella used to shade a vase. Betty was resourceful; under the afternoon sun, the fresh flowers would stay vibrant.

I returned to Kristeene and settled on the lawn. She chatted with a stuffed rabbit, now cradling it in her arms, now letting it recline while playing with its long ears. I smiled at Kristeene, then glanced at Betty. I saw numerous metal table legs beneath the white tablecloth, slender and cool...

Soon, one vehicle after another arrived, filling the space in front of the main building with parked cars. I wasn't well-versed in cars, but I was certain that most of them were high-end models.

When Kristeene took her nap, I had lunch in the kitchen. Betty was there at the time. She introduced me to the other American servants—the cook and his assistants. Their names escaped me. Lunch was packed in a plastic container: steak, potatoes, creamed spinach, and a slice of chocolate cake. I couldn't manage to eat it all and cream didn't appeal to me. I finished about two-thirds of the steak and considered storing the rest in the refrigerator. Betty tugged at my hand, saying, "Throw it away. We'll have fish for supper." It suddenly dawned on me that they didn't store food in this refrigerator, let alone leftovers. Still, I didn't want to throw it away. It was a bad habit to waste such a good steak and potato.

After finishing my lunch, I returned to my room on the third floor. Peering down from the window, I saw more cars arriving. Two police officers were stationed at the gate, directing cars to park behind the building.

The revelation from the baby monitor left me trembling. George and Anna's heated exchange laid bare their troubled relationship. George expressed a desire for divorce, hoping Kristeen could have a mother who was truly present, not just in name. He granted Anna the freedom to see her friend, but on the condition that she prioritized Kristeen's well-being. Anna's response,

我走到柯丽丝那里，坐在草地上。她正在和一个绒毛白兔对话，一会儿抱在怀里，一会儿让它躺下，一会儿玩弄它的长耳朵。我朝柯丽丝笑了笑，回头再去看蓓蒂，只看到了白桌布下面无数条金属的桌腿，细细的，孤零零，阴森森，冷冰冰……。

过不了多久，一辆辆汽车鱼贯而入，把主楼前面的空地几乎停满了。我是车盲，但是我敢肯定大部份都是豪华车。

柯丽丝去睡午觉的时候，我去厨房吃了午餐。刚巧蓓蒂也在厨房里，她给我介绍了其他几位美国佣人，有的是厨师，有的是帮手，我记不住他们的名字。午餐在一个塑料盒子里，牛排，土豆，奶油菠菜，还有一块巧克力蛋糕。我根本吃不了那么多，而且不喜欢吃奶油的东西。我吃了三分之二的牛排，想把剩下的存在冰箱里。蓓蒂拉拉我的手，说，倒掉，晚餐吃鲑鱼。我突然意识到，这里的冰箱里是不存食品的，更不要说吃剩的食品。

但是，心里真有点舍不得，那么好的土豆和牛肉白白浪费了，多么可惜！

吃完，我回到三楼客房，往底下望去，汽车还在继续进来，大门口已经站了两个警察，指挥着汽车停到楼背后去。本来想躺一会儿，一来不困，二是不知道柯丽丝什么时候醒来。平时，我都是躺在她那儿的地毯上的。我忽然想起了那个“窃听器”，就把开关打开。心想，如果柯丽丝醒了，应该有信号给我。不料，窃听器里传来一男一女的对话，就像收音机一样。我仔细一听，老天爷，是乔治和安娜，他们在吵架！

我应该马上关掉它，但是，我听到了他们在讲柯丽丝的事情。乔治说，我希望我们能够离婚，给柯丽丝找一个名符其实的妈妈，但是，我考虑到你，你的名声和你的将来。我允许你去找你的同伴，但是，前提是必须把柯丽丝照顾好。安娜，你没有孩子，为什么不能把女人的母爱给这个可怜的女孩？

乔治吵架的声音和说话一样，不紧不慢，用词很精炼，没有多余的话。我不明白的是，他为什么要说柯丽丝可怜而不是可爱？

接着是安娜如泣如诉的女低音。安娜的话不很清楚，断断续续的，大意是：谁不知道我们的关系？……我不愿意再偷偷摸摸地下去。同性恋并不可耻，别人能正大光明地公开同居，我为什么不能？……你是为了你的面子。你自己宁可在外面混女人，不同意我离婚。你也太过份了。……希望我们好合好散，不要搞到法庭上

though tearful and fragmented, hinted at her own struggles. She spoke of their public image, her own identity as a lesbian, and her plea for a peaceful separation, eschewing court battles and seeking her freedom.

It was a stark and heartbreaking truth. Anna was a lesbian, and George led a life largely apart from her, involved with other women. The complexity of their situation was staggering. I turned off the monitor and hurried to Kristeen's room, driven by an impulse to shield her from the painful discord between her parents.

However, as I stood in the room, I was met with a surprising silence. It was as if the echoes of their argument still resounded in my ears, but here, serenity prevailed. Was this a daytime nightmare, or perhaps my own illusion? How had I come to this conclusion about Anna? It occurred to me that the soundproofing was so effective in this room that I couldn't hear the dispute next door. I even searched for a "listening-in device," but found none. Regardless of whether their quarrel was real or a mirage, I resolved not to sleep on the third floor. Instead, I would stay here beside Kristeen, on the carpet, just as I had done every afternoon before.

去。……求求你，让我走，我不需要很多钱，给我自由吧！

我听得手脚发抖，不敢再听下去。这会儿所有的疑问都有了答案。可谓真相大白！原来安娜是同性恋，乔治在外面混女人。这对夫妻也够离奇和出色的了。关了机器，我即刻去了柯丽丝的房间。我有一种要保护柯丽丝的冲动，鼻子酸酸的，忍住眼泪，假装笑脸，别让父母的吵架伤害她幼小的心灵。我真想把柯丽丝抱回家！

小乖乖睡得那么甜蜜，那么美丽。看着她，我的眼泪止不住喷涌而出。老天爷啊，为什么要恶作剧，将不幸落在一个纯洁无辜的孩子身上？奇怪的是，柯丽丝的房间里什么声音都没有。静得出奇。这是不是白日的一场恶梦？还是我的幻想？我怎么可能有那样的幻想呢？我怎么可能知道安娜是同性恋？一定是房间的隔音材料太好，所以，听不到隔壁的吵架。我在房间里到处搜寻，没有找到那个窃听器的插头。那就对了，一定是谁插错了窃听器，插到主卧室去了。我即刻做出决定，不管乔治和安娜的吵架是真是假，今晚我不睡到三楼去。我睡在这里，守着柯丽丝，就像每天下午一样，睡在地毯上……。

Chapter 9

As Kristeene woke, I followed our routine, bathing and dressing her in her finest attire for her father's birthday. A white dress with a red heart, paired with a red silk scarf bearing the words "Happy Birthday, Daddy!" adorned her. She looked adorable, and as we descended the stairs, the joyous atmosphere enveloped us. Warm greetings and endearing nicknames for Kristeene filled the air. She responded with cheerful waves and a sweet "Hi, hi!"

The lawn outside was a lively scene, with tables laden with delectable offerings, wine, and salads. A band played dance music, setting a backdrop of vibrant colors against the sunset. I paused, asking Kristeen, "Where are mummy and daddy?" To my delight, she echoed, "Mummy, daddy."

"Good, good. Mummy, daddy," I praised, giving her a kiss. Her progress amazed me, learning to walk in the morning and now speaking these words in the evening.

Spotting Anna in her shimmering silver dress, I couldn't help but notice her slender figure. She was engrossed in conversation, a wine goblet in hand. George approached us, his spirits high, dressed in a sharp black tailed suit. I encouraged Kristeene to present the scarf, and she chimed in with "Daddy, daddy!" George, while stern, accepted the gesture with gratitude, his eyes revealing a touch of vulnerability.

As the last rays of sunset faded, I glimpsed glistening tears in George's eyes. In that moment, he appeared more human, his vulnerabilities on display. My perception of him shifted slightly, seeing him in a softer light. He draped the red scarf around his neck like a Tibetan Hada, wearing it throughout the evening.

While George attended Kristeen, I seized the opportunity to enjoy my meal. The fish, mentioned by Betty earlier, was beautifully presented. I sa-

第九章

柯丽丝睡醒以后，我像往常一样，给她洗个澡，换上干净的衣服。我想，既然今天是她父亲的生日，作为女儿应该穿得出众一些。我在她的壁橱里挑出一件白色的背心连衣裙，胸前印着红色的爱心。我找到了一条红绸子的围巾，用孩子的涂料笔，写上了“生日快乐，爸爸！”几个白色的大字，披在柯丽丝的肩膀上。

我们从楼梯上下去的时候，楼下闹哄哄的，到处是人。柯丽丝！宝贝！美人儿！……不绝于耳，客人们不停地和小女孩打招呼。柯丽丝扬手说，哈哎，哈哎。

外面的草地上，人更多。长桌上摆满了各种食品，有的喝酒，有的吃冷餐。草地的另一头，还有一个乐队，正在演奏舞曲，有人在那里跳舞。绛红的天空如天幕一般垂在后面，鸟儿当空飞过，交织在霞光与花香之中，留下无形的弧线，如长虹曼舞一般。

我走了没几步，就停住了，对柯丽丝说，爹地妈咪在哪里？柯丽丝居然跟着我说，爹地，妈咪。

对呀，对呀，爹地，妈咪！我亲了她一下，心里高兴极了。这个女孩简直像神仙一样，早上学会了走路，晚上叫起了父母。

我先在人群中找到了安娜，她穿一件银色的连衣裙，衣料像有鱼鳞一样闪闪发光。更加瘦骨如柴，好像一条垂挂的银蛇。她一手端着酒杯，一面在和几个女人说话。

乔治是自动走过来的，他穿黑色的燕尾服，头发一丝不乱，神采奕奕。我让柯丽丝把红围巾举起来，代她说：

生日快乐，爹地！柯丽丝跟着说“爹地，爹地”。乔治看了围巾上的祝贺词，一把将柯丽丝抱过去，不停地亲吻，然后，朝我看了看，说了声“谢谢”。他的脸上并没有笑容，反而有点严肃。但是目光真诚，充满了感激之情。

最后的一抹霞光在这个时候落了下去，我看到了乔治眼睛里泛起了晶莹的泪花。就在这一刻，我看到了一个活生生的乔治，他像

vored its tender, smoky flavor, though the meat was slightly overpowering. There were a variety of cream-based dishes that were unfamiliar to me, so I opted for fruit and sweet treats. A fluffy cake, akin to cotton candy, caught my eye. Betty suggested a spoonful of strawberry jam, which elevated its taste to perfection.

I observed the American guests on the lawn, as if watching a film. Men in black and women adorned with jewelry exuded elegance and refinement. Their demeanor and hushed conversations were a far cry from the carefree gatherings I was accustomed to at school. These adults inhabited a different sphere of life. I couldn't help but wonder how they looked in their youth. Were they always this composed, or did they wear masks of pretense?

Kristeene, not one to be shy, was passed between guests, her laughter ringing out joyfully. Eventually, a heavily perfumed woman returned her to my arms. The fragrance was overpowering, making me sneeze uncontrollably. I couldn't fathom how such a pungent scent could be sold. My nose itched intensely, and I sneezed repeatedly

The commotion caught the attention of nearby guests. Apologizing, I turned to Kristeene and asked, "So many guests here today. Do you want to perform something?" I hummed a child's song:

"And on this farm, he had a cow—EIEIO With a moo moo here, And a moo moo there, Here a moo, there a moo, Everywhere a moo, Old McDonald had a farm—EIEIO."

Kristeene, standing by my side, clapped her hands and swayed to the rhythm. Her joy blended with my song, resonating with those around us. The guests joined in, clapping and mimicking moos. George approached, clapping, and suggested, "Come on, Susu, play a piece of music for us."

He lifted Kristeene and, holding my hand, led us into the house. I followed him to the living room, where he opened the piano and placed a music book in front of me. Flipping through the pages, I looked up at George and admitted, "Sorry. I can only play children's songs for Kristeene." Gesturing to the band outside, I added, "Ask them to play. I'm afraid that I can't." George's hopeful gaze turned to a frown.

I was on the verge of conceding, willing to grant this affluent host some satisfaction. Yet, I stood my ground and refused to play. I suspected George's intention was to draw attention to me among the guests. But who was I? Why

平常人一样有软弱的一面。他的形像在我的心里好像从天外掉入人间亲切了不少。乔治把红围巾挂在自己的脖子上，就像西藏人的哈达一样，一个晚上没有取下来。

趁着乔治把柯丽丝抱了过去，我抓紧吃晚饭。蓓蒂提及的鲑鱼，有两尺多长，被去掉了鱼头，，对剖开，整条地躺在盘里，鱼身上覆盖着许多澄黄的柠檬片和密密麻麻的香草料。我切了一点尝尝，烟熏味很重，很嫩很鲜美。厨师站在烤牛肉腿和猪火腿面前，用特殊的刀给客人切成薄片。我要了两片，牛肉很嫩，带点血，火腿太咸，不敢多吃。许多奶油制品，都是我第一次看见，碰都不敢碰。还有各种生菜色拉和水果甜点。我吃了些水果和甜点。有一种蛋糕蓬松得像棉花糖一样，我切了一块，蓓蒂正巧在旁边，说，要淋一勺草莓酱在上面才好吃。我试了试，果然味道奇美。我问蓓蒂，为什么一个热菜和热汤都没有？是不是因为夏天的关系？蓓蒂说，PARTY都这样，下雪天也如此，不在外面办就是了。

吃饱了以后，我像看电影一样，看着草地上的美国人。男人都是一身黑的，女人个个珠光宝气。人人轻声轻语，文雅可鞠，不像学校里的PARTY，随心所欲，肆无忌惮。到底都是成年人，生活的舞台不一样。我想像着这些绅士淑女，在年轻的时候是什么模样？是不是也像现在这样假惺惺？不知怎么地，我想起了我的哲学老师，他是成年人中的异数，真不容易。

柯丽丝在客人们的手里传来传去。她生来不怕陌生，时不时传来那铜铃般的笑声。最后，一个香气冲天的女人把柯丽丝送到我的手里。这种香味刺激得我只想打喷嚏。女人走了，味道留在柯丽丝的衣服上，挥之不去，难受得我真想回楼把她的衣服剥下来，换一身干净的。我简直怀疑香料厂里有人的嗅觉出了问题，怎么出售这种比中药还要难闻的香水？竟然还有人买！鼻子里突然奇痒无比，我马上转过脸去，用手捂着脸，打了一个接一个的喷嚏。

这一来吸引了旁边一些客人的注意力。我向他们表示抱歉，然后对柯丽丝说，今天有那么多客人，你要不要表演一下节目？我哼起了一首童谣：

OLd McDonald had a farm – EIEIO
And on this farm, he had a cow – EIEIO
With a moo moo here,
And a moo moo there,
Here a moo, there a moo,
everywhere a moo moo,

did he want them to notice me? To my surprise, he swiftly reverted back to his composed self. He patted my shoulder and said, "You're right. It doesn't matter, doesn't matter." He turned to leave, a smile on his face. After all, he was a VIP, experienced in handling all sorts of situations, able to control his emotions with no trace left behind. It was no small feat.

As he turned to go, I began to play "Happy Birthday to You." The guests joined in, singing, "Happy birthday to you, happy birthday to you, happy birthday dear George, happy birthday to you." I repeated the tune, and the singing continued. Kristeene leaned on the piano bench, dancing with abandon. The party had reached its peak.

I believed George was satisfied, though he didn't return. He remained outside with the guests. Anna, somewhat unsteady from drinking, came over to thank me. She kissed Kristeene before leaving.

That night, after the party concluded, I tucked Kristeene into bed and returned to my third-floor bedroom. I took a bath and slipped into the sleeping attire Charlie had given me. I admired myself in the mirror, wondering how many compliments Charlie would offer if he saw me in this outfit. In a lighthearted moment, I greeted Charlie's mysterious girlfriend. "Sorry, I got here first." I grinned at my reflection, then rolled up my bedding. Quietly, I crept into Kristeene's room with the bedding in hand. I spread it out on the carpet and settled in. Awake, I replayed the day's events in my mind, sensing that something else was on the horizon.

I couldn't discern how much time had passed when I was jolted from my slumber. There was movement in the room, and a hand touched my foot. Startled, I sat up, peering through the haze of sleep. A man, shirtless and in his underwear, crouched at my feet, his back turned to me.

"Who is this?" I whispered, retreating to the farthest corner, my body shrouded in sheets, trembling.

"It's me, Susu. Don't be afraid."

It was George. I quickly covered my eyes with my hands.

"I came to adjust the listening device. They placed it in the wrong room earlier, in my bedroom."

"I don't need the listening device. Why would I need it? Please go. I'll sleep here and look after Kristeene."

"Susu, how can you sleep on the floor?"

Old McDonald had a farm—EIEIO.

她听到了歌声，就靠在我的腿旁边，一边拍手一边摇晃身体。她的快乐伴随在我的歌声里，一波一波地传给了大家。周围的客人也跟着击起掌来，发出牛羊叫声。乔治拍手走过来，说，素素，来，给大家弹一支曲子。

他抱起了柯丽丝，拉上我的手，往楼里走。我跟着他进了客厅，他为我打开了琴盖，取出一本五线谱，搁在琴架上。我稍稍翻了翻，抬眼看乔治。我说，对不起，我只为柯丽丝弹儿童歌曲。我指了指外面的乐队，说，请他们演奏吧，我恐怕不行。乔治的眼睛里充满着期待。听我这么说，不免扫兴，站在那里，微皱着眉，一声不吭。我差一点作了让步，准备给这个富裕高贵的主人一点面子，但是，我狠了狠心，不弹。我隐约感到，他好像是为了转移客人们的注意力，而要我弹琴的。我是谁？为什么要让客人注意我？令我吃惊的是，一眨眼，他变得若无其事，拍了拍我的肩膀，说道，你是对的，没有关系，没有关系，嘴角挂着笑容，转身走了。毕竟是大场面里来去自如的人物，能把情绪控制得不留痕迹，也是难得。

就在他转身离开的那一刻，我弹起了“生日快乐”的乐曲。客人们都和着音乐唱起来，生日快乐，生日快乐，祝乔治生日快乐，生日快乐！我弹了一遍又一遍，钢琴不停，歌声不止。柯丽丝扶在琴椅上，任意地扭动着身体，像疯丫头一般……。Party在这个时候达到了高潮。

我相信乔治对此很满意，但是，他没有再进来，一直留在外面招呼客人。倒是安娜，喝得醉醺醺的，脚步不稳地走过来，眼神朦胧，好像困得不行马上要倒下来一般。她谢了谢我，抱起柯丽丝亲了亲，走了。

那天晚上，PARTY结束以后，我安顿好了柯丽丝，便回了三楼的客房，洗了澡，换上了查里送我的内衣和睡裙。我对着镜子欣赏了一会儿自己的体形，心里想，查里如果看到我穿这件睡衣，不知道要创作出多少赞美的词儿？我暗暗地对查里的神秘女朋友打了一个招呼，对不起啦，让我捷足先登。我对着镜子傻笑。然后把床罩卷了起来，夹在肢窝下悄悄地去了柯丽丝的房间，铺在地毯上，睡下了。我迟迟没有入睡，想着白天的一幕幕情景，心中有一种预感，好像要发生什么事情。

不知道过了多久，我在睡梦中被人惊醒。有人在房内活动，碰到了我的脚。我睁开眼睛一看，是一个男人，穿着短裤，光着上

"Please go. Leave me alone, I beg you. Go, please go!"

We spoke in hushed tones, careful not to wake Kristeene. If anyone entered the room now, George and I would have a hard time explaining ourselves, like dirt that clung stubbornly, defying even the vast Pacific

He stood before me, bare-chested, bathed in moonlight filtering through the shuttered gaps. "Sorry to let you sleep on the floor. Now, you can return to your own bedroom," he said.

I rushed out like a phantom, nearly stumbling on the stairs. Once in my room, the first thing I wanted was to lock the door, but there was no lock. I hastily pushed a sofa against it, my breath quickening. Then, a knock on the door jolted me, like a fish hook snagging my heart, sending a painful jolt. Trembling, I dared not make a sound.

"Susu, try your monitor." It was George again, the George with the bare torso. I was so frightened I couldn't bring myself to respond.

"Susu, turn on the monitor, please," he urged.

"I will. You can go," I whispered, anxiety coursing through me.

"Turn it on right away. I'll go downstairs. Let me know when you hear my voice."

I switched on the monitor, but it remained silent. Panic set in. Should I go downstairs and tell him? But I didn't have the nerve. What if the monitor was faulty? Who would look after Kristeene tonight? What if something happened to her? Why did we rely on this contraption? It would be safer to sleep on the floor. But did I dare to? No lock on the door. No one would come to my aid if I were assaulted in the dead of night. The thought sent shivers down my spine.

"Susu, did you hear my voice?" He was back again! What was he doing? Why did he keep coming to me? I was just a poor student, a Chinese girl. He was wealthy, surely able to find a willing companion. Why me? I thought he was right outside my door. I couldn't help but run to the window and wrap myself in the curtains, so fearful I might jump out. When he spoke again, I realized his voice was coming from the monitor.

I swiftly moved the sofa from the door, squeezed out, and raced downstairs. Halfway down, I collided with George. Oh my goodness! Oh my goodness! Disaster had found me. The little lamb had finally fallen into the jaws of

身，正蹲在我脚边的地上，背朝着我。

“你是谁？”我睡眼惺忪地坐起来，压低了嗓音说，“你在这里干什么？”

说话的同时，我迅速地退到了离他最远的墙角落里，裹着床罩，全身发抖。

是我，素素，不要怕。

那是乔治！我赶紧用双手蒙住了眼睛。

我来把监听器插上，白天，他们插错了，插到了我的睡房里。

我说，不要窃听器，为什么要用窃听器？你走吧，我睡在这里照顾柯丽丝。

乔治说，素素，你怎么能睡在地上呵？

我说，你走吧，不要管我，求求你，走吧，走吧！

所有的对话都像窃窃私语，为了不吵醒柯丽丝。任何人要是在这个时候闯进来，我和乔治就是跳进了太平洋也洗不干净。

他还是不走，裸露着上身，站在我的面前。月光穿过百叶窗的缝隙照在他的肌肉上，一道亮一道青。他说，非常抱歉，让你睡在地上，现在，你可以回房去了。

我一溜烟地跑去出，跌跌撞撞差点儿在楼梯上绊倒。进了房，第一件事就是去锁门。但是，门上根本没有锁的装置！我赶紧把一个单人沙发推到门口，坐在沙发上直喘气。就在这个时候，我听到了敲门的声音。一下子，我从沙发上弹跳了起来。这种用手指关节嗑门的声音，虽然很轻却像飞来的鱼钩一样，挖心割肺地疼。

我一阵哆嗦，不敢出声。

素素，试试监听器。那是乔治，那个光着膀子的乔治！我吓得不敢回答。

素素，请把监听器打开。

我说，你下去吧，我会打开的。

他说，你现在就打开，我下去，你听到了声音要告诉我。我把机器打开，什么声音都没有。我不知道应该怎么办？出去告诉他？我哪里敢呵？但是，如果机器坏掉了，今天晚上谁来照顾柯丽丝？万一出个差错怎么办？要什么鬼机器呵，还不如让我睡在地上！但是，现在我还敢去睡吗？门上都没有锁，半夜被人强奸了都没有人来救我！想到这里，我浑身都是冷汗。

素素，你听到了我的声音吗？不一会儿，他又来了！他这是在干什么呀，为什么要缠着我？我是一个穷学生，中国人，你有的是钱，找个女人玩玩多么容易，为什么来找我呀？我以为他在我的门

the gray wolf. I felt like I was crumbling.

"Sorry." He steadied me, inquiring, "Did you hear my voice?"

I was deeply embarrassed, yearning for a hole in the floor to swallow me. "Yes, I heard. Now I need to sleep. Please don't bother me again," I implored, rushing upstairs, barricading the door once more.

As I lay in bed, I spotted the full moon. Was it the Mid-Autumn Festival today? For some reason, tears began to flow, dampening the pillow. I got up to draw the curtains. There's a saying, "On every festival day, one will doubly think of one's kinsfolk." Poor me! I didn't even dare to gaze at the moon. The more I tried to hold back, the more my family occupied my thoughts. Memories of past Mid-Autumn Festivals surged forth like a geyser. When I was a child, I once snatched a mooncake before my older brother could grab one. I sat on my father's lap, listening to the tale of the moon goddess. I even believed I'd seen the cinnamon tree and the rabbit on the moon. Later, in the countryside, we may not have had mooncakes to eat, but at least the whole family gathered together.

As the saying goes, "Extreme happiness will be followed by sorrow." Just a few days ago, I'd allowed myself to believe that good fortune was on my side, even dreaming of a future here. But fate had a different plan. Now, what should I do? Should I stay here tomorrow? If not, where could I find another job? Must I remain until I secure new employment? But what about Kristeene? Despite my exhaustion, I tossed and turned, unable to find sleep.

外，身不由己冲到窗前，把自己卷在窗帘里。我吓得差点儿从三楼的窗口跳下去。当他说第二遍的时候，我才发现那声音原来是窃听器里的！

我赶快把沙发往后拉，挤出了房门，直奔楼下。我腾腾腾地跑下楼，想不到在楼梯上和乔治撞了个满怀。完了，完了，灭顶之灾，小羊羔终于落入大灰狼的手中。我全身软了下来。

对不起，他一把扶住了我，问道：有声音吗？

我狼狈至极，恨不能有个地洞让我钻进去。我说，我听到了，我要睡觉，请不要打扰我，好不好？说完，我连爬带跑地上了楼，回客房，再把沙发顶住房门。

我往床上一倒，迎面遇到了一轮满月。该是中秋节了吧！心里一酸，眼泪淌湿了枕巾。我赶紧起来把窗帘拉上。

每逢佳节倍思亲。我可怜得连月亮都不敢看！越不看，越想家，许多许多中秋节的往事像喷泉一样冲出来。小时候，和哥哥抢月饼吃，坐在爸爸的腿上听长娥奔月的故事，看到了月亮上的桂花树和小白兔。后来在乡下过没有月饼的中秋节，却有一家人的团圆……。

中国人说“乐极生悲”，前两天还自以为交了好运，还幻想着将来能够住进来呢！上帝保佑，我没有走得那么远！我该怎么办？明天还要不要在这里？到哪里去找新工作？要不要忍声吞气地坚持到下一份工作到手？但是，柯丽丝怎么办？……我困得要命，翻来复去睡不着。

Chapter 10

The next day, I awoke well past ten in the morning. I drew back the curtains, and sunlight streamed in like eager customers rushing into a store for a sale. I smoothed out my sheets, banishing the wrinkles with my hands. In an instant, dust particles swirled like tiny dancing ants in the sunbeam. They formed a hazy veil, stubbornly refusing to disperse. It felt like they were mocking me, saying, "Are you ashamed to sleep in? You're just an employee here." I retorted silently, "Where were you yesterday? Do you know how frightened I was last night? Since I can't continue this job, why does it matter if I sleep in? I won't even take the pay, alright?"

I gathered my belongings and headed downstairs, but something felt off. The entire house was deserted – no sign of Anna, Betty, or any other servants. It was as if I had wandered into the wrong house. I stomped my foot on a step, but all I got was an empty echo. As I reached the first-floor hallway, the space seemed to grow, making me feel smaller. I looked around, met with an eerie silence. How could the kitchen be so far away? Why did the hallway to the main door seem endless? The air felt unfamiliar, as if it had turned icy. My breath grew heavy. What was wrong? I seemed to have lost my sense of the house. Was it because of last night's fright? Or had I been abandoned because I slept in? The living room was immaculate, no paper scraps on the sofa, no cups on the coffee table. Only rows of vacuum cleaner tracks etched into the carpet. No one was in sight. Everything felt like stage props, strangely unreal.

There were four bedrooms on the second floor. I gently called out, "Anna? Kristeene? Are you here?" I didn't dare call George's name before checking his room. I knocked, but there was no response, so I carefully pushed the door open. It was empty. The exercise room had a glass wall, but with no lights, it was vacant.

"Is anyone there?" I shouted, standing on the landing and sending my

第十章

第二天醒来，已经过了十点。拉开窗帘，阳光一涌而进，像一群抢购紧销商品，在门口等了很久的消费者。我拉直了被单，用手把表面的皱纹撸平。霎那间，扬起一片灰尘，像千万只小蚂蚁在阳光里跳集体舞。它们像一道雾蒙蒙的屏幕，在我的眼前迟迟不肯散去，好像在笑话我，在别人家里打工还要睡懒觉，难为情吗？我在心里说，你们昨天在哪里？知道我夜里被吓得半死吗？反正这份工是不能再打下去了。晚起睡懒觉有什么不可以？不拿钱就是了。

我把东西收拾完，走到楼下，感到气氛不对。整栋楼空空荡荡，不见安娜，也不见蓓蒂等一大群佣人，好像走错了人家。我蹬了一下脚下的楼梯，一声沉闷的反响，连灰尘都看不见。我走到底楼的过道上，越走越觉得自己变小了。前看后看，死气沉沉，厨房怎么那么远？直通大门的走廊怎么变得那么长？哎哟，仿佛空气也变得陌生，冻住了似的，呼吸起来特别沉重。这是怎么回事啊？我完全失去了对这栋房子的感觉。是因为昨晚受惊？还是因为我睡懒觉，被他们抛弃的关系？客厅已经被收拾得干干净净，皮沙发上没有一张纸片，咖啡桌上没有一只杯子。地毯上留下了吸尘器轮子滚过的一条条长长的痕迹。没有人，一切都像道具一样，变得那么不真实。

走上二楼，四个睡房，我一间一间地推门进去看。我轻声地喊着：安娜？柯丽丝？你们在吗？我进主卧室之前，没有喊乔治的名字。敲了敲门。没有回音，就推了进去，也是空的。健身房是玻璃墙壁，里面的灯关着，没有人。

有人吗？我提高了嗓门，站在楼梯口，对空喊了一声。声音一出口，就给吸走了，连个回声都没有。

有人在这里吗？我喊第二遍的时候，已经回到了底楼。我想喊

voice into the air. But once it left my lips, it seemed to vanish, leaving no echo.

"Is anyone there?" I called again, now back on the ground floor. I wanted to shout louder, but hearing my own voice, my courage waned.

There were only two rooms left unexplored, both on the ground floor. One was the study, and the other was that bedroom beneath the staircase. I hesitated to enter the latter. In my imagination, it must be low-ceilinged and dimly lit. If there was anyone inside, it couldn't be Kristeene or the homeowner. In movies I'd seen, such rooms were often used to hide bad guys or their tools. Just thinking about it sent a shiver down my spine, and my hands and feet trembled. I turned quickly, half expecting to find someone sinister behind me.

So, the fear from last night returned in the daylight. I panted heavily, my back pressed against the wall. The study was on my left, about twenty paces away. I sidestepped, inching towards it, step by step. The back of my clothes made a soft rustle against the wall. I gripped the handle, determined that if no one was inside, I'd call Charlie right away. I couldn't stay here any longer; this place, haunted or not, terrified me to my core. The metal handle was colder than my hand, but I held it until it warmed. I turned it carefully. As the door cracked open, a voice floated out, startling me.

"Please, come in."

It was George. If he was there alone, I didn't dare to enter.

"Is it Susu?"

"Yes." I hesitated, hiding behind the door. "Is Kristeene there?"

"She's here. Kristeene's here," said George.

I pushed the door open inch by inch. When it swung wide, I saw Kristeene sitting beside George, engrossed in cartoons on TV. The house had impeccable soundproofing; not a sound escaped, not even if someone struck a gong inside.

"Good morning, Susu," greeted George. He looked weary, distant, still in the same sleepwear, with disheveled hair.

"Good morning," I replied absentmindedly, surveying the study with its towering bookcases, a massive desk like a front tooth facing the door, and a sofa tucked into a corner, almost as broad as a bed at a right angle, with two end tables on either side, each with a lamp. If not for the window, the room would have been a dark abyss.

"I'm sorry I'm late," I offered.

"Didn't sleep well last night?" George asked.

得响一点，但是，在听见自己的声音以后，知道勇气已经所剩无几。

这栋楼里，只有两个地方我从来没有去过，都在底楼。一是书房，二是楼梯底部的那间卧室。我不敢去卧室，想像中，那房间肯定很低矮很阴暗。如果有人，也不会是柯丽丝和这家的主人。以前看的电影里，藏坏人死人和犯罪工具的，往往在楼梯底部的房间里。想到这里，突然觉得背脊发凉，手脚打颤，我猛地转身，怕有坏人跟在后面。

昨晚的恐惧就这样在光天化日之下找上了我。背贴着墙壁，我大口大口地喘气。书房就在我的左边，大概有二　十步远。我横着走，一步步向书房移动，背后的衣服和墙壁磨擦得“赤赤”作响。我抓到了门把。我已经想好了。如果书房里没有人的话，我得赶快给查理打电话。不能多停留。这个鬼地方，简直要了我的命。金属门把比我的手还要凉，我捏了一会儿，捏到它接受了我的体温以后，小心翼翼地拧了一下，门一开，有声音飘了出来，反而把我吓了一跳。

请进。

乔治，那是乔治的声音。如果只有他一人的话，我是不敢进去的。

是素素吗？

YES。我犹豫了一下，躲在门后面说。柯丽丝在吗？

在这儿。柯丽丝在这儿。乔治说。

这时我才把门一寸一寸地往里推。打开一看，原来，柯丽丝正坐在乔治的旁边，观看电视里的卡通片。这栋房子隔音太好，即使里面敲锣打鼓，外面也听不到。

早安，素素。乔治和我打招呼。他显得有些疲倦，表情淡漠，穿着昨天早上相同的睡袍，头发松散。

早安。我心不在焉地答道，一边打量着这个四面被书架包围了的房间，一张巨大的写字台，像一颗大门牙似的，对着房门。转角沙发很宽，像一张转弯的睡床，两头都有茶几，台灯亮着。如果没有那扇窗，这里几乎像阴间一样。

我说，对不起，来晚了。

乔治说，昨晚没有睡好吧！

还可以。我说，找不到你们，真有点着急。

乔治说，你的早饭在微波炉里。

"So-so," I replied. "I couldn't find you, and I was worried."

"Your breakfast's in the microwave," George informed me.

I pretended not to hear him. He wasn't as polite or warm as he'd been yesterday. He must be irritated with me.

Upon seeing me, Kristeene waved and called my name. I went over to her, giving her a kiss. "Kristeene, sweetheart, Susu's leaving. You'll have to play by yourself."

George suddenly turned towards me, his expression puzzled. It seemed he didn't quite understand. "Oh, do you have something urgent? Anna mentioned you'd be leaving in the evening."

I lowered my gaze, looking at the hardwood floor beneath me. With effort, I managed to say, "I want to quit this job. There's too much to do. It takes up a lot of my time coming here every day."

"Oh." When George said his second "Oh," he stood up and paced the study. I could tell he was trying to regain his composure. After a few rounds, he said, "Alright, I understand."

"I didn't do anything over the weekend, so you needn't pay me," I interjected, seizing the opportunity while he paused. "I'm leaving. Take care of yourself." And with that, I left. Once outside that dreadful place, I felt an overwhelming sense of relief.

From the moment I passed Kristeene on the sofa to when I reached the study door, George remained silent. Even as I walked down the corridor and approached the main door, he gave no indication that he wanted me to return. It was only when I realized I had no car to return to my dorm that I decided to go back and speak with him. Perhaps he might offer to drive me back. At the very least, I could call Charlie.

George looked surprised when he saw me return to the study door. He gazed at me with wide eyes, which made me hesitant to ask for his help. I managed to stammer out, "Can—I—use—the—phone?"

He extended his arm in a gesture that said "Please," and handed me the receiver.

Casually, I inquired, "George, where's Anna?"

"Anna?" He repeated her name, now pacing the study. This time, when he reached a tall bookcase against the wall, he stopped. He stood there for a moment, as though searching for a book. I unfolded a nearby chair and sat down, placing the phone set on my lap. Just as I was about to dial, I heard his cold voice.

我装着没有听见。他没有了昨天的客气和热情，一定在生我的气。

柯丽丝看到我，一边叫着我的名字，一边招手。我上前去亲了亲她，说，柯丽丝，小宝贝，素素要走了，你自己玩。

乔治猛地转过脸来，不解地说，噢，你有事吗？安娜说，你到晚上才走呢！

我低下头，看着脚下的硬木地板，为难地说，我想把这份工作辞了。功课太多，每天来这儿，要化很多时间。噢。乔治第二次说“噢”的时候，站了起来。他在房内来回地走。看得出来，他在用脚步安定自己的情绪。几个来回以后，他说，是这样啊，我理解你。

我说，这个周末，我没有做什么事情，不必要付我工钱。

乘他还没有反映过来，我忙说，我走了，你们保重。

说完，我就出来了。离开这个鬼地方，我感到一阵轻松。从柯丽丝的沙发旁走到书房门口，乔治一直没有回话。我走到走廊上，走到楼门口，乔治都没有要我回来的表示。是我自己意识到，没有车，是回不了家的。只能转回来，想给他打个招呼，或许送我回家，或者借打个电话通知查里？

对于我重新出现在书房的门口，乔治着实吃了一惊。他瞪大了疑惑的眼睛看着我，看得我不敢开口求他。我含含糊糊地说，能否……借……打个……电话？

乔治手臂一伸，做了个“请”的动作，从写字台上取了电话传过来。

我顺便问了一句：乔治，安娜到哪里去了？

安娜？他重复着她的名字，再一次在房内走动起来。这一次，他走到了墙边高大的书架旁，停了下来。他在那里站了好一会儿，好像在找书的样子。我拉了旁边的一张折椅坐下，把电话放在腿上，拿起了电话筒，正准拨号，突然听见了他冷冷的声音。安娜，再也不回来了，她走了。

安娜走了？我心里想，难怪今天的气氛这么奇怪。手指像僵硬了一样，拨不动电话，心往下一沉，好像装上了一大堆石头。

我说，也许过几天，她会回来的。

不会了。他的背对着我，在和书架说话。她早就想走了，恐怕永远不会回来了。

我不禁一阵哆嗦。第一念头就是柯丽丝怎么办？对于安娜的出

"Anna won't be back any more. She's gone forever."

Anna was gone? No wonder everything felt so strange today. My fingers felt stiff, unable to dial. My heart plummeted, heavy as a bag of stones.

I said, "Maybe she'll return after a few days."

"She won't." With his back to me, he seemed to be addressing the bookcase. "She wanted to leave long ago. I'm afraid she won't come back, ever."

A chill ran down my spine. My first thought was of Kristeene. I wasn't surprised or shocked that Anna had left, as I'd overheard the argument between the couple yesterday. But I wasn't prepared for her to leave so abruptly. Didn't she have any regard for Kristeene? Why hadn't she made arrangements before leaving? Ah, no wonder she was so drunk yesterday.

Could it be that she left so suddenly because of my presence? If Anna knew I was planning to leave soon, would she change her mind and stay? She didn't strike me as someone so irresponsible towards a child. I suddenly felt ashamed. It was I who had been thoughtless. I didn't give any prior notice when I decided to leave. That was like adding fuel to the fire, pulling the rug from under a boiling pot. But why? Was it because the father had planted a listening device for his daughter? When he came in to do that, how could he have known I'd been sleeping on the floor? When he finished, he wanted to test if it worked. Had he done something wrong?

The cartoon on the TV sounded like a mosquito's hum.

Something suddenly clicked in my mind. Just as I was about to speak, George turned to face me and said, "Oh, sorry. I forgot you don't have a car. Let's go. I'll drive you back."

"No," I said, "George, I'm sorry. Anna left so suddenly. I'd better stay until you find another babysitter."

George was momentarily stunned by my change of attitude. He leaned against the bookcase and said, "Anna's departure wasn't unexpected."

I thought he might tell me why Anna left. I strained to hear his explanation, but he stopped short. I raised my eyes to meet him and saw him sigh, his eyes glistening with tears.

"It's you who finds it sudden."

"I'm sorry, sorry." I fidgeted, feeling like I'd made a mistake. I muttered, "I shouldn't have declared my departure so suddenly. Now I won't leave, and neither will George. I love Kristeene and will take good care of her."

"Susu, many things can't be explained in a word. I'll tell you when we have a chance," he said with a wry smile.

走，我并不感到十分意外，因为昨天无意中窃听了他们夫妻的吵架。但是，说走就走，走得那么快，还是毫无思想准备。难道她对孩子都没有一点留恋？为什么不做好了安排再走？……唉，难怪她昨晚喝得半醉。

是不是因为有了我，安娜走得心安理得？如果安娜知道我要走，会不会改变主意？她不见得对孩子不负责任吧！我突然感到一阵内疚，不负责任的恰恰是我。事先不给通知，说走就走，等于给乔治雪上加霜，釜底抽薪。这究竟为了什么？是因为这个当父亲的为女儿插了一个监听器？他来插的时候，怎么知道我睡在地毯上？插完了，要检验一下机器是否工作正常，做错了吗？

电视里的卡通片像蚊子一样“嗡嗡”作响。真奇怪，我怎么一下子开了窍？正想说话，乔治转过脸来对我说，噢，对不起，我忘记了你没有车。走，送你回家去。

不用了。我说，乔治，很抱歉，安娜走得那么突然，我还是留下吧！等你找到了新的人选再走。

乔治怔了一下，侧身靠上了书架。他说，安娜走，一点不突然。

我以为他要给我解释安娜出走的原因，拉长了耳朵，聚精会神地等着下文。他却停顿了下来。我抬眼去看他，正好和他的视线接上。他叹了口气，摇摇头，眼睛里好像有泪光。他说，突然的是你。

对不起，对不起。我像犯了错误一样，坐立不安。我喃喃地说，我不应该突然宣布要走。我不走了，乔治，不走了，我喜欢柯丽丝，一定好好照顾她。

素素，许多事情一言难尽，以后有机会，我慢慢给你说。他说话的时候，嘴边挂着一丝苦笑。

柯丽丝是我的命根子，你待她好，我都看在眼里。昨天晚上，我看见你睡在她房间的地毯上，感动得直流泪。我要到哪里去找一个人那么爱她，嗯？

说到这里，我看见他的眼泪一颗一颗地滚出来，亮晶晶地挂在两颊，我也哭了起来。我扔了电话，冲过去把柯丽丝搂在怀，一边哭，一边说，乔治，我不走了，你放心，我保证把孩子带大。

乔治默默地点了点头。

我说，请你原谅我，好吗？不是你的错。

他目光柔和地看着我，问道，是不是昨天晚上，把你吓着了？

"Kristeene is my life. You treat her so well. I see it all. Last night, when I saw you sleeping on the carpet in her room, I was so moved, tears streaming down my cheeks. Where can I find another babysitter who loves her as much, eh?"

As he spoke, tears welled up and hung on his cheeks. I cried too, dropping the receiver and rushing to Kristeene, embracing her tightly. Through my tears, I promised, "George, I won't go. Don't worry. I promise to take care of the child."

George nodded in silence.

I said, "Forgive me, okay?"

"It's not your fault." He looked at me with gentle eyes. He asked, "Did I frighten you last night? I should be the one apologizing. But there's no need for us to apologize to each other. We have plenty of time ahead of us; let time speak for us."

He handed me a box of tissues and said, "Let's go have breakfast."

I looked at his back and followed. By the time I carried Kristeene there, he'd already turned on the microwave oven. It hummed softly, its light blinking.

"Let me do it myself."

He said, "After breakfast, I'll teach you how to drive."

I wished he would leave soon, so I could have a moment alone. I needed time to process the events of the past few minutes. Anna's departure had disrupted George's entire routine. He seemed to have devised a new plan after giving it serious thought that morning. If he intended to put his plan into action, he would need my cooperation. Yet he didn't give me sufficient time to catch my breath; he was eager to push me along his intended path.

Learn to drive? I was greatly surprised. Since coming to America, I hadn't truly resolved the issue of making a living. How could I possibly expect to learn to drive? What I was thinking must have shown on my face and conveyed itself to George through my eyes. He simply nodded, as though he understood everything.

I retrieved breakfast from the microwave oven. George sat beside me, holding Kristeene on his lap. Breakfast was in a white plastic box, containing pieces of onion and potato covered with two fried eggs. George poured me a glass of orange juice, saying, "Kristeene and I already had our breakfast."

As I ate, I considered asking him why Anna had chosen to leave. But since I already knew, I moved on to a different question (that was my first mistake).

我对不起你。素素，来日方长，我们不必信誓旦旦，让时间来说话吧！

他传给了我一盒面纸，说道，走，吃早饭去。

望着他的背影，我跟了出去。抱着柯丽丝赶到那里，看到他已经把微波炉开上了。机器“呜呜”响着，里面的灯光一眨一眨。

我自己来。

他说，吃完了早饭，我教你开车去。

我希望他马上离开，独自坐一会儿。刚才几分钟里发生的事情，需要重新梳理。安娜的出走整个地改变了乔治的生活秩序，他好像经过了一个上午的苦思，重新设定了计划。这个计划必须有我的配合才能实现。但是，他不给我喘气的机会，迫不及待地推着我朝他的轨道上走。

学开车？我大吃一惊。来美国，生计还没有解决，哪里敢有那样的奢望？我的心理变化一定表现在自己的眼睛里，并且通过眼光传给了乔治，他胸有成竹地点点头。

我取出了早餐，乔治抱着柯丽丝坐在旁边。那是一个白色的玻璃盒子，里面是洋葱土豆丁上面加了两个鸡蛋。

乔治给我倒了一杯桔子汁，一边说，我和柯丽丝已经吃了。

吃早餐的时候，我应该问他，安娜为什么要出走？但是，因为我已经知道了其中的原因，便跳跃成这样的问题

（这是我的第一个错误）：为什么不叫蓓蒂帮帮忙？

乔治说，蓓蒂眼睛不行，怕出差错，不敢带孩子。

我说，他们平时在后楼干些什么？

他说，蓓蒂退休了，在当地教会里很活跃，和安娜关系不很好，所以，如果我不在，他们一般不来这儿。

我说，安娜为人不错的，她待我很热情，很慷慨。

他说，我不是这个意思，安娜从来不小气。我是说，蓓蒂他们对安娜不理解。

这时，我已经吃完了早餐，拿着玻璃盒子走向水池子。我说，他们是否对安娜的同性恋不理解？（这是我的第二个错误，如果要算错误的话。）

乔治的脸色和口气一下子变得严肃起来，提高了嗓音问道：同性恋？你怎么联想起同性恋呢？

我的脸涨得通红，吞吞吐吐地说，我，我不知道，是猜的，对不起，猜错了。

"Why not ask Betty for help?"

George replied, "Betty has some trouble with her eyes. She's afraid to care for the child, worried she might do something wrong."

I inquired, "What's happening in the back part of the building?"

He explained, "Betty is retired and now volunteers at the church. But she and Anna didn't have a good relationship. So if I'm not here, they generally don't come to this part."

I said, "Anna is a good woman. She's been kind to me and paid me fairly. I mean, Betty and the others don't understand Anna."

Finishing my breakfast, I disposed of the box in the garbage bin. I thanked him, realizing I must choose my words carefully, but...

I asked, "Don't they realize Anna is a lesbian?"

After my comment about Anna, George's face turned serious. Noticing my face turn red out of embarrassment, he swiftly changed the subject, asking about Chinese kung fu and Qi Kung. I managed to steer the conversation with a playful remark, which earned a smile from him.

We spent most of Sunday in the car. I learned to drive, and we had lunch at KFC, where I followed George's lead in choosing what to eat. The fried chicken was enticing, and the sweet corn covered in butter was a delightful surprise.

In the afternoon, while Kristeene napped, George had Betty look after her so he could continue teaching me to drive. We practiced in various settings, from parking lots to mountain roads. George's patience and lack of temper were remarkable, especially considering it was my first time behind the wheel.

For dinner, Betty cooked a delicious meal featuring roast mutton with mustard and honey. She explained how marinating it in cumin powder eliminated the mutton smell. We also had steamed string beans and carrots. I fed Kristeene with care, and Betty cleaned up the leftovers.

Afterward, George helped me with the dishes, placing everything in the dishwasher. He then drove me back to my dorm and handed me three hundred dollars. I hesitated, feeling it was too much, but George insisted, explaining that it was a small sum to him. He also made a generous offer: if I chose to live in his house to care for Kristeene, he would cover my tuition. He urged me to take some time to consider the offer and let him know my decision.

这个时候，只要有一点点的认真，我就无处藏身。乔治应该问我，什么不能猜，要猜同性恋？

但是，他很克制，马上转移了话题，说道，你究竟来自哪个世界？我听说中国人懂一种功夫，可以隔墙看人。你有这样的功夫吗？

我什么功夫都没有。

给我说说，气功到底是怎么回事？

我调皮地说，气功吗，就像上帝，信就有，不信就溜。

乔治笑了。

我就这样轻易地混过去了。

这个星期天，我们几乎是在车上度过的。上午出去学开车，中午，在肯塔基吃炸鸡。我到美国以后，自己没有化钱喝过一罐汽水。在肯塔基吃饭，就像和查里上意大利饭店一样，我不懂菜名，也不知道如何吃。乔治吃什么，我也吃什么。炸鸡很香，还有玉米，甜津津的，要涂牛油，真是好吃极了。

下午，柯丽丝睡觉的时候，乔治请蓓蒂看着，再带我去学开车，一直到天黑才回来。怎么说呢，乔治是个非常耐心，没有脾气的男人。这是我第一次学开车，以前，连方向盘都没有摸过。在学习的过程中，因为胆小，反映迟钝，出了许多错误，他没有一声批评。我们到大停车场练习基本动作，十遍，二十遍，五十遍地练习，然后上路，从大街小巷到高速公路到弯曲陡立的山路。

我在他们家吃了晚饭，是蓓蒂过来烧的，烤羊肉，肉上涂芥末酱和蜂蜜，上桌以后，自己撒胡椒粉和盐。我问蓓蒂，为什么没有羊肉的膻气？她说要用CUMIN粉腌一腌。她拉开了一个小柜子的门，里面都是装调料和香草的瓶子。晚餐还有一些清蒸的四季豆和胡萝卜。柯丽丝坐在儿童高椅上，我给她系上了围兜，把羊肉切成了小块，她用手抓着吃。吃剩的菜肴，蓓蒂都拿走了。

乔治帮助我一起收拾了餐桌，把所有的盘子刀叉都放到洗碗机里，让机器洗。然后他送我回宿舍，并给了三百美金。我无论如何不肯拿。他说，三百美金对于我来说，并不是一个大数目，拿着吧。如果你愿意搬进来住在我们家里照顾柯丽丝，我把你的学费付了。你考虑一下，给我答复。

Chapter 11

As George raised the topic of gifting me a car, I hesitated. The idea of driving felt daunting, especially in such a luxurious vehicle. I couldn't afford any potential repairs, and with Kristeene in the car, the stakes felt even higher.

That evening, as George prepared to drive me back, he suggested, "Let's head to the garage. Tonight, you'll drive your own car."

This offer wasn't entirely unexpected; George had mentioned it before, but I thought it was a distant prospect, contingent on me obtaining my driver's license. Maybe I misheard, or perhaps I wished I had. "I'd rather not," I admitted.

"What's holding you back, Susu?" he inquired.

"I'm just afraid of accidents. I'm not ready to take the wheel yet."

He reassured me, "I'll be right there with you until you pass your road test."

Curiosity piqued, I asked, "Where's the car? There's no extra vehicle in the downstairs garage."

"It's in the main garage. I have a thing for collecting antique cars. Let's go take a look."

The moonlight illuminated our path, casting long shadows as we made our way to the garage. The door rumbled upward, revealing a cavernous space that could easily accommodate a crowd. Inside, an array of cars greeted us, four of them imposing and large. Nestled in a far corner was a small red car, resembling a half-spherical turtle. George gestured towards it. "Just this BEETLE."

"Beetle? More like a turtle," I quipped, slipping into the driver's seat.

He chuckled. "Originally, the Germans called it a BUG when they advertised it. It caught on, and everyone started driving BEETLEs."

第十一章

在我拿到驾驶执照以前，乔治天天留守在家。他像安娜一样，每天到宿舍来接我，晚上送回家。我的工作时间比以前延长，一般都是在吃了晚饭以后再走。蓓蒂过来做晚餐，我在旁边学。吃完了，我收拾餐桌，陪柯丽丝玩一会儿。有时候讲故事，有时候唱歌弹琴，一直到她上床睡觉。乔治有时候和我们在一起，大部份的时间，在他的书房里。柯丽丝上床以后，我得打电话给蓓蒂，等她过来，乔治才能开车送我回宿舍。在回宿舍的路上，只有他和我两个人。我们有许多机会聊天。但是，双方都很谨慎，只谈柯丽丝。

那天下午，乔治带我去考交通规则的笔试，考完了，他让我开他的车回家。我不敢开高级车。万一出什么事情，我赔不起。再说，柯丽丝在车上，我怎么敢开？

那天晚上他送我回宿舍的时候，说道，素素，来，我们去车库，今晚你开自己的车回家。

他要给我一辆车。说了好几次，还为我买了保险。但是，我以为是很遥远的事情，最早也得把执照考出来。不知道是听错了还是希望自己听错，我说，我不要。

素素，什么意思？

怕闯祸，我不要自己开车。

他笑着说，我陪着你，一直到考出驾驶执照。

是这样啊！我也笑了，问道，车子在哪里？楼下的车库里没有多余的汽车。

他说，在大车库里，我喜欢收藏一些古典汽车。走，我们去看看。

大车库坐落在房子的西面，是一栋独立的平房。我跟在他的后面，心里充满了好奇。月光照白了后花园一条弯 曲的小石径，青

As I drove onto the highway, George commended, "Impressive, Susu. You've got a knack for this."

He went on to extol the virtues of German car engineering, from Mercedes to BMW. Then, he fell silent, resting his arm on the window frame, lost in thought.

"George, is everything okay?" I inquired, turning to face him. "Did my lack of car knowledge lose your interest?"

He shook his head. "No. Do you know who the previous owner was?"

"Who?"

"Kristeene's mother, Laura."

Suddenly, it struck me that perhaps George had been waiting for the right moment to share his family's story. This car provided the catalyst, but as he began to speak, a wave of shock and disbelief washed over me. My hands trembled, and my feet seemed to have a mind of their own. The car surged forward, a wild, untamed force. George sprang into action, guiding the wheel. With a racing heart, I slammed on the brakes, the screech of tires filling the air. We came to a halt beside the cold, unyielding cement wall. It was a close call, a reminder of just how close we came to a devastating accident.

As I caught my breath, I realized I was enveloped in George's arms. Instinctively, I stirred, attempting to extricate myself. He gently patted my back, his voice soothing, "Hush, don't move, don't move." His fingers grazed my hair as he asked, "Susu, were you scared? Are you okay? Need to go to the hospital?"

Exhaustion washed over me, rendering me speechless. I simply shook my head, assuring him it wasn't serious, no hospital required. With care, he lifted me from the driver's seat to the back, securing the seat belt. When we arrived at my dorm, he assisted me out of the car, concern etched on his face. "Your hands are freezing. I'm a little worried. I won't let you go upstairs alone. I'll keep you company for a bit." I protested, "Kristeene is waiting for you. You must hurry back." When he tried to help me once more, my words were sharp, "No. You must go."

Inside my room, I collapsed onto the soft bed, which felt like a trap – easy to enter, but hard to leave. Lying there, fatigue coursed through me. I wished someone would pull me up and let me rest on the carpet. Yet, it wasn't even ten o'clock. Lisa hadn't returned. I lacked the motivation to move. I thought, "Let

蛙在河边鼓噪。我们好像走在电影里一样，两条黑影，一前一后，鬼鬼祟祟，面目模糊。

库门徐徐地往上升，乔治开了灯。我俩走了进去，那车库看上去就像开会的大礼堂一样，可以容纳几百个人。里面一，二，三，四，停着五辆汽车，其中四辆车身都很宽。最里面，停着一辆红色的小车，那样子就像乌龟一般，呈半圆形。乔治开了车门，坐进去说，就是这辆Beetle（甲壳虫）车。

我说，甲壳虫？它更像Turtle（乌龟）。我坐上了驾驶员的位置。

乔治大笑，说道，当初德国人做广告的时候，叫它Bug，人们好像得了病毒传染一样，都开Beetle车。

一路很顺利，我们上了高速公路。我加大了车速，乔治说，好，素素，开得真好！他说，Volks Wagon是德文，意思是老百姓的运输工具。Beetle很省油，不要换机油，马达靠空气冷却，比其他汽车少许多麻烦。他滔滔不绝地从Marcedes讲到BMW，对德国的汽车技术赞不绝口。后来他沉默了，胳膊支在窗框上，一手托着前额，好像在想心事。

乔治，你怎么啦？我扭过脸去问他。是不是我不懂汽车让你扫兴？

NO，他说，你知道原来的车主人是谁吗？

谁啊？

柯丽丝的妈妈劳瑞。

事后我想，可能他一直想说他们家的故事，但是，没有机会。这车给了他一个讲故事的理由。可是，当时的我，听他这么一说，就像丢了魂似的，全身都瘫痪了，手脚完全失去了控制。汽车像野马一样横冲直撞。说时迟，那时快，乔治扑过来把住方向盘，我只听到他说，素素，踩刹车，踩刹车！我闭着眼睛踩了刹车。车在长长地尖叫声中停了下来，停在路中间的水泥墙旁。幸亏不在高峰时间，否则，一场大车祸难免。我们死里逃生！

等我缓过气来的时候，发现自己被乔治拥抱着。我本能地动了动，想从他的怀里挣脱出来。他像哄孩子一样，拍着我的背，说道：嘘，别动别动。他抚摸着我的头发，问道，素素，吓着你啦。ARE YOU OK？我们要不要去医院？

我觉得筋疲力尽，连话都不想说。我摇摇头，表示没事，不要

me drift into sleep like this. No need for a bath or a change into sleepwear."

I closed my eyes, instantly finding myself back in that turtle of a car, seated in the rear. Anna was beside me, and George was at the wheel. Another woman occupied the front seat. The car glided over the water like a boat, swaying with the gentle waves. I grasped Anna's hand, but her face transformed into Charlie's. He was speaking to me, his lips moving, yet no sound reached my ears. What are you saying, Charlie? Why can't I hear anything? But, my own voice seemed trapped, unable to break through. We gestured to each other, unable to communicate. Suddenly, the car split in two. George drove away with the woman, leaving Charlie and me adrift on the water. Charlie, we must catch up – they've taken our child. Then, Anna morphed back, ignoring me. A chill settled over me. I said, "Kristeene... Kristeene is with them. Don't you care?" Then, Anna vanished. All around me was darkness. I felt the boat sinking, deeper and deeper. I screamed, but no sound emerged. Then, there was a deafening explosion, a resounding BANG. Everything shook...

It was Lisa's return that jolted me awake. The sound of the door closing pierced through my haze.

"Lisa, Lisa..." I called weakly.

"Susu, what's wrong?" Lisa came over and stood by my bed. She reached for the light switch, but I halted her.

"Just a nightmare. Lisa, help me up, please!"

I sat up, and Lisa propped a pillow behind me. Then, she illuminated the living room, bringing me a glass of water. With the light filtering in, the room took on a warm glow.

I confided, "Lisa, I might move out at the end of this semester."

"Sounds good. I'll move too, and we can find another place to share."

"As you have some free time, can you work, perhaps taking care of a child?"

Lisa seemed puzzled. "How does moving out connect to looking after a child?"

"I have a job offer, but I'm worried about handling it on my own. Any thoughts?"

As I recounted George's family situation, we sipped water. The story was straightforward, touching on divorce, the absent mother, and the child in need of care. Lisa listened intently.

去医院。他把我从驾驶椅上抱到后座，让我躺下，上了保险带，到了宿舍。扶我出车的时候，他说，你的手冰凉，你一个人上去，我不放心，让我陪你一会儿。我说，柯丽丝等着你，赶快回去。乔治再来扶我的时候，我很粗暴地说，NO，回去！

一进了房间，我就倒在床上。床如陷井似，进去容易出来难，睡着很累。希望有人来拉一把，让我起来，躺在地毯上。可是，还不到十点，莉莎没有回来。懒得动，心里想，就这样睡去吧，免了梳洗和换衣服。

闭上眼睛，就是那辆乌龟汽车。我在后座上，旁边是安娜。乔治在开车，另有一个女人坐在前面。车在海上开，好像船一样，起伏不定地摇晃着。我拉了一下安娜的手，见她转过脸来，那张脸却变成了查里。查里对我说了一通话，只看见他的嘴唇不停地变动，没有一点声音。查里，你说什么呀，我怎么听不见？但是，我的声音也传不出去，我们互相比划着，相互都听不见。就在这时，汽车一分为二，乔治和那个女人开着车跑了，把我和查里留在海上。查里，我们必须追上去，他们把我们的孩子抢走了。这时，查里变成了安娜，冷冰冰地不睬我。我说，柯丽丝，柯丽丝被他们带走了，你就不管吗？这时安娜也消失了。周围一团漆黑。只觉得船在往下沉，往下沉。我大声呼叫，却发不出声音来。只听见“轰”的一声爆炸，天动地摇！……

原来，莉莎回来了，关门声把我惊醒。

莉莎，莉莎……。我有气无力地喊着。

素素，怎么啦？莉莎来到了我的床边，要去开灯，被我阻止。

做恶梦，莉莎，拉我起来。

我坐了起来，莉莎在我的背后加了一个枕头。然后，开了客厅的电灯，送来了一杯水。房门开着，灯光流进来，照亮了门旁的一个角，室内如点了蜡烛一样，朦朦胧胧，有了温馨的气氛。

我说，莉莎，这个学期结束，我可能要搬出去住。她说，好哇，我也搬，我们仍旧分租一个公寓。

我说，你平时有多少空余时间？能打工吗？比如，照看孩子？

莉莎说，怎么啦，搬出去住和看孩子有什么关系？

我说，我有一份工作，恐怕一个人干不了。你有什么好主意？

我一边喝水，一边讲述在乔治家的故事。故事讲得很简单，无非是夫妻闹离婚，老婆出走，孩子没有人带，等等。莉莎却听得津

"I'm thinking, the best way to care for the child is for me to pause my studies, while also asking George to assist with my green card application. Maybe in three to five years, once Kristeene starts school, I can return to college."

"Well, if it were me and I cared about the child, I'd move in if he asked. Think about it – why are you going to college? Isn't it for a good job, better pay, a brighter future? Now, he only asks you to look after the child. If you do that, you have it all. You don't have family in America. How long will you struggle for a car, a house, and legal status? But if you work and stay there, because you love the child, isn't that a win-win? When you have money, why bother with college? Do you really think all those courses we pay so much for will be useful in the future? Doubtful. Don't be so stubborn. Many inventors don't hold degrees, but they succeed because they do what they love."

"I believe if you assist me, it's a mutually beneficial arrangement. You can look after the child while I'm in class and earn some money. Sounds like a win-win, right?"

Lisa chuckled, then teased, "Susu, you're sharp. Why don't you rope George in?"

"What nonsense! Why would I 'rope in' George?"

"Look at the books you're reading: philosophy, psychology, education, economics, logic, history, literature. You can self-educate on all of that. You don't need college."

"I'm working there not for him, but for his daughter and myself. I'm young and not looking to marry for money." Then, I thought of Laura. "I forgot to mention," I added, "the child isn't his wife's. Kristeene's mother is Laura."

Lisa gasped, "Oh my gosh! Another woman in the mix!"

"It was because of Laura," I reflected, "that we nearly had an accident tonight."

I recounted the car incident to her.

"Laura is an enigma. Why did George let you drive Laura's car?"

"Maybe, like Anna, Laura also left George."

"But you said he still thinks about Laura."

"I think when he talks about Laura, he's in a somber mood."

Lisa commented so casually, but her words hit me with distaste. A difficult scene to act in? I didn't want to be a part of a scene. It seemed I wasn't the one with the final say in getting involved. This wasn't acting out a scene. It was an

津有味。

我说，要把孩子照顾好，一了百了的出路是我暂时休学，让乔治办身份，双方得利。也许三年五年以后，等柯丽丝上了幼儿园，我再回来读书。

她说，如果我是你，爱他的孩子，他让搬进去住，我就去了。素素，想一想，读书究竟为了什么？不就是为了能找一份好工作，工资高一些，生活好一些吗？好，现在他对你只有一个要求，就是把孩子带好。带好了孩子，你就有了一切。你在美国举目无亲，要奋斗到哪一天，才能有汽车？有房子？有身份？而你，就是因为爱那个孩子，才愿意在他们家工作。这不是两相情愿吗？有了钱，还读什么书呵？你觉得我们化那么多钱学习的课程将来都有用处吗？不要太死心眼。多少创造发明家是没有学位的，他们能够创造发明，是因为他们做了喜欢的事情。

我说，我在想，如果你能帮一把，我读书的时候，你去看孩子，不就两全其美了吗？

莉莎“哈哈”大笑：素素，你那么聪明，为什么不能把乔治搞到手？

我说，你胡说什么呀？我为什么要把他搞到手？

她说，瞧你看的那些书，哲学的，逻辑的，心理学，教育学，经济学，历史和文学，你完全可以自学，不用来学校上课。

我说，我不是为了他，而是为了他的女儿和自己去工作的。我还年轻，不想为了钱去定终身。说到这里，我突然想起了劳瑞。

我说，忘了告诉你，那个孩子不是他太太生的，柯丽丝的妈妈叫劳瑞。

莉莎说，天哪，还有一个女人夹在中间。

我说，因为这个劳瑞，今晚差点儿酿成一场车祸。

我讲了车的故事和事故过程。

莉莎说，劳瑞很神秘。乔治为什么让你驾驶劳瑞的车？

也许劳瑞像安娜一样弃他而去。 我说。

但是，你说，看上去他对劳瑞很留恋？

我说，看上去他谈劳瑞的时候，心情很忧郁。

这是一场难唱的戏。素素，看来他是要把劳瑞娶回来的。等劳瑞一来，他就不需要你了。

莉莎说得随便，但是，到了我的耳朵里，很不是味道。难唱

actual competition, an unexpected one. In this contest, I was powerless, akin to a pawn. Once my limited use was up, I could be ejected from the game at any time. How had I not seen this? When Anna left, the vacancy wasn't meant for me. It was for Laura, Kristeene's mother.

"So, maybe we don't need to move. I'll have to find another job," I decided.

Lisa gave me a sly wink. "That's up to you and how savvy you are, Susu."

It was clear Lisa was encouraging me to vie for George's affections. She was pragmatic. Were all Americans this practical?

We talked until midnight. Lisa shared the details of her relationship with David. She explained that when David first visited her, he already had a girlfriend. Nonetheless, she managed to win him back. David was on the verge of transferring to the local college. If neither of them had a change of heart, they might be married within a year. I offered my congratulations to Lisa, and she expressed her gratitude. She firmly believed that any man could be won over by Susu. I pleaded my case, saying, "It was all for you that I once had to play a role. Do you think I'm naturally deceitful?"

She cut in, "You should take pride in your ability to capture hearts."

Lisa returned to her room, and I settled on the floor to sleep. It was peculiar that night; the fragrance of Kristeene lingered on me, her soap's scent filling the air, and her infectious laughter echoed in my ears. The unforgiving floor beneath me felt akin to Kristeene's room. A subtle melancholy settled deeper into my heart, tugging me further away from Kristeene.

I realized, no matter how far I journeyed, I always ended up back in the same place.

的戏？我才不愿意卷进去唱戏呢！但是，好像卷不卷不由我说了算。这哪里是戏呵，分明是一场竞争，一场出乎意料的竞争。在这场竞争中，我毫无实力，就像一个无名小卒，在微弱的价值被利用以后，将随时被踢到场外。我怎么没有看到呢？为什么要卷进去？事实明摆着，安娜出走以后，那个空缺并不在等着我，那是给劳瑞的，柯丽丝的妈妈。

我说，那么，不必再搬家了，应该去重新找一份工作。

莉莎狡黠地眨了眨眼睛，说道，看你的本事啦，素素。

看得出来，莉莎在鼓动我去竞争乔治太太的位置。她很实际，美国人是否都很实际？

我们聊到半夜。莉莎说了她和戴维德的关系。她说，戴维德来看她的时候，已经有了女朋友。但是，现在她把戴维德夺回来了。戴维德正准备转学回来，如果大家都不再三心二意的话，也许，一年以后要订婚。

我祝贺莉莎，莉莎感谢我。她认为，任何男人都会成为素素手下的败将。我辩护说，还不是为了你，我做了一回骗子？你以为我骗人成性？

她打断我说，让男人折服应该感到骄傲，云云。

莉莎回房以后，我睡地上。很奇怪，那晚，柯丽丝的气息一直在我身边缭绕。空气里有她身上的肥皂香，耳朵旁时不时响起那铜铃般的笑声。还有身下那个硬绷绷的地板，好像睡在柯丽丝的房间里。

Chapter 12

On the night before the road test, I asked George if I could make a call before I left. I wanted to subtly convey that I had a boyfriend.

I wasn't Lisa; I was Susu from China, making a living through hard work. I had no connection to George, regardless of his wealth or the number of women in his life. Laura, if you could return to care for Kristeene, I, Susu, would pack my things and go.

But when it came to leaving, it felt like there was something lodged in my chest. I could let go of everything, except Kristeene. The little girl, though not yet speaking much, was enchanting and clever. We communicated through glances, expressions, and gestures. I knew when she was lost in thought, she needed a nap, and when she fiddled with her food, she wanted a drink. I also knew that music lifted her spirits, and without a bedtime story, she couldn't sleep well. We had an unspoken understanding. There had been a time I contemplated leaving, but I reconciled with George due to a misunderstanding and stayed, unable to bear leaving her alone. Yet this time, if it was also a misunderstanding, it might be alright.

However, George had informed me that Laura was Kristeene's mother. If this Laura was still alive, there would come a day when Kristeene would inevitably be separated from me. So, the entire afternoon, I watched the girl, unsure of what to do. It felt like attending a funeral. I sang and danced to pass the time, but my heart remained heavy.

The initial plan was for me to drive myself back, but I asked George, "Could you drive me to my boyfriend's place? I'm not very familiar with this area." George glanced at the address and agreed.

Once in the car, he inquired, "I heard from Anna that you have a handsome boyfriend. What's his name?"

第十二章

在考驾驶执照的前一天晚上，我故意在回家前，要求打一个电话。我要向乔治显示，我有男朋友。

我不是美国姑娘，不是莉沙，是来自中国的素素。我靠自己的劳动过日子。乔治有再多的钱，再多的女人，和我没有关系。去你的劳瑞，有本事回来好好照顾柯丽丝，素素我，打起背包就走人。

说到要走，心口像被堵住了似的。什么都能舍，就是舍不下柯丽丝。小姑娘虽然说不了几句话，但是，耳聪目明，懂得用眼睛和面部表情，以及肢体语言来进行交流。我知道她心不在焉的时候要睡觉，知道她挑食的时候要喝水；我知道她听到音乐就兴高采烈，知道她没有故事睡不安稳。我们俩已经心心相印。上一次，本来已经要走，因为舍不得她，和乔治消除了误会，留了下来。这一次，如果也是误会多么好！但是，乔治说得清清楚楚，劳瑞是柯丽丝的妈妈。只要这个劳瑞还在世界上，柯丽丝总有一天要和我分手。整整一个下午，我的心情就像在开追悼会一样，痴痴地看着这个女孩，不知道应该怎么办。我用唱歌跳舞来打发时间，心里却越发悲伤。

本来应该自己驾车回家的。我对乔治说，能否帮个忙，开到我男朋友的家里去？对这一带的地形我不熟悉。他看了看地址，说没问题。

上车后，他主动搭腔，说道，听安娜提起过，你有一个长得很英俊的男朋友，叫……什么来着？

查里。我说，查里．汤姆斯。

你们在一个学校吗？

是的，他是老师，哲学系新来的。

"Charlie," I replied. "Charlie Thomas."

"Are you both at the same college?"

"Yes. He's a teacher, new in the philosophy department."

"Oh," George acknowledged.

I steered the conversation back to Kristeene. "Kristeene has a new tooth. She's starting to talk more, like a little parrot. Today she learned to sing 'Twinkle, Twinkle Little Star.' She followed me, singing 'Strar, Strar.'"

"So?" George was visibly delighted. He began to tap the rhythm on the steering wheel, humming the tune.

I couldn't help but hum along, feeling as though Kristeene were right beside me.

George shared, "I'm amazed at how Kristeene is growing every day. It's like living in paradise."

"Uh-huh," I replied, feeling a tickle in my nose, as if I'd pressed a button.

George continued, "I even thought about hiring someone to take care of my work so I wouldn't have to."

"If you don't work, you won't need me anymore."

"That's not the case." George turned to look at me. "I can only offer her a father's love. Your position isn't affected. No one can replace you."

I almost wanted to say, "But Laura, you have Laura. What do you need me for?" A sort of resentment welled up in me, itching to spill out. Yet, I held it back. Once I started, I might lose control, and I didn't know what the outcome would be. Regardless, it wouldn't be favorable, considering there was a woman involved, the mother of Kristeene. I didn't want to bring up Laura's name.

"Susu, why so quiet?" George asked.

I mustered a smile and suddenly felt a wave of sympathy for him. "I'm just thinking about my homework."

As the night rolled on, I mumbled, "Sorry for the interruption, George."

"It's cool," I murmured, "Just pondering over next semester."

"Take your time," he assured, "Finish this semester strong."

I hesitated, almost ready to spill about moving into his home if he could aid my situation. No, courage failed me.

Before I knew it, we arrived at Charlie's place.

George mentioned he'd take his leave once I was inside. I pressed the doorbell, and there was Charlie, wrapping me in a tight hug. Tears streamed

噢。乔治答道。

我把话题扯回柯丽丝。我说，柯丽丝长了新牙，话也越来越多，像个学舌的鹦鹉一样。今天，她学唱

Twinkle, twinkle little star, Strar Strar地跟着我唱呢！

是吗？乔治很高兴，便在驾驶盘上打拍子，哼起了那支歌曲：

Twinkle, twinkle little star,

How I wonder where you are.

Far above the world so high,

like a diamond in the sky.

Twinkle, twinkle little star,

How I wonder where you are.

我也情不自禁地轻唱起来，好像柯丽丝就在身边一样。

乔治说，看着柯丽丝一天天长大，每天有惊喜，好像活在天堂里。

我“嗯”了一声，好像按了一下开关似的，鼻子酸了起来。

乔治说，我真想雇人照顾生意，不上班了。

我说，你不去上班的话，就不需要我了。

哪里的话？乔治回头看了看我，说道，我只能给她父亲的爱。你的位置是没有人能够替代的。

我想说，劳瑞，你还有劳瑞呢？你要我干什么？有一股怨气，不明不白地在体内流动，只差没有冲出来。忍住了不说，是因为怕自己一旦开口，难以控制情绪，不知道会有什么结果？怎么说也不会有好结果的，因为中间隔着一个女人，她是柯丽丝的母亲。很不愿意提劳瑞这个女人的名字。唉……乔治是个好父亲，为了柯丽丝宁可不去上班。劳瑞却忍心把孩子扔给一个男人，这哪里像母亲的样子？乔治为什么要接受这样的女人？

素素，你怎么很安静？

我勉强笑了笑，突然可怜起他来。我说，在想功课呢！

噢，对不起，我打断了你的思路。

没有，没关系。我说，在想下个学期的事情呢！

Take Your Time。他说，把这学期的书读完再说。

我想告诉乔治，愿意搬到他那里去住，如果给我办身份。…

down, oblivious to George's presence. His departure was a blur.

Charlie inquired, "I'm stationed on the fifth floor of the library. I hope you'll swing by. Where were you this weekend?"

I remained in tears.

Charlie guided me to sit and went to whip up some tea. When he returned, he gently wiped away my tears.

"How'd you spend the weekend?" he probed. What could I say?

Over the weekend, I juggled reading, homework, learning to drive, tending to Kristeene, and handling George. The uncertainty of my next move loomed. Could I make such a monumental sacrifice for Kristeene? The prospect of losing my job as a caregiver didn't daunt me, but the thought of parting with her was unbearable.

At first, Charlie misread my tears, assuming they stemmed from our weekend separation. This led to a string of suggestive gestures, kisses, and caresses. Yet as my tears persisted, he sensed something amiss. He pressed for an explanation, wanting to know what had happened over the weekend, and who the man was who brought me here. I could only shake my head, tears flowing.

He grew slightly exasperated, rising to his feet. "Susu," he urged, "if you don't share, how can I ease your burden? Let the tears flow if it brings relief."

His words were a jolt. I snapped to attention. Wasn't this behavior akin to that of a fallen woman? Why burden Charlie with my troubles? I wasn't a fragile soul. With my face hidden, I hastened to the bathroom. I dabbed my eyes, blew my nose, and doused my face with warm water. A steaming towel rested on my eyes, granting solace for a long stretch before I emerged.

I couldn't bring myself to sit close to Charlie. I stood at a distance, eyes red and swollen, and murmured, "I'm sorry, Charlie. My emotions got the better of me. I'm fine now. Don't worry."

"Did someone mistreat you?" he inquired.

"No," I replied, "I made three hundred dollars last weekend, and this week, I'll make thirty dollars every day. I'll repay you for the sleepwear."

Charlie pressed, "But why cry when you've earned so much?"

"My tears," I confessed, "have nothing to do with money. Just tell me the cost of the clothes."

Charlie said nothing, his gaze a silent skeptic. I couldn't help but smile. "The money came from caring for the child. My employer even provided a car.

…不，不，我哪里敢说？哪里有这么大的勇气？

不一会儿，查里的家到了。

乔治说，要等我进去了以后再走。我按了门铃，查里出来，一把抱住我。我便扑在他的肩膀上哭了。完全忘记了乔治的存在，也不知道他什么时候开车走了。

查里说，我天天去图书馆的五楼，我以为你会来的呢！这个周末，你到哪里去了？

我还是不停地哭。

查里让我坐下，去泡茶，回来帮我擦眼泪。

查里的问题，该如何回答他？

这个周末，对付了读书和功课还要对付学车，照顾柯丽丝，和乔治周旋。更难的是，不知道下一步该如何走？不知道应该不应该为柯丽丝做出如此大的牺牲？我不怕失去一份照顾孩子的工作，但是难以承受失去柯丽丝。

开始，查里误解了我，以为是想念他而留眼泪。他做了一些性感的暗示，吻我，抚摸我。见我越哭越凶，以为是我遭受了别人的欺负，询问出了什么事？周末那两天如何度过？刚才开车的人是谁？我一边摇头一边抽泣。他有点生气了，站起来说：素素，你不说话，我没有办法分担你的痛苦。你要哭就哭个够吧！

他这么一说，倒是像一盆冷水，把我浇醒了。这不是在耍无赖吗？有什么理由把自己的苦恼转移到查里身上？我可不是脆玻璃那样碰不起的女人。我捂着脸急步跑去了厕所，擤鼻涕，擦眼泪，用热水把脸洗了又洗，然后把热毛巾敷在眼睛上，好一会儿才出来。

我不敢坐回到查里的旁边，离开他老远地站着，红肿的眼睛望着地面，惭愧地说，查里，对不起，没有控制好自己的情绪。我没事，你不要担心。

他说，没有人欺负你？

没有。我说，周末我赚了三百元，这个星期每天三十元，我把内衣的钱付给你。

查里说，为什么你拿了钱还那么伤心？

我说，钱和伤心没有关系。告诉我，内衣裤总共多少钱？查里没有回答，盯着我看，好像在说，不相信你。我忍不住哑然失笑，

I'm swamped with driving lessons."

"And yet, you cried?"

I said, "Share a secret, and I'll spill why I shed those tears. Seems fair, doesn't it?"

Charlie pondered, "What secret do I hold?"

I pressed, "Who was the lucky recipient of those sleepwear?"

He hesitated, "You might not like my answer."

"Why's that?"

"Because it's not much of a secret. She was an ex, living states away. When we parted ways, she handed back all the gifts I'd given her."

I bit back questions about the coincidence, their parting, and her allure. Men prefer not to dwell on bygones. It's a dance best left untouched. How many women stumble and bleed, shackled by their inability to accept their partner's past? So, I decided, it wasn't worth mentioning, let alone repaying him.

An instinct nudged me, urging me to offset my prior misstep. I needed to reclaim the part of me that seemed to have slipped away in that moment, sparing Charlie the weight. And so, I unraveled the intricate web of George's recent family dramas—the suspense, the misunderstandings, the fabricated accident. We talked and talked until fatigue overtook us, and we slumped into slumber on the sofa.

The transition to the bed eluded my senses. The sensation of being lifted, suspended in the air, faintly echoed memories of George's arms, ferrying me to the backseat of the car. As Charlie drew near, my reflexes kicked in, jolting me awake.

Charlie caught on in an instant. "Susu, if George overstepped, you can take legal action for harassment."

I shook my head, "No, he didn't. Maybe I'm just a little wary of him. I heard from Anna that he's involved with someone. But who can blame him? Anna's a lesbian." Charlie mused, "But you brought up Laura, Kristeene's mother."

"Don't speak of Laura. Don't even say her name, alright?" I snapped.

"Susu, Sweetheart, is something bothering you emotionally?" Charlie's words fueled my simmering frustration.

"Emotional problem?" I retorted. "Put yourself in my shoes. Imagine an

说道，钱是带孩子挣来的，主人给了一辆车，这几天忙学车呢！

那么，你哭什么哭呵？

我说，你说你的秘密，我告诉你为什么哭，平等交换，如何？

我有什么秘密？

我说，那套内衣是买给谁的？

查里说，你不会喜欢我的答案的。

为什么？

因为不是什么秘密。是我原来的女朋友。她在另外一个州，我们分手的时候，她把以前送的礼物都还给了我。

我想说，这么巧，她的个子和我一样？你们为了什么分手？她长得是否漂亮？等等。但是，男人不喜欢纠缠旧事，过去的事情就过去了，没有什么好说的。多少女人因为小心眼难以和男人的过去共存，跌了个头破血流？我不再提付钱的事了。

我本能地感到，必须作一些努力来抵消刚才的“拙劣”表现，必须让自己的灵魂回来而不成为查里的负担。于是，我把这几天在乔治家里的事情有声有色滴水不漏地告诉了查里。有悬念有误会，还有那场虚惊。我们谈呵谈，谈到体力不支，东倒西歪地靠在沙发上睡了。

不知什么时候，被人抱到了床上。那种离开地面，腾空而起的感觉，朦朦胧胧地回到了乔治抱我到汽车后座的情景。所以，当查里用身体来接近我的时候，出于本能，推了他一把，惊醒了。

查里马上领悟了，说道：素素，如果乔治真的欺负了你，可以告他性骚扰。

我说，没有，他没有。可能是因为心里有点怕。听安娜说，他在外面混女人。

老婆同性恋，混女人有什么奇怪？查里说。不过，你不是说，还有个劳瑞，柯丽丝的妈妈？

不要说劳瑞，不要说，好不好？我叫了起来。

素素，亲爱的，你的情绪有问题。

他这么一说，就像火上加油一样，我更生气了。我说，我的情绪有问题？换了你来试试看。如果有一个神秘的人物，从来没有露面，却影响着你的生存，比如说，你随时有可能因为她的原因，失

enigmatic figure, never seen, but poised to upend your life. Picture losing your job at any moment because of her, sacrificing your happiness. Tell me, wouldn't that stir up some emotions?"

Charlie posed some sharp questions. Have I ever seen this elusive figure? Why didn't she make an appearance at George's fiftieth? Why remain unseen after Anna's departure? If this person truly existed, why lavish me with a car, bump my pay, and promise tuition? Why not let Laura take over?

Charlie's logic sent shivers down my spine, evoking images of the madwoman in "Jane Eyre" and the foreboding atmosphere of the castle. Fear gripped me, numbing my extremities. I curled into myself. "Charlie, could Laura be unhinged or battling some incurable ailment in isolation?"

"Perhaps Laura's already gone," he suggested.

I clamped my hand over his mouth. "Enough of this nonsense. She's Kristeene's mother, after all."

Charlie reasoned, "If not this, then what? Susu, Laura belongs to George, and we're not in this equation. Rest well—you've got that road test tomorrow."

Charlie embraced me.

"Tighten that hug."

"Alright."

"I worry Laura might slip into my dreams."

"Don't fret. I'm right here with you."

Charlie's warmth coursed through me, from shoulders to toes, as we melted into each other, the night draped in our shared warmth.

去工作，失去欢乐，你的情绪会不会有问题？

查里说，也许这个人物根本不存在。你见过她吗？乔治五十岁的生日宴会她为什么不来？为什么在安娜离家以后，没有出现？如果确实有这个人物，乔治为什么要给你汽车，加你工钱，付你的学费，为什么不让劳瑞来代替你……？

查里说得好吓人。我想到了“简爱”里的疯老婆，哎哟，和城堡里阴森森的气氛挺相近的。我一时吓得手脚冰凉，缩成了一团。我说，查里，劳瑞会不会是个疯子或者嗑白粉的？或者得了不治之症被隔离在什么地方？

查里说，也许劳瑞已经死了。

我赶忙用手去堵他的嘴巴，说道，不要乱说，她毕竟是柯丽丝的妈妈。

查里说，除了这样猜，还有什么其他的可能？素素，劳瑞是乔治的，不管我们的事。明天你要考驾照，好好睡一觉。

查里抱抱我。

嗯。

抱得紧一点。

嗯。

我怕劳瑞爬到我的梦里来。

别怕，有我呢！

查里的热量从肩膀往下传，通过胸口，腹部，大腿，直到脚跟，我们互相摩擦，翻来滚去，大汗淋漓。

Chapter 13

I aced the road test for my driver's license. The temporary license paper felt surreal in my hands—should I celebrate or reflect on the missing 15 points? The tester, a man with a subtle accent, announced my score of 85, leaving me curious about the passing grade.

As I headed back to the building, George and Kristeene awaited, Kristeene chirping "HI" to the world. George wore a faint worry, aware we might need a second or even a third attempt if I failed. With the sun on my face, I shielded it with the temporary license, while Kristeene wriggled free from George's embrace, wobbling towards me. I scooped her up, declaring, "Home, let's go home." Then, I handed the paper to George, awaiting his verdict.

"Susu, you're brilliant. Passed on the first try!" George's relief painted his face.

"Passed? Passed what?" I questioned.

"The driver's license." He waved the paper triumphantly.

"Driver's license? I passed the test?" I exclaimed, perplexed by the paper.

George clarified, "You just need to take a photo and provide fingerprints inside. Your license will arrive in the mail soon."

"George, I actually passed!" My elation made me leap, still cradling Kristeene. "I can drive solo now and go wherever, whenever! Beach trips and zoo adventures await!" My jubilation set Kristeene into peals of laughter—a rare moment of open joy in front of my employer.

George coaxed Kristeene to him. "Come to Daddy, Kristeene. Susu has other things to attend to." As he approached, I slung an arm around him, beaming. "Thank you, boss, for the training and the car."

He didn't mind the address, giving me a congratulatory pat. I gazed at him with newfound appreciation, taking in the details of his face: strong cheekbones, deep-set eyes, a straight nose, a hint of silver at his temples, and the gentle sag of his skin.

With a winsome smile, I dashed into the building, breezing through the

第十三章

我很快地结束了驾驶执照的考试，接过考官递过来的一张纸片，称之临时通行证，我两眼一摸黑，不知道该喜还是该悲？考官说八十五分。我既不知道另外十五分跑到哪里去了，也不知道究竟需要多少分才算及格？接过临时通行证，不知道和原来的那个学车证明有什么不一样？考官是个黑人，说了一通走样的美国话，我连想带猜还不能全部听懂。

乔治和柯丽丝原来等在大厅里，看到甲壳虫车开了回来，便向停车场走来。柯丽丝对着来回的车流和人们时不时地说“Hi”，乔治的脸上挂着焦虑，我知道，如果不争气的话，我们还要来第二次或者第三次。我朝他们走去的时候，正好太阳迎面射过来，我皱着眉头，举着通行证遮太阳。柯丽丝挣脱出乔治的保护，摇摇摆摆地朝我跑过来。我一把抱起她，说道，回家，我们回家。然后把那张纸给了乔治，就像在等候判决一样。

素素，你真行，一次通过！乔治愁云密布的脸顿时阳光灿烂。

通过了吗？通过什么呀？我问道。

驾驶执照！他把纸片举过了头，在空中挥舞。

驾驶执照？我通过了驾驶执照？那么，他为什么仍旧给我一张纸片？看着我一脸的疑惑，乔治笑了。他说，你要到大厅里去拍照片，按手印，过不了多久，驾照就寄来了。

乔治，你是说，我考出了驾照吗？哎呀呀，我可以自己开车了？我心花怒放，抱紧了柯丽丝就像抱个枕头似地在地上跳跃。我说，素素能自己开车啦！素素有了行动自由啦！素素可以带你到海边到动物园去玩儿啦！柯丽丝被我颠得放声大笑。毫不掩饰地在雇主面前宣泄自己的快乐感情，对于我来说，这是第一次。

乔治说，柯丽丝，来，爹地抱，素素还有事呢！在他来接柯丽

procedures.

"Let's head home!" I called out, almost singing. "I'll be the one behind the wheel today—I've got my driver's license."

The journey back was marked by a gentle drizzle, raindrops dancing around my car, bestowing it with a refreshing cleanse. I cracked my window just a bit, letting in the crisp air and the delicate touch of rain on my hair—like Heaven's gifts in handfuls.

After dropping them off at their place, I made a beeline for college, just in time for the last philosophy class before lunch. Today, the professor dished out feedback on the test papers we'd handed in a couple of days ago. The question was a head-scratcher: "The familiar person at my side." It called for a philosophical spin, using the knowledge we'd soaked up in his lectures to dissect the subject. I initially thought about scribbling on Kristeene—the little dynamo who couldn't chatter or feed herself, yet sparked my creativity. Through her innocence, I could sift out the muck of adult life. But my English wasn't up to the task for such a brain-bender. So, I opted for an easier question: "Monk Jigong in red pants." I took a lighthearted approach, spinning yarns about the Chinese monk Jigong—always half-lit, riding a bamboo stick in the sky, carefree. His tattered robes hitched a ride on a mythical bird, soaring to America. Upon touchdown, he adapted to local customs, ditching the shabby threads but keeping his cheeky demeanor. I jotted that he once roamed the streets, now he's hitting the books in college. His frayed fan transformed into a self-flipping set of papers—impressive and inspiring. I wrapped it up with a nod to his loose-fitting, old-fashioned attire, with the bold choice of red pants. And that, my friends, was the Americanized Monk Jigong, training a fresh crop of young acolytes.

The professor gave my piece a thumbs-up, even summoning me to read it aloud. I was a bundle of nerves, speeding through the words like a runaway train. My mind raced, trying to flee the anxiety. Images of the highway I'd just navigated flashed before me. The summer wind raced, bringing rain along for the ride. They embraced me, planted kisses, and sang joyously in my ears. My eyes remained glued to my paper. Each word marched in orderly lines, and when their march concluded, so did my reading.

Applause and laughter filled the room. I glanced around, baffled by the commotion. Did I stumble over some words? Sweat broke out all over as I used my papers as a makeshift fan, rustling them and making a racket. "Sorry, sorry," I stammered. "If I flubbed something, please let me know." More laughter followed. I shielded my face with the papers, terrified I might spill the beans about my absent-minded driving. At last, I blurted out, "I just got my driver's license today. I'm over the moon. Forgive me if I blathered on."

丝的时候，我勾住了他的肩膀，快乐地说，老板，谢谢你的训练，谢谢你的车！

他好像很满意，不在乎我如何称呼他。他拍拍我的背，一边说，祝贺你，素素。

也许是出于感激的原因吧，我多看了他一会儿。第一次近距离地看清楚了他的容貌。高高的颧骨，眼睛深深地凹进去，高鼻子挺得像条木头。鬓角上暗藏着零星的白发。我还注意到他脸上开始松弛的皮肤。

我丢给他一个妩媚的微笑，连蹦带跳地往大厅飞奔。一会儿就把公事办了。

回家，回家！我走到他们身旁时，大声嚷嚷，好像在唱歌一样。今天我开车，我有驾照啦！

在回家的路上，天下起来蒙蒙细雨。雨帘跟着汽车走，好像淋浴的水龙头一样，把车身洗个干净。我把窗摇开了一道缝，清新的空气夹着雨珠飘进来，落在我的头发上，好像上苍送来一把把珍贵的礼物。

把他们送到家，再到学校去上课，我赶上了午餐前的最后一节哲学课。今天的内容是教授评讲我们前两天交上去的小测验。题目是“身边一个熟悉的人”。当然不是一般的记叙文，必需运用所学得的哲学知识对人物进行分析。我原来想写柯丽丝，这个不会说话不会自己吃饭的小精灵，通过她的天真和无辜来过滤成人生活中的精神杂质，我有许多感想要写。但是，我的英文不允许写很深奥的哲学道理，于是，换了一个比较容易写的题目：“穿红裤子的济公”。我几乎是用开玩笑的口气写的。介绍了中国的济公，醉眼朦胧，糊里糊涂，假作真来真亦假。我说他乘竹竿而起，飘飘逸逸不小心，破衣服挂上了飞来美国的金属鹏鸟。来美国以后，他入乡随俗，衣服没有中国那样破烂，也改变了蓬头垢足的模样，但是内在的素质非但没有改变而且有了发展。我说他本来在民间游荡，现在进了高等学府。他的破扇子变成几张讲义，扑簌簌翻动起来，也有清神醒目的作用。我说，他的衣服肥大陈旧，下面穿一条红色的裤子。那算是济公的美国特色，而且调教出一批批的小济公。

这篇文章很讨教授的喜欢。他请我站起来，在同学面前念了一遍。我紧张得要命。念得很快。越念越快越忘掉了自己在念什么。可能是脑袋想逃避紧张的状态，本能地一心二用。我的思绪倒回到了高速公路，夏风驾着速度，伴着雨珠，扑上来拥抱我，亲吻我，

Suddenly, a pat on my back jolted me. I nearly leaped out of my skin, swiftly clamping a hand over my mouth. It was the philosophy professor. "You did splendidly, Susu. Congrats on the license," he beamed, extending his hand. I shrank back, then realizing who it was, I extended mine, too. I murmured, "Why were they laughing, then?" He pointed to the end of my article, remarking, "Someone added a little joke there." It was the professor's own comment, which I'd inadvertently read aloud in my distracted state. He'd written, "Hahaha, very funny. Susu is the young Jigong. Please come to my office for a chat when you are free."

And then it hit me. It wasn't my fault—it was the professor's blunder! At least, that's what I thought back then. My thoughts were all over the place.

I mustered up some unexpected courage and said, "Inviting just me to your office isn't enough. What if we all went together?" The classroom buzzed with agreement, and someone even suggested visiting the professor at his home. Surprisingly, he agreed. Another student proposed going that very night, and he gave the green light. He was the most laid-back person, never putting on airs.

After class, I called George right away, filling him in on the impromptu plans for the evening. How could I back out now when I was the one who suggested it? Plus, I was genuinely intrigued by the professor. But was it too much to ask for some time off on the very day I earned my driver's license?

George didn't sound thrilled on the phone, but he phrased it delicately, "Why didn't you tell me sooner?" I was at a loss for words. After a long pause, I mustered an apology, "Sorry, George. You're right. I should have told you earlier."

As I said it, any remnants of the intimacy we shared that morning at the road test site evaporated. I didn't even feel inclined to explain. Tell him earlier? There was no "earlier" to this. It all unfolded mere minutes ago. I recalled not long ago when I'd contemplated giving up the job. He'd been surprised, but hadn't said no. Now, his stance had shifted noticeably. I chalked it up to my employer's dignity. He was the boss; what could I say?

After a quiet spell, I stated, "I'll come after school." He paused for a beat and replied, "We'll discuss it when you get here."

I returned to the "castle" promptly at half-past three. The party at the professor's place was slated for seven.

I did my best to act like everything was business as usual. I played with Kristeene for a bit and managed to get her down for a nap. George was holed up in his study. Not a word about the evening's party was uttered. If I wanted to make it to the gathering, I'd have to leave by half-past six. I ventured downstairs, my intention to knock on the study door. But I wavered, pacing in front

呜呜地在我的耳边欢乐地唱歌。眼睛看着稿纸，文字像排队似的，秩序井然地进入眼底。字走完了，我也念完了。

课堂里，又是拍手又是大笑。我朝周围看看，不知道发生了什么事情？心想，我只是把一个个单词念了出来，是不是说错了话？顿时，浑身是汗。我用稿纸不停地当扇子，在耳旁叭嗒叭嗒地摇晃，一边说，对不起，对不起，如果念错了请大家指正。又是一阵欢笑。我不得不把稿纸蒙在脸上，怕只怕自己把开车的体会胡乱

地说了出来。我说，今天我考到了驾照，如果有胡说八道，请大家原谅。这时，有人从背后拍了我肩膀一巴掌，吓得我捂住“伤口”，差点儿跳起来。回头一看，原来是哲学教授。他说，念得很好，素素，祝贺你考出了驾照。说完，他把手伸过来。我缩手缩脚地往后退，看准了是这个满脸络腮胡子的哲学教授，才敢把手伸过去，轻声地问，他们为什么要笑我？他指了指文章的结尾，说，有人写了几句废话。我一看，原来是教授的批文，被我一不小心也念了出来。教授写的是：哈哈哈，很有趣。素素小济公，请有空来我办公室坐坐。

哦，我恍然大悟。原来是教授闯了祸！到了这个地步，我还不知道问题出在自己身上，可见在当时，我多么糊涂！

不知道哪里来的勇气，我说，邀请我一个人去坐坐，多么不够意思！要去大家一起去，对不对？

YES！全场轰动。有的同学甚至建议要到哲学教授家里去访问。他居然同意了。有个同学说，今天晚上就去，他也同意了。反正，教授是个最没有规矩最随和的人。

下了课，我马上和乔治打电话，告诉他今天晚上的活动。怎么能不去呢？一切都是从我开始的，而且，我确实对哲学教授充满了兴趣。但是，考出驾照的第一天就要求请假，是不是太过份了？

果然，乔治在电话里不高兴。他说得很婉转，你应该事先告诉我一声。我欲答无词。许久才抱歉地说，对不起，乔治，你是对的，应该事先通知你。

当我这样回答他的时候，上午考车时的亲近感消失得无影无踪。我连解释的兴趣都没有。事先给通知？这件事根本没有事先，而是刚刚发生，就在几分钟之前。我想起了不久前我突然辞职的那天，他虽然吃惊却没有说一个“不”字，相比之下，他的态度明显地有了变化。我很简单地将这种变化理解为主人的威严，我是被雇佣的，有什么好说的？

of it, unable to gather my resolve. I retreated to Kristeene's room, attempting to tackle some homework. The letters on the page swam before my eyes like a school of alien tadpoles.

En route here, I'd resolved to sit down with George and negotiate. He'd be awaiting my answer about moving in. My condition would be that he helped with the green card. If he wanted me to pause college, then we'd discuss compensation. And there'd be other details to iron out, like having some time off during the week, figuring out holiday pay, and so on. But the moment I stepped inside the house, my courage waned. I dreaded the thought of losing Kristeene forever if our negotiations fell flat. Truth be told, I was willing to do whatever it took for that child, even without a paycheck.

I checked my watch repeatedly. The second hand ticked away steadily, like the steady beat of a heart. Round and round it went. I'd already mapped out the route. The professor's place wasn't far, right on the hillside next to the estate. I'd traced the path with a colored marker. Everything was set, except for hitting the road. I pictured countless students gathering for a wild, free-spirited party at the professor's home. It thrilled me just to think about it. I even had my outfit planned.

Now, it was time to head downstairs for that final talk with George, hoping he could grasp my feelings and let me go.

I went up to the master bedroom to fetch the baby monitor, then made my way back downstairs and entered the study. George sat there, perched on the bridge of his nose, engrossed in a document.

I said, "Sorry, George, I need to trouble you for a moment."

"That's quite alright," he replied, "Is this about the party tonight?"

I purposefully sidestepped the question and handed him my article, saying with a smile, "I got praised for this by the professor today. Would you like to give it a read?"

Without waiting for his response, I laid the article before him and continued, "After you're done, I'll share a little joke about it."

He pushed his glasses up and delved into the text. The article wasn't particularly long. He smiled as he read and commented, "If I were the professor, I'd praise you too."

I said, "But my fellow students couldn't help but laugh."

"Why's that?"

"Finished already?"

"Yes."

"Well, when the professor wanted me to read it, I even read out his comment. I was in a daze, only thinking about the driver's license thing at the time."

我沉默了一会儿，说道，我下课了就回来。

他也沉默了一会儿，说道，回来再说吧！

我三点半准时回到了那个城堡，教授家的Party定在晚上七点锺。

我尽量装成什么事都没有发生的样子，和柯丽丝玩了一会儿，就哄她睡午觉了。乔治在书房里，也不提晚上的事情。如果要赶上Party，必须六点半离开。我走到楼下，想敲书房的门，走过来走过去，就是下不了决心。我回到柯丽丝的房间，打算做一会儿功课，书上的文字就像一群陌生的小蝌蚪，在眼前游来游去。本来，我在路上就想好了，今天必须和乔治进行一场谈判。他在等我的答复，是不是要住进来？我的条件是，办绿卡。如果他提出休学的问题，我就提出工资的要求。还有一些细节，比如应该有每周的休息时间，假节日如何计算，等等。可是，进了这个房子我就失去了勇气。我怕谈判不成功，最后失去柯丽丝。说实话，为了这个孩子，哪怕不给钱，我也是愿意的。

我时不时地看手表，秒针像心脏一样，有规则地跳动着，走了一圈又一圈。我已经查好了地图，哲学教授住得

离这儿并不远，就在旁边的一个山坡上。我用颜色笔把路线勾划了出来，只等着上路呢！想像着今天晚上将有那么多的同学相聚一堂，无拘无束地在哲学教授的家里疯狂，心里真是激动极了。我把晚上应该穿什么衣服都想好了。现在，我必须下楼，必须和乔治摊牌，希望他能理解我的心情，批准我走。

我到主卧房去拿了监听器，携带着下楼进了书房。乔治的鼻梁上架着老光眼镜，正在阅读一份文件。

我说，乔治，对不起，打扰你一下。

没关系。他说。是不是晚上的Party？

我故意回避不谈，而把那篇文章递给了他。我笑着说，这份作业，今天受到了老师的表扬，你要看看吗？

我不等他回答，就把文章放到了他的面前，一边说，等你看完了，讲个笑话给你听。

他推了推镜架，仔细地看了起来。文章不长，他一边看一边笑，说道，如果我是老师也要表扬你的。

我说，我的同学都笑话我呢！

为什么？

你看完了吗？

He leaned over to read the comment. After he finished, he tossed the paper down and burst into laughter, his face turned up towards the ceiling. It was the first time I'd seen him so at ease, laughing wholeheartedly.

He gasped for breath, then asked, "This is for the party tonight?"

"Yes," I confirmed. "Initially, the professor wanted to talk with me alone, but word got out, and now all the students are heading to his place."

"Oh." He took off his glasses, still smiling, and said, "Alright, you can go. A Chinese monk in American red pants—that's quite amusing."

I thanked him profusely and said, "The party starts at seven."

He glanced at his watch and advised, "You might want to leave a bit earlier. You'll need time to change and put on some makeup."

I was deeply touched and lost for words. I couldn't resist giving him a warm hug. He patted my back and said with warmth, "Enjoy yourself." As I stood at the study's doorway and turned to smile at him, he nodded, his eyes following me, radiating happiness.

In that moment, I felt both joy and surprise. I couldn't dare to dwell on why his demeanor had changed so swiftly.

看完了。

我说，老师让我念给大家听，我把评语一起念了。当时，我心不在焉，想着考驾照的事情。

他凑近去看老师的评语，看完后，把作业本往写字台上一仍，笑得仰面朝天。我第一次看到他如此放松地开怀畅笑。

他上气不接下气地问我，这就是今晚的Party?

是啊，我说，教授本来只是想和我一个人聊天，因为泄漏了秘密，现在，全班同学都要到他家里去了。

噢，他把眼镜取了下来，依旧笑容满面，说道，去吧，去吧，中国的和尚穿上美国的红裤子，太有意思了!

我忙谢了谢，说道，晚上七点。

他看了看手表，说，早点走吧，你还要梳洗换衣服!

我一下子感动得不知道说什么好，情不自禁地走上去给他一个拥抱。他拍拍我的背，亲切地说，玩得高兴。

我走到书房的门口，再回过头去朝他笑了笑。我说，如果有好玩的故事，明天告诉你。他点点头，用目光送我，很开心的样子。

当时因为又吃惊又高兴，我没有去思考为什么他的态度转变得那么快。

Chapter 14

"I need tell you, George, that philosophy professor is like an alien." I couldn't wait to share the events of last night as we sat down for supper.

I had deliberately waited a day and a night before talking to George. Even though I'd thought of calling him from the dorm hallway last night, it somehow didn't feel right. I preferred face-to-face conversations. The philosophy professor was just too amusing and captivating. I knew George might not align with his lifestyle, but I hoped he could appreciate something from it. Even with their differences, George could still find happiness and ease in his own way.

The reason the philosophy professor was so popular with his students was that he lived and breathed his philosophy: when you live, you must focus on what you "could" do, not what you "should" do. Opening the door to "what could be" made the world vibrant and full of color.

Sharing this philosophy wasn't my only intention. It was also a gesture of gratitude towards George. When I called him from school yesterday for his opinion, I'd unfairly judged him, thinking he was just asserting his employer's authority over me. It turns out, I'd misjudged him due to my own narrow perspective. In moments of anxiety, crisis, or failure, it's easy to view everything negatively. Negative thinking acts like a vacuum, sucking the joy out of life and often turning into a blade to cut ourselves. This revelation came courtesy of the philosophy professor and was a reflection of my own journey. I wanted George to know that since he'd given me permission to go, I'd experienced such a wonderful time last night.

"Alien?" George quipped, "Is he growing extra eyes and noses?"

I chuckled, "No, not like that. I mean his lifestyle, it's just so different from the mainstream."

We sat across from each other at the table, Kristeene by George's side, facing me.

I'd gotten the hang of preparing some simple American dishes by now. Tonight's menu consisted of a fresh lettuce salad, succulent steak filets, roast potatoes, and tender boiled green beans.

With Kristeene napping, I seized the opportunity to whip up dinner. George appreciated home-cooked meals and wasn't a fan of fast food. I wasn't sure who did the shopping, but perhaps it was George himself. He seemed

第十四章

乔治，我必须告诉你，那个哲学教授，嘻嘻，简直像外星人一样。

我已经等了一天一夜了。昨晚回到宿舍，本来想到走廊上去给他打个电话，犹豫再三，觉得不妥，因为我们从来不在电话上聊天。所以，一直等到今天和他见面。哲学教授实在太好玩，太吸引人了。虽然我知道乔治不会喜欢哲学教授的生活方式，但是，我希望他了解，即使不一样的生活方式，也可以活得很轻松很愉快。哲学教授之所以受到学生的尊敬和爱戴，是因为他身体力行他的哲学：人活着，不是“应该”如何如何，而是“可以”如何如何？“可以”的大门一旦被打开，这个世界就变得丰富多采，充满了活力。

这还不是急着要告诉他的主要原因。我想和乔治分享这些体会，是出于对他的感激。昨天，在学校里打电话征求他意见的时候，曾经把他想得很坏，以为他在玩弄雇主的权利。事实证明，是自己心胸狭隘做出了错误的判断。人在焦躁紧急和失败的的情况下，太容易从消极的方面来思考问题。而消极的思维就像吸尘器一样，把人生中本来的快乐抽走，转为变成伤害我们自己的刀刃。这些想法都来哲学教授，我正好被他言中。我想让乔治知道，因为有了他的批准，我昨天晚上玩得很开心。

外星人？乔治问道，不见得多长几个眼睛和鼻子吧！

No，No，我是指他的生活方式，完全和主流社会不一样的生活。

我们俩面对面坐着，柯丽丝在乔治的旁边我的对面。

我已经能够做一些简单的美国菜了。今晚的菜单是：生菜色拉，腓利牛排，烤土豆，和水煮四季豆。

我利用柯丽丝睡觉的空余时间用来准备晚饭。乔治喜欢在家里用餐，讨厌美国的快餐食品。不知道谁是这里的采购员，也许就是乔治自己。因为他好像对食品的质量要求很高。比如牛肉，以前在国内吃的西餐，那肉都有点筋筋拉拉的，叫牛腩，要煮很长时

to have a preference for high-quality ingredients. Take beef, for instance. In China, it tended to have a bit of fat due to its location on the cow's abdomen. It needed lengthy cooking to become tender. But here, the steak came from the side, devoid of excess fat. A mere five or six minutes in the oven at high heat rendered it perfectly chewable. I seasoned the steak with a blend of black pepper, crushed garlic, and olive oil. No salt was necessary; anyone who wanted it could add their own. I'd prepped the lettuce earlier, letting it dry in the fridge. There was an array of salad dressings, from the rich French style with heavy cheese to the spicy Italian varieties. George preferred a homemade concoction—two spoons of olive oil mixed with three spoons of German black vinegar, whisked together like eggs before drizzling over the salad. As for the green beans, I opted for boiling rather than cooking in oil. They were drained in a colander, then tossed with butter. The potatoes got a generous coating of olive oil before roasting in the oven

When there were no visitors, we'd have dinner in the kitchen at a round table by the windowsill, offering us views of the backyard, the sunset, and the babbling brook. On guest days, Betty would take charge of the cooking, and I'd step in as her assistant. Our meals were held at the long dining table in the dining room. Kristeene had her own high chair, complete with a half-round tray to keep her secure. It served as her makeshift plate. I'd carefully cut her food into bite-sized pieces, and she'd use her little hands to feed herself.

I started, "Have you heard of the Eastern philosophy of Yin and Yang?"

"Yes," he replied, "the symbol of half black and half white."

"That's right, but it's not a straight divide. It's curved. Have you noticed?"

"I didn't at first, but thinking about it now, I see it." George was quite precise in his dining etiquette. If he wanted to speak, he'd finish chewing, set his utensils down, place his hands in his lap, and sit up straight.

I went on, "His house is split between tile and thatch. The tiled portion faces west, while the thatched section is on the east. Even the garden follows suit: flowers flourish in the west, while vegetables thrive in the east. The kitchen and living room are in the tiled area, and the bedroom is in the thatched part. But it's bare, no furniture, no electricity, no carpet—just soft cushions. Large ones for sleeping, small ones for sitting. He sleeps on the floor and uses candles. The only mobile thing in the house is him."

George mused, "Is this division a blend of history and modernity, Eastern and Western?"

"Some of my classmates think so. But I believe it's all for fun. He's quite the big kid."

"And how old is he? Treating architecture like toys?"

"It's not really about age. Living joyfully is his philosophy."

As George focused on his plate, he lifted a forkful of green beans to his mouth before delicately slicing through the tender steak, which yielded easily to the pressure.

Seeing he hadn't spoken, I quickly added, "He has a white beard like yours." It slipped out, and I hurriedly followed up, "But you look younger

间，煮烂了才能吃。这里的牛肉，从来没有这种东西，是里脊肉的部份，烤的时间非常短，五六分钟的最高温，即烤箱的上层火，就成了。牛排必须用黑胡椒粉，大蒜末和橄榄油周身抹一边，不能放盐，盐是上桌以后各人自己撒的。生菜要提前洗尽，吸干水份，进冰箱冷藏。色拉酱品种很多，法国式的重奶酪，意大利的重香料。乔治最喜欢现做的，二匙橄榄油，三匙德国黑醋，要像打鸡蛋那样把油和醋拌匀，淋在色拉菜上面。四季豆不用油炒，而是放入沸腾的一大锅水里煮，用大火，水很多很烫，一会儿就捞出来，沥干水份，拌白脱油。土豆也要抹上橄榄油以后进烤箱。

没有客人的时候，我们都在厨房的圆台子上吃。台子在窗台边上，窗外有后花园的景色，落日和潺潺溪水。有客人的时候，蓓蒂过来掌厨，我当帮手。我们在晚餐厅的长桌子上吃饭。柯丽丝有自己的高餐椅子，坐下以后用一个半圆形的小台子把她“锁”在里面。台子代替盘子，我把食品切成小块，她用手抓来吃。

我说，你听说过东方的阴阳哲学吗？

YES，他答道，一半黑一半白的象征符号。

对了，对了，但不是对切的一半，而是弯曲流动的，你注意到了吗？

没有注意。不过，现在想起来好像确实是弯曲的。他说话的时候，总是要把嘴里的食品先咽下去，把刀叉放在盘子上面，双手垂在腹部。身板直挺挺，坐得规规矩矩。

我说，他的房子一半是瓦房，一半是茅草屋。瓦房在西，草屋在东。花园也是，西面种花，东面种菜。瓦房里是厨房和起居室，草屋是主卧室，里面没有家具，没有电灯，没有地毯，只有软绵绵的软垫。睡的是大软垫，坐的是小软垫。睡地铺，点腊烛。流动部份，就是他自己。

乔治说，这样分开，是不是为了历史和现实，东方和西方的结合？

有些同学是这样认为的。我觉得，主要是为了好玩。他是一个大孩子。

有多少年纪了？把建筑当玩具？乔治问道。

我说，这事儿和年纪没有关系。活得开心是他的人生哲学。

乔治垂下眼睛，吃了一叉四季豆，再把叉子横过来，去切牛排。腓利很嫩，像豆腐一样，轻轻一压，就分开了。

见他不说话，我着了急，忙说，他有白胡子了，大概和你差不多。说完了我很后悔。马上补一句，你看上去比他年轻。

那么说也有一把年纪了。

是啊，正因为有一把年纪了，才显得难能可贵。

than him."

"So, he's an old man."

"Yes, he's special because of his age."

"Ah, I see. Quite special." He echoed my words. Then, he gazed at me with a hint of suspicion. "Susu, do you think I'm getting old?"

I shook my head earnestly. "Not at all, not in the slightest."

He confessed, "I am, both in years and in my heart. It's only when I'm with Kristeene that I feel young." Then he met my gaze. His eyes seemed to say, "I feel young with you too," but for some reason, he didn't voice it.

Changing the subject, I continued, "He's hung up this enormous photo of a woman in his bedroom, black and white." I stopped there and chuckled.

"Why the laughter? I've never put up photos. The past isn't worth revisiting."

I hadn't expected him to connect it to himself. I'd already noticed the absence of any life chronicles in this house. I wanted to steer the conversation towards his own history, hoping he might share some of his secrets. Yet, I was too caught up in the joy of recounting the professor's stories to stop just yet.

"And here's the thing— we all wondered if the woman in the photo was his wife. She doesn't resemble any of his girlfriends. Oh, I forgot to mention, he's very open-minded, with a few girlfriends, none of them wives. They all know each other. We've met them all— Jessie, Mimi, and Alice. Alice has African-American roots, a lovely brown complexion, and a great figure, you know."

Unlike me, who was thoroughly engrossed in the story, George responded with a hint of disdain. "Open-minded, indeed."

I couldn't suppress another round of laughter as I continued, "Can you even guess who the woman in the photo is? I bet you can't."

George, not finding it as amusing, saw me chuckling and exchanged a smile with Kristeene.

"Listen to me, George," I said, trying to catch my breath.

"I'm listening. Please, continue. Don't keep laughing like a maniac," he said, smiling. He raised an eyebrow at Kristeene. "What do you think, sweetheart? Is Daddy right?"

"The professor said that he will never get married. That woman… Is his monitor."

"What? Say that again," George asked, his tone incredulous.

"We have a baby monitor, and he has one too."

"A monitor? What on earth is it for?" George questioned.

"Monitoring love-making. Haha—haha!" I set down my fork and knife, covering my mouth with my hand, fearful of erupting into more laughter.

"What did you say? He allows a woman on the wall to monitor his love-making? Who is that woman?"

"A stranger, would you believe it?" I almost shouted, "George, it's a strange woman. An artifact he picked up at the flea market."

George retorted, "He's just messing with you. Who would let anyone

呵呵，难能可贵。他重复着我的话，突然抬起怀疑的眼光望着我，问道：你不觉得我老吗，素素？

我一边摇头，一边认真地说，不老，一点不老。

他说，我老了，心老了。只有和柯丽丝在一起的时候，感到年轻。然后，他朝我看看。他的眼睛分明在说，和你在一起也感到年轻。但是，不知道什么原因，他没有说。

我说，他的卧室里，挂着一张很大的女人照片，黑白的。我没说完，就“咯咯咯”地笑起来。

乔治说，你笑什么呢？我不挂照片，往事不堪回想。真没有想到他又把自己联系上来。我早注意到这栋房子内是不存历史记录的，很想在这当口转移话题，去打听他过去的事情。也许，他会打开话匣子，告诉我许多秘密？但是，我正沉浸在讲述教授的快乐中，不舍得停下来。

我说，我们都问，照片里的女人那么漂亮，是你的原配老婆吧？因为和他的几个女朋友都不像。噢，忘了告诉你，他很开放，有几个女朋友，她们相互都认识，没有结婚。我们都看到她们啦！婕西，咪咪，还有爱蜜丽。爱蜜丽有黑人的血统，皮肤是棕色的，体形特别棒，腿好长。

乔治并不如我那么有兴致，不屑地说，确实很开放。

我禁不住又笑了起来，一边笑，一边断断续续地说，你猜照片里的女人是谁？你怎么也猜不到的。

乔治一点都不觉得好笑。倒是柯丽丝看到我大笑不止，在一旁笑我。

乔治，你听我说呀！我捧着肚子笑弯了腰。

乔治说，我在听呢！你自己不说只顾着傻笑。说完，他也笑了起来，挤着眉毛问柯丽丝，你说，爹地说得对不对？

教授说，我从来没有结过婚。那个女人是，嘻嘻，他说，那个女人是他的……监视员。

什么？什么？乔治问道，再说一边。

我们有监听器，他有监视员。

监视员，监视什么呢？乔治问。

监视做爱。哈哈……哈哈！我放下刀叉，双手捂住嘴巴，怕把饭喷出来。

你说什么，让墙上的女人监视他做爱？那个女人是谁呢？

陌生人。你相信吗？我差一点叫起来。乔治，那是一个陌生的女人！他从跳蚤市场买来的艺术品。

乔治说，他给你们开玩笑，谁愿意在做爱的时候，让别人监视？

monitor their love-making?"

"It's his philosophy," I explained, "A photo is just a photo. The professor wants to share the joy of love-making with others."

George scoffed, "Several girlfriends not enough for him, eh? He needs a monitor? This society is twisted thanks to these liberals."

"He's a skeptic," I said, "He never trusts others to make the right judgment or draw the right conclusion. He has to try everything himself."

"If everyone was like this, society would descend into chaos," George stated firmly.

I countered, "But not everyone is like them. They're just a handful, and mainstream society can't accept it. So, imagine the courage and confidence people like the professor must have to face the situation."

I was taken aback by my own impassioned response. How did I end up debating this so fervently?

George finished his meal, wiped his mouth with a napkin, and calmly remarked, "I hope he has the strength to face himself." His words were delivered casually, as if we were discussing something mundane. But as they settled in my ears, I sensed I needed to look at George in a new light. Why did he say "face himself"? Could he be considered to have truly faced himself, living this way? His financial standing was solid, yet he seemed eternally burdened. There was a distinct lack of joy here, unlike in the professor's home. Although the professor looked older than George, in some ways, George seemed the older of the two. Why couldn't he find happiness? It struck me then that the reason I had waited a whole day and night to share the party story was because I wanted him to be happy.

I mulled over the phrase "face oneself." Was it because he had confronted his past and wiped it clean, leaving no trace of family history? Was it because he had faced himself, making me feel safer living in this "castle"? Since Anna's departure, I'd never seen him bring a woman home for the night or receive calls from any. Was it a different level of "facing oneself" that he loved the child more than his business, even willing to sacrifice it for her?

As George stood up, he cleaned Kristeene's hands with a damp towel, laughing and playing with her. There was a substantial amount of food left on the plate, a result of my nonstop chatter. Kristeene had eaten her fill. So, I stood up, intending to retrieve Kristeene from her high chair, but George gently nudged me back down. He stood behind me, hands on my shoulders, and said, "Warm your food in the microwave."

I looked down at the plate, noticing that the food had indeed gone cold. The fat from the beef had solidified into delicate specks, floating on the surface of the juices.

那是他的心理。我说，照片还是照片。教授希望让别人来分享做爱的快乐。

乔治说，有几个女朋友还不够，嗯？加一个监视员？这个社会就是被这些自由主义分子搞得乱七八糟。

他是怀疑主义者。我说，他不相信别人的结论永远正确。他要自己去尝试。

乔治说，都像他们那样，社会就没有了秩序。

我说，怎么可能都像他们一样呢？出了几个不一样的，主流社会就难以接受。像教授那样，需要多少勇气，多少自信？我说完了不禁大吃一惊，自己怎么不知不觉地和他辩论了起来？

乔治已经吃完了晚餐，用餐巾擦了擦嘴，说道，希望他有勇气战胜自己。他说得轻描淡写，好像我们没有分歧和争论一样。但是到了我这里，却不得不对他刮目相看。他为什么要说“战胜自己”？像他那样地生活能算战胜了自己吗？他的条件那么富裕，却总是心情沉重，这个城堡里没有一点哲学教授家里的快乐气氛。看上去，教授比乔治老得多，实际是，真正苍老的是乔治。他乔治不能活得开心一点呢？这时候，我才醒悟到，等了一天一夜要把昨晚的Ｐarty告诉他，就是为了让他开心起来啊！

我把“战胜自己”几个字反复地回味：这个没有历史记录的家庭，是不是因为“战胜自己”的原因，而把过去一笔勾销？是不是因为他的“战胜自己”，让我感到了在城堡里生活的安全。是的，自从安娜出走以后，从来不见他带女人回家过夜，也没有女人的电话来打扰他。他对孩子的热爱超过了自己的事业，甚至愿意放弃工作，难道这是另一个层面的“战胜自己”？

乔治说完就站了起来，用湿毛巾给柯丽丝擦手，嘻嘻哈哈地逗女儿玩。我只顾着说话，盘子里还剩下许多。柯丽丝也吃得差不多了。我赶快站起来，想把柯丽丝从高椅子上抱下来，却被乔治按了下去。他站在我的背后，

双手搭住我的肩膀，说，用微波炉把饭热一下吧！

我往盘子一看，果然，菜冷了，漂浮在汤汁上的牛油已经凝固成薄薄的小片。

Chapter 15

The first semester was drawing to a close, and a week-long break loomed between the summer and autumn sessions. Most of my fellow students would scatter, either returning home or heading elsewhere. As for me, where could I go? Charlie? It was only natural for his name to cross my mind at such an intimate stage with him. But my rationality held me back. I needed to push the notion of a vacation to the back of my mind. My circumstances didn't permit a carefree getaway. In other words, even if Charlie had made plans, they wouldn't align with my situation.

Just as I pondered this, Charlie came by with a proposal.

While working in George's household, my schedule was meticulously planned, down to the minute, because time equated to money. Charlie was understanding and never intruded. After all, he was a philosophy teacher, inherently more mature than the average young man. Our connection likely stemmed from my lack of youthful disposition—my maturity, in other words. Living in a foreign land, I had to rely on myself for everything, growing under a certain pressure, much like some American youths who were pushed out of their homes by their parents. When hormones surged, opposite sexes naturally gravitated toward each other, yet they lacked the means to form a family. We were both aware of this. Marriage, to a large extent, wasn't for the couple themselves, but for posterity. That was the mutual understanding between Charlie and me, explaining why love and intimacy were our sole connection, not matrimony.

Every evening, I would take Kristeene out for a stroll in her pram. Sometimes, I'd invite Charlie to join us, but he couldn't make it every time, nor did I always need him. However, when he did join, the three of us would walk, soaking in the afterglow of sunset and the intentionally gusting autumn breeze. At times, a pang of longing would flicker in my heart. How fervently we wished to form a warm family like this. In those moments, I'd steal a glance at Charlie, wondering if he, too, entertained such daydreams. After careful scrutiny, I realized he wasn't as ensnared in them as I was.

The weather turned brisk, yet it retained a touch of warmth around noon. Only in the evenings did a hint of early autumn permeate the air. One evening, Charlie came to the "castle," and we strolled together within the walled yard. I wore a white jacket, and Kristeene was cozily swathed in a thin pink

第十五章

第一个学期马上就要结束了。暑期和秋期中间有一个多星期的假期。同学们都回家或者去度假去了，我到哪里去呢？查里？到了这个时候，自然而然地想到查里。但是，理性上不允许，必须把度假两个字移到了脑后。我的处境根本不具备度假的条件。也就是说，即便查里有度假的计划，在我这里也是行不通的。

果然不出所料，查里来看我了，并且有他的计划。

在乔治家工作期间，每天的时间排得很紧，可谓分秒必争，时间就是金钱。查里知趣得很，从不缠我。他毕竟是哲学专业出身，比一般年轻人要成熟得多。我们能相伴，恐怕和我缺少孩子气也有关系。身处异乡，什么都要靠自己，被逼着长大。这和美国的一些年轻人被家长赶出家门，逼着独立是一样的道理。人在荷尔蒙高峰阶段，最容易男女相吸却没有成家立业的资本。我们好像都明白这一点。结婚，从很大的程度上来说，不是为了自己，而是为了后代。这是我当时对查里的理解，也是对我们之间有爱有性，到此为止的解释。

在傍晚的时候，推着儿童车带柯丽丝外出散步，有时候，我请了查里来陪伴我。他不能每次来。我也不需要他每次来。但是，如果他来了，三个人走在落日的霞光和徐徐的秋风里，心头常常划过一丝丝的遗憾。多么希望我们能够有个温馨的小家庭啊，就像现在这样！在这种时候，我会瞟一眼查里，看看他是否也有一个白日的梦想？看来看去，看不出他像我这般陶醉。

天气渐渐地凉了起来，中午仍旧很热，到了晚上，就有了早秋的气氛。那天傍晚，查里来了城堡。我们在围墙内的院子里散步。我披了一件白色的夹克衫，柯丽丝的小车盖上了条粉红的薄绒毯。查里不在乎，穿了件紫色的短袖体恤。

一群群的小鸟朝南飞。草地上的落叶时不时被秋风吹起来，打一个转又落下来，像跳舞 一样。

查里说，放假了，我们应该好好玩一玩。

blanket in her pram. Charlie, seemingly impervious to the chill, still sported his customary purple T-shirt.

Flocks of birds soared southward across the sky. Fallen leaves on the lawn were periodically lifted by the autumn breeze, now soaring high, now gently descending, occasionally executing a graceful pirouette before settling, as if dancing in tandem with the wind.

Charlie remarked, "The vacation is nearly upon us. We should make the most of it."

"Where do you want to go, Charlie?" I inquired.

"Susu, would you be willing to meet my parents?" he proposed.

"Meet your parents?" I chuckled, adding, "Has our relationship reached a stage where we must be introduced to your parents?"

"No, no, that's not what I meant. We don't have that tradition in America. But I thought you might be interested in meeting them," he clarified.

Abruptly, he stopped, standing before me. He likely knew my response, understood that the outcome would be the same whether he asked or not. Yet he still wanted to take a chance.

I must say, I was feeling pretty content. If a good time was on the cards, why not grab the chance? But I didn't give an immediate response. I mulled it over, thinking, "If I say yes, what's the outcome? Sure, I might relax and have some fun, maybe even please Charlie's parents and keep him happy. But it would mean leaving Kristeene, and who knows if I'd ever be back at the 'castle'. Still, I can't afford to lose this job. And if I say no, what happens then? Lose Charlie? Not likely. Charlie should understand my situation."

Eventually, I replied, "I've got to take care of Kristeene. How can I just get up and leave?"

"Susu, you need a break. Why don't you know where Kristeene's mother, Laura, is? And why doesn't George hire someone else to ease the load on you?" Charlie pushed.

I shot him a glance, then turned to the edge of the brook. I gathered some blackberries and placed them in Kristeene's tiny hand. Then, I picked a handful more and handed them to Charlie. Betty had made a pie with these blackberries, and let me tell you, it was delicious. I couldn't give Charlie a straight answer to his questions. But I needed this job, so I had to do everything in my power to keep it.

As I savored those blackberries, a sudden thought hit me.

"Charlie, what if I put college on hold for a year or two and ask George to help me apply for a green card? Do you think it's worth considering?" I tossed out.

Charlie looked stunned, his lips stained with blackberry juice, but he didn't say anything. He just stood there, seemingly speechless.

I went on, "With a green card, I can work legally. If I can't get legal status, I'll have to hightail it back to China after finishing college."

He nodded, like he was catching on.

"If George can get me that green card, I'll dive back into my college educa-

我说，你想到哪里去，查里？

他说，素素，愿意去见见我的父母吗？

见你的父母？我笑了，说道，我们的关系已经到了要向父母摊牌的地步吗？

不，不是这个意思。美国没有这种规矩，但是，我想，你是愿意和我的父母见面的，不是吗？

说这番话的时候，他突然停下来，挡在我的面前。他大概是知道我的答案的，知道问与不问其实是一回事情。但是，他还是打算碰一下运气。应该说，我还是高兴的。有玩白不玩。但是，没有马上答复他。我对自己说，如果答ＹＥＳ，将是什么结果？最多是轻松地去玩一阵子，讨一下他父母的喜欢，让查里得到一些满足，但是，我将离开柯丽丝，甚至可能永远不再回到这个城堡来。我付不起这样的代价。如果答Ｎo，将是什么结果？失去查里？不至于吧，他应该理解我的处境。

我说，我有柯丽丝，怎么走得开？

素素，应该休息一下了。你怎么到现在还不知道柯丽丝的妈妈劳瑞在哪里？乔治为什么不另外请人，而要把负担压在你一个人身上？

我朝他看了看，转身走到小河边，采了几粒野生的黑莓，放在柯丽丝的手心里。再去采了一把，给查里。蓓蒂曾经用这种黑莓做成攀（Ｐie），很好吃。我无法答复查里的问题，但是，这份工作是我需要的，必须尽力做好它。

就在吃黑莓的时候，我的脑子里突然转过一个念头。

我说，查里，如果我休学一两年，让乔治办身份，你觉得是否值得？

他怔了一怔，留着黑莓汁的嘴唇动了动，楞在那里。

我说，有了身份就能合法工作，可以收入高一点，支付读书和生活的费用。他赞同地点点头。

我说，我是外国留学生签证，没有身份的话，读完书应该回国去。

他略有所悟地点了点头。

我说，如果乔治帮我申请永久居留的身份，我再读书，拿学位以后，就可以在美国留下来了。

他好像听明白了，说道，素素，很对不起，我没有能力帮助你。看来这是一个最好的办法。

那场谈话，让我觉得很失落，很灰心。他一点不在乎我住进乔治的家里以后，对我们俩的关系会有什么影响。他也不是一点不能

tion, snag a degree, and then I can live in America permanently," I explained.

Charlie seemed to get it and said, "I'm sorry, Susu, but it's beyond my power to help you. Your idea does seem like the best option for now."

Our talk left me feeling like something was missing. I also felt a sense of isolation. Charlie didn't seem to care at all whether my living arrangements would impact our relationship. He acted like he was powerless to help, but I knew he had more say in it than he let on. He placed himself in the role of an outsider, as if my decision had no bearing on him. He didn't even stop to ponder it, didn't ask for more details.

Suddenly, I realized that Charlie was emotionally distant from me. It was painful, but afterward, I found myself somewhat proud. I had the ability to resolve my own problems without relying on others. Maybe that's why, that very night, I made up my mind to put my college education on hold.

Charlie left earlier than I would have liked, leaving in disappointment. I had declined his invitation multiple times to keep this job. How significant was he to me? That remained a big question mark. However, I had no other option. If he couldn't understand my situation, there was nothing more I could do.

After Kristeene went to bed and I bid her good night, I descended to the living room. George was engrossed in his newspaper.

I asked, "George, do you really want to stay at home and look after Kristeene?"

This seemed to catch him off guard. He gazed at me and said, "I've been waiting for your answer. Remember, I can cover your tuition next semester if you choose to live in and care for Kristeene."

I pressed on, "What about when I'm in classes?"

"I'll find someone else," he assured.

I couldn't help but ask, "Where is Laura, Kristeene's mother? Why hasn't she come to look after her daughter?"

"Laura?" George seemed startled, a hint of alarm flickering in his eyes. "Laura, Laura, Laura," he murmured repeatedly, almost as if trying to calm himself. His voice grew softer and softer, his face growing longer. After the last utterance left his lips, his facial muscles stiffened, as if locked in place, and his eyes fixated on a point, unyielding.

I was taken aback and quickly said, "I'm sorry, George, I shouldn't have asked."

As if roused by my words, he blinked, "No, no, don't think that." He elongated the word 'no' and said it slowly, as if he'd been in a far-off place and was gradually returning. He furrowed his brows and bit his lower lip, gazing at me and then looking away.

He gazed at the night sky through the half-closed windows, his expression like a prayer, seeking answers from the heavens. After what felt like an eternity, the tightness in his face began to relax. "You're not wrong to ask. Where is Kristeene's mother? Why hasn't she come for her daughter? These are normal questions," he murmured, repeating it like a mantra. Then, in a

帮助我。他完全把自己放到了局外人的地位，好像我的选择和他毫无关系。他连想都不想，问都不问。

我们俩近在咫尺，却发现内心深处相隔很远，我的心隐隐作痛。但是，在伤害之余，多少有那么一点骄傲，那就是，我有能力解决自己的问题，不需要依靠别人。大概就是因为这个原因，那天晚上，我作出了休学的决定。

查里比我早走，走得很失望。为了这份工作，我已经不止一次地拒绝了他的邀请。他在我的心目中究竟重要到什么地步？其实也是一个大问号。但是，没有别的选择呀！如果他真的不理解，我也无能为力。

等到柯丽丝上床和我说了晚安以后，我下楼到客厅，乔治正在看报纸。

我说，乔治，你真的准备让我留家照顾柯丽丝吗？

他朝我看了看，平静地说道，我在等你的答复。记得吗，下学期的学费我来付，你住进来照顾柯丽丝？

我说，那么读书的时候怎么办？

他说，我另外找人。

我说，劳瑞，柯丽丝的妈妈在哪里？她为什么不来照顾女儿？

劳瑞？乔治很意外，眼睛里闪过一道惊慌。劳瑞，劳瑞，劳瑞，他喃喃地重复着，像是为了镇静自己。他的声音越来越轻，脸越拉越长，在发出最后一个音节之后，脸部的肌肉僵在那里，再也收不回来。眼睛也像定格一般，再也不动了。

我吃了一惊，忙说，对不起，乔治，我不该问的。

他眨了一下眼睛，好像被我唤醒了似的，No，No，不要这样想。他把No拖得很长，说得很缓慢，好像去了一个遥远的地方，正在一点一点地倒回来。他拧起了眉，咬着下唇，看了看我，又把目光移开。

他望着外面的夜空，半眯着眼睛，好像在祈求上帝来回答。过了好一会儿，他那痉挛的脸松弛了下来。他说，你没有问错。柯丽丝的妈妈在哪里？为什么不来照顾她？这是很正常的问题。很正常的问题。他说了两遍。

他深吸一口气，嘴唇动了动，没有声音。我觉得有句话好像在他的嘴里难产了一样。我开始微微颤抖，十指发麻。他终于说出来了。柯丽丝的妈妈……已经不在人世了。她……在柯丽丝……出生以后……离开了我们。

他说得很轻很轻，断断续续，像呜咽似的，音节不全。他没有说完，我已经泪水涟涟。我一边抽泣一边说，乔治，对不起，是我

voice barely above a whisper, he confessed, "Kristeene's mother is no longer in this world. She... after Kristeene's birth... left us forever."

Tears welled up in my eyes before he even finished. Through my own sobs, I stammered, "I'm so sorry, George. It's my fault for bringing it up. Don't worry about Kristeene. I'll move in. I'll put my studies on hold for a year or two and take care of Kristeene full time."

George turned to me suddenly, his eyes reddened, struggling to hold back his own tears.

"Yes," I affirmed, "I've made up my mind. You can go back to work, and I'll look after Kristeene."

He continued to gaze at me, a mixture of disbelief and understanding in his eyes.

"But I have one condition," I added.

"What is it?"

"Help me get a green card, a permanent legal status."

"Ah, right. You're in student status. Very well, I'll consider it."

"And we need to discuss my pay and days off."

After a brief moment of thought, he said, "Yes, we'll need to talk about your pay and time off. Susu, please, sit down. Let me think about it."

He rubbed his temples, muttering to himself, "My God! Everything's going to be alright." Half-turning to me, he said, "Susu, I need some time to think. I wasn't prepared for this."

I stood up and said, "That's alright. I'll leave now."

"Leave?"

"Yes," I nodded, "Let me know once you've decided."

He approached me with open arms, embracing me like a protective bird with both wings. "Susu, how can I ever thank you?"

"No need for that. You're helping me too."

He sighed, "Worry has given me quite a few white hairs."

I couldn't help but smile. "Let me see."

Standing tall and dignified before me, he was so humble. I couldn't help but be moved. I gently touched the hair at his temple and teased, "Time for a trim, I think."

In that close proximity, he pulled me into his arms once more and planted a gentle kiss on my hair. "You've made me so happy, Susu," he murmured.

I offered him a sweet smile, and he returned it with pure happiness.

As the semester came to a close, I settled into the "castle," taking up residence on the third floor. George granted me a day off every week and provided a monthly stipend of one thousand five hundred dollars. He returned to his company, focused on his own affairs.

Charlie, meanwhile, journeyed to another state for a visit with his parents.

的错，我不该惹你伤心。不要为柯丽丝担心，我搬进来住，休学一到两年，全心全意照顾柯丽丝。

乔治猛然转过脸来看着我，眼睛通红，强忍着不让泪水掉下来。

我说，是的，我不去上学了，你去上班，我来照顾柯丽丝。

他还是看着我，脸上挂着两行泪。

我说，你答应我一个条件。

什么条件？

给我办身份，在美国的永久居留权。

噢，对了，你是留学生身份。可以，可以考虑。

还有，我的工资和假期？

他稍微想了想，说道，是的，我们需要商量你的工资和假期。素素，你坐，坐下，让我好好想一想。

他用手拍了一下自己的前额，自言自语地说，天！这下全解决了。他侧过身来对我说，素素，我要想一想，我还没有思想准备呢！

我起身说，那么，我走了。

走了？

是的，我说，你想好了以后答复我。

这时他已经走了过来，一边走，一边张开双臂，然后，像巨鸟一样把我夹在怀里。

素素，应该怎么感谢你？

我说，谢什么呀？你也帮助我么！

他说，我愁白了许多头发。

我笑着说，让我看看。

他站在我的面前，又高又挺拔，却是那么谦卑。我不由地一阵感动，顺手去抚摸他的鬓发，笑着说，剃掉它，剃掉它！

就在我靠近他的时候，他第二次拥抱我，并且吻了一下我的头发，说道，你让我快乐，知道吗，素素？

我甜甜地朝他笑了笑，他也开心地笑起来。

学期一结束，我就搬进了城堡，住在三楼。乔治给我每星期一天假期，每个月一千五百美金。他回公司上班去了。查里去了外州探望他的父母。

Chapter 16

Living in the "castle," I never anticipated the profound impact this decision would have on my future. It was for my livelihood and the pursuit of a green card, wasn't it? At the time, I couldn't fathom the monumental shift this would bring about.

The baby monitor sat in my bedroom, granting me moments of reprieve when Kristeene was asleep. In those times, I'd read, jot down my thoughts in my diary, or steal a moment's rest. When Kristeene was awake, we'd play, sing, stroll, or dive into storybooks together.

With my move-in, George enlisted his lawyer to spearhead the green card application process. I readily agreed to have the fees deducted from my pay, resulting in a monthly reduction of five hundred dollars. Each morning, George would wait for Kristeene to stir, offering her a farewell kiss before heading off to work. His breakfast routine typically involved a cup of coffee and a selection of fruits. In the afternoons, he'd call to confirm whether he'd be home for supper or not. If he was, I'd make a trip to the supermarket to fetch his desired items. However, with his return to work, his presence at home dwindled. There were nights when he'd return past midnight, and others when he'd be away until morning. Anna had mentioned that he worked in international trade, so I surmised that his extended absences were due to business ventures in distant places.

One night, as I drifted into slumber, it seemed as if I heard a voice murmuring in my ear. I thought Kristeene was calling me, prompting me to awaken and check the baby monitor. Yet, no sound emanated from it. In my wakefulness, I noticed the voice was external, coming from beyond the window. I hadn't fully closed it, leaving a narrow gap. Slipping into my nightgown, I widened the window and peered below. The full moon cast a luminous glow, painting the scene in black and white. Two figures wrestled with each other.

I heard George's voice, "I'll drive you home."

Another voice, unfamiliar and feminine, mumbled in reply.

George persisted, "You're in no condition to drive. Let me take you."

Repeated attempts proved futile; the woman seemed to resist his offer. Then, I watched as George unlocked his own car, gently lifted the woman inside, and settled her in. She struggled to escape, but George firmly held her in place. The car door slammed shut, and he drove away.

第十六章

我就这样住进了城堡，不就是为了解决生存和绿卡而住进来的吗？我根本没有想到这个决定改变了以后整个的人生。

我的房间里放着柯丽丝的监听器，在她睡觉的时候，我可以看书，写日记，也可以休息。其他时候，我和柯丽丝一起玩，唱歌，散步，念故事给她听。

乔治在我住进去以后，关照了他的律师给我办身份。我同意把申请经费从工资里扣除，每个月减去五百元。每天，在去公司以前，他等着柯丽丝起床，然后亲亲她再走。他在家吃早饭，只喝一点咖啡，吃一些水果。下午的时候，会来电话，告诉我是不是回来吃晚饭。如果回来，我就开车去超市买一些他要求的菜。

他回公司去以后，回家吃饭的频率很低，有时候半夜才回来，也有不回来的时候。我记得安娜说过，他的生意是国际贸易，在我的脑子里，不回来就是外出做生意去了。

有一天晚上，我已经睡着了，睡梦中好像听到耳边有人在说话。我以为是柯丽丝在叫我，赶快开灯，把耳朵贴上了监听器，结果，里面一点声音都没有。等自己完全清醒以后，再听听，发现声音是从窗外传来的。我的窗没有完全关闭，留了一条小缝。我穿上了睡袍，把窗开大一点，往楼下看。正巧是满月，楼下特别亮，就像一幅黑白的风景照。有两个人影，正在推来推去。我听到了乔治的声音。他说，我送你回去。

另一个声音不熟悉，是女人，口齿很含糊。

乔治说，你醉了，不能开车。

乔治不断地重复上面的话，好像受到了女人的拒绝。后来，我看见乔治开了自己的车门，走过去把女人抱起来，塞进车里。女人还想挣扎出来，乔治把她推回去，“砰”地关上门，开车走了。

因为已经打了一个磕睡，不觉得困，我便开了台灯读小说。不知道过了多久，眼睛有点累了，我把书合上，放到枕头底下，准备睡觉。突然，听见乔治的车开回来了。我本能地去关台灯，不希望

Having dozed off earlier, sleep now eluded me. I switched on the bedside lamp and reached for a novel. I couldn't discern how much time had passed before fatigue overcame me. Setting the book beneath my pillow, I prepared to surrender to sleep just as I heard George returning. Instinctively, I extinguished the lamp, hoping to conceal any evidence of my having witnessed the scene between him and the woman. However, it was too late. As he entered through the gate, he surely caught sight of the light in my room. Reflecting on it, I realized he must have known the commotion had roused me. That would explain his hasty departure with the woman. Perhaps he simply didn't want me to witness it. If he were to address it or inquire about what I'd heard, I resolved to feign ignorance.

Lying in bed, sleep eluded me. Those two shadows writhed in my mind, dancing in their twisted ballet. If I didn't know Laura was gone, I might have suspected that woman was her. Now, I suspected she was George's girlfriend. Had they argued so fiercely that she refused to stay the night? Or was she merely inebriated? I quickly dismissed that notion. Maybe their relationship wasn't based on love. If not, why would they be drinking together until midnight? It felt as if I were concocting a plotline from a novel until sleep finally claimed me.

The following day, George rose later than usual. While Kristeene and I frolicked on the lawn, I noticed his car still parked in the garage. Kristeene had grown steadier on her feet, so I began teaching her a simple dance routine. We practiced steps, hands resting on our sides, one leg slightly ahead, heel off the ground, then balancing on the ball of the foot, switching to the other leg. Kristeene put in earnest effort. Sometimes she'd lose balance and tumble onto the grass. After helping her back up, I'd ask if she was hurt. She'd shake her head. When I inquired if she wanted to continue, she'd reply with an emphatic "yes." During our breaks, I demonstrated finger patterns mimicking orchid blooms, promising, "Tomorrow, we'll learn this finger dance, Kristeene." Observing my hand movements—thumb and pinky splayed, index finger extended like a bird in flight—Kristeene clapped her hands in delight, exclaiming, "Bird, bird!" She wanted to try the bird pattern herself. After mastering the orchid pattern, we moved on to wrist-twisting exercises, seated on the grass, mirroring each other's movements.

Next, I taught her to stretch her arms overhead, palms turned outward. Kristeene tackled it with vigor.

At noon, we retreated inside for lunch. George was sipping coffee in the kitchen.

"Ah, George," I feigned surprise, "Skipping work today? Want me to whip up some lunch for you?"

"Just some sandwiches, keep it simple," he replied.

I raised the subject of Chinese wontons, frozen and stashed away in the freezer. George admitted he hadn't tasted them before. As I pulled them out to show him, he likened them to Italian tortellini, a floury pasta stuffed with cheese. We chatted about their similarities and differences.

他知道我看到了刚才的一幕。但是，已经太晚了。他在开车从大门进来的时候，肯定看到我房里亮着灯光。后来再一想，其实，在他离开之前，已经知道吵醒了我。他急匆匆地把女人塞进车内送走，不就是为了宁人息事？我想，如果明天他来作解释或者问我听见了什么，我准备装聋作哑，一无所知。躺下来，却是睡不着，脑子里一直出现两个黑影，扭来扭去。如果不知道劳瑞已经过世，我一定会怀疑这个女人就是她。现在，猜想她是乔治的女朋友，两人发生了口角，女的不愿意在这里过夜？或者她本来就是一个酒鬼？我马上否定了酒鬼的想法。乔治是个有地位有品味的绅士，怎么会和酒鬼谈恋爱？也许他们不是恋爱关系？那么为什么深更半夜在这里喝酒？我像猜测侦探小说的情节一样，想着想着就睡着了。

第二天，乔治起得很晚。我和柯丽丝在草坪上玩的时候，看到他的车仍旧停在车库。柯丽丝走路走得很稳了。我在草坪上教她跳舞，双手插腰，一腿跨前，点脚跟，再点脚尖。换腿，点脚跟，再点脚尖。柯丽丝学得很努力。有几次重心没有把握好，不小心摔倒在草地上，我前去扶她，问她摔疼了没有，她摇摇头。问她还要不要学？她连说了三遍“yes”。休息的时候，我做兰花指头给她看，说道，柯丽丝，手指舞蹈是这样的，我们明天学。她看我中指突出，小指和母指外翘，五指分开，如一只正在飞翔的鸟儿。开心地拍起手来，一边嚷嚷，小鸟，小鸟。意思是她也要做小鸟。我们学了兰花手指以后，学转动手腕。我们俩坐在草地上，不停地练习手指和手腕的动作。后来，我再教她把手臂举过头，手心外翻。柯丽丝学得兴致勃勃。

中午，我们进楼吃午饭。这时，乔治在厨房里喝咖啡。

呵，乔治。我假装很吃惊的样子。你没有去上班？要不要我做午饭？

他说，做个三明治吧，简单一些。

我说，昨天，包了一些中国的馄饨，在冻箱里。你知道馄饨吗？尝试过吗？

没有。

我开了冻箱的门，把冰冻的馄饨端到他面前。

他说，噢，大号的tortelini，很好。

tortelini是意大利的一种面食，形状和馄饨很像，个子很小，只有馄饨的三分之一，里面包奶酪。以前蓓蒂从商店里买回来，放在水里煮熟，像意大利面条一样，撒上干酪粉或者调料酱就能吃了。

我托着玻璃盘，突然间对一个个金元宝般的馄饨产生了特殊的

Carrying the glass tray, a sudden fondness washed over me for the golden yuanbao-shaped wontons. They evoked memories of my childhood, a time of communal wonton-making with the family gathered around. I'd lay a wonton skin on my palm, chopsticks poised in my other hand, meticulously placing the filling in the center before folding and sealing it. For George, the wonton held a newfound value, distinguishing itself from the machine-made Italian tortellini. It was a nostalgic piece of my life.

"Wontons are not just food," I explained, "They're handmade art. The stuffing is a blend of vegetables and minced meat, a balanced nourishment. Plus, they're often enjoyed in soup. You can include various vegetables, or none at all, just the pure broth."

With a coffee cup in hand, George chuckled, "Susu, you should open a restaurant, exclusively serving wontons. Why haven't I seen them in Chinese eateries?"

I had never ventured into Chinese restaurants until then, so I couldn't comment on their absence.

"So, shall we have wontons for lunch?" I proposed, inwardly relieved that George hadn't mentioned the events of the previous night.

I set a pot of water to boil and worked on chopping onions and tomatoes, sautéing them in oil. Meanwhile, I prepared a smaller pot with chicken soup, diluting it with some water and adding finely chopped scallions. When the water reached a rolling boil, I tossed in the frozen wontons, stirring them occasionally.

Observing my kitchen ballet, George came over with Kristeene in his arms. Together, we watched the culinary performance. As the wontons surfaced, I fished them out, draining them before adding them to the chicken soup. With the fire turned off, I settled Kristeene into her high chair and set the round table with napkins, cutlery, soup spoons, and glasses of chilled water.

Kristeene's wontons needed a little extra care, cooling before she could enjoy them. I poured the soup into her spill-proof cup, adding a dash of ice. The spout made it safe for her to sip away. Thirsty, she eagerly gulped down the nourishing broth.

"Kristeene, time to dance. Show Daddy your moves!" I announced, prompting her to wriggle free from her high chair.

"Dance like a little bird," I encouraged. Her eyes sparkled with joy, and she called out, "Daddy, Daddy," her tiny hands flitting about. George, arms folded, watched in delight. After a playful performance, he raised his arms and twirled, eliciting giggles from Kristeene and me. I dished up the wontons in a big bowl and handed it to him. Serving myself a bowl, I noticed George hesitating.

"Eat while they're still hot," I advised. "I'll join you."

"I was waiting for you," he admitted, "Let's start together." I figured he was concerned about the heat, so I tossed an ice cube into his bowl. Then, I tested a wonton's temperature for Kristeene. Satisfied it was suitable, I sliced it into

感情。以前在中国的时候，习以为常，大人拌馅，孩子围在桌旁，一手摊开馄饨皮，另一只手用筷子把馅儿夹起来，放在皮儿的中央，对折再对折，两边角搭上，就成了一个馄饨。但是，在乔治面前，馄饨变得身价百倍，意大利的tortelini哪能和馄饨相比，都是机器做出来的。中国的馄饨，有我的童年回忆，馄饨代表了我一部份的生命。

我说，馄饨是艺术品，手工包出来的，这是一。第二，里面的馅也不一样，馄饨馅是蔬菜和肉末的混合，营养平衡。第三，馄饨有汤，汤里可以放各种蔬菜，也可以什么都不放，纯粹的broth（清汤）。

乔治捧着咖啡杯“呵呵”笑了起来，说道，素素，你应该去开一个中餐馆，专门出售馄饨。我怎么不见中国饭店里出售馄饨呢？

馄饨引开了他的注意力，大幸，大幸，他没有提昨天半夜里的事情。

我烧了一大锅水，切了一些洋葱丝和西红柿丁，在油里炒了一下，加了一罐鸡汤在另一个锅里。等水开了以后，便把冰冻的馄饨扔到水里，时不时搅拌一下。在鸡汤的锅里加点清水和青葱末。

乔治看我在两个大锅之间忙来忙去，抱起了柯丽丝，站在旁边看。

我把煮熟的馄饨，沥干了水，倒入鸡汤里，关了火。让柯丽丝坐进了高椅子，在圆台子上放了餐巾，刀叉，汤匙和冰水。

柯丽丝的馄饨必须和鸡汤分开，等冷却了以后才能给她。我把鸡汤倒入柯丽丝的杯子里，并加了一点碎冰。杯上有个盖子，盖上有一个突出的“嘴”，孩子从“嘴”里吮吸里面的液体，很安全。柯丽丝很渴，一口气就把鸡汤喝完了。

我说，柯丽丝会跳舞呢，做给爹地看。听我这么一说，她吵着要从高椅子上下来。

我说，跳小鸟。小女孩眼睛一亮，笑着“爹地，爹地”不停地喊，一边转动那玲珑的小手。乔治双臂交叉在胸前，兴高彩烈地看了一会儿，随后也把手举过头顶，转了一个圈，惹得我和柯丽丝哈哈大笑。我用一个大汤碗装了一碗馄饨端给他，也给自己装了一碗。

乔治在腿上铺了餐巾，楞楞地坐在那里。我说，吃呵，趁热吃。他说，等你一起吃。我以为他怕烫，去拿了一小块冰扔进了他的碗里，然后，转身去尝试柯丽丝的馄饨，不烫了，用刀对切再对切，放到她的盘子里。柯丽丝抓起来就往嘴里送。我说，嚼的时间长一些，不要马上吞下去。记住了？她点点头。

bite-sized pieces for her. She eagerly grasped them, one after another, popping them into her little mouth.

I advised, "Chew a little longer, don't swallow too quickly, okay? Remember?" She nodded.

Upon my return to my seat, George sat upright, seemingly motionless.

"Why aren't you eating? It won't taste as good if it gets too mushy," I queried.

He replied, "Waiting for you."

"Why wait for me? Start eating now," I said, then realized he might not know how to eat wonton, much like my initial confusion with Italian macaroni when I first arrived in America.

Smiling, I shook my head and instructed, "Use the soup spoon to scoop up one wonton at a time. Then, eat it with the soup. Like this," I demonstrated. George followed suit, gingerly spooning a mouthful. Yet, he couldn't see how I managed the wonton and soup together. The Chinese typically sip the soup first, then focus on the wonton. George, however, held both in his mouth, his face contorted, lips pursed, cheeks puffed out like he'd been slapped. I struggled not to burst into laughter, encouraging him, "That's right, good job. Swallow the soup first, not the wonton. Yes, now chew, you don't need to keep your mouth so tightly shut, relax a bit. Right. It's okay to open your mouth a little. Right." Oh my! How did the wonton transform from an angel to a demon once inside George's mouth? He polished off the first one as if trying to atone for a sin. Sweat dotted his forehead, and I, too, felt a sheen of perspiration, as if I'd run a marathon.

"Can I eat the soup and wonton separately?" he inquired.

"Like Kristeene does?" I asked.

He widened his eyes, asking eagerly, "May I?"

"Why not?" I thought to myself that he was approaching the wonton like Italian tortellini.

So, I handed him an empty plate and explained, "You can take out the wonton one by one and place them on the plate. Then, enjoy the wonton while sipping the soup."

He didn't quite follow my instructions. He used the spoon to slurp up the soup, then extracted a wonton and deposited it on the plate. He sliced it in half, dusted it with powdered cheese, and savored each portion. "Delicious, delicious," he praised.

I couldn't help but smile and thought, "Even though he's not eating it the Chinese way, which is richer in flavor, he still finds it delicious."

By the time I reached the bottom of my bowl, George still had half his left. The wontons in his bowl formed a mound, like defeated soldiers collapsing in exhaustion. I inquired, "How tasty is it?"

He responded, "There's all sorts of stuff inside, though I'm not sure what. It's mysterious." Such comments left me in fits of laughter.

Kristeene played for a while before needing a nap. As I descended the stairs, George was still in the kitchen. I approached, smiling, "Skipping work

我坐回自己的椅子，对面的乔治还正襟危坐，一动不动。

我说，你怎么不吃呢？馄饨烂掉了就不好吃了。

他说，等你。

为什么要等我呢？快吃快吃！说完，我才醒悟到，原来他不知道如何吃馄饨！就像我刚来美国的时候，不会吃意大利的面条一样，不好意思说。

我一边摇头一边笑，说道，用汤匙，一个馄饨一汤匙，连汤一起吃。就这样，看着我。我吃给他看。他照做了一遍。满满一大匙，规规矩矩地被他送进嘴巴。但是，他不知道馄饨和汤水入口以后如何运作。中国人是先把汤咽下去，再来对付馄饨的。乔治把汤和馄饨都留在了嘴里。他的脸就变了形。双唇外翻，面颊鼓起来，像被打肿了脸一样。看得我哭笑不得。我忍住笑，对他说，把汤咽下去，是汤，先不是馄饨。对了，咀嚼，对了，嘴唇不必闭得那么紧，放松一些。对了，张开一点也没有关系。对了，老天爷啊，这馄饨到了乔治的嘴巴里，好像天使变成了魔鬼。他像赎罪一般地把第一个馄饨吃完，前额沁出了汗珠。我和他一样，好像长跑回来，满头是汗。

他问道，为什么不能像柯丽丝那样能把汤和馄饨分开来吃？

我说，为什么不可以呢？心里想，他还是把馄饨当成意大利的tortelini了。于是，我给了他一个空盘，说道，你把馄饨捞出来，装在这里，边吃边喝汤。他没有照我说的做，而是把碗里的汤一匙一匙地吃完。然后，取一个馄饨放在盘子上，对切，散了一些干酪纷，半个半个地吃。他嚼了几下，对我说，好吃，好吃！

我忍不住笑了，心里想，把中国风味都扔掉了，好吃个鬼！

我差不多在打扫碗底的战场了，乔治还有一半馄饨没有动。这些馄饨就像战场上的残兵败将一样，软塌塌地聚在一起。我问，好吃在哪里？他说，里面有各种东西，不知道它们是谁，很神秘。他的话令我捧腹大笑。

柯丽丝玩了一会儿，就去睡午觉了。等我下楼来，看到乔治还在厨房里。我笑嘻嘻地走过去，问道，今天不上班？晚上想吃什么呢？中国炒面？酸甜猪肉？

他说，我们晚上出去吃。你，我和柯丽丝。我们到中国餐馆去。

我说，那还是由我来做吧，不见得比餐馆差。

乔治说，我说不清楚要哪些中国菜。你知道mushoo pork吗？

我说，无锡猪肉啊？是不是有很多软骨在里面？

他说，没有，没有骨头。有点像墨西哥菜。

today? What would you like for supper? Chinese chow mein or sweet and sour pork?"

"We'll dine out tonight. You, Kristeene, and I. At a Chinese restaurant," he proposed.

"Let me cook instead. I can whip up something as good as the Chinese restaurant," I offered.

"I can't quite explain what Chinese dish I'm after. Do you know about mu shu pork?" George inquired.

"You mean moo shu pork?" I clarified. "The one with a lot of cartilage?"

"No, it has no bones, more like a Mexican dish," he clarified.

I was puzzled. I had no knowledge of Mexican cuisine. Which Chinese dish was akin to a Mexican one? How could I even begin to guess?

Seeing my confusion, George reassured, "You'll understand when we get to the restaurant."

He settled into a chair by the window, wearing a blue T-shirt with red stripes and a pair of jeans, appearing quite unassuming. Beyond the window, Japanese red maples stood amidst the pine trees. The autumn wind, akin to a playful child, danced through the trees, sweeping up leaves and sending them floating away.

Engrossed in the scenery, I was brought back by George's voice, "Susu, I'd like to discuss something with you."

"Sure," I replied. "What is it?"

"It's about Kristeene's birthday party."

"A birthday party for a two-year-old?" I queried.

"Yes," he affirmed. "But Kristeene is too young for a party with all the adults. How about going away on a vacation? Will you come with us?"

A vacation? I was overjoyed. Finally, a chance for a break, and with Kristeene!

I beamed, "My job is to look after Kristeene. Of course, I'm in."

"Another person will join us. Her name is Nancy," George added.

Nancy? Who was Nancy?

George explained, "Nancy is a friend of mine from business. I want to take this opportunity to get to know her better."

My heart gave an anxious flutter. I'd feel awkward. A wonderful vacation could be spoiled by a stranger. But after a moment's thought, I realized it was Kristeene's vacation and George's plan. I had no say in it.

I inquired, "Where are we going?"

George sketched out a plan on a slip of paper.

Checking the calendar, I found that Kristeene's birthday fell on a Monday.

"We'll leave on Friday afternoon, okay?" George suggested.

"Okay," I responded.

We had two days to prepare.

我更糊涂了。我对墨西哥菜一无所知，哪个中国菜和墨西哥有联系？我怎么可能想出来？

乔治看我为难的样子，说道，到了餐馆你就知道了。

他坐在窗台旁的椅子上，上面穿一件藏青红条的体恤，下面是牛仔裤，一介平民百姓的样子。窗外，日本的红枫树夹在密密的松林里，秋风像个淘气的孩子，时不时地爬上绿男红女的肩膀，掠走一批秋叶，往空中撒去，飞飞扬扬。我正看得出神，听见乔治在问我。

素素，我想和你商量一件事情。

好哇，我说，什么事情？

关于柯丽丝的生日。

两周岁的生日Party？

是呵，他说，柯丽丝太小，不适合开群体Party。我的意思是，成人的PARTY。我们出去度假怎么样？你愿意和我们一起去吗？

度假？心里好高兴啊！我终于也要度假啦！而且和柯丽丝一起去！

我笑着说，我的工作就是照顾柯丽丝，哪有不愿意的呢？

他说，还有一个人和我们同行，她叫南西。

南西？谁是南西？

乔治说，南西是我的生意上的一个朋友。我想借此机会了解她。

我的心里“格登”了一下，好端端的假期，插进来一个陌生女人，多么别扭啊！但是，我马上想通了，这是柯丽思的假期，乔治的计划，我没有什么好说的。

我问，去哪里？

乔治在纸上画了一张草图。

我翻了一下台上的日历，柯丽丝的生日在星期一。

乔治说，我们星期五下午走，好吗？

我说，好哇。

我们有两天的时间作准备。

Chapter 17

Having spent my time in America living in a student dorm and now tending to a white man's child, I had little contact with other Chinese people. Tonight, George, Kristeene, and I ventured to a Chinese restaurant. It marked the first occasion I found myself in a place populated by fellow Chinese.

The restaurant stood at the city's heart, a single-story establishment flanked by two sturdy pillars. On these pillars were painted golden dragons, their features, scales, and claws distinctly visible beneath the spotlight-like lamps. The Chinese dragon, believed to hail from Heaven, held great significance in our culture. It served as a guardian spirit for Chinese establishments abroad, instilling a sense of security for the proprietors. I tried to explain this to George: the golden dragon holds a place for the Chinese similar to God in America.

I couldn't be sure if he grasped the depth of my explanation. Soon, our conversation shifted to the tank of goldfish before us. The vibrant fish swayed and swirled, capturing Kristeene's rapt attention.

"Why display goldfish when there's another tank of live fish nearby?" George queried.

"The live fish are for the kitchen, while the goldfish are for ornamental purposes," I explained.

"I see," he nodded. "That makes sense, it's common knowledge."

"Don't mistake me for an expert. We're on equal footing in this regard," I chuckled inwardly. I pondered, "What symbolism lies behind the goldfish tank? Elegance, perhaps? Sympathy? Or is it akin to a woman applying lipstick?"

When a waitress came to seat us, I mustered the courage to ask her about it, but she shyly shook her head.

第十七章

餐馆地处市中心，平房，门口有两根粗圆的柱子，上面画着金龙。玻璃橱窗内陈列着各色烧烤，里三层外三层，金灿灿，油亮亮，还有悬在半空的一排烤鸭，锦上添花般地使橱窗的气氛更加热闹。

两道灯光从屋檐上射下来，正巧落在金龙的身上，把龙眼龙须龙鳞龙爪都照得一清二楚，栩栩如生。中国的龙来自天堂，是神的像征，海外的中国饭店，门口立着一对金龙，从心理上来说，比金狗和金狮子都安全。我就是这样向乔治解释的，金龙意味着美国人的上帝保佑。

不知道他是否听懂，话题转向迎面而立的金鱼水池箱。摇头晃尾的鱼群，色彩绚丽，柯丽丝正看得眼珠子骨碌碌地转。

乔治问我，为什么有了里面的活鱼水池，还要搞一个金鱼展览？

活鱼水池的鱼是吃的，金鱼水池是看的。

噢，他说，这点常识我还是有的。

我说，别把我当专家。我们都是半桶水。

餐馆是乔治选的，他说以前曾经来过，有许多问题找不到答案。

我说，东方人讲究神秘主义，没有答案就是答案。

这倒是个好答案。他笑着说。

外出吃晚餐，乔治穿得很正宗，西装领带，皮鞋。我穿了件紫红色的连衣裙，外披一件黑色的风衣。女招待和柯丽丝打招呼的时候，说到爹地和妈咪。我当作没有听见。茶来了。先给乔治倒，再给自己倒。乔治在茶里加了糖，再加了一点酱油。

这是干什么呀，乔治？我说，鸡尾酒吗，中国式的？

他说，要不要试试？味道很独特。

我连忙摇头，说道，盐和糖都不是好东西。

乔治已经一饮而尽。

The choice of the restaurant was George's. He mentioned having been here before but harbored unanswered questions.

"The Oriental people have a penchant for mysticism. Sometimes, no answer is the answer," I ventured.

"That's a good way to put it," he agreed with a smile.

For our dinner outing, George donned a suit, tie, and leather shoes. I wore a long purple dress covered by a black raincoat. The waitress kindly addressed Kristeene, mentioning her daddy and mommy. I chose not to acknowledge it.

Tea arrived first. I poured a cup for George and then myself. To my surprise, he added some sugar and then a bit of soy sauce.

"What's this, George?" I inquired. "A Chinese-style cocktail?"

"Care to give it a try? It has a unique flavor," he suggested.

I declined, shaking my head. "Sugar and salt don't mix well."

George, undeterred, downed the concoction from his cup.

He motioned for me to draw nearer, suggesting we peruse the menu together so he could point out his selections. I shifted my chair accordingly. He handled the English section while I focused on the Chinese. Though the menu was brief, he flipped through it a number of times. In the end, he settled on fried wonton, spring rolls, broccoli and beef stir-fried in oyster sauce, sweet and sour pork with onion and pineapple, mu shu pork, and rice. Throughout his ordering, he repeatedly asked if the choices were good.

I reassured him, "In the realm of Chinese cuisine, every dish is a good one."

He grinned, adding, "In the Chinese way."

Our smiles exchanged spoke volumes, a shared understanding that connected us. I recalled the first time I learned to barbecue outdoors with George. He'd used a long-handled fork, while I wielded chopsticks. His surprise was evident as these two slender sticks managed to turn over beef weighing over a pound. My response? A simple, "That's the Chinese way." I'd also prepared Western-style dishes in a Chinese wok, taking less time yet rendering the meat more tender. George would nod and say, "That's Susu's Chinese way." It became a bridge that drew us closer.

"George, which pork did you order? Wuxi pork?" I inquired.

"No, I ordered Muxu pork," he corrected, pointing at the menu.

Muxu pork? What was that? It seemed I'd misheard. I'd mistaken Muxu

他招呼我靠得近一点，合用一份菜单，便于指点给我看。我把椅子挪了挪，他看英文，我看中文。薄薄几页纸　被他翻来复去，看了好长时间。他点的是：锅贴，春卷，绿椰菜炒蚝油牛肉片，酸甜猪肉炒洋葱菠萝，木须肉，还有白米饭。一边点，一边向我证实是不是好菜？

我说，中国菜都是好菜。

他说，Chinese Way。

我们俩都笑了。这是他知我知的暗语。记得第一次学习室外烧烤，乔治用一把金属的长叉子翻牛排，我用筷子。他很吃惊两根短小的筷子竟能把一磅多重的牛肉翻过来。我回答说，Chinese Way。后来，我用中国的煎锅做一些西餐，时间短，口味比烤出来的还要嫩。他说，素素的Chinese Way。总之，Chinese Way就像一座桥似的把我们俩连接了起来。

我问道，乔治，你要的那个猪肉呢？无锡猪肉？

要了呀！他哗啦啦地翻菜单，指了指木须肉说。

木须肉？原来我把“木须肉”误听成“无锡肉”啦！

我说，第一次听说，从来没有尝过。无锡肉骨头才真正有名呢！女招待过来的时候，乔治问，你们有，素素，你说什么猪肉很有名？

我说，无锡肉骨头？

无锡，肉骨头？女招待说，没有，没有，太太，我们只有豆豉排骨。

我说，木须肉是什么意思？

她说，薄饼啊，包着菜吃。

噢。我说。其实我也不懂，不再问了，怕闹笑话。

来美国以后，我住学生宿舍，带白人的孩子，基本上和中国人没有联系。今天晚上，是我第一次回到中国人集中的地方去。我和女招待说的是普通话。乔治坐在旁边听得很认真。等女招待一走，他便“哈哈”大笑。

你笑什么？笑我们说中国话？

他说，像开机关枪一样。一边叠起双臂，做出开枪的样子，嘴里“突突突”地叫着。

我忍不住放声大笑，说道，柯丽丝，你父亲是一个优秀的战士。同时，侧过身去用拳头顶在乔治的后腰，压低了声音喊道：缴枪不杀！

乔治假装投降，翻起了白眼珠，扑倒在餐桌上。柯丽丝拍手鼓掌，大叫“爹地！”“爹地！”。这一叫，引来了许多注意力。我

for Wuxi. I admitted, "This is the first time I'm hearing of it. I've never tasted it before, but Wuxi pork is quite famous."

When the waitress approached, George asked, "Do you have—Susu, what was the famous pork you mentioned?"

"Wuxi pork?"

"Wuxi pork?" The waitress shook her head. "No, Madam. We only have pork chops cooked in fermented soybeans."

"What about Muxu pork?" I inquired.

"It's meat and vegetables cooked together, wrapped in thin pancakes when eaten."

I nodded, but I still couldn't grasp it fully. I decided to stop asking, fearful of making a fool of myself.

As the waitress and I conversed in Mandarin, George sat nearby, listening intently. When she left, he burst into laughter.

"What's so funny? Our Chinese conversation?" I asked.

George explained, "You spoke like a machine gun." He mimicked the sound, pretending to fire a machine gun.

I couldn't help but laugh. I turned to Kristeene, joking, "Your daddy is a soldier." Then I half-turned to George, playfully pressing my fist against his waist, whispering, "Put down your gun, or I'll get you."

George feigned surrender, rolling his eyes and collapsing onto the table. Kristeene clapped her hands, chanting, "Daddy, daddy!" Her enthusiasm drew attention, including my friend, the son of my mother's friend, who had picked me up from the airport. He worked as a waiter here, attending to another table.

"Susu!" He called from afar, then approached, glancing at George and Kristeene. "Long time no see. Are you married?"

Still wearing a smile, I replied, "Oh, you work here. It's a nice restaurant."

He grinned. "I had no other choice. Had to work here."

I explained, "I'm not married. Just looking after the child. They're helping me get a green card."

He looked at George and Kristeene again, a hint of curiosity in his eyes. As if he didn't entirely believe my explanation, he switched to English and told George, "We're close friends."

George was thrilled. Upon learning of our friendship, he declared, "Susu

的朋友，我母亲朋友的朋友的孩子，也就是来飞机场接我的的那个中国朋友就是这样走过来的。他本来在招待另一个桌子的顾客。

“素素！”他老远地打着招呼。走近以后，朝乔治和柯丽丝看看，问道“好久不见，结婚啦？”

笑容还挂在我的脸上，我说，原来你在这里上班！挺不错的餐馆。

他笑了笑，说，没有办法，凑合着干。

我说，没结婚，照顾孩子，他们给办绿卡。

他再看了看乔治和柯丽丝，露出警惕和窥视的眼神，好像不相信我的解释。然后，用英文和乔治打招呼，说，我们是很熟悉的朋友。

乔治本来正在兴奋中，见他是我的朋友，便说，素素是我见到的最漂亮的女孩子之一。

别吓说了。我说，你喝醉了，乔治。然后用英语对朋友说，你知道吗，他把酱油和茶，糖混在一起喝，比喝酒精还要厉害！

来，来，来！你也来一杯。乔治说，真的很好喝，要不要试试？说完，利索地配制了一杯。

朋友连忙摆手，一边退一边说，不用，不用，谢谢，谢谢！说完，朝我再看了一眼，说不出是为我高兴还是为我忧愁，皮笑肉不笑地工作去了。

我说，乔治，你相信吗？我差一点来这里打工了。

他说，刚才还说是第一次来中国饭店，怎么可能在这里工作？

说来话长啊！我说，要不是找到你们家，朋友要介绍我来洗碗呢！

洗碗？能赚多少钱？

许多中国留学生都在干。我说，都是读硕士和博士的，没有合法工作的权利，来这里打黑工。

噢，乔治说，不容易，是不是？

是的，非常不容易。我的眼睛一直盯着男女招待看，一边自言自语地说，离开家乡，无依无靠，没有选择的余地，什么活都要干。

乔治说，素素，我的家就是你的家。他说这话的时候，一把捏住了我搁在台面上的那只手。我没有回头，依旧看着眼前的中国人。

女招待送来了锅贴和春卷，在我们面前操起剪刀，把锅贴一剪为二，把春卷一剪成三，再淋上酱油。我感到莫名其妙，中国菜哪有这种吃法？可是，乔治好像并不见怪，说了声谢谢，用筷子把春

is the most beautiful girl I've ever seen."

"Nonsense," I retorted. "You're just tipsy, George." Turning to my friend in English, I added, "You know he put soy sauce and sugar in tea. It's more stimulating than spirits."

"Come on. Have a cup," George insisted, offering a freshly concocted mixture.

My friend waved his hand, stepping back. "No, no. Thank you, thank you." He glanced at me and returned to his duties with a wry smile. I couldn't tell if he was happy or concerned for me.

"George, can you believe I almost ended up working here?"

"You just said it's your first time in a Chinese restaurant. How could you work here?"

"It's a long story," I replied. "If I hadn't come to work for you, my friend would have recommended me to wash dishes here."

"Wash dishes? How much would you earn?"

"Many overseas Chinese students take up such jobs. When they come to study for master's or doctorates, they often lack legal permission to work. So they resort to illegal employment in places like this."

As the dishes arrived, George and I delved into our Chinese meal. He was eager to learn the art of using chopsticks and I guided him through it. Kristeene was contentedly enjoying her food with her tiny hands.

When the Muxu pork arrived, I was taken aback. It was nothing more than a few thin slices of pork. George, however, expressed his love for this dish and deftly prepared a rolled pancake with sautéed eggs and vegetables. His enjoyment was palpable, humming a lively Mexican tune in sheer delight. It was a rare sight to see George so relaxed.

Kristeene couldn't manage the pancake, so I improvised and served her the components separately. I finally identified the "muxu" in the dish - it was black edible fungus.

As the meal went on, George's tendency to mix up cuisines continued. He ordered a variety of dishes, and we couldn't finish them all. I suggested inviting Nancy over to try Chinese food at our home.

As we prepared to leave, the waitress handed us several food boxes, carefully packed in plastic bags. George and Kristeene's chairs were now vacant, but I felt reluctant to move. The sound of an Erhu, a traditional Chinese mu-

卷夹到了自己的盘子里。

我说，你会用中国筷子？

乔治说，瞧，很中国，是不是？说罢，又去夹锅贴，没有夹住。他看了我一眼，伸了伸舌头。

我说，把筷头对齐，对了，保证夹住。

乔治，你不觉得锅贴很像意大利的面食？应该撒一点干酪粉？

Good idea，他说，你能做锅贴吗？以后在家里可以这样吃。

我朝他白了一眼。在他的概念里，凡是能和自己熟悉的菜肴接上联系的，绝不会轻易地另立新的门户。他把馄饨当作意大利的面食，把木须肉归类于墨西哥食品，同出一辙。我转身照顾柯丽丝，把春卷切得再小一点，让她用手抓着吃。

木须肉上来的时候，我真是跌破了眼镜！准确地说，是惊讶得有点愤怒！木须肉木须肉，原来就是胡须那么几根猪肉丝！

乔治说，这是我最喜欢的中国菜之一。他在圆圆的薄饼上均匀地涂了甜蜜酱，就像平时在面包上涂白脱那么熟练，然后，把那些乱七八糟的包心菜炒鸡蛋的混合物夹在薄饼中央，卷起来，封住两头，捏在手里，像啃甘蔗一样地咬了一口。

呵，他扬起了眉毛，说道，好吃，很好吃。

我问，很墨西哥？

非常墨西哥。他点点头，轻轻地哼起了节奏感强劲的墨西哥歌曲，一付陶醉的样子。难得看到乔治如此放松自己。柯丽丝不能这么吃。我把饼撕成小块，另外给了她一些填充料。这时，我才找到了木须肉中的“木”字，这个“木”，原来是黑木耳！

乔治问我，自己做，难不难？

我说，做菜不难，不知道有没有现成的薄饼出售。

他说，墨西哥的玉米饼到处都有。

这个美国人，竟然如此移花接木，简直乱弹琴！我顺便问了问女招待。她说，中国菜场有卖的，并告诉了我一个很远的中国超市的地址。乔治知道了以后很高兴。

菜太多，我们根本吃不完。 乔治，为什么不请南西一起来？

不知道她是否喜欢中国菜？

我说，以后请她来家里，我来烧，让她试试看。

那倒是个好主意。乔治一边说，一边吃着酸甜肉。红酱留在他的唇上，像口红一样，看得我直想笑。柯丽丝也喜欢酸甜的食品，脸上一道道红杠，像大花脸似的。我一边擦柯丽丝的脸，一边对乔治说，其实中国的蔬菜很好，炒茄子和四季豆，有独特的风味，还有豆制品，有许多种类，不知道你尝过没有？

sical instrument, played softly in the background. It was both soothing and poignant, stirring memories of my homeland.

The aroma of ginger and scallion cooking permeated the air, a familiar scent that comforted me. It filled my chest, like reuniting with an old friend. The waitstaff bustled around me, their figures blurring as my eyes welled up with tears. The scenes around me began to shift, merging with images of my mother's home, the hills, the streams, and the familiar landscapes. Was I in a dream, or had time and space transformed?

When George called out to me, I was in the midst of drying my eyes with a white napkin, lost in a moment of nostalgia and emotion.

他说，好哇，那么我们订一些带回家，明天吃。

于是，临走的时候，女招待给我们打了包，许多盒子重重叠叠，被装在两个塑料袋里。

该走了，乔治和柯丽丝的位置上都空了，我却懒得动。扬声器传来二胡演奏的乐曲，并不好听，却是那么熟悉，音符划过，揪心揪肺，好像琴弦就在我的身体里，一根根脆弱得就要崩溃。空气中的油烟姜葱味，久违了，吸进去，好舒服，却堵在胸口，不肯出来，就像遇到了知己的老朋友。男女招待在眼前穿梭而过，渐渐地被泪水蒙住，好像罩上了一层粗玻璃，越来越模糊。什么都不清楚，什么都换成了家乡的符号，我的娘家，娘家的山水和土地。我是在梦中，还是变换了时空？

乔治搀着柯丽丝的小手已经走得很远，当他回过头来招呼我的时候，我正在用白色的餐巾擦眼睛。

Chapter 18

As the next day unfolded, George extended an invitation to Nancy for dinner. It was around three in the afternoon when George called home. Kristeene had just settled in for her usual nap, and I was engrossed in a book in her room. The ringing phone reached my ears through the slightly ajar door, prompting me to hurry to George's master bedroom to answer.

Upon picking up the receiver, he inquired if the invitation was on short notice. I assured him that we had plenty of leftover dishes from the night before, which we could make use of. George then asked if I needed Betty's assistance, to which I replied that Betty wasn't familiar with Chinese cuisine and I could handle it myself. He seemed pleased and mentioned that he would bring some wine home.

This marked the first time I entered his bedroom without prior consent. It was a necessity, though. After hanging up, I took a moment to look around. The bed wasn't neatly made, with the sheets unevenly hanging on either side. I adjusted them, making sure everything was in order. On the night table near the window, I noticed some books, primarily biographies. I left his notebook untouched and left the room to prepare dinner in the kitchen.

There's a Chinese saying that even a clever woman can't prepare a meal without rice. In this case, I would turn the leftover Chinese food into a new dinner. I retrieved the containers from the refrigerator and placed them on the round table. With a pen and paper, I listed out what we had. There were five containers: broccoli cooked in oyster oil, eggplants with smashed garlic, green beans with fermented soya beans, hot bean curd, and Chinese BBQ pork, all ordered later. The restaurant leftovers were sautéed beef filets with cauliflower and sweet-sour pork. After some consideration, I decided on a new menu: 1. Chinese BBQ pork with green beans; 2. Sweet-sour pork with hot bean curd; 3. Eggplants with smashed garlic; 4. Sautéed sea shrimps with green peas (which I would buy from the supermarket); 5. Beef cooked with broccoli (also to be bought). The sautéed beef filets and cauliflower would be saved for my later meal.

Following Betty's protocol, I preheated the plates in the oven to keep the

第十八章

第二天，乔治果然把南西请来吃晚饭。打电话来的时候，大约是下午三点钟。柯丽丝刚刚睡下不久。我正在柯丽丝的房里看书，幸亏房门没有关紧，听到电话铃响，我赶快奔到了乔治的主卧室，抓起台灯旁边的电话。

他问我，是不是太仓促？我说，昨晚不是带回来许多菜？正好把它们打扫干净。

乔治说，要不要蓓蒂来帮忙？

我说，蓓蒂不懂中国菜。我能应付。乔治很高兴，说，他带酒回来。

这是我第一次擅自进乔治的房间，出于不得已。挂了电话，朝周围看了看。他的床没有铺好，外翻的床单两面不对称，靠窗的那边长出一大截。我把床罩，毯子和床单全部重新铺了一遍，还把他的枕头拍得松软一些，叠整齐。靠窗的那个床边柜上除了电话，还有几本书和一个记事簿，翻了翻那些书籍，都是人物自传。没有动他的记事本，就出来了，到厨房去准备晚餐。

俗话说，巧妇难为无米之炊。现在是巧妇巧搭配。从冰箱里把昨晚上带回来的中国菜整理一遍，一个个白色的塑料盒放在圆台子上，我拿了一支笔，在纸上涂来涂去。数了数，一共五个菜。蚝油芥榄，蒜蓉茄子，豆豉四季豆，麻婆豆腐，叉烧肉，还有就是吃剩下来的炒牛肉片和甜酸肉。几经“周折”，菜单出来啦！

1，叉烧肉片配四季豆。2，甜酸肉配麻婆豆腐。3，蒜蓉茄子。4，我去超市买一磅海虾，做个青豆炒虾仁。5，买一点牛肉和芥榄炒在一起。那个椰花菜炒牛肉，显得陈旧，晚上就不用了，以后我来吃。

根据蓓蒂的规矩，客人晚餐用的盘子必须在烤箱里预热，有利于热菜的保温。我把这些盆子都放入了烤箱，到时候扭一下开关就是了。再把家里的银餐具检查了一遍，其它都铮亮发光，有几个不

dishes warm. When dinner time approached, I'd simply switch on the oven. I checked all the silverware, ensuring they gleamed, and gave a little extra attention to some less frequently used spoons. Afterward, I meticulously cleaned the kitchen, tidying up the floor and countertops, and disposing of unnecessary leftovers in the bin. Somehow, I took special care in preparing this dinner.

During the cleaning, I came across some expired oatmeal. I went out to the back door and emptied it onto the ground. I gazed at the sky, half-expecting a flock of birds to swoop down, but all I saw were dried leaves scattered about. A gust of wind swept them into a pile of fallen leaves.

In the evening, as deep autumn settled in, the setting sun seemed weary. The sky near the horizon shifted from yellow to purple, and then to black, in the blink of an eye. The once lush trees of summer now stood naked, bracing themselves for the chill of the approaching winter winds. I sat on the doorstep, lost in thought, arms wrapped around my knees, and let the wind play with my hair. My mind wandered to Kristeene. The poor child had lost her mother shortly after birth, and then her stepmother had abandoned her. Now, another woman named Nancy would enter her life. I wondered if she would be kind and caring.

George had mentioned that Nancy was a business associate. Did this imply that if they married, Nancy would continue working? And would I remain here to care for Kristeene? I hoped Nancy would be a kind woman who would get along with me

A creaking noise disrupted my thoughts, and I turned to find George entering. Surprised, I greeted him, "Back so early?"

He explained, "I'm afraid you might be too busy to get everything done in time, so I came back early to have a look," loosening his tie.

I reassured him, "Don't worry, everything is ready-made," and headed toward the hallway to check on Kristeene upstairs. George, however, sensed my worry and inquired, "Susu, anything wrong?"

Ignoring his question, I continued upstairs, but George brought up another topic. "Susu, your boyfriend Charlie, I haven't heard anything about him in so long. How is he?"

Stopping midway on the stairs, I replied, "Charlie went to visit his parents in another state." Internally, I wondered why Charlie hadn't called me, considering the school term had already started.

Returning with Kristeene in my arms, I rejoined George in the kitchen. He was busy pouring ice cubes into a metal container to chill the wine. Kristeene had just woken up and called out for her daddy. George lovingly picked her up and kissed her cheek. I had hoped he might mention the visitor, Nancy, and give Kristeene a chance to practice saying her name, which would

常用的大匙子有点氧化，把它们都擦干净了。然后，把厨房地上和柜台台面都整理清洁了一遍，把一些吃剩的没用的东西都扔进了垃圾箱。不知道什么原因，我对这顿晚餐格外地仔细和小心。

整理橱柜时，发现一些过期的的干麦片，便开了厨房的后门，倒在后花园的地上。朝天空望了好久，盼望着叽叽喳喳地飞来一群小鸟，看到的却是漫天干枯的树叶。一阵风吹来，像扫地似的，把麦片赶到了落叶堆里。深秋的傍晚，落日显得有气无力，天边由黄变紫，由紫变青，就是一眨眼的功夫。夏日茂盛的树林到了秋冬却被剥光了衣裳，赤身露体地在冷风中经受磨练。我呆呆地坐在台阶上，双手抱膝，任凭头发被风吹来吹去，心里想着柯丽丝。可怜的孩子，出世不久失去了母亲，继母安娜走了。现在，有一个叫南西的女人要进来，不知道善良不善良？

乔治说，南西是他生意场上的朋友，那意思是否意味着如果他们结了婚，南西还要去上班？还要继续留我照顾柯丽丝？希望南西是好人，能和我和睦相处。

“吱呀”一声，背后有人开了门，吓了我一跳。回过头，看到了乔治。

回来了？这么早？

怕你忙不过来，回来看看。他一边说，一边解领带。

没事，都是现成的。我站了起来，转身朝走廊上走，准备到楼上去看柯丽丝。

素素，怎么啦？乔治在背后说，你好像有心事？不要为晚餐发愁。

我继续往前走，没有搭理他。

素素，你的男朋友，查里，好久没有他的消息。他好吗？

我已经上了楼梯，停下来说，查里去外州探望父母了。心里想，查里应该回来了，学校已经开学，怎么也不来个电话？

把柯丽丝抱下楼，回到厨房时，乔治正在把一袋碎冰块倒入金属的盛器里，那是冻酒用的。

柯丽丝刚醒，亲昵地叫了声“爹地”。乔治把她接了过去，亲她的脸蛋。我以为他接下来的话就是告诉她，今晚我们家有客人，她的名字叫南西。如果柯丽丝能够反复地念几遍南西的名字，将给南西很大的面子。但是，乔治没有说。

我说，我要去超市买一点菜，一会儿就回来。柯丽丝，留在家和爹地玩。

乔治说，我去，我去。

surely delight Nancy. However, he remained silent on the matter.

Deciding to head to the supermarket, I announced, "I'll go buy something. I'll be back soon. Kristeene, stay home and play with daddy."

"I'll go, I'll go," George offered.

"You? To buy Chinese things?" I quipped, smiling.

"Alright, I'll give you money," he replied.

"I still have some from the last time you gave me," I assured him.

George often handed me a couple of hundred dollars for groceries and other expenses, never asking for an itemized list. However, I meticulously kept track of every expenditure.

In the supermarket, I gathered all the necessary items and paid. As I carried the shopping bags out, it struck me that the careful preparation for tonight's dinner was to leave a positive impression on Nancy.

Returning home, a question weighed on my mind. Tomorrow was the day we had planned to travel, but George hadn't mentioned anything about preparations. Had he forgotten or had the plan changed? I asked, "Are we still leaving tomorrow?"

"It depends on how things go tonight," he replied.

Perplexed, I pressed, "What does Kristeene's birthday have to do with tonight? If you don't mind me asking, why invite Nancy instead of Anna? After all, Anna cared deeply for Kristeene. She must be thinking about her."

George seemed uncomfortable, shutting his eyes and offering no answers. After a moment, he retrieved a box from a cabinet and lit a cigar.

Watching him smoke, I realized my questions had hit a sensitive nerve. Questions, apologies, and painful memories seemed to be the essence of our communication. This time, if I refrained from apologizing, would it alleviate his pain?

He continued to smoke, and I kept quiet. On the kitchen floor, Kristeene's toys were scattered around a small rug. Next to it was a plastic table, where Kristeene sat happily coloring with crayons.

White smoke billowed from George's mouth, dissipating gradually until it was no longer visible. Yet the weight of his sorrow lingered, growing thicker and closer, as if it were fermenting and swelling in the silence, threatening to crush me.

I needed to say something, even if it led to an argument or the smashing of a plate. Anything was better than this stifling silence. Summoning my courage, I exclaimed, "George, can you smoke outside?"

He replied, "Yes," and extinguished his cigar before leaving for the study.

As I watched him go, I felt a sense of regret. This wasn't my intention. I only wanted to remind him that Nancy wasn't as crucial to Kristeene as he believed. If plans were being changed for Nancy's sake, it was turning things

我笑着说，买中国菜，你去？

乔治说，给你钱。

我说，上次给的还没有用完呢！

乔治经常给二，三百元家里用的钱，从来不要报帐。但是，我都记录得清清楚楚。

在超市里，选完菜，付了款，拎着口袋出来的时候，我才明白，今晚如此认真地准备晚餐，是为了给南西一个好印象。

回来的路上，突然想到了一个问题。明天，应该是外出旅游的日子。乔治为什么不交待？是不是忘记了，还是改变了计划？所以，一到家，就问他，明天走不走？

他说，看看今天晚上的情况再说。

我说，柯丽丝的生日和今晚上有什么关系？如果你不介意的话，我要问你一个问题，为什么柯丽丝过生日，不请安娜请南西？无论如何，安娜是爱柯丽丝的，安娜一定非常想念她。

乔治显得很难堪，随即闭上了眼睛，一个问题都没有回答。过了一会儿，他走到一个柜子前，拿出了一个盒子，点上了一支雪茄烟。

第一次看到他抽烟，知道自己又问错了问题。问题，道歉，痛苦的回忆，成为我们之间经常的一种交流模式。

那么，这一次，如果不道歉，是不是会减少他的痛苦？

他只顾着抽烟，我一句话都不说。

厨房的地上有一块小地毯，都是柯丽丝的东西。傍边放了一张彩色的塑料桌子，柯丽丝握着蜡笔在纸上涂鸦。

白烟从他的口里吐出来，缓缓地向四周散去，越来越淡，直至肉眼看不见，却留下浓浓的的悲哀，无处不在，越来越浓，越来越近。僵持在沉默中发酵膨胀，好像要把人压扁。

我必须说什么，哪怕是吵架，或者摔破一个盘子，都比半死不活来得舒畅。我狠了狠心，叫道，乔治，不能到外面去抽吗？

YES，他掐断了烟火，起身走了。他去了书房。

望着他的背影，好像看到了一个失败的士兵，被缴下了枪支一样。这完全不是我的本意。我无非是想提醒他，对于柯丽丝来说，南西并不重要。如果因为南西的关系而改变了原来的计划，那是本末倒置。但是，想到这里，已经后悔了。我是谁？有什么权利来指挥他？他是爱女儿的，怎么可能做出不利于柯丽丝的事情呢？我把拳头堵在嘴上，低头在厨房里来回地走，思忖着是不是应该去作一点说明？我就这样走到了书房的门口，轻轻地敲了敲门，问道，乔

upside down. Yet, reflecting on this, I felt remorseful. Who was I to give orders? He loved his daughter, and how could I accuse him of acting against her best interests?

I paced back and forth in the kitchen, my hand over my mouth, head hanging low. Contemplating whether to offer an explanation, I finally gathered the courage to knock lightly on the study door. "George, may I come in?"

After a long pause, I heard his voice, "Come in."

Entering, I stood before him. At that moment, I could tell I'd made yet another wrong move. George's eyes and nose were red, as if he'd been crying. I chose to pretend I hadn't noticed. No words came to mind, and I contemplated leaving. Men's tears, especially George's, always unnerved me. But if I left, it might only make things more awkward. After wracking my brain, I found something to say.

"I was just wondering if you'd like Kristeene to dress up nicely for tonight."

"It's not necessary," he replied.

I didn't dare look at him, so I couldn't gauge his expression. I wasn't sure if discussing his daughter brought him happiness.

"Is there anything else you need, apart from the Chinese food?" I asked.

"No, Susu, thank you."

"George, I'd like to take back what I said earlier. You don't have to answer any questions."

George responded, "I hope there's a day when I can tell you everything."

"No, no," I insisted. "Don't take it to heart."

"No one wants to hear my story. Maybe you're interested."

"Interested? Of course I am," I assured him. "But when you're feeling better."

Nancy arrived promptly at half-past seven. I could hear the doorbell from the kitchen, and George's face lit up as he went to greet her. They chatted in the living room for a while, and my job was to deliver two glasses of wine later, just as Betty had done whenever a guest came over. However, this time, George led Nancy directly into the kitchen.

"Susu, this is Nancy," he introduced. "Nancy, this is Kristeene."

Nancy gave a polite nod and extended her hand, saying, "Pleased to meet you, Susu."

"Likewise," I replied.

I didn't dare to scrutinize her, but I could tell by her movements that she had been trained for social occasions. When she shook hands, her upper body leaned slightly forward, her abdomen moved back a little, creating a curve to maintain a subtle distance. When she spoke, her head turned slightly to the side, her neck remained straight. Every movement adhered to strict rules of

治，可以进来吗？

好一会儿，才听到他的答复：进来。

我进去了。走到他面前的时候，知道这一步也走错了。乔治的眼睛鼻子通红，好像刚刚哭过。我赶快装着什么也没有看到。一时无语，真想回头就走。最怕男人的眼泪，尤其是乔治的。但是，如果离开，不是更令他难堪？挖空心思，想出了这么一句话。

我说，想问问你，今天晚上，要不要把柯丽丝打扮得漂亮一些？

他说，不必了。

不敢看他，不知道他说话时的表情，不知道谈及他宝贝的女儿，是不是能让他开心一点？

我说，除了中国食品，还有什么其他的要求吗？

没有，素素，谢谢你。

乔治，我把刚才说的话收回。你不必回答任何问题。

他说，希望有这么一天，把所有的事情都告诉你。

不，不。我说，你不要太当真啊。

他说，没有人要听我的故事。也许，你有兴趣。

有兴趣，当然有兴趣。我说，等你开心一点的时候。

南西是七点半到的，很准时。乔治在听到了门铃以后，很高兴地走过去，热情地拥抱了她。他们应该先在客厅里聊一会儿天，然后我送两杯葡萄酒过去。以前蓓蒂都是这样对待客人的。不料，乔治直接把南西引进了厨房。

素素，这是南西。南西，这是柯丽丝。

南西很有礼貌地点了一下头，伸手过来，说道，很高兴遇见你，素素。

我说，我也是。我不敢很仔细地打量她。根据她的身体动作，很明显，是经过待人接物的专门训练的。她握手的时候，上身往前倾，腹部却收得很紧，以弧度拉开与对方的距离。说话的时候，头往一边侧，脖子是直的。她的每一个移动都有规有矩，一板一眼，以求得到最佳的效果。这种动作，乔治一定很满意，很熟悉，在商场上见怪不怪了。

但是，作为局外人，我能区别出南西和安娜的不同。安娜是真诚的，南西是在演戏。

柯丽丝被介绍给南西的时候，乔治把她从地上抱了起来。南西对柯丽丝格外地热情，亲了她不够，还要把柯丽丝抱过去。柯丽丝扑在乔治的背上，不停地摇头，把身体一起摇了起来。我大吃一

standard social conduct, aimed at achieving a perfect effect. George must have been familiar with and appreciated such behavior in the business world. But as an outsider, I could discern the contrast between Nancy's movements and Anna's. Anna's gestures exuded spontaneity, while Nancy's were more like a performance.

When Kristeene was introduced to Nancy, George lifted her up from the floor. Nancy made an extra effort to endear herself to Kristeene. She gave her a kiss, but it seemed she thought it wasn't enough. She then attempted to take Kristeene into her arms. However, Kristeene clung to George, shaking her head vigorously until her tiny body wiggled along with it. Both George and I were taken by surprise.

After a short time, the trio moved to the living room. I remained in the kitchen to continue preparing dinner. Before long, George returned with Kristeene. She rushed into my arms, calling out, "Susu, Susu." George left with two wine glasses, a container of ice, and a bottle of wine.

I wasn't sure if a child without memory possessed unique talents or if these talents would fade as her memory developed. Regardless, that night, Kristeene was restless, emitting a sound akin to crying but not quite. She refused to let me out of her sight.

I figured she must be hungry, so I decided to feed her first. I chopped some shrimp into small pieces, microwaved them for a few minutes, added some ketchup, and mixed them with rice. I placed the dish in front of her along with some green beans, and she eagerly used her fingers to eat.

When Betty cooked here, she displayed a remarkable ability to control multiple tasks with impeccable timing. She could work at the roast oven, microwave, and gas burners simultaneously, managing it all seamlessly. That evening, I thawed the green peas first. Then, on two burners, I sautéed beef and shrimp separately while heating eggplant and tofu in the microwave, and preheating plates in the roast oven.

George had initially planned for all four of us to dine together, but I had disagreed. After some persuasion, he relented. Once I finished serving the dishes on the long dining table, I retreated to the kitchen to heat the beef with cauliflower that had been leftover from the previous night's dinner at the restaurant, and enjoyed it on my own.

The next morning, George and Nancy were still in the house when I got up. I felt awkward about intruding on their time together, so I quietly went about my usual routine. I prepared coffee for George, knowing he would appreciate it. The machines would automatically turn on and off, so he could enjoy a freshly brewed cup.

As I went outside to take care of the garbage, I noticed Nancy's car was still parked there. It seemed she had stayed the night. I assumed they had

惊。乔治也感到意外。

他们三人去了客厅，我留在厨房准备晚餐。过不多久，乔治抱着柯丽丝回来，柯丽丝扑到我身上，“素素”“素素”叫着。乔治拿了两个酒杯和那个盛冰块的容器走了。容器里放着一瓶酒。

不知道没有记忆的孩子是不是有其他方面的特异功能？这种功能是否在自我能力加强以后逐渐地丧失？反正，那天晚上，柯丽丝很不安分，发出呜哩呜哩非哭非笑的声音，而且很粘人，不让我离她很远。

我想，也许是饿了，不如先喂饱了她。我挑了几个虾仁，剁碎了，放到微波炉里转了转，然后淋了一点番茄酱（Ketchup），和米饭混在一起，我喂她米饭，再给一些四季豆。她自己抓着吃。

蓓蒂在这儿做菜的时候，一再显示其对时间的控制能力（Timing）。也就是说，烤箱，炉头，微波炉，要同时工作，统筹兼顾。今晚，首先要把青豆化冻，然后在两个炉灶上同时炒牛肉和虾仁，在微波炉里加热茄子和豆腐。还有，要开烤箱，把盘子预热。

乔治原来是打算四人一起上桌的。我不同意。他和我争执了几句，便放弃了。我把菜端去晚餐室的长台子以后，自己在厨房里把昨晚的椰菜炒牛肉热一热，吃了。

过了好久，乔治来厨房，说他们吃完了。我问，要不要把柯丽丝抱过去？乔治摇摇头。他又拿了一瓶酒，走了。不一会儿，南西进来了，拥抱我说，每个菜都很好吃，尤其是那个讨妇（豆腐），又酸又甜又辣，有益于健康，第一次尝试，非常好。她说，过几天也要到那个中国餐馆去，再吃一遍“讨妇”。

我没有吭声，心里想，这样的“讨妇”哪个餐馆也不会供应的，让她去碰一鼻子灰吧！

我把餐盘刀叉放进了洗碗机，抱着柯丽丝上了楼。柯丽丝最喜欢睡前有人坐在床边讲故事。有的儿童书，图文并茂，还有儿歌相配，只有按一下开关，音乐就起来了。这种书，重复了几遍以后，柯丽丝就记住了。如果问问题，她能用单词回答，万一答不上，就指着图画来表达自己的意思。我们每天晚上要“共同学习”半个多小时。

柯丽丝睡下以后，我到楼下准备乔治第二天喝的咖啡，机器到时会自动跳上开关。

明天是垃圾日，我把垃圾捅拉到了城堡的大门口，南西的车还停在那里，估计今晚她可能要在这儿过夜。心里想，正巧，乔治的床铺好了。

made up after their disagreement.

When I returned inside, I overheard George and Nancy having a discussion. It was a disagreement, but their tone remained polite and composed. I only caught snippets of their conversation.

Nancy asserted, "I don't believe you."

George replied firmly, "This is the rule."

Nancy pressed on, "The house is not without women."

George repeated, "I've said it several times. I won't say it again."

I couldn't help but feel my heart race. It was evident that Nancy was talking about me. I couldn't understand why my presence was a topic of their quarrel. Was it that she didn't believe the true nature of George's and my relationship, or had George rejected something she wanted? George and I never exchanged bitter words, so it must have been Nancy who had provoked him with her unreasonable demands. Since George had chosen Nancy, he must have had his reasons. I wondered why they couldn't discuss things calmly and why he had hurt her feelings.

As I headed back upstairs, I decided to leave a note for George in his bedroom:

'George,

Please make arrangements for Kristeene's birthday. It's very important.

Susu'

I left the note by the lamp on his night table. They shouldn't let their disagreement affect Kristeene. Since they had spent the night together, tomorrow would be a perfect opportunity for them to bond further.

回到大楼的时候，听到乔治和南西正在吵架，那是文明人之间的吵架，双方都很克制。我听见了一部份。

南西说，我不相信你。

乔治说，这是规矩。

南西说，这楼里不是没有女人。

乔治说，我已经说了好几遍，不愿意再重复。

这些话都是在上楼梯的时候亲耳听到的。我的心怦怦乱跳，很明显，南西在说我。真不明白，为什么要把我拉进他们的争论里去？是不相信我和乔治的关系还是乔治拒绝了她的什么要求？他们为什么要吵架？我和乔治从来吵不起来。一定是这个叫南西的女人骄横无理，把乔治惹火了。但是，他选择南西，一定有喜欢她的道理。难道不能好好说吗？为什么要伤她的心呢？

回三楼的时候，我拐到乔治房里给他写了一个便条。

乔治：

请安排好柯丽丝的生日。此事最重要。

素素

我把纸条放在他的床头柜的台灯旁，心里想，他们不应该在柯丽丝的问题上有分歧。等度过今晚的鱼水之夜，第二天，应该是一个艳阳天。

Chapter 19

As we embarked on our train journey to the south of America, it was just the three of us—George, Kristeene, and me. I couldn't help but wonder why Nancy hadn't joined us. What had transpired between her and George? Where had she spent the night? Why had George changed his plans? These questions lingered, but George offered no explanations. He simply expressed gratitude for my reminder about Kristeene's birthday that morning in the kitchen. Later in the day, he called to confirm our travel plans.

Before we departed, the phone rang persistently. When no one answered, I picked up the receiver. It was Charlie, asking if I would be free that evening. I explained that we were leaving for a week-long vacation, but I would get in touch with him upon our return.

During the train journey, I inquired with George about Nancy's absence. He responded, "Was this her call?"

"No, it was Charlie," I clarified, "He's back from school since it's begun."

"How is he?" George inquired.

"I didn't ask, I was afraid of missing the train," I admitted, feeling somewhat preoccupied.

At the train station, George went to purchase our tickets, while Kristeene and I waited in the bustling terminal, tending to our luggage. He returned with one-way tickets, explaining that we would be flying back home. He had shown me the route on a map, but I was still unfamiliar with American geography.

With Kristeene riding on her father's shoulders like a young rider on a horse, she observed the surroundings with excitement. I pointed to the train, explaining, "Look at that, it's a train. See how many wheels it has underneath? It's like a tall house on wheels, and it moves!"

Kristeene echoed, "Train… wheels…"

The lower deck of the train was equipped with sleeping berths and storage for luggage, while the upper deck served as a seating area and dining car. We secured two compartments, each equipped with upper and lower berths concealed within the compartment walls. Special keys were used to access them. Every compartment also featured its own toilet and shower. Kristeene and I shared one compartment, while George used the other. Once we settled in, we made our way to the upper deck for supper. Returning to our compartments, exhaustion began to set in. George inquired, "Would you like some wine? I'll

第十九章

我们在星期五的傍晚搭上了开往美国南部的列车。三个行，乔治，柯丽丝和我。

南西为什么不随行？昨晚吵架的结果是什么？南西在哪里过夜？乔治为什么改变主意？什么解释都没有。他只说了一句话：素素，谢谢你提醒我记住柯丽丝的生日。

那是今天早晨，他临出门前在厨房里说的。然后，在中午的时候，他打来电话，说，我们三人将搭乘晚上的火车，去南部一个城市度假。

出门前，电话铃响了。响了很久，没人接。我跑过去拿起话筒一问，原来是查里。问我晚上有没有空？我说，我们正要出门旅游，大约一个星期，回来后，再和他联系。

上路后，我问乔治，南西为什么没有来？

他说，是不是她的电话？

不是她，是查里。我说，开学了，他回来了。

噢，他好吗？

我笑着说，怕耽搁时间，没有来得及问呢！

到了车站，乔治去办手续，我和柯丽丝在候客厅里看管着我们的行李。据乔治说，我们买的是单行票，回来的时候坐飞机。昨天，画草图的时候，他给我讲了沿途的路线和城市，但是，我对美国非常不熟悉，仍旧是一头雾水。

火车八点准时开。乔治把柯丽丝扛上肩膀，给了我一个手推行李箱，其他都雇人送进了车厢。柯丽丝骑马一样高高在上，东张西望，得意洋洋。我指着火车，告诉她，那是“TRAIN”，瞧，底下有那多轮子，哇，两层楼，比汽车高大，大房子一样，会开着走呢！

柯丽丝附声道“Train”，“Wheels”，……

火车底层是卧铺和行李房，楼上是客座和餐厅。我们有两个包厢，每个包厢有两张床，一张在底下，另一张在上方，隐藏在墙壁里。要用特殊的“钥匙”打开，才能放下来。每个房间有厕所和淋浴。我和柯丽丝用一间，乔治单独用隔壁的。

go get some."

"I don't drink wine," I stated. Then, as he opened the compartment door to leave, I added, "No smoking, no alcohol. No coffee or tea for me. I'm a clean-living woman."

George turned back, chuckling, "Clean-living woman? Haha, that's amusing. Clean-living woman. Very amusing."

I regretted my comment, feeling somewhat nervous about traveling alone with a man. However, there was no reason to distrust him, or else I should have declined the trip. Ultimately, there was little difference between sharing the same house and having separate train compartments. Despite this, I couldn't shake a subtle feeling of unease.

Most of our luggage was for Kristeene—clothes for daily changes, books, toys, snacks, and various other items for her birthday celebration. As I organized Kristeene's belongings, I pondered our three-day train journey. What would we do aside from gazing at the passing scenery, reading, or listening to George's stories? I did look forward to hearing George share his past during the trip. He remained a mystery to me, as I only had fragments of information about him. He had mentioned early on that he would eventually share his story, but whenever the moment arrived, I found myself avoiding it. The more this happened, the more enigmatic I found him. I even theorized that perhaps he hadn't shared his story not because he didn't trust me, but because it was too heartbreaking, and my nerves may not be able to handle it. After all, when he revealed that Laura was Kristeene's mother, I had nearly lost control and nearly caused an accident. I considered myself a 'coward,' and George must have recognized this.

When George returned, he brought two glasses of wine. He sat at the low table near the window, while I settled on the bed by the door. He removed his jacket and tossed it on the bed, revealing a white T-shirt underneath. He handed a glass to me.

I hesitated, then declined with a smile, "I don't drink wine. Do you doubt me?" In truth, I almost accepted, recalling the night at the Italian restaurant with Charlie when spirits had disarmed me. I didn't want to risk a repeat tonight, only to regret it.

He replied, "Then both are mine." Taking a hefty sip, he added with emotion, "Ah, the feeling of leaving home is so wonderful!"

Cushions lined the berths, and George leaned back, propping his feet up on a nearby chair, savoring his newfound freedom

The sensation of leaving home seemed to hold a profound weight for George. It was evident that he harbored deep-seated pain and sorrow associated with his home life. The words he uttered carried a heavy undertone of melancholy. How many hidden wounds lay within the confines of that house?

After a few swigs of wine, he declared, "You asked why Nancy didn't come. Once I finish this, I'll tell you."

I bathed Kristeene, dressed her in a sleeping gown, and settled her on the lower berth. Placing two chairs in front of her berth, I took precautions

把东西安顿好了以后，我们到楼上的餐车去吃了晚饭。回到包厢，大家都很累。乔治问我，要不要喝点酒？他到楼上去买。我说，我不喝酒。他开门离开的时候，我再补充了一句：我烟酒不粘，不喝咖啡和茶叶，是个干净的女人。

乔治回头说，干净的女人？呵呵，有意思，干净的女人，很有意思。

我说完了有些后悔。跟一个男人单独出门，我有点紧张。但是，对他不放心，是没有道理的，否则为何不拒绝？再说，分住两个房间和同住一个大楼，有什么区别？我想了想，觉得还是自己有点心虚。

柯丽丝的行李最多，除了替换衣服，书籍，玩具，点心，还有为生日准备的许多用品。我整理着柯丽丝的东西，心里想，我们要在火车上住三天，除了看风景，还能做些什么呢？看书？听乔治讲故事？我倒是期待在旅途上听他讲讲自己的过去。乔治像个大谜团，我只看到一些蛛丝马迹。对于他，除了柯丽丝的父亲身份，其他方面都不了解。而他从一开始的时候起，就说要慢慢告诉我他的故事。但是，每次到了关键的时刻，却闭上眼睛加以回避。越是如此，越让我觉得神秘。我也考虑过，他不说，可能并不是不信任我，而是因为故事太悲惨，怕我经不起。我不是在他告诉了劳瑞是柯丽丝的妈妈以后，就失去了控制，险些出车祸吗？我是个胆小鬼，乔治一定看透了我。

乔治回来的时候，还是端了两杯酒。他坐在靠窗口的那一头，旁边是个茶几。我坐在床尾，靠门的一边。他脱了夹克衫，扔在床上，里面是一件白色的体恤。他把一杯酒递给了我。

我没有接，笑着说，我不喝。你不相信我？其实，我差一点要把酒接过来。我想起了和查里在意大利餐馆的那个晚上，自己被酒精解除了武装，不希望今晚做出后悔的事情。

他说，那么都是我的了。他喝了一大口，情不自禁地说，啊，离家的感觉多么好！

火车上的床有软垫靠背。乔治往后一仰，双腿伸直了架在前面的椅子上，好像得到了解放一般。

离家的感觉多么好！他不喜欢那个家，所以，家里没有任何的历史记录，所以，在中国餐馆里，他表现得像孩子一样。他脱口而出的一句话，到了我这里，变得很沉重，很悲凉。那个家，那栋房子里究竟隐藏了多少伤害他的东西？

几口酒下肚以后，他说，你不是问我，南西为什么没有来？等我喝完了，我再告诉你。

我帮柯丽丝洗了洗，换了睡衣，让她上了床。床边用两张椅子

to ensure she wouldn't roll off during the night. I would take the upper berth, and George assisted in lowering it. Kristeene slept by the window, so George shifted to the end near the door, requiring me to adjust my position to accommodate him.

Kristeene lay in her berth and implored, "Susu, tell me a story."

Of course, we needed our bedtime stories.

"Kristeene, can't you read by yourself?" George interjected, "Susu is tired."

Kristeene pouted. "No, Susu, no."

"Alright, let's read together. Which book would you like, Kristeene?" I retrieved a stack of books from the duffel bag and let her choose.

"This one, and this one," she picked five with glee.

George observed, smiling, "Kristeene, why don't you look at the scenery outside the window? Trees, houses, everything is moving."

Kristeene allowed me to lift her and draw back the curtains to peer outside.

The outside world was already enshrouded in darkness, with only some moving lights visible. So Kristeene opted for reading. I suggested, "Today, daddy will tell stories, and Susu will sing. Does that sound good?"

Kristeene agreed, "Yes, yes."

Thus, George read a children's poem, and I sang a children's song. Kristeene followed along with George's reading and joined me in singing, sounding like a cheerful lark. Once we concluded, Kristeene grew tired and swiftly drifted into sleep after we bid each other goodnight.

George finished the wine bottle and gestured towards the glass he had offered me, remarking, "Susu, are you truly so 'clean'?" I smiled and inquired, "Is being clean not a good thing?"

"To be clean, you must have paid a high price," he suggested, implying something deeper.

I understood his allusion. So I took a sip from the glass and then handed it to him, jesting, "Now, I'm not clean anymore."

He let out a hearty laugh.

"Shh," I reminded him, "Kristeene's sleeping."

He stood up, patting my shoulder, and suggested, "Let's go to my compartment."

I hesitated briefly, considering saying, "Tomorrow. Let's rest for now." Yet, I feared this might dampen his enthusiasm for conversation. After all, I had been eagerly anticipating hearing his story. His recent tales had revolved around Nancy, then Anna, and Laura. All these women remained enigmatic figures to me. At home, George lacked the courage to speak openly. Was it that I lacked the courage to listen now? I told myself, "What do I have to fear? Is he some kind of devil? I'll go."

"Um," I said, "You go ahead. I'll join you a bit later."

当围墙，避免晚上滚下来。我的床在上铺，乔治帮忙放了下来。柯丽丝睡在靠窗口的那一头，乔治只好往门边移，我让出了自己的空间，坐了对面的椅子上，否则太拥挤。

柯丽丝上床后，说道，素素，讲故事。

呵，对对，我们讲故事。

柯丽丝，不能自己看吗？乔治说。素素很累了。

柯丽丝翘着小嘴说，NO，素素， NO。

好吧，好吧，我们一起读书。柯丽丝，你要读哪一本？说完，我从旅行包里取出一叠书，让她选。

这本，这本，她眉开眼笑地翻来复去，选了五六本。

乔治在一旁看着笑，说道，柯丽丝，为什么不看看窗外面的景色，树呵，房子呵，都在动？

柯丽丝让我把她抱起来，拉开窗帘看外面。

天已经黑了。窗外，只有流动的灯光，其他什么也看不见。柯丽丝还是要看书。

我说，今天，爹地讲故事，素素唱歌，好不好？

柯丽丝说，YES，YES。

于是乔治念了一首童谣。我唱了一首儿歌，柯丽丝跟着念，跟着唱，像个百灵鸟一样。唱完了，她也累了，道晚安后，不一会儿就睡去了。

乔治已经喝完了一杯酒，指着另一杯，说道，素素，你真的那么干净？

我笑了笑，问他，干净不好吗？

他说，干净的代价很大。

我知道他话里有话，接过酒杯，喝了一口，还给了他，说，好了，不干净了。乔治大笑。

“嘘！”我提醒他，柯丽丝在睡觉。

他站了起来，拍着我的肩膀，说，走，到我那边去。

我犹豫了一下，想说，明天吧，早点休息。但是，又怕他有了聊天的兴致，被我浇冷水。我不是一直在期待听乔治讲故事吗？南西，安娜，劳瑞，这些女人没有一个不是谜。平时，是乔治没有勇气讲，难道现在反而是我没有勇气听？我对自己说，你怕什么呢？他是魔鬼吗？去就去吧！

嗯。我说，你先去，我马上过来。

Chapter 20

George's voice trembled as he asked, "Do you really want to hear my story?"

"Of course," I replied, my tone sincere.

He drained his goblet, exhaling softly. "Do you remember the night we woke you up? It was Nancy."

"Nancy?" I feigned ignorance, masking my knowledge of the drunken woman.

"We had a heated argument that night, outside the house. Did you hear it?"

"No," I continued to feign, hoping his tale didn't intersect with me.

"We had another last night. You must have heard."

"I heard voices, but I didn't pay much attention," I confessed.

"That's a relief," he said, placing the empty goblet on the small table beside him. He interlaced his hands, offering a reluctant smile.

"The argument was over something simple: Nancy wanted to stay, but I couldn't allow it."

He was direct, leaving out the intricacies. It surprised me, but I felt oddly at ease, as if listening to someone else's story. George wasn't drunk; there was no flush on his face. I sat across from him.

The train's rhythm swayed us gently, everything in the compartment swaying with it. The air was stale, the window and door sealed tightly.

"People are more accepting now. Nancy didn't do anything wrong. Did you love her?"

"Love?" He murmured, a wry smile tugging at his lips. "I don't even know what love is. Is it love when a man and woman share a bed? What about same-sex relationships? If I let her stay, does that mean I love her?"

He grew restless, hands on the edge of the berth, as if about to stand. He scanned the compartment, eyes darting around. Maybe he was looking for a

第二十章

他笑了笑，问我，真的想听我的故事？

想听。我认真地说。

就让我们从南西开始吧！他把杯子里剩下的那点酒一饮而尽，轻轻地叹了口气，说道，那天半夜里，把你吵醒了，是不是？

哪个半夜？我假装糊涂。原来那个喝醉的女人是南西！

素素，许多天以前的半夜里，我和南西在楼外争吵。你没有听到吗？

没有。我继续否认，希望他的故事和我没有丝毫的联系。

那么，昨天晚上，我们再一次争吵。你一定听到了吧！

我说，听到你们在争论，没有注意听。

噢，是这样。他松了一口气，把手中的空杯子放到了身旁的小台子上。随后，双手交叉，作了一个很勉强的微笑。

吵架的原因很简单，南西要在我们家过夜，我没有同意。

他说得那么直接了当，割断来龙去脉，很出乎我的意料，却让我感到安全，好像在听他诉说别人的事情一样。

乔治一点没有醉，脸都不红。我坐在他的对面。

火车有规则地晃动着，地面，椅子和桌子都不很稳定。窗和门都关得紧密，空气都是旧的。

我说，现在人们都很开放，南西没有什么错，是不是你并不爱她？

爱不爱她？他动了动嘴角，似笑不笑地说，我已经不知道什么叫爱了。两个男女睡在一起，是爱吗？女人同女人，男人同男人发生性关系，是爱吗？我留下了她，就爱她了吗？

他说得有些激动，双手撑住床沿，好像要站起来的样子。他的眼睛左顾右盼，似乎在寻找什么东西。我想，是不是他要找雪茄烟抽。我知道他的烟盒在哪里。乔治，你想找什么？雪茄烟？

不，他摇摇头，不找什么。我没事。说完，他坐得安分了些。

我说，你和安娜一起生活了多少年？

cigar. I knew where his stash was.

"Looking for a cigar, George?" I inquired.

"No," he shook his head. "It's nothing. I'm fine." He settled back in.

"How long were you with Anna?" I asked.

"How long?" The hesitation revealed it was a significant stretch.

"Seventeen years," he sighed. "We grew up together, family friends. I'm thirteen years her senior. We got married when she turned twenty. Happy times in the beginning. There are plenty of photos as proof. But..." He stopped abruptly, gaze dropping.

He no longer met my eyes, staring at the floor, burdened by something. After a pause, he stumbled, "Our intimacy, it just didn't align. Not at all."

Once those hard-to-say words were out, he seemed to find some solace. He repeated himself, voice thick with emotion.

"Back then, attitudes towards homosexuality weren't as open," I noted.

He suddenly fixed his gaze on me, sharp and intense. "You've mentioned homosexuality twice now, Susu. Where are you getting this?"

"No one else knows, except for you and Anna."

"My parents knew, but they've passed. No one else knows that Anna is a lesbian. Did she tell you?"

"No, George," I quickly denied. "It wasn't Anna. It's... it's..."

"Did you meet her partner? The woman who wants to be with her?"

"No, George." Nervous sweat pricked my forehead. "I don't know any lesbians. I... I found out during your birthday party through the baby monitor. You were arguing, remember? Someone plugged it in wrong, in your master bedroom."

"The monitor? God!" George smacked his own leg. "I remember now. Anna did that. She made the mistake because she was leaving." He craned his neck, asking, "So, you knew our secret from the very first day we met?"

"Yes, George. But I didn't tell anyone, except Charlie. I'm so sorry."

"I told Charlie. Charlie told Peter. Peter told Mike. Haha, now the whole city thinks George's wife is a lesbian." He laughed bitterly.

"Sorry, George. I'm exhausted. I need some rest. Good night." I rose and left.

As I reached for the doorknob, I heard George weeping. I withdrew my hand as if it were scorched. I turned back, and there he was, head buried in his arms, shoulders shaking.

I returned to the bathroom, grabbed a small towel, wet it with warm wa-

多少年啊？

凭他的口气，我已经知道是很长很长的岁月了。

十七年了。他叹了一口气。我的父母和她家是老朋友，我们从小就在一起玩，我比她大十三岁，她一直喜欢和男孩子玩，我保护她，不让她受其他男孩子的欺负。我等到她满了二十岁和她结婚。我们是甘心情愿的。我们结婚的时候是快乐的，有许多照片为证。

他突然煞住了。他不再看我，望着地面，好像犯了错误似的。隔了一会儿，吞吞吐吐地说，我们的性生活不和谐。很不和谐，很不好。

难以启齿的事情，一旦说了出来，他便不在乎了，重复了好几遍，声音有些哽咽。

你们是不是很守规矩，婚前没有同居？我问道。

没有，没有。我们在婚前从来没有性关系。

十七年前，同性恋的常识没有今天普及。我说。

他突然抬起头来，目光峰利地看着我，问道：这是你第二次提到同性恋的问题。素素，你哪里得来这个结论？

我支支吾吾地说，除了你和安娜，难道别人都不知道吗？

我的父母知道，他们都已经去世了。除了他们，再没有了，再没有别人知道安娜是同性恋。素素，是安娜告诉你的吗？

不，不！我忙解释道，不是安娜，是，是……。

素素，难道你认识她的爱人？那个每天要在她身上胡闹的女人？

不，乔治。我急得虚汗直流。不，不是的。我不认识任何同性恋的女人。我，我，我是在你五十岁生日的PARTY时，通过监听器，柯丽丝的监听器听到的。你们在吵架。记得吗，有人把监听器插错了，插在你们的房间里。

监听器？呵，上帝！乔治一巴掌击在自己的大腿上，说道，想起来了，是安娜插的，插错了。她吵着要搬出去，把监听器插到了我的房间里。他伸长了脖子问我，那么说，你第一次见到我，就已经知道了我们的秘密，是不是，素素？你没有透露一点风声？没有对别人说吗？

我，……我说了，告诉了查里。我低下头，说得很轻很轻，轻到自己几乎听不见。

你告诉了查里。查里告诉了彼得，彼得告诉了麦克，哈哈哈哈，整个城市都知道了乔治的老婆是同性恋。

乔治发出一阵冷笑，声音越来越高。

我说，对不起，我累了，想去睡了。晚安，乔治。说完，我起

ter, and wrung it out. Then I went to him, offering the towel. He didn't look up, his voice breaking as he said, "Don't leave, Susu. Don't leave me alone." He sounded so fragile, like he was pleading for solace.

"Alright, enough tears. Here, take this." I sat by his side, offering the towel. Like a compliant child, he accepted it, wiping his cheeks.

"Thirsty?" I inquired. He nodded, and I handed him a glass of water. He took a sip and settled back into his previous posture.

"There are so many lesbians, George. It's not their fault. They bear more pain than most. They deserve understanding."

George looked up, his eyes reddened. He gazed at me, a sadness etched on his face. "She's the woman I love. At first, I thought she was just reserved. Women often hide their feelings from men, right? The more she did, the more I pushed. Back then, I believed that's how women liked it. But later, things weren't that way. She seemed tormented, crying every time. I told her if she was afraid, we could stop. We could be like two kids, just loving each other. But, Susu, I was fooling myself."

He took a deep breath, shaking his head in helplessness. "I was young, and though I was a man, I didn't always act like one. She lay beside me, and I couldn't help myself. I thought I was failing her. So—" He trailed off.

The train raced through the night, the vibrations intensifying. The chair shuddered, and so did my legs.

His eyes resembled those of a man lost, drained of vitality.

"So I did something foolish. Very foolish," he confessed, his voice heavy. He lowered his head, resting it on the hand between his thumb and forefinger, fingers shielding his eyes. Only the lower half of his face was visible. His lips quivered slightly, his Adam's apple bobbing, as if he were tightly sealing his words.

"Have some more water," I urged.

He drank, nearly finishing the glass. When he set it down, he confessed, "I went to a brothel."

Everything fell into place. No wonder this memory was so agonizing. He uttered "brothel" as if it was a painful secret he could barely utter.

He went on, "I wanted to learn how to be with a woman. So I sought out the best girl to teach me. It cost me a fortune."

I interrupted, "But it's pointless, given Anna's orientation."

"But, Susu, I didn't want to accept that. Who wants to think that way? Even Anna wouldn't. When I returned, I instructed her on what to do. She

身走了。

在开门的时候，我听见他哭了。握住门把的手像烫着了似地，收了回来。我不由回过头去，看见他趴在床边的小台子上，肩膀抽动得很厉害。

我不得不退回来，到浴室去取了一条小毛巾，用温水弄湿了，搅干了走过去，递给他。

他的头仍旧埋在手臂里，“哦……哦”地嚎哭着，一边说，不要走，素素，不要走。

他一下子变得那么软弱，好像在求我一样。

好吧，我不走，别哭了。来，把脸擦了。我坐到了他的旁边，把毛巾递给他。他就像一个听话的孩子，接过了毛巾，擦眼泪。

我说，要喝水吗？他点点头。我给他倒了一杯水。他喝了一口，又趴倒了。

我说，同性恋的人有好多，不是他们的错。他们比正常人更痛苦，值得同情。

乔治抬起红肿的眼睛，悲哀地看着我，说，她是女人，是我爱的女人。

他停了停，目光下垂，彷佛难以启齿。

他说，开始的时候，我以为她怕羞。女人在男人面前常常躲躲闪闪的，不是吗？她越躲，我越受刺激，越有攻击性。我以为这是女人喜欢的方式。后来，我发现不是那回事。她好像在受刑一样，每一次都要掉眼泪。我说，你怕过性生活，那么我们就不过。我们就像小时候一样，相亲相爱。

素素，我没有做到。我是为了安慰安娜，我在欺骗自己。

他深深地吸了一口气，一边无奈地摇摇头。

我是个男人，那个时候，我还年轻。她睡在我的旁边，我做不到不要她。我以为是自己没有做周全。于是，……他又停了下来。

火车在夜里加快了速度，震动得剧烈起来。椅子抖，我的腿也一起抖。

他的眼睛像盲人一样，黯然失色。他喃喃地说，

于是，我做了一件非常愚蠢的事情，非常愚蠢的事情。他说了两遍。说完，垂下了头，一手托着前额，张开的手掌正巧遮住了眼睛。我只看到他的下半张脸。嘴唇在哆嗦，喉结滑上滑下，好像咬紧了牙关，要把语言咽下去。

我说，再喝点水吧！

他喝了，一口气把水喝完。在他放下杯子的时候，他说，我去

followed my lead. She tried her best, even to the point of sickness. From then on, she slept in a separate room, away from my touch."

He added, "Things spiraled. Those women in the brothels were so skilled. They satisfied me. Later, I bought an apartment and brought them there."

"When you argued, I overheard Anna mentioning you being with other women," I said.

"Yes. I'm a terrible man, truly terrible."

"Let the past go. In my eyes, you're a good man, a devoted father. Don't always blame yourself."

He cut me off. "Susu, you don't understand how awful I am. Laura knew. It was during that time she got to know me."

"Laura?" I was taken aback. "The mother of Kristeene?"

"Yes. She was one of those I brought to the apartment."

Laura was a... I was nearly stunned.

George nodded, his eyes wide and honest.

"No," I said, tears streaming down my cheeks. I had no idea why I was crying. Since he told me of Laura's passing, she'd seemed so pitiable, it almost shattered my heart. How could she have been involved in that life?

"Ah!" I exclaimed, "George, you can't tarnish Kristeene's reputation. Laura wasn't involved in that. She was your lover, wasn't she? You cared for her. You even bought her a car. If you didn't love her, why did you take in her daughter? Can you explain that?"

I felt propelled by an indescribable force, making my way to the window. Tugging the curtain aside, I tried to gulp in some fresh air. The effort to open the window proved too much. My sobs echoed, a desperate plea, "George, help me!" He rose swiftly, allowing the wild wind to rush in like a roaring tempest. Just as swiftly, he shut it again.

I leaned against the window frame, my legs refusing to budge. The weight of his revelation, of Laura's past, had been unbearable. Yet, I had tried to console him, affirming he was a good man. I hadn't realized the truth he'd shared would be more brutal than his visit to a brothel. Laura, Kristeene's mother, reduced to such a life! I couldn't, and didn't, want to hear more. What did his history have to do with me? I wished he'd stop there, say no more. I should have left long ago.

But he was like a runaway car with no brakes, hurtling forward, unstoppable.

"I only paid attention to Laura when she told me she was pregnant. I'd

了妓院。

“妓院”两个字说得含糊不清，这个词好像是从他的牙缝里挤出来的。

他说，我想学一学男人和女人在床上应该如何配合。我找最高级的女郎，化了很多钱。

我打断了他，说道，因为安娜是同性恋，怎么学也没有用。

可是，素素，我不可能往那里想，谁愿意往那里想呵？连安娜自己都不愿意往那里想。我回家来就告诉她，应该如何如何做。她照着做了，她很努力地照着做了。但是，她把晚饭都呕吐了出来。从那以后，她睡到了另外的房间，不准我碰她。

他说，我一错再错。妓女很专业，很让我满足。后来，我买了一套公寓，招女人上门。

我说，你们吵架的时候，听到安娜说，你在外面混女人。

是的，我是一个非常坏的男人，非常坏。

我说，过去的事情就让它过去吧！我看你是个好男人，好父亲，你没有必要和自己过不去。

他打断我说，素素，你不知道我有多么坏。劳瑞知道，劳瑞就是在那个时候认识我的。

劳瑞？我大吃一惊！柯丽丝的妈妈劳瑞？

是的，劳瑞，她就是我招来的女郎之一。

劳瑞是妓女？我高声问，只差没有跳起来。

乔治瞪大了诚实的眼睛，缓缓地点点头。

NO，我说，NO，乔治。我开始流眼泪，完全不知道为什么在这个时候哭了起来。自从他说了劳瑞已经不在人世，我心中的劳瑞可怜得令人心碎。她是柯里斯的妈妈啊！怎么会是妓女啊！我说，乔治，你不能这样毁坏柯丽丝的名声。劳瑞不是妓女，她是你的情妇，你是爱她的，是不是？你不是给她买了汽车？你不爱她，为什么接受她的女儿？你说呀！

我好像是被什么东西弹出去似的，一直冲向窗口，拉开了窗帘，想吸一口新鲜的空气。我想把窗打开。可是，一点力气也没有。我一边抽泣，一边喊，乔治，快来帮帮我呀！乔治站起来，打开了一条窗缝。霎那间，狂风像恶魔似的“呜呜”吼着钻进来，他又把窗关上了。

我靠在窗框旁，几乎迈不动自己的腿。从他谈妓院开始，我已经承受不住了，强打精神去劝慰他，说他是个好男人。哪里知道他给我的回复比上妓院还要残酷！劳瑞，柯丽丝的妈妈变成了妓女！我不能也不想再知道他的任何故事。他的过去和我有什么关系？我

been with too many women. I couldn't distinguish who was who, which day they'd come to me. I asked Laura if she could be certain the child was mine, given her history. She said, 'I know it's your child. But if you want to disown it, I'll raise it.' She believed God would help her, and if she gave birth, she'd leave that life behind. The child... is Kristeene."

With those words, he crumbled, tears and mucus streaking his face. His mouth opened wide, as if ready to shout, but no sound emerged, as if choked. He gasped, as if surfacing from deep waters. "George, you're exhausted. Go to bed," I urged.

"I'm already dead. My soul's left my body. Laura, why make me look back? Why not let me go with you? Oh, Laura, Laura..." He cried, his head buried in his hands, repeating her name.

Fear gripped me. I feared he might lose his mind. Yet, he seemed so pitiful, like a lost child unable to find his way home. The strain on his nerves had been too much, the suppression too long. Perhaps unburdening himself was the best way, letting the words flow out rather than fester in the shadows of his mind. But who knew how this tale would unfold?

George was spent. He closed his eyes. I helped him lie down, gently removing his shoes. I sat by him until he slipped into slumber.

Dragging my weary legs back to my compartment, I shut the door and checked on Kristeene. After a few steps, darkness descended. I couldn't see a thing. I floated, weightless, in a void. My outstretched hands grasped for something, but found only emptiness. Finally, I landed on the floor, fingers brushing the carpet. I crawled to the berth, reaching out for Kristeene. She was there. My heart, suspended in worry, found its anchor.

Opening my eyes, I beheld the child's serene face, deep in dreams. A smile graced her lips, lost in some sweet reverie. I leaned against the berth and slipped into sleep.

希望他到此为止，不要再说了。我早该走了。

他好像是一辆坏了刹车的汽车一样，一发而不可收拾。他说，我是在劳瑞告诉我怀孕了以后，才注意上她的。我接触的女人太多了，我分不清她们谁是谁，哪一天和我睡在一起。我问劳瑞，你睡过那么多的男人，能保证是我的孩子吗？她说，我知道是你的孩子，如果你不想认，我也要把孩子生下来。她说，这是上帝在帮助她，生下了孩子，她就不再做风流事了。这个孩子……就是……柯丽丝。说到这里，他崩溃了，涕泪交垂。他的嘴张得很大，好像要喊口号一样，发不出声来。他大口大口地喘气，好像淹水了以后刚刚浮出水面。

乔治，你累了，睡吧！

我已经死了。素素，我的灵魂早就死了。劳瑞，你为什么要让我回头？为什么不让我和你一起走？哦……劳瑞，劳瑞……，他抱头痛哭，一遍又一遍地喊着劳瑞的名字。

一种无名的恐惧开始围绕着我，我害怕了。一方面担心他走火入魔，精神崩溃。另一方面又觉得他可怜，好像一个迷了路的孩子，到现在还没有找到自己的家。他受的刺激太重，太压抑，应该让他说出来。说出来，就让他说给我听吧，总比闷在心里好。但是，我不知道自己能否承受？不知道打开了这个黑匣子，结果将会如何？

乔治已经精疲力竭，双目紧闭。我扶他躺下，帮他脱了鞋，坐在旁边陪着他，直到他沉沉地睡去。

拖着沉重的两条腿回到自己的包厢，关上门，直奔柯丽丝。未走几步，只感到眼睛一黑，什么都看不见了。呵，我怎么变得那么轻？好像飘起来了一样，飘到了邈无人烟的荒野之中，睁眼瞎一样什么也看不见。我伸长了双臂在空中摸索，移来移去，都是一场空。我摸到了毛茸茸的地毯。我顺着地毯往前爬，总算摸到了床架，摸到了毯子，摸到了柯丽丝。这时，悬在半空的心终于落了下来。我睁开眼睛，看到了孩子美丽的脸孔。柯丽丝睡得正甜，脸上露出微笑，好像在做美梦一样。我趴在床边睡着了。

Chapter 21

The next day, George arrived at our compartment after we'd finished breakfast in the dining car above. After our meal, the little one indulged in a long bout of play, darting back and forth in the passageway. With the train racing across a plain, we spotted cows and horses grazing. Together, we sang and tried our hand at mimicking their sounds.

Upon our return to the compartment, George appeared. He still seemed weary, eyes slightly puffy. Otherwise, he seemed his usual self. Upon entering, he scooped up Kristeene, planting a kiss on her cheek. He then gave me a gentle peck on my forehead and greeted me with a warm "good morning."

I mentioned the satisfying breakfast in the dining car and how they offered nearly everything. But he claimed not to have much of an appetite. I suggested, "You look after Kristeene, and I'll grab some food for you." He took my hand, saying, "Wait a moment. Let's go for lunch together."

I fetched some snacks I'd brought along for Kristeene—biscuits and cheese. He nibbled a bit and said, "That's enough for now." After making a quick excuse to step out, I went upstairs to buy him a cup of coffee. He was genuinely grateful when I handed it to him.

The train pressed southward, transitioning from plains to mountains. It frequently dove into tunnels, each one a shroud of darkness. The first time, Kristeene was a bit frightened. So, I wove a tale about Mr. The Sun winking his eyes. I told her, "Close your eyes, Kristeene. What do you see?" She shut them and shook her head. I explained, "We're in the eyes of Mr. The Sun. When he closes them, we can't see anything. That's why we need lights." She nodded, though I wasn't entirely sure she understood. Every time we entered a tunnel, she followed suit, saying, "Close eyes," and obediently shutting them. Then, as the train emerged into sunlight, we'd declare, "Open eyes." The distant mountains were capped with snow, streams flowed at their feet. It was Kristeene's first glimpse of such sights. I found some children's books and pointed out pictures that matched the scenes outside. This way, she learned a slew of new words.

When Kristeene dozed off, George asked me to join him in his compartment. He said, "We need to plan Kristeene's birthday party."

"Of course," I agreed with a smile. "This vacation is all about Kristeene.

第二十一章

第二天，乔治过来的时候，我和柯丽丝已经在楼上餐厅里吃了早饭。吃完饭，小姑娘在长长的走廊上来来回回，疯疯癫癫，玩了好一会儿。火车经过平原的时候，牧场上有牛有马，我们一起唱歌，学牛羊叫。

我们刚刚回到包厢，乔治来了。他面带倦容，眼睛有些肿，其他如常。进门后，他抱起了柯丽丝，亲了又亲。还亲了我的前额，问早安。

我说，楼上的早餐挺好的，什么都有。他说不觉得饿。我说，你看着柯丽丝，我给你去买回来。他拉住了我的手，说再等等，我们一起去吃午餐。

我拿出一些柯丽丝的点心，饼干和干酪片，他吃了几片，说够了。我借口到外面看看，去楼上给他买了杯咖啡，端回来的时候，他非常感激。

火车往南开，穿过了平原，进入了山区。火车时不时钻进山洞，一片漆黑。开始的时候，柯丽丝有点害怕。后来，我给她讲了一个太阳先生眨眼睛的故事。我说，柯丽丝，把眼睛闭起来，你看见了什么？她闭上眼睛以后，左右摇头。我说，我们就在太阳先生的眼睛里头。他闭上眼睛的时候，我们什么都看不见，必须用灯光来代替。她似懂非懂地点点头。到火车进山洞的时候，她跟着我一起说“CLOSE”，并把眼睛闭上。阳光普照的时候，我们说“OPEN”。车厢里有了笑声。远山上覆盖的白雪，山脚下流淌的山泉，柯丽丝都是第一次看见。我把儿童书籍找出来，让图画照片和现境相配，她学会了许多单词。

柯丽丝睡觉的时候，乔治邀请我去隔壁的房间。他说，我们应该讨论一下柯丽丝的生日Party。

好哇。我笑着说，本来就是为了柯丽丝出来度假的，我们得策划出一个漂亮的生日Party。

我们将在星期一上午下车，停在南方的一个城市。星期一就是柯丽丝的生日。所以，星期天的晚上，我们和餐厅联系好，邀请列车上所有五岁以下的小乘客参加柯丽丝的Party。

Let's make sure she has a beautiful celebration."

We were set to disembark on Monday morning, the train stopping in a southern city. And wouldn't you know it, Monday was Kristeene's birthday. Come Sunday evening, we coordinated with the dining car. We invited all the little ones under five on the train to join in her celebration.

Early that Sunday morning, George was up and about. When he opened our door, he found me asleep on the floor. He let out a sigh, berating himself. He apologized profusely, explaining it was his responsibility to lower the upper berth daily, but he'd completely forgotten. I quickly ushered him into the next compartment to avoid waking Kristeene. I assured him that I didn't need a berth and that I was accustomed to sleeping on the floor.

"Sit, Susu. There's something I want to discuss," he said. Wearing a blue-and-white pinstripe shirt, he settled in the sunlight, looking particularly animated.

I sat across from him, but he asked me to sit beside him. So I moved to his side, curious about the weight of his words. He looked at me earnestly and said, "Can you give me your hand? I need to hold it to find the courage to say what's on my mind."

I obliged, a smile playing on my lips. "You're quite serious. What's on your mind?"

"Susu, I've pondered this for a long while. I should've shared it sooner."

"Out with it. I'm all ears."

As I extended my hand, I felt an unusual tension. Instead of clasping it, he lowered his gaze and let my hand rest on his palm. He studied it, as if examining an antique. Then, he gently caressed and kneaded it, as though he could extract courage from my hand. It sent a strange thrill through me, and I began to wonder what this 'courage' entailed. I grew anxious. What would happen if he found it? Should I let him kiss my hand, or pull it back? Just as I felt trapped, he stopped kneading.

He explained, "I didn't initially agree to divorce Anna, so we bickered incessantly. Now, I realize it's best for both of us. It would free her, and it would free me."

He added, "I thought about finding a girlfriend, someone who could be a mother to Kristeene. But now, I don't need any woman. You are Kristeene's mother."

I nodded, saying, "Yes, Kristeene sees me as her mother, and I see her as my child."

"Do I need to find a girlfriend? Aren't you my girlfriend now?"

I feigned composure, but my heart raced. "You employ me. How can I be your girlfriend?"

He looked at me intently and then suddenly grasped my hand tightly. "My dear Susu, do you think I'm too old for you? Will you marry me?"

My heart pounded. How could I marry him? I pulled my hand away

星期天早上，乔治起得较早，来敲门的时候，发现我在地上搭了一个铺，他跺脚垂首，后悔莫及，一而再，再而三地向我道歉。他说，每天把上铺翻上翻下的工作应该是他的责任，居然彻底忘记。我赶快把他拉到隔壁，因为柯丽丝还没有醒来。

我解释说，不需要上铺，我睡地板习惯了。

他说，素素，坐下，我想和你商量一件事。他穿一件蓝白细条的衬衫，坐在射进来的阳光里，显得很有精神。

我坐在他的对面。他要求我坐到他的旁边。我坐到了他的旁边。这时，他看着我说，素素，能把你的手给我吗？我要拉着你的手才有勇气说。

我把手伸给他，笑着说，看你这严肃的样子，有什么重要的事情？

素素，这些话已经想了好久，早就应该告诉你了。

嗯，说吧，我听着呢？

他把我的手托在手心里，双目低垂，好像在鉴赏文物似的看了又看。然后轻柔地抚摸，搓来搓去，好像要把勇气搓出来。我的心就在这来来回回的摩擦中被吊了起来，隐约感到，他所说的勇气究竟意味着什么。我开始担心，一旦他获得了勇气，将是什么结果。让他吻一下我的手背？还是把手抽回来？就在在进退两难的时候，他停止了搓动。

他说，原来我不同意安娜离婚，她总是和我吵。现在看来还是离了好。否则，拖累了她，也拖累了我自己。他说，原来我想寻找一个女朋友，希望柯丽丝有个妈妈。现在我什么女人都不需要，因为你就是柯丽丝的妈妈。

我说，是啊，柯丽丝确实把我当妈妈，我也把她当成自己的孩子。

他说，我还需要找女朋友吗？你不就是我的女朋友吗？

我？是你的女朋友？我装出很镇静的样子，心里像翻江倒海一般。我说，你付我工钱呀！我怎么成了你的女朋友呢？

他两眼直直地盯着我，突然捏紧了我的手，说道，亲爱的素素，你会嫌我太老吗？你是否愿意嫁给我？

他在说什么呀？我怎么可能嫁给他？我用力地把手抽出，起身就走，跑进自己的房间，锁住了门。

柯丽丝已经醒了，不吵不闹，独自在床上玩字母游戏。二十六个字母要按秩序镶进木板，镶对了，游戏机会发出声音。每一个发音，柯丽丝都要重复一边。多么聪明的孩子啊，离两周岁还有几天，就自己学习了起来。我看着她那认真的样子，禁不住扑上去抱住她，一边说，柯丽丝啊，素素有话没人说，你赶快长大呀！

and hurriedly left, locking the door behind me. Back in my compartment, Kristeene was already awake, quietly playing with her alphabet game. I watched her so intently. She was just days away from turning two, yet she was already learning the alphabet on her own. I hugged her tightly, tears streaming down my face. "Oh, Kristeene, Susu has no one to talk to. You must grow up quickly."

She was startled by my outburst and started to cry.

"Don't cry, Kristeene. It's Susu's fault."

She protested, "No, no."

"Alright, alright. Susu won't cry. Susu won't cry."

She reached out her tiny hand to wipe away my tears and then put her finger in her mouth to suck on it. I scolded gently, "You can't suck away tears, Kristeene."

She frowned, looking at me with wide, teary eyes, as if saying, "I'm trying to help you."

I washed her hands and face, assuring her, "Susu's not crying now. Let's smile." I gave her a warm smile.

She smiled back, and I encouraged, "Keep playing, sweetheart. Susu will take a bath." She replied, "A, B, C." I praised her, "Good job with the ABCs. Isn't it fun?" She nodded, fully engrossed in her game.

Stepping under the shower, I let the water wash over me. It felt like a barrage of bullets. I pressed my hands to my head, curling into a small, shivering ball. Memories flooded in, a carousel of men I'd known. Why did they always fall for me, only for things to end in disappointment? My first love, a naive hope for forever, had crumbled. Charlie's love, though deep, was impractical. The same lesson echoed in my mind: "Depend on yourself, not on men."

Hadn't I learned enough?

Now, an American man over fifty, affluent but devoid of love or romance, wanted to marry me for the sake of a motherless girl. Is this what marriages were like in the world?

In truth, my affection was reserved for Kristeene. She had woven herself into the fabric of my life, and I gladly set aside my education for her sake. I had entered George's world solely on account of her. Were it not for Kristeene, I wouldn't have stepped foot in this "castle," nor embarked on this vacation with her father. The hearts that intrigued me belonged to Kristeene, not her father. The idea of being George's wife never once crossed my mind. We knew so little about each other. How much of him did I truly understand? He hadn't even inquired about my relationship with Charlie. Why was that? Couldn't I simply work as a caregiver for Kristeene, much like I was doing now?

With these thoughts, I switched off the shower, quickly dressed, and made my way to George's compartment. The door was still slightly ajar, just as I'd left it. I pushed it open a bit wider and stepped inside. George was gazing out the window, and upon seeing me, he appeared somewhat uneasy. He turned his

我哭了，柯丽丝被我吓着了，也跟着我一起哭。

不要哭，不要哭，柯丽丝，都是素素的错。

她说，NO，NO。

我说，好的，好的，素素不哭，素素不哭。

这时，她把小手伸过来，抹了一把我脸上的泪水，然后把手指放到嘴巴里吮吸。我转悲为嗔，责问道，你怎么能吃眼泪呢？好吃不好吃，柯丽丝？

她皱着眉摇摇头。

我说，不可以吃眼泪。

她睁大了泪眼望着我，好像在说，我想帮助你。

我给她洗了手，擦了脸，对她说，素素不哭了。来，我们笑笑。我给了她一个笑脸。她也笑了。我说，你自己去玩，素素要去洗个澡。她对着我说，A，B，C。我说，对，玩ABC，很好玩，是不是？她点点头，自己玩去了。

打开了水笼头，站在浴池里，眼泪随着浴水流。水珠如密集的子弹，劈头盖脑地射出来，很难抵挡很难招架。我抱着头，蹲下去缩成一团。往事就这样爬上了心头，一个个男人像走马灯一样，围着我转。为什么到最后，总是被男人打上了主意？总是以失望而告终？我想起了自己的初恋，年纪轻轻不知天高地厚地投入一个男人的怀抱，希望他能爱惜我，结果一场空。我想起了查里，对我那么有感情，可是，离现实却是如此遥远。漫长的经历重复着一个简单的道理：不要靠男人，要靠自己。我的教训还不够多吗？

现在，出现了这个五十岁的美国人，家产万贯，和我没有恋爱，没有浪漫，因为一个没有妈妈的女孩，要娶我做太太。天底下哪有这样的婚娶方式？

我确实爱他的女儿柯丽丝，这个孩子已经成了我生命的一部份。为了她，我放弃了学业，放弃得甘心情愿。因为她，我和乔治成为朋友。如果没有柯丽丝，我绝不会进那个城堡，也不会擅自和她的父亲度假旅游。如果没有柯丽丝，我对劳瑞，安娜毫无兴趣，更不会去听乔治那悲惨的过去。我爱的是柯丽丝，不是她的父亲。我从来没有想到要做乔治的太太。对他，我一无所知。同样地，他对我又了解了多少？他甚至都不问一问我和查里的关系。这究竟是为了什么？难道我不能像现在一样，做孩子的保姆？想到这里，我关了水从浴缸里出来，穿好了衣服，去了隔壁。

门半掩着，就是刚才我出去的时候留着的样子，一推就进去了。乔治正对着窗口发呆。看到我进来，显得很不自在。他随即把脸转向窗外，好像是在拒绝我。我摇摇头，笑了笑。这个世界上，只有女人追求他，而他从来没有被拒绝，除了同性恋的安娜。他是

face towards the outside world, as though avoiding conversation.

I shook my head, smiling to myself. Perhaps, in his world, it was always women who pursued him, vying for his attention. He had never faced rejection, except from Anna, the lesbian. He seemed like a lord, the master of his domain. But today, he had met resistance. Had he yet recovered from this rebuff?

Approaching him, I gently touched his shoulder. "George, we lack love. How can we marry? Aren't you concerned a stranger might take your possessions?"

He still paid me no mind, gazing out the window.

"What a beautiful view outside," I remarked, leaning my head nearer his shoulder to peer outside. The scenery rushed by in a blur, making me slightly dizzy, as if I were on a spinning carousel at an amusement park.

"I'm not as perfect as you might imagine," I confessed. "I sleep on the floor, on the carpet in Kristeene's room, because of a back injury from China. I relinquished my education for the sake of a green card. I cherish freedom and have a fondness for my philosophy professor due to differing value systems from yours. George, you know nothing about my family or my past. Why take such a risk?"

He turned to me, his expression stern. His eyes bore into mine, intense and fiery. What would he do? I began to retreat, step by step.

He spoke, his voice resolute. "We've always loved each other. You're afraid to face it, to acknowledge it. Sometimes I even find myself in doubt. It wasn't until last night that I realized I can't imagine a life without you. Susu, I can't fathom ever being happy without you by my side. And I finally understand that I've lived in Laura's shadow for far too long. I despised myself for being unable to bring her back. Were it not for Kristeene, I'd have longed to join her in the heavens. But last night, after unburdening myself, I bid farewell to my past. Susu, I've discovered that I can face the future with hope, because of you."

I was stunned.

He stood up, as if delivering a speech. "You believe in freedom and equality. I hold the same convictions. Yet you've felt small in the face of my social status and wealth. You see this 'castle,' this emblem of prestige, and you withdraw to the sidelines. Unconsciously, you let material things create distance between us. But you forget, at our core, we're all equal. If I were an ordinary person, and we both loved the same child, would you still reject me?

He held his head high, exuding confidence, using expressive gestures to underscore his words. "Susu, it is I who believes in equality. That's why I loved Laura, even with her occupation. It is George Dickson who believes in equality. So he loves Susu. My dear, I don't need to know your past or your family background because what I love is you, the present you." As he spoke, he drew closer, step by step. "Susu, don't you truly love me? A towel, a cup of coffee.

大亨，上天入地，指点江山，易如弹灰一般。可是，今天失败了。他还没有想通呢！

我走过去，推了推他的肩膀，说道，乔治，我们没有恋爱，如何谈婚约？你不怕自己的家产被一个陌生的女人卷走？

他仍旧不理我，眼睛看着外面。

有什么好风景呵？我问道，凑到他的背面往窗口看，只见景物在飞快地后退，令人眼晕目旋，好像骑上了游乐场的电马一般。

我说，我没有你想像的那么好。我睡地板，睡在柯丽丝房间的地毯上，是因为我的背曾经在中国受过伤，不能睡软床。我放弃学位来照顾柯丽丝是为了得到绿卡。我支持美国的自由派，欣赏我的哲学教授，和你的价值观念不一样。乔治，你对我的家庭，我的过去一点都不了解，为什么要冒这个险？

这时，他转过脸来，神色非常凝重地看着我，一直看着我，目光如炬。哎哟，他要干什么呀？我开始一步步往后退。

他说，我们一直在恋爱，你不敢面对，不敢承认。连我自己，也是时而清楚时而糊涂。到了昨天晚上，我才发现，自己已经离不开你。素素，我不能想像，在我的生活中，没有你，我能快乐得起来？我原来一直活在劳瑞的影子底下，我恨自己不能让她起死回生，要不是为了柯丽丝，我早想到天堂里去和她相会。但是，昨天晚上，当我把心中的积郁都吐出来以后，我和过去作了了结。素素，我发现这个重新开始的希望是因为有了你。

我目瞪口呆。他站了起来，严肃得像在作演讲一般。他说，你相信自由平等，我和你的信仰相同。但是，在我的地位和财产面前，你自觉矮了一截。你看到那个城堡，看到那些地位显赫的名流，便退到了墙角边。你不知不觉地让物质拉开我们的距离，而忘记了我们之间本质上的平等人格。如果我是一个普通人，我们爱着同样一个孩子，你会不会这样拒绝我？

他的下巴翘得高高的，气宇盎然的样子，一边说一边挥动手势。

素素，相信平等的是我，所以，我爱劳瑞，尽管她是一个风尘女子。相信平等的是乔治·笛克荪，所以他爱素素。亲爱的，我不需要知道你的过去，不需要了解你的家庭和背景，因为我爱的是你，一个现在的你。

他一边讲，一边走，一步一步逼近我。

素素，你难道不爱我吗？一块毛巾，一杯咖啡，我的喜怒哀乐都影响着你的情绪。你不期待我说甜言蜜语，是因为你知道我多么看重你，重到不需要用言语来表达。你看不到死去活来的爱情，但是，问问你自己，如果几天不见我，你会不会着急？你对查里有这

My happiness, my anger, and my sorrow all influence your feelings. You don't expect sweet words because you know how much you mean to me, and there's no need to express it in words. You may not have witnessed a life-and-death kind of love, but ask yourself, if you don't see me for a few days, will you be worried? Do you feel this way about Charlie? And consider this, if another woman comes between us, will you be concerned? That's why I didn't allow Nancy to stay overnight in our home. She could see that you hold a greater place in my heart than she does."

I had retreated to the door. One push would set me free, closing him inside. But he stopped, standing right in front of me, tears glistening in his eyes.

"Susu, admitting my love for you isn't easy for me. If you think it's only because of your youth and beauty, that's not entirely true. I love you so profoundly that it becomes irresistible, like the very air I breathe."

He repeated it, and I heard every word clearly. This American man always managed to stir sympathy and a sense of sorrow within me. I understood him. He had everything, yet he needed me to make his life complete. But was this the kind of love I longed for?

"George, don't say any more," I murmured, my gaze fixed on the last button of his shirt, which hung loosely. I plucked it free and slipped it into my pocket. "I'll sew it back on when we're back home."

As I looked up to speak, George encircled me in his arms. He stood there, still as a statue, as though waiting for my response. All I could hear was the rhythm of his heart. He simply wanted me to feel his heartbeat, to be aware of his living, breathing presence. This was why he held me so tightly.

He gently tilted my chin upward, causing my eyes to flutter half-shut. "Susu, since you believe in freedom and equality, should I seek your consent before I kiss you?" I pondered for a moment and smiled, eyes still closed. "I never rely on love, as it's an outcome of education. So, I must give it careful thought." He chuckled and released me. I had managed to escape him so effortlessly. I couldn't help but feel surprised.

We moved on to the next compartment, putting the recent exchange out of our minds. This was the George I knew. His maturity wasn't just evident in his self-control, but also in his ability to influence others. I'd suspected this before, but it was crystal clear to me now. When I'd contemplated resigning, he hadn't pleaded with me to stay. Instead, I'd altered my decision independently, remaining here until now. When I'd forsaken my education, he hadn't asked me to do so. Still, I chose to, to his satisfaction, without a single complaint, as if I were running on the tracks he'd laid out. He must have honed this skill over the years in business. But he possessed a knack beyond other businessmen—a proficiency in touching people's hearts. This time, I'd resisted his advances, turned down his kiss. But I wasn't certain if I'd continue to follow his lead. He claimed his love for me was irresistible. Could I truly resist him?

种感觉吗？再问问你自己，如果有一个女人闯进我们之间，你会不会担心？素素，这就是我不愿意让南西在我们家过夜的原因。她都看得出来，你在我的心目中，份量比她重。

我已经退到了门框旁边，只要一拉门，我就能从这里逃出去，把他关在里面。

就在这时，他停了下来，直挺挺的站在我的面前，眼睛里饱含泪水。

素素，承认自己爱上了你，对我来说，不是一件容易的事情。如果你以为是你的年纪和容貌打动了我，那是不完整的。我爱你，爱得无法抗拒，好像不呼吸就活不下去一样。

他说得断断续续，但是，我还是听清楚了。这个美国人总是让我心软心碎。我能理解他。他什么都有了，只需要和我相依为命。但是，这就是我期待的爱情吗？

乔治，不要再说了。我低下头去，正巧看到他衬衫最下面的一粒钮釦松动了。我干脆把它扯了下来，放进了口袋，说道，回家我给你缝上。

就在我抬头说这句话的时候，乔治一把搂我在怀里。他一动不动，好像在等待我的回答。耳旁没有了他的话音，却听到他的心"咚，咚，咚，咚"地跳跃，他就是为了让我体会他的心跳，感受他那有血有肉的躯体，才把我搂得那么紧。

他弯下腰来，托住了我的脸。因为太接近，我几乎睁不开眼睛。他问道，信仰自由平等的素素，吻你一下是否要征得同意？我想了想，闭着眼睛笑了笑，说道，教育出来的爱情不算数，我要考虑考虑。他大笑，真的放开了我。这么容易就摆脱了他，我不禁暗自吃惊。

我们就这样来到了隔壁，把刚才的一切都丢到了脑后。这就是我认识的乔治。他的成熟，不仅在于控制自己，更在于把握对方。对于这一点，以前我稍有察觉，但是，还没有看得像今天这样清楚。

我很清楚地记得，在我要求辞去工作的时候，他没有来求我，结果是我自己改变了主意，主动要求留下来的。在我放弃学业的时候，他也没有要求我，是我自己最终进入了最符合他理想的轨道，而且毫无怨言。他的敏锐也许是在做生意时培养出来的，但是，他能攻心，却不是一般生意人的水平。这一回，我拒绝了他的求婚，拒绝了他的接吻，但是，我不知道是否早晚要进入了他的轨道？他说，他爱我爱得不可抗拒。我抗拒得了他吗？

Chapter 22

The three of us had lunch together, but both George and I were lost in thought. At the table, George and Kristeene chatted and laughed loudly, completely abandoning his earlier demeanor of a gentleman. After lunch, Kristeene and I played hide-and-seek in the passageway, running and giggling until we returned to our compartment. George avoided looking at me, and I, in turn, focused all my attention on Kristeene.

Yet, in truth, we were both watching each other stealthily, as if we had grown a third eye. His third eye was on my side, like a sharp needle aimed at my heart. My third eye lingered behind him. I thought he couldn't see it, but he sensed it. It felt uncomfortable. I finally realized that hidden feelings couldn't truly stay hidden.

After playing for a while, Kristeene went to nap, and George moved to the next compartment. I let out a sigh of relief and sank into a chair, feeling utterly drained. I wanted to take a nap too. Closing my eyes, I began to count in my mind: 1, 2, 3, 4. Before I reached 10, I slipped into a reverie again. So I started counting once more: 1, 2, 3, 4. I drifted into daydreams again before I could reach 10. I repeated this several times but couldn't fall asleep. So, I picked up a newspaper to read. Strangely, not a single word registered in my mind. Instead, it was filled with question marks, and nothing else could penetrate.

Why didn't he ask me to join him in the next compartment? Why did the words on the newspaper seem to echo his voice? Why did George's tall figure appear in the photo when I looked at it? Could such things happen between human beings? Did I really love him?

Doubt crept into my mind. Initially, I believed my relationship with George was distant, but suddenly I realized we had become dependent on each other. At first, I thought my relationship with Charlie was close, but later I discovered we both held some reservations in our hearts. What was love, really?

I couldn't deny that I had feelings for George, but he was my employer

第二十二章

三人一起去吃了午餐，我和乔治都心不在焉。他和柯丽丝在饭桌上大声说笑，完全丢掉了昔日的绅士风度。吃完饭，我在走廊上和柯丽丝捉迷藏，东奔西跑，玩得气喘吁吁。回到包厢。乔治不看我，我也不看他，所有的注意力都集中在柯丽丝身上。但是，实际上，谁都没有放松对另一方的观察。我们好像都长出了第三只眼睛，他的眼睛在我的侧面，像长针一般对准我的心口。我的眼睛躲在他的背后，以为他看不见，却被他识破。这种难堪，让我真正地见识了一回什么叫“心中有鬼”。

柯丽丝玩了一会儿，要睡午觉了。乔治去了隔壁。啊，我终于松了一口气，倒在椅子上像瘫痪了一样。好累啊，也应该睡一个午觉了。我抱着椅背闭上了眼睛，心里数着1,2,3,4,不料，思想开了小差，重来。1,2,3,4,一遍又一遍，数不到10，又溜了号。睡不着，看报纸吧！奇怪，一个字都进不了脑袋。脑袋里除了问号，什么也装不进去。

为什么？，为什么？他没有拉我一起去隔壁？为什么？为什么？念着报纸上的文字，文字变成了他的声音？为什么？为什么？看着报纸上的照片，照片里出现了乔治高大的身影？人与人之间原来可以如此接近，难道我真的爱上了他？

我开始怀疑自己的判断。原来以为查里和自己很近，后来却发现在内心，我们守护着各自的领地。原来以为乔治离自己很远，突然间，发现我们相依为命。爱情究竟是个什么东西？

对于乔治，不能说我对他没有感情，但是，他是我的老板，我是他的雇工，他是美国人，富人，我是中国人，穷学生，他的人生和我的是那么地不同，连他吃的饭，用的餐具都和我不一样。在我的心里，他一直在一个可望而不可及的地方。可是，现在，那些距离好像都不存在了，那些不同都变得无足轻重。乔治好像成了

and I was his employee. He was a wealthy American, and I was a struggling Chinese student. There was a vast gulf between our lives. In my heart, he was somewhere I could see but not touch. But now, all those differences seemed inconsequential. George felt like my shadow, omnipresent. It was all because he had said those words, as if an oracle had traversed countless mountains and rivers to reach me. He had said, "We love each other."

Could love truly hold such power? He was right when he said that whatever he did or said affected my emotions. I'd never regarded any other man as important as him. Yes, I felt jealous of Nancy, always hoping there would be no other women between us. This must be love! Love transcends differences in age, skin color, status, money, and even nationality, leaving two "naked" human beings, nothing but equals. This is an absolute love, unlike any I'd known before. I had always associated love with physical touch and romantic emotional exchanges, never with day-to-day coexistence. George was different. We were like two laborers building a house from the ground up, stacking bricks one by one, unaware of the end result. But one day, we both suddenly realized we had constructed a home and could live safely within it, sheltered from rain and wind. Love like this is more stable and enduring, isn't it?

I stood up and looked at little sleeping Kristeene. I whispered to myself, "Sweetheart, do you know? You don't need to worry about who will be your new mom. Susu will be your mom." I began to walk to the door, but after a couple of steps, I turned back. Why did he leave me here? Was he giving me time to think? Did he believe I was a woman who hesitated in love? Or was he playing a love game with me? Why did he avoid me during lunch? Was he treating me as something unimportant for some reason? Was he still angry with me? Was he so sure that Susu loved him? Or was he just too nervous and afraid I would reject him? I imagined that beyond the compartment wall, everything was the same as here—his presence made that compartment as attractive as a magnet. What was he doing right now? Was he sleeping? Was he having a drink? Or was he feeling just as restless as me?

Why was I thinking like this? We didn't need to evade each other. George had said, "I love you to such a degree that it is irresistible." I should tell him that I loved him too. Why did I lack the courage?

I went to the next compartment. "Come in," he called when he heard the knock on the door.

"Kristeene's taking a nap, so I popped in for a quick check," I mentioned.

He looked up from his newspapers, unfazed, as if nothing out of the ordinary had happened earlier.

Tonight was all about Kristeene's birthday bash. We'd already gathered

我的影子一样，无时无处不在。因为，就是因为他说了一句话，这句话像纤语一样，穿透了间隔在我们之间的千山万水。他说：我们相爱。爱情真有这么大的力量吗？他说得一点不错。他的一举一动都影响着我的情绪。我还从来没有把任何一个男人看得如此重要。是的，我妒忌南西，不希望我们之间出现任何女人。原来这就是爱情！爱情可以把年龄、肤色、地位、钱财，甚至国籍都像秋天的树林一样剥得精光，只剩下赤裸裸的两个人，想不平等也不行。这是一种多么不一样的爱情啊！以前我理解的爱情都是介入了肌肤的接触和性的愉悦，都是浪漫无比的情感交流，但没有脚踏实地的共同生活。和乔治恰恰相反，我们是从脚下开始，好像两个建筑工人，当我们把一块块砖头砌上去的时候，并不知道它的结果。但是，突然有一天，我们不约而同地发现，原来造成了一栋房子，可以安全地住在里面，挡风避雨。这样的爱情是不是更牢固更经得起考验？

我站起身，看了看熟睡的柯丽丝，心里说，小宝贝，你知道吗？你不用担心别人做你的妈妈，素素要做你的妈妈啦！我朝门外走，刚走了几步，又退了回来。他为什么要留我在这里？是为了给我考虑的余地？还是把我看成了欲爱还休的女人？他不会在和我玩感情的游戏？刚才吃饭的时候，他为什么故意回避我？是他在生我的气？是他真的那么自信，认定素素会爱他？还是心里紧张得要命，怕遭到我的拒绝？我想像着墙那一边，和这里一模一样的空间和摆设，因为一个男人的存在，使得那房间有了那么大的吸引力。他在干什么？在呼呼大睡？在喝酒浇愁？还是和我一样坐立不安？

哎，我这又是为什么呢？我们没有必要互相躲避，乔治说，爱你爱得不可抗拒。我应该告诉他，素素也爱你！我难道连这点勇气也没有吗？

我去了隔壁。

听见敲门，他说了声“进来”。

我说，柯丽丝睡着了，来这里看看你。

什么事？他在看报纸，若无其事的样子。

哎哟，他的神经为什么还是绷得那么紧？今天晚上就是柯丽丝的生日Party，我们已经买了许多的礼物，比如糖果，玩具，书本和背心，帽子等等，准备送给来参加Party的孩子们。我还设计了一个摸彩游戏，谁得了奖，得一个金色的巧克力糖果盒，里面有二十元的现金，一元五元十元的面值，都是崭新的钞票。

up a bunch of goodies—candies, toys, books, clothes, and hats—all set to be handed out to the kids. I cooked up a game where they could pick a prize. The kid who scored it would walk away with a golden box of chocolates, twenty bucks in cash—a ten, a five, and five ones, all crisp and clean.

"What's the deal? For tonight's event," I grinned, "George, you up for giving a speech?"

He asked, "A speech?"

"The one for Kristeene's party. You can talk in front of a crowd, right?"

A sly smile tugged at his lips, showing he got my teasing. "Depends on the scene and the crowd. But tonight, you should do it. You're her mom, after all."

I let out a chuckle. "You're joking. We're not married yet."

"Not married yet? Does it matter? They won't know."

I said, "Alright, alright. No speeches. Let's sing. You pick a song, deal?"

He said, "If I'm singing, it's gonna be a love song."

I couldn't help but laugh. "What's gotten into you? You've turned into a whole different person."

He held out a finger and drew a circle in the air. "That's right. You'll have to be more careful in the future."

"I swear, I've seen you act like this before," I racked my brain, finally recalling it. "It was at that Chinese restaurant. You were playful."

He beamed. "They thought we were a couple, right?"

I said, "So, in that Chinese place, you were already hoping we were an item? How come I didn't sense any of that back then?"

"Didn't you think we looked like a real family there? Remember when I held your hand? What did I say then?"

I looked at him without answering. Of course, I remembered. It was his words that made me think of my homeland.

"You don't remember, do you?" He said, "You didn't take me seriously."

I avoided his gaze, stammering, "How could I forget? You said, 'Susu, my home is your home.'"

"Ah," He said, thrilled, "You really didn't forget. You thought I was just joking, didn't you?"

"No. I believe you meant it because you're Kristeene's dad and I'm like her mom. We really are like a family."

"Like a family?" He emphasized 'like'. "We actually are a family, aren't we?"

"No, no. I don't see it that way. We're under the same roof because of Kristeene. We truly rely on each other."

"Rely on each other," He echoed. "Nice choice of words. We rely on each

什么事？他问。

晚上的事情啊！我笑着说，乔治，晚上你有什么演讲吗？

他说，什么演讲？

柯丽丝生日Party的演讲呵，你不是很会讲吗？

他用嘴角笑了笑，表示领会了我的讽刺，说道，那也要看时间地点和听讲对像的。今天晚上应该你讲，你是她的妈妈，比爸爸更合适。

我“扑嗤”一笑，说道，别开玩笑了，我们还不是夫妻。

不是夫妻？他说，有什么关系？乘客哪里知道？

我说，好了，好了，那就不要演讲了，唱个歌吧！你唱歌，好吗？

他说，要我唱，就唱情歌。

我捧着肚子，笑弯了腰，说道，你怎么啦？好像变成了另外一个人。

他伸出一个手指，往空中绕了一圈，说道，是呵，你要小心一点。

我说，好像在什么地方看到你这付模样的。是在……哪里呢？我冥思苦想，终于想起来了。

我说，在中国餐馆里，你就是这么调皮的。

他喜形于色地说，他们把我们当夫妻了，是不是？

我说，原来在中国餐馆里，你就希望我们是夫妻？我怎么一点没有感觉呢？

他说，难道你不觉得我们是名符其实的一家人？记得我拉着你的手，说了什么话？

我朝他看看，没有回答。我当然记得。因为他的那句话，勾引出我绵绵的思乡之情。

你不记得了吧！他说，你当时就没有把我的话当回事。

我避开他的目光，不好意思地说，怎么不记得？你说，素素，我的家就是你的家。

啊，他得意地说，真的没有忘记。你以为我是说着玩的，是不是？

不，我相信你是真心的，因为你是柯丽丝的父亲，我像柯丽丝的妈妈。我们确实像一家人。

像一家人？他把“像”字的发音拉得很长。他说，实际上，我

other."

I said, "That's a down-to-earth, day-to-day kind of love."

"Oh," He mused, "Does such love exist in this world?"

I nodded. "Yes. We love. It's no cakewalk. This kind of love shines in the little things, in everyday moments."

"Not an easy love?" He repeated, his expression somber. "Yeah. Love's no walk in the park. Let me tell you my last tale."

I grinned and asked, "Another story?"

"Do you want to know why Laura committed suicide?"

I slipped from the chair, my knees grazing the floor, my upper body resting on his legs. "I can't bear to hear it. I can't." I shouted, clutching his clothes and burying my head against him.

Then, silence enveloped us, broken only by his rapid breaths. I couldn't bear for him to bring up Laura again. No, I couldn't let him unravel like that.

I settled on the floor, holding onto his knees, pleading with him, "George, let's forget the past. I love you. Let's start anew, alright?"

He didn't respond. He always withdrew into silence when pain gripped him. How could I help him? Just then, he ran both hands through my hair, from the crown of my head to the nape of my neck. Up and down, over and over. He massaged me, tracing each vertebra down my spine.

With concern, he asked, "Where does it hurt on your back? Are you feeling better now?"

"Um, thank you." My eyes grew moist.

"I'm here for you. You won't suffer any more. No one will harm you again."

I wept, my sobs wracking my body, still on his knees. It was as if I were a lost child who'd finally found a home after wandering in loneliness for so long, with no one to provide warmth or support. There had been a hollow space in my heart, sensitive to touch, but now it was suddenly filled. The tears, held back for months, surged like a released floodgate. I wept and wept until my heart was content.

He observed me with a profound emotion. His hand gently grazed my face, wiping away my tears, but he said nothing in consolation.

"Why did Laura commit suicide? Was it because of you? Or because of the child?" I asked softly, my voice close to a murmur.

He said, "It was because of me."

I raised my face to meet his gaze, his eyes fixed ahead, as if lost in a void, devoid of tears but brimming with sorrow.

Even now, I struggle to put into words the depth of George's grief and remorse over losing Laura. In truth, the tale was rather straightforward. Laura's

们已经成为一家人，不是吗？

没有，没有。我没有那么想。因为柯丽丝，我们生活在一起。我们确实相依为命。

相依为命。他重复道，说得好，我们相依为命。

我说，那一种很实在的，天天存在的爱。

噢，他说，世界上原来还有这样的爱？

我点点头说，是的，我们相爱，爱得不容易。这种爱都表现在一些非常琐碎的小事情上。

爱得不容易。他重复道，脸色一下子变得严肃起来。是呵，爱情不是一件容易的事情。让我告诉你最后一个故事。

我笑盈盈地说，还有什么故事？

他说：想知道劳瑞为什么自杀吗？

天！我从椅子上滑下来，膝盖落地，上身倒在他的大腿上。不要听，不要听！我抓住了他的衣服，用头去撞他的身体，大声喊起来。

顿时肃静，静得能听见他急促的的呼吸声。不能让他再提劳瑞了，不能，不能！不能让他再一次崩溃。我坐在地上，抱着他的膝盖，苦苦地哀求他，乔治，把过去都忘掉了吧！素素爱你的呀！让我们重新开始，好不好？

没有答话。最痛苦的时候，他总是一言不发。我应该如何帮助他？就在这时，他把双手插进了我的头发，从头顶到后颈，上上下下地移动。他一遍又一遍地为我按摩，按摩了头部再按摩我的后背，他的双手，沿着我的瘠椎骨一节一节地往下走。

他关切地问，背上的伤在哪里？这样好受些吗？

嗯，谢谢你。我的眼睛一下子潮湿了。

他说，有我在，不会再受伤了。没有人敢欺负你。

我哭了，趴在他的腿上拼命地痛哭。好像一个流浪的孩子孤零零地四处寻找，没有温暖没有依靠，突然发现家已经到了。好像心里有一个空洞，一碰就要痛，突然间被填满了。积蓄了几个月的眼泪，此刻像开了闸门似的，统统放了出来。我哭呵，哭呵，哭得真痛快。

他深情地望着我，抚摸我的脸，擦去我的眼泪。一句劝慰的话都没有。

哭够了，我才想起了他要说的故事。我轻轻地问他，劳瑞为什

social standing couldn't align with his. He'd been hesitant to wed her, preferring to keep Anna as his public wife, while sharing his days with Laura in that apartment building. It marked the first time George had shared his intimate life daily with a woman he adored. He'd been content then, especially when Laura became pregnant. Yet, he could never decide whether Laura should be his wife or mistress. He couldn't offer her a definitive answer. Initially, Laura insisted that even if he disavowed the child, she'd raise it on her own. However, as their love deepened, Laura yearned for more than being a hidden lover; she wanted to be his wife. Additionally, she knew Anna was a lesbian. George and Anna's marriage was but a facade. Still, George couldn't acquiesce to Laura's desire for marriage. He sought to protect his reputation on two fronts: he didn't want others discovering Anna's sexual orientation or that Laura worked as a prostitute. Consequently, after giving birth to the child, Laura overdosed on sleeping pills, ending her own life. From the day he met her to her tragic passing, less than a year had transpired. He concluded, "She left just like that, leaving behind a new life for me." It had been the longest year of his life, etched into his memory every day.

I offered, "Laura might have experienced postpartum depression. I've read about such things in books."

He replied, "Susu, don't absolve me of blame. If I'd married Laura, none of this would have happened."

I fell into a prolonged silence, struggling to find the right response.

The train rolled into the station, a bustling hub with throngs of people scurrying about.

My thoughts turned to Laura. She had been frail in the face of life's challenges, yet remarkably steadfast in love. Beneath it all, she possessed an audacious spirit. Laura was undoubtedly a fearless woman. Then my mind shifted to Anna. She, too, was a woman of courage, though more pragmatic than Laura. Taking one's own life is not arduous. What's truly challenging is to persist in living, regardless of circumstances, without stumbling or falling flat. In times past, lesbianism and cohabitation without marriage went against prevailing moral norms. Yet, those who persisted in such relationships have gained a measure of acceptance. Anna's determination to uphold her beliefs in life was no small feat.

Laura could have found happiness if she'd persevered until now. Her passing hadn't been in vain; she'd saved George at the cost of her own life. How else could he confess his love for a Chinese student of modest means and court her so ardently? I recalled his words about conquering oneself, a lesson or experience he must have cherished deeply. If I claimed he criticized our

么要自杀？是因为你吗，还是为了孩子？

他说，是我，是我害了她。

我抬起头来，看见他的眼睛干干的，空如枯井，没有一滴眼泪，满脸的悲哀。难以用文字来形容乔治对于失去劳瑞的悲痛和悔恨。其实故事很简单。

劳瑞的身份和他不配，他一直不愿意和劳瑞结婚。也就是说，明处，他的太太是安娜，暗处，他和劳瑞生活在一起，住在那个公寓里。那是乔治第一次和自己有感情的女人过性生活，每天朝夕相处，确实很幸福，而且劳瑞怀上了他的孩子。但是，在情人和太太之间，他始终不能给劳瑞肯定的答复。开始的时候，劳瑞说，哪怕他不认这个孩子，也将抚养孩子长大。但是，两个人情甜意蜜以后，劳瑞便不满足于偷偷摸摸地当情人，希望成为他的太太。何况，安娜是个同性恋女子，他们的婚姻本来名存实亡。但是，乔治没有答应他。他想保两个面子，一个是安娜同性恋的面子，一个是劳瑞风尘女子的面子。结果，劳瑞在孩子出生以后，服安眠药自杀了。

从认识劳瑞到她去世，加起来不到一年。这一年是他一生中最长的一年，每一天都留在记忆里。他说，她就这样走了，留给了我一条新的生命。

我说，劳瑞可能得了产后忧郁怔，我看过这样的书。

他说，素素，不要为我开脱，如果我和劳瑞结了婚，一切都不会发生。

我沉默了好久，想不出合适的话来回答他。

火车进站了，好像是一个大站，月台上有很多人，有的上，有的下，来去匆匆。我想着劳瑞，在为生存折腰的时候，她是那样柔软，而在爱情面前，却是那么刚烈。这一柔一刚的背后，是敢作敢为的性情。劳瑞真是一个无畏的女人。我想到了安娜，也是敢作敢为，却比劳瑞 来得现实。人要结束自己，其实并不很难，难的是为自己活，而不被别人绊倒。同性恋和非婚同居，在过去是那么大逆不道，但是，因为每一个个人的坚持，今天，多少得到了社会的承认。安娜坚持了下来，多么不容易呵！劳瑞如果能够坚持到今天，就是一个幸福的女人。但是，劳瑞并没有白死，她以生命拯救了乔治。否则，今天乔治怎么可能承认自己爱上了一个中国的穷学生，并且不顾一切地向她求婚？我想起了他在评价我的哲学教授

philosophy professor, it would be more accurate to say he criticized himself. George had paid a steep price to master his inner struggles.

I reminisced about the moments we'd shared. I'd sat alone in the garden outside the kitchen before Nancy arrived. He'd returned home early to lend me his support. He'd said, "Susu, you seem burdened." So, as soon as Nancy appeared, he ushered her into the kitchen to see me. I remembered how he hadn't initially agreed to my attending the party at the philosophy professor's home. But upon reading my article, he'd allowed me to go even earlier than planned, relieved by my achievement. He'd observed Charlie and me, concluding that our connection had likely been a youthful whim or an immature affection. Otherwise, why would he have agreed to help with my green card application?

I'd spent all this time nestled between George's knees, pouring out my thoughts. I said, "You've faced a tough internal struggle, no matter the cost. You sought to affirm your feelings, hence the recounting of the past."

George responded, "I witnessed it all unfolding unconsciously. Perhaps, it's divine guidance leading my steps. Susu, you're the most astute woman I've ever encountered. The first day I glimpsed you in my bedroom, crouched there playing with Kristeene, I sensed you were extraordinary. At the party when you gifted me that red scarf, I realized how meticulously you consider everything. You play the piano beautifully. You swiftly aced the driver's license tests. Your writing is both witty and well-crafted. Your culinary skills excel in both Chinese and American fare. You hold Kristeene dear. Oh, my dear Susu, how could I not fall in love with you? Countless times, when you drew near, I yearned to embrace you, to kiss you. That night when I clashed with Nancy, I longed to ascend the stairs, knock on your door, and lay bare my feelings. But I hesitated. You're so young, so lovely. You could find a man better suited than me. Susu, the more I love you, the more I cherish you. It's because I hold you in such high regard that I'm resolved to prove myself worthy of your love."

My heart melted. I'd often heard that love was noble, but now I grasped that its nobility didn't spring from birthright or social status. On the contrary, it emanated from humility, from modesty. Suddenly, an urge surged within me to hold him, to give myself wholly to him, to meld into him. We were akin to two opposing magnets irresistibly drawn together. His tears fell onto my face, warm and gentle, trickling down one by one.

时说的话：人要有勇气战胜自己。这大概就是他一生的教训和经验吧！与其说他在批评哲学教授，不如说他在批评自己。对于乔治来说，为战胜自己，付出了多么昂贵的代价啊！

我回想着过去发生在我们之间的许多事情。记得南西要来之前，我独自坐在厨房外面的花园里。他提早回来帮助我。他说，素素，你好像有心事。所以，南西一到，他马上引她进厨房，和我见面。记得去参加哲学教授的Party前，他不同意我去。但是，在看了我的文章以后，让我提前走。因为他对教授放心了。他一直在仔细观察查里和我的关系，知道我们之间充其量是年轻人的激情而不是成熟的爱情，否则，为什么需要他来为我申请绿卡？

我一直偎在乔治的两腿之间，滔滔不绝地讲我的感觉。我说，尽管如此，你还是经过了一番内心的挣扎。你要证实你的感情，所以，把过去的事情都倒了出来。

乔治说，一切都是在不知不觉中进行的，也许是上帝在指导着我。素素，你是我一生中遇到的最聪明的女人。第一天见到你，在我的房间里，见你蹲在地上向柯丽丝发口令，就觉得你不同寻常；Party上，你献给我那条红绸带，想得那样细致入微；你恰如其分恰到好处地弹钢琴；你迅速地考出了驾驶执照；你的文章幽默清新；你做的菜可口美味，不论是中国菜还是美国菜；你深爱着柯丽丝，……亲爱的素素，我怎么可能不迷上你？

他换了一口气，继续说，不知道有多少次，在你靠近我的时候，我想拥抱你，想亲亲你。和南西吵架的那个夜晚，我想到楼上来敲你的门，想把自己的感觉告诉你。但是，我有顾虑呵，你那么年轻，那么漂亮，可以找到比我更好的男人。素素，越爱你，我越珍惜你。也正因为这一点，我一定很努力很努力，来证明我值得你爱。

我的心就这样被溶化了。都说爱情是高尚的，直到今天我才懂得这份高尚并非来自高贵，恰恰相反，高尚的底蕴是歉卑。我突然有一种冲动，想贴近他，把自己献给他，想和他合为一体。我们就像南北两极的磁铁，牢牢地吸在一起。他的眼泪滴到了我的脸上，烫烫的，缓缓地往下滑，一滴接着一滴，……。

Chapter 23

Kristeene awoke from her nap. I busied myself, adorning her in a pink dress, a bow adorning her hair, and a pair of soft leather shoes. A touch of rouge on her cheeks and a light-colored lipstick completed her look. She grew more beautiful with each passing day. Her big eyes blinked, as if contemplating weighty questions in her studies. Her long lashes fluttered rapidly, and her tiny mouth babbled with enthusiasm. She grew bolder, wanting to explore and try everything. My affection for her deepened; we shared a special bond.

George donned a striking red shirt and dark blue pants. I wondered why he chose such eye-catching attire. Perhaps he feared people might forget he was Kristeene's father. What should I wear? George remarked, "That dress you wore on my birthday was stunning." I inquired, "The cream-colored backless one?" He nodded, saying, "It perfectly complements your vivacity." I clarified, "I didn't wear it for your birthday. I didn't even know it was your birthday. I wore it boldly because I was feeling envious of Lisa, who had reconciled with her boyfriend."

Truthfully, I wasn't fond of that dress. It wasn't the provocative style; rather, it had become a symbol of loneliness and disappointment in my life. But to George, it had left a lasting impression, that of a daring Susu in a cream-colored, alluring dress that immediately caught his attention. And so, I chose to wear it once more.

George suggested, "Once we step off the train, let's find some even sexier clothes. You're the most beautiful woman in the world."

I stole a glance at him. He was positively beaming.

The party was hosted at one end of the dining car. There weren't many children under five, just a little over ten. Some were still infants cradled in their parents' arms. However, parents, older children, and other passengers gathered to watch. Vibrant helium balloons bobbed behind the chairs, and paper plates and plastic cups, each bearing the words "Happy Birthday," were set before every seat at the long table. At its center stood a specially crafted birthday cake. Perched atop the cake was a plastic doll in a white dress, forming the creamy peak of the three-tiered confection adorned with green leaves and red roses. It was a thoughtful touch. All of this had been brought onto the train after George coordinated with the head of the train crew during its last stop.

第二十三章

柯丽丝午睡醒来以后，我就忙着打扮她。粉红色的连衣裙，蝴蝶结和软皮鞋。在她的脸上抹了点胭脂，点了淡淡的唇膏。这个孩子真是越长越漂亮，大眼睛一眨一眨，好像总是在学习在思考。长长的眼睫毛，一闪一个笑。小嘴唠唠叨叨没个停，胆子也越来越大，什么东西都想碰一碰，试一试。

乔治穿了一件大红的水洗绸衬衫，下面是藏青的西裤。不知道他为什么要穿得那么引人注目，好像害怕别人忘了他是孩子的父亲一样。我穿什么衣服好？乔治说，过生日时你穿的衣服挺好看。我说，那件露背的米色连衣裙？他点点头，说，很有灵气。我说，你还记得。当时才不是因为你的生日才穿这件衣服的。我根本不知道你要过生日，而是因为妒忌我的朋友莉莎和男朋友重归于好，想穿得性感一点安慰自己。我并不喜欢那件连衣裙，倒不是因为式样太性感，而是因为它成了我生活中的一个代号，一个代表孤零和失望的代号。但是，在乔治看来，那是我给他的第一个印象，一个穿着米色性感连衣裙的素素，一下子吸引了他。所以，我穿上了它。

乔治说，等下了火车，我们去买衣服，买得再性感一点，你就是天下最漂亮的女人。

我朝他看了一眼，他很得意。

Party设在餐车的末端，五岁以下的小朋友并不很多，十几个，有的还是抱在怀里的Baby。但是，孩子的家长，许多大孩子和乘客都来看热闹。五颜六色的氢气球，被系在一张张的椅子背上，印着“生日快乐”的纸盆和纸杯，已经分放在每个座位前面的长台子上。桌中央是那个特殊的生日蛋糕，上面有一个塑料的洋娃娃，穿着白色的连衣裙，蛋糕上的奶油就是娃娃的裙子，上面画着有绿叶和玫瑰花，把一个三层的蛋糕全部覆盖住，可谓别出心裁。这些东西都是乔治和列车长联系了以后在停站的时候运上来的。

我们进去的时候，大家都齐声招呼柯丽丝：Happy Birthday！

"Happy birthday!" The children cheered for Kristeene as we entered the dining car.

George carried Kristeene in, and she waved, shouting back, "Happy birthday!" Laughter filled the air.

I asked Kristeene, "Sweetheart, what's your name?"

"Kristeene Dickson."

"And how old are you?"

"Two." She held up two tiny fingers.

"And what are your names, little ones?"

The children began to clamor, calling out their names. I intervened, "No, no. You must say it one by one. Let's start with her." A girl of Kristeene's age stood to my left. I asked, "My lovely little girl, what's your name?"

"Lucy."

I greeted, "Hi, Lucy!"

Kristeene followed suit, saying "hi, Lucy!" I was overjoyed. Whatever I said, she echoed. It was the best way for her to learn independently.

Each time a child shared their name, I wrote it on a name tag and affixed it to the front of their clothes. Then, I distributed the gifts. Everyone received a plastic bag filled with bubbles, blindfolds, candies, and stationery. The children eagerly explored their new treasures.

George sat beside me with Kristeene on his lap throughout. He whispered in my ear, "Susu, if I could buy a diamond ring right now, I'd propose to you on the spot. There are so many witnesses here."

I whispered back, "You're… incorrigible. Don't think of such things at your daughter's birthday party. You deserve a playful swat on the hand." He extended his right hand, and I playfully obliged. Kristeene joined in, giving his hand a pat. Lucy and Monica, two nearby children, joined in, too. Kristeene repeated the action multiple times. After her last swat, she clapped her hands and giggled. Suddenly, George pulled his hand away. Kristeene tapped the table in response. George cautiously extended his hand once more, only to be met by another child's playful swat. Soon, a crowd of children had gathered, eager to join in the fun. George wore a resigned expression, and I laughed so hard that I had to retreat to a corner, thoroughly entertained.

When Kristeene saw me step away, she wanted to follow, which gave George some freedom. As he carried Kristeene over, I was still laughing. "Susu dear," he said, "you shouldn't leave when you saw me get playfully scolded." I teased, "You lie in the bed you've made. Will you dare to daydream in the future?" George assured, "I won't dare next time. I'll be completely focused on you." I couldn't help but laugh again.

After supper, George lit the two candles on the cake. Kristeene blew them out, with other children eagerly joining in. Children are quick to make friends without any prejudice. They clapped their hands and sang "Happy Birthday." Then, each received a slice of cake. Kristeene got the doll to top it off, and she was overjoyed.

乔治抱着柯丽丝，柯丽丝扬着小手，高声应道：：Happy Birthday。大家都笑了。

我问柯丽丝，小姑娘，你叫什么名字呵？她说，柯丽丝·笛克荪。

几岁啦？

她伸出了两个手指头。

我说，各位小朋友，你们的名字呢？

孩子们杂声一片，各自报名字。我说，不行，不行，一个一个来，从这儿开始。我的左面是一个和柯丽丝差不多大的女孩。我说，美丽的小姑娘，你叫什么名字？她说，露西。我说，露西，你好！柯丽丝跟着说，露西，你好！我真是高兴极了。我说什么话，她都要模仿一遍。这是她自学的最佳途径！

孩子报一个名字，我就写在有粘性的卡片上，贴在他们的胸前。贴完了我分发礼品。每人有一个塑料袋，里面有Blowing Bubbles（肥皂泡的液体），Blid Fold（蒙眼睛的套子），还要其他吃的和用的礼物。孩子们拆开了口袋以后，各自玩了起来。

乔治一直坐在我的旁边，柯丽丝坐在他的腿上。他在我耳朵边悄悄地说，素素，如果现在能买到一枚钻指，我要向你求婚，因为有那么多的人作证。

我压低了嗓门回他，你真是不可救药啦！给女儿开Party，还要三心二意，该打手心。

他把手心摊给我，我拍了一下，柯丽丝也拍了一下。旁边的孩子，露西，莫尼克，都过来打乔治的手心。柯丽丝拍得最起劲，拍完了乔治，自己鼓起掌来，“咯咯”地笑。乔治突然把手抽掉，柯丽丝打在台子上。乔治再把手摊开来，被旁边一个孩子拍着了。结果很多孩子都涌过来，要打他的手心。他朝我做了一个无可奈何的表情，笑得我不得不离座，躲到角落里去。

柯丽丝看到我走开了，吵着要我。这才给乔治解了围。他抱着孩子过来的时候，我还在笑。他说，好一个素素，看到我挨打，你拔腿溜走了？我说，这叫搬起石头打自己的脚！以后还敢三心二意吗？他说，不敢了，一心一意就是了。又惹得我大笑。

吃完了晚餐，乔治点上了蛋糕中的两支蜡烛。柯丽丝对着蜡烛吹，孩子们个个翘起了嘴唇，身体前倾，意在帮助柯丽丝吹蜡烛。孩子是最没有偏见的，见面就成了好朋友。大家拍手，唱“生日快乐”之歌。然后分蛋糕。柯丽丝得了那个洋娃娃，高兴得合不上嘴。

最后，Party在“驴尾巴”的摸彩游戏中结束。孩子们排着

Finally, the party concluded with a game of pinning the tail on the donkey. The children formed a line, and the one with the turn would be blindfolded, spun around, and then attempt to pin the tail on a drawing of a tailless donkey. The child who came closest to the mark received a prize. Kristeene was the winner, perhaps because the other children used their right hands, and some even raised their hands too high. Kristeene, however, used her left hand, and the donkey's behind on the drawing was on the left side.

When Kristeene opened the chocolate box, the other children eagerly shouted, "Money, money!" I suggested to Kristeene, "Why not share your prize with the other children?" She happily distributed the bills one by one to those around her.

After we returned from the party, we were all exhausted. George suggested, "I'll sleep here tonight. You can take the next compartment. It's quiet." He moved towards the upper berth, but I stopped him. "No need. I'll sleep on the floor. Kristeene always sleeps well and never gives me any trouble at night."

He stood there, looking at me intently. I smiled at him, saying, "Get some rest early tonight. Tomorrow, we'll get our luggage ready to leave the train." I took Kristeene to the bathroom to wash her face. When we returned, George was still standing there. I lay the child on the lower berth and turned to George, asking, "What's on your mind?"

He was gazing straight ahead, deep in thought about something important.

"I wish, I wish we had a larger bed," he said somewhat abstractly.

Leaning towards him, I raised my head to meet his gaze and asked with a smile, "Have you learned your lesson? Do you want to live together first and get married later?"

"Yes, yes," he replied. "You can call it a trial for marriage."

I wrapped my arms around his neck and inquired, "Do you really think we'll get married?"

At that moment, his eyes brightened. He said, "Why don't I keep you company and we'll sleep together on the floor tonight?" He moved the chairs behind the door.

Hearing his words, my heart raced. I said, "I'm going to take a bath. George, stop. You should take a bath, too." I hoped he understood my intention. George abruptly turned his head, as if he understood this romantic gesture of bathing together. However, it seemed he didn't hear me, as he was still preoccupied with his preparations, sweat glistening on his brow.

I sympathized with him. He was unaccustomed to such gestures at home, where he was used to a life of luxury, with servants attending to him. I felt touched and content. At any rate, we would be sleeping together tonight. If we were in separate compartments, who could sleep peacefully?

When I returned from my bath, I found a double bedding arranged on the floor. He'd brought his pillow and blanket from the next compartment. The lights were turned off, and Kristeene was already asleep. I turned off the

队，一个一个地被蒙上了眼睛，原地转几圈，然后上前走几步，把手里的“驴尾巴”订在一幅图画上，图画是一头没有尾巴的驴。这个游戏的名字叫：Pin the Tale on the Donkey。谁订得最接近驴的尾部，谁就得奖。结果订得最准的居然是柯丽丝！因为别的孩子都把手伸直了去订，有的还手臂举得很高。柯丽丝用了左手，驴的尾部正巧在左面。

柯丽丝打开了巧克力的盒子，大家都叫了起来：Money，Money！

我说，柯丽丝，为什么不和你的朋友分享礼物？她笑了笑，把里面的钞票一张一张地抽出来，分送给了周围的朋友。

Party回来，我们都累坏了。乔治说，今晚我睡在这里，你去我的房间睡，安静一些。说完就去拉上铺。我拦住他说，不用了，我睡地上，柯丽丝很乖，晚上没事的。

他站在那里，出神地看着我。我朝他笑了笑，说道，早点睡吧，明天要整理行李，准备下车。说完，便抱着柯丽丝到厕所给她洗脸。洗完了，我们出来，乔治还是站在那里。

我把孩子放到床上，转身问道，乔治，怎么啦？

他目光迟钝，好像在考虑什么问题。我希望……，希望有一张大床。他说得含糊不清。

我笑了，倚靠着他，仰头问道，吸取教训啦？先同居后结婚？

对，对。他说，试婚试婚。

我环着他的脖子，问道，你真的以为我们会结婚吗？

这时候，他的眼神起了变化，好像暗淡的灯光忽然亮了起来。他说，为什么今天晚上，我不陪你在地上睡一夜？说完，他把椅子都叠了起来，搬到了门后面。听他这么一说，我的心“通通通”地跳起来。我说，我要洗个澡。乔治，不要搬了，你也去洗洗吧！心里盼望着乔治突然回过头来，马上领会这个浪漫的要求，和我一起去洗澡。但是，他好像没有听见，忙进忙出，手脚不停，累得满头大汗。

我真有些心疼他。这些事情，如果在家里，都不是他做的。他习惯了养尊处优，让一群佣人跟在身后。我已经很感动很满足了，因为无论如何，今晚我们将睡在一起。如果分睡两个房间，谁能睡得安宁？

洗完了出来，看到地上已经铺成了一个双人床的样子，他把隔壁的枕头和毯子都拿了过来。电灯关了，柯丽丝进入了梦乡。我关了厕所里的灯，轻手轻脚地走出去，却不见了乔治。看看墙壁上，那个上铺没有被拉下来。

bathroom light and walked out quietly, but George was nowhere in sight. I looked towards the wall. The upper berth was still up. Where had George gone? I stood in the dark, wondering if he'd returned to the next compartment. But if he had, why had he prepared the double bed and brought his pillow and blanket here? Was he taking a bath in the next compartment? If so, I'd wait for him.

I put on my sleeping gown and stepped outside. The passageway was empty, and I felt a slight chill. I knocked on the next door, but there was no response. What could be the matter? I softly called his name, but still no answer. I thought that perhaps he was so exhausted that he'd fallen asleep wherever he'd laid down. I, too, was weary and yawning incessantly. In any case, I'd return to my compartment.

So, I walked back with a weary step, feeling a sense of regret. As soon as I entered, I settled onto the floor. As I lifted the blanket, I discovered George lying there, right beside me. I threw myself onto him and asked, "Where were you? I was looking for you."

He embraced me, his face pressed against mine. "I hid under the berth, just teasing you."

"Do you have a guilty conscience about sleeping with me before marriage? Are you afraid the police will come to arrest you for it?"

"No," he said, laughing, "I just wanted to see if you'd miss me at night." I playfully punched him, saying, "You made me worry, and you're taking it so lightly." "Ouch!" He feigned a cry. "We've only just started living together and you're hitting me. How will I endure this for the rest of my life?" I restrained my laughter and playfully punched his bare shoulder again.

It was the same man, now lying beside me, with bare shoulders and just underwear on. But on that night of the full moon, he had nearly scared me out of my wits, and I had almost leapt out of the third-floor window.

I recounted that night to him, and he held me even tighter. "How wonderful it would have been if we could have slept together back then, like we are now."

I mused, "If I really had jumped that night, where would you be now?"

He said, "Sweetheart, I'm truly sorry I scared you."

I replied, "Thank goodness I didn't actually quit the next day."

"Yes," he said, "When you said you wanted to leave that day, my tears welled up."

"Oh," I said, "If I had left that day, where would I be now?"

"Susu is here with me. I'm so happy," he said.

We talked and talked, our hearts pouring out in endless conversation. Sleepiness seemed to have eluded us completely.

他到哪里去了呢？我站在黑暗里，想来想去，是不是回到隔壁去了？但是，为什么要在地上铺双人床？还把枕头毯子都拿了过来，他在隔壁如何睡？是不是在隔壁洗澡？那么，我就等他一会儿。

我坐在床沿上，身上裹着一条大浴巾，等了好久，不见他回来。心里好纳闷，难道他是想在半夜里来袭击我吗？那又何必呢？我没有反对铺双人床呵！我决定到隔壁去把他叫回来，并且告诉他，我想和他睡在一起。只是床太小，只能睡地上，委屈他了。

我穿上了睡衣，跑了出去。列车的走廊上空无一人，有点冷飕飕。敲敲隔壁的门，也没有回音。这是怎么回事呢？轻声喊他的名字，仍旧没有声音。我想，他一定是累得不行，睡着了。我也累了，接连不断地打呵欠。算了，回房去吧！

没精打采地走回来，心中觉得很遗憾。回到自己的房间，我倒下就睡。在掀毯子的时候，突然发现乔治睡在地上，就在我的旁边。我扑到他的身上，问道，你躲到哪里去了？让我好找啊！

他一把搂着我，脸贴脸，说道，开个小玩笑，躲到床底下去了。

你心中有鬼啊！怕警察来抓，是不是？

他笑着说，想证实一下，你在晚上是否需要我？

我赌气地给了他一拳，说道，把我急死了，你说得好轻松！

他说，哎哟哎哟，才开始同居，就挨揍了，受不了，受不了。

我不敢笑出声来，再往他的肩膀上加了一拳。

就是这样同一个的男人呵，光着膀子，只穿一条短裤，此时躺在我的旁边。可是，在那个圆月的晚上，却把我吓得魂不附体，差点儿从三楼跳下去。

我把这个想法告诉了乔治，他把我抱得更紧。他说，如果那天晚上，我们能这样抱着睡，该多么好哇！

我说，如果真的跳了，岂不是又一条性命？

他说，真是对不起啊，我的宝贝，吓着你了。

我说，幸亏第二天辞职没有成功。

他说，那天你要辞职，急得我掉了眼泪。

是呵，我说，如果真的走了，今天的我将在哪里？

他说，素素在这里，和我在一起。我太幸福了。

我们聊呵，聊呵，心里话说也说不完，居然赶走了困意。

Chapter 24

The next morning, we both slept in, waking up together. He smiled at me as I stirred.

"Good morning, Mr. Dickson. Did you sleep well? Any backaches?" I inquired.

He kissed me gently. "I'm not quite used to it, to be honest."

We sat up on the bedding. I playfully massaged his back. "Feeling the effects of our first night together?"

He grinned. "It was a fantastic first night, unforgettable. My bed partner is wonderful, even if the bed itself isn't."

I teased, "Considering a retreat, are you?"

He pointed at the tip of my nose. "I can't have you sleeping on the floor any longer. I promise to find a suitable bed for you in America."

Kristeene's little friends came to see her one by one when they learned we'd be leaving the train that day. George answered a knock at the door, a bit tousled. He told the children to wait in the dining car, promising we'd join them soon.

Kristeene was awake, playing on her berth. When she heard her name, she wanted to go out. I quickly washed her up and suggested George take her to the dining car for breakfast. He insisted I go first, assuring he'd look after her. So, he ended up taking a bath first, and neither of us had a chance for a shower. We only managed to retrieve our bath supplies from our suitcases.

In the dining car, the children and their parents were already waiting for us. I announced, "Today is truly Kristeene's birthday," and they burst into song once more. Many parents thanked us for the party and asked for our contact information. They vowed to send Kristeene gifts when they got home, since they hadn't brought any along. Kristeene and the children posed for photos and videos, her crescent-moon eyes gleaming with delight.

As we disembarked, we lingered, reluctant to leave. The head of the train crew and the attendant bid us farewell. Kristeene didn't grasp the feeling of parting, waving and smiling goodbye incessantly. Tears welled up in George's and my eyes.

George had an office in the city, and a car was sent to pick us up. We arrived at a hotel, and George promptly requested a new bed.

第二十四章

第二天，我和乔治起得比较晚。我醒来的时候，他也刚刚醒，笑嘻嘻地看着我。

早安，笛克荪先生，睡得好吗？是不是腰酸背痛？

他吻我，说，很不习惯，很不习惯。

我们都坐了起来。

我帮他捶背，一边说，同居第一夜，受罪了，呵呵。

他笑了，说道，美好的第一夜，难忘的第一夜，人好床不好。

我说，不想打退堂鼓？

他点着我的鼻尖说，不能再让你睡地上了，我就不信在美国买不到适合你睡觉的床。

柯丽丝的那些小朋友知道我们今天要下车了，络绎不绝地来看她。听到敲门声，乔治披上了睡袍去开门，显得很狼狈。他对客人说，请大家到餐厅等，我们马上就来。

柯丽丝已经醒来，自己在床上玩。听到有人叫她的名字，吵着要出去。我赶快给她洗了洗，让乔治抱柯丽丝先　上去吃早饭。乔治不同意。他要我洗澡，自己留下干苦力。我俩互相推让，便谁也没洗成澡，倒是把行李都给整理出来了。我们到餐厅的时候，许多孩子和他们的家长已经等在那里。我说，其实今天才是柯丽丝真正的生日。于是，大家再唱一曲生日之歌为柯丽丝祝贺。许多家长感谢我们昨天的Party，向我们要电话和地址，说孩子们玩得很高兴，拿了礼物却没有什么东西送给柯丽丝，回去以后补寄来，等等。柯丽丝和孩子们一起拍照片，上录像镜头，大眼睛笑得像一勾弯月。餐车里闹哄哄乱成一片。

下车的时候，我们依依不舍，列车员和列车长都来送行。柯丽丝还不懂离别的滋味，小手臂不停地挥舞，笑着说再见，再见！我和乔治的眼睛里都含着泪花。

乔治在这个城市里有一个办公室，公司派车来接我们。到了酒

However, he returned with frustration, suggesting we try another hotel. As we waited in the atrium, I chatted with the clerk at the front desk, mentioning my preference for a firm bed. She mentioned a bed-sofa in one of the rooms, which could be converted into a bed without springs. I agreed, "That'll do."

When George returned, clearly annoyed, he proposed switching to a different hotel.

I reassured him, "Don't be so serious. I can manage on the floor."

He insisted, "Susu, you can sleep anywhere you want, but not on the floor when you're with me."

He clenched his teeth as he spoke, a reaction that caught me off guard. I wondered how he could be so irritable over such a small matter. He must have had an argument with the manager. Initially, I considered mentioning the bed-sofa, but now I chose not to. If he wanted to leave and I objected, he would likely become even more agitated. So, I decided not to mention that the bed-sofa could solve my problem. I could appreciate his good intentions, but I couldn't tolerate his bad temper. Eventually, the desk clerk came over and said, "Mr. Dickson, there's a bed-sofa in that suite. It's a bit firm. Would you like to take a look?"

"Why didn't you mention it earlier?" George snapped.

The clerk glanced at me, as if expecting me to answer.

I smiled and said, "That sounds great. Let's have a look."

The suite was exquisite, located at the top of the hotel, offering a panoramic view through its windows. After the attendant, who had brought in our luggage, left the suite, George pulled out the bed from the sofa and sat on it to test its comfort. Then he gestured to me, saying, "Lie down, see how it feels."

I complied, lying on the bed. "It's perfect, just fine," I assured him. He let out a sigh of relief and wiped sweat from his forehead, smiling at me.

I returned his smile, extending my hand for him to help me up. I leaned against his shoulder and whispered, "Our plan almost hit an obstacle on the second day of living together."

"I understand these things aren't easy," he observed. "Living together is important. Let's sleep here tonight."

He began to make a series of calls, scheduling appointments and ordering various things, including a massage for me, a sauna for him, a hair-styling session, buying some new clothes for me, and arranging room service for lunch, among other things.

I remarked, "How can you make so many arrangements for me without consulting me?"

He replied, "My dear, my office is hosting a cocktail party tonight. We're attending together. I want you to look like a star."

"Look like a star?" I asked, furrowing my brow. "Why would I want to

店，他说要一张新床。结果，酒店的经理请他去了办公室。我和柯丽丝在大厅里等。酒店很豪华，四周都是玻璃，有墙的地方镶着杨木浮雕。柯丽丝在铺着红地毯的过道上跑来跑去玩。玩累了，扑到我的身上，吵着要抱。我们等了好久，不见乔治回来。我便和服务员聊上了天。我告诉她，我不能睡软床，背痛。她说，套房的外间有沙发可以翻成床，上面没有很厚的席梦斯。我说，那就行了。

乔治回来的时候，脸上带着怒气，说要换地方。

我说，你干吗那么认真？不行就睡地上么！

他说，素素，你可以睡在任何地方，只要不被我看见。和我在一起，不准睡地铺！

他说得咬牙切齿，把我吓了一跳。心里想，这么一点小事，就要发脾气。大概和酒店的经理发生了争吵。本来想告诉他沙发床的事情，干脆不说了。他要走，我不同意。他更加扫兴，更加不愿意留下。我则越不想告诉他沙发床能解决问题。我理解他的好心，但是难容他的坏脾气。结果，那个服务员过来打圆场，说道，笛克荪先生，套房的沙发床很硬，要不要去看看？

你怎么早不说呢？

服务员看看我，好像应该由我来代她回答问题。

我笑了，说，那么，我们就去看看吧！

套房很漂亮，在酒店的最高层，往外看，风景一览无余。送行李的服务员走了以后，乔治马上拉开了沙发床检查，坐在上面，试弹性。然后喊我过去，说，躺下试试。我躺了下来。不错，很好。他舒了长长的一口气，抹了一把额上的汗，看着我笑了。

我也笑了。伸直了手臂，让他拉我起来。我趴在他的肩膀上悄悄地说，嘻嘻，同居第二天，差点儿蹦了。不容易，不容易。他说，同居很重要。今晚，我们就睡在这里。

他打了许多电话，联系和预约了许多事情。其中包括我的推拿，他的桑拿浴，给我做头发，去楼下买衣服，以及请人送午餐上门，等等。

我说，你怎么可以自说自话，为我安排那么多的事情，也不征求我的意见？

他说，亲爱的，晚上公司里有个酒会，我们一起出席，我要你成为明星。

要我成为明星？为什么要我成为明星？

他说，我是总裁，你是我的未婚妻呵！

我说，不对，不对。乔治，我不去。

look like a star?"

He explained, "I'm the president. You're my fiancée."

"No, no. George, I won't go."

He widened his eyes, looking at me in surprise. He gazed at me for a long moment. I met his gaze, my lips pursed. I wouldn't back down. He couldn't remain silent any longer and asked, "Are you joking or playing a trick?"

"Who's playing a trick on you?" I responded. "The person I love is Kristeene's father, not the president of some organization. I don't want to be the president's fiancée."

"But I am the president," he argued. "Do you want to split me in two?"

"You can be the president. Regardless, I won't go."

With that, he let his hands drop, turned his back to me, and went to the window. From there, you could see the boundless ocean, waves shimmering like a surface-broken mirror, reflecting dazzling light. He stood there for a long while, one hand on his side, the other under his chin. I couldn't fathom what he was thinking. Was he angry with me? What did I say wrong? I didn't want to attend his work party. Was that a mistake? He often employed silence in such situations. Why wouldn't he speak? Why try to reason with me? Suddenly, I remembered him saying that our cohabitation was just a trial before marriage. Did that mean if the trial didn't go well, we wouldn't get married? Thinking about it, my spirits sank. We had no issues in our physical relationship, but today we'd already had two arguments. If we kept bickering, how could we get along?

Lunch was served: salad, soup, and noodles. I fed Kristeene first, then she played by herself. The little girl seemed to sense something amiss between her father and Susu. At times, she clung to my leg; at others, she climbed onto my lap. She wouldn't leave me be.

All the plates were covered with silvery metal lids to keep the food warm. George sat down to fill his plate with salad. He glanced at me. I told him I wasn't hungry. I settled Kristeene on my lap and watched him eat.

George appeared unhappy. After a few mouthfuls, he set his plate aside, saying, "If you're not eating, how can I?"

He got up and walked to the window, then back again. He stopped behind me, wrapping his arms around me and resting his hands on my chest. He murmured, "Are you on a hunger strike? Do you think it's worth it?"

I couldn't help but smile. I gently removed his hands and said, "Who said I'm on a hunger strike?"

He took Kristeene and sat across from me. Looking at me, he said, "You eat, and I'll eat." So I took some soup. It was delicious, with tomatoes and chopped-up shrimp. George finished his salad.

He turned to Kristeene and said, "Daddy will play with you. Susu is going for a massage and hair styling." Then he handed me a card key to our room. "Put all the expenses on our hotel account," he instructed.

他瞪大了眼睛，惊愕地看着我，看了好长时间。我也看着他，咬紧了嘴唇，毫不示弱。最后，他忍不住了，问道，你这是开玩笑还是耍小孩子脾气？

谁和你开玩笑啦？我说，我爱的是柯丽丝的父亲，不是一个什么集团的总裁。我不要做总裁的未婚妻。

我就是总裁。他说，你要把我一劈为二？

我说，当你的总裁去吧！反正我不去。

这时，他双手一甩，背我而去，走到了大玻璃窗前面。

窗前是大海，一望无际，波光粼粼，好像一面破碎的镜子，亮得有点刺眼。他站在那里，一手插在腰间，一手托着下巴，站了好久。不知道他在想什么？是被我的话伤了心？我说了些什么呢？我不愿意介入他的工作，错在哪里？他总是用沉默来对付我。为什么不说话呢？为什么不给我讲道理？想到他说的"试婚"，心里凉了半截。我们在性生活上没有问题，但是，今天已经吵了两次。人与人靠得太近，反而难以相处。今后，如果吵架不断，日子怎么过？

午餐来了。有色拉，浓汤和面条。我把柯丽丝喂饱了，让她自己玩。小姑娘好像感觉到父亲和素素之间的气氛不对，一会儿趴在我的膝盖上，一会儿靠在我的腿旁边，不肯离开。

所有的盘子上都罩着保温用的银色金属盖。乔治坐下来取了一盘色拉，然后朝我看看。我说我不饿，把柯丽丝抱在膝上，看着他吃。

乔治心事重重的样子，吃了几叉，把盆子一推，说道，你不吃，我怎么吃得下去，嗯？说完便站了起来。

我说，你吃你的，我不饿。

他走到窗边，又走回来，然后，在我的背后停住了。他的手从后面绕过来，搁在我的胸前，轻声问，绝食啦？值得吗？

我没有吭声。但是，心里好受了许多。

喂你，喝点汤，好吗？

我忍不住笑了，瓣开他的手说，谁要你喂？

他把柯丽丝接过去，坐到了对面。看着我，说，你吃我也吃。于是，我喝了一些浓汤，里面是西红柿和切碎的虾仁，挺好吃的。他把色拉吃完了。

乔治对柯丽丝说，爹地和你玩，让素素去推拿和做头发。然后转过身来给了我一把房间的钥匙牌，说道，把账都记在房间的号码上。

我一声不响地走了，关门的时候，听到了柯丽丝的哭声。多么

I left without saying anything. As I closed the door, I heard Kristeene crying. I wished I could go back into the room. What was the point of buying clothes and getting my hair done? It felt like I was spending money to buy unhappiness. Was it all for a party I had no interest in? Kristeene could sense my unease. Why couldn't George?

I didn't go anywhere. Instead, I wandered alone in the corridor, back and forth. I sat down on a chair across from the bank of elevators. Memories of George's fiftieth birthday party flooded back. I had met all those wealthy people and celebrities. I also remembered the forced politeness of Nancy. I asked myself, "Is this the future I want for myself? Am I willing to become like that?" I didn't want to be Mrs. Dickson. I wanted to be Susu.

I took out the card key and tried to open the door following the instructions. I slid the key in multiple times, but the small light above the lock stayed red. If it didn't turn green, the door wouldn't open. I grew frustrated. The more I tried, the less likely it seemed I would succeed. So, I knocked on the door. George answered, looking surprised to see me. He said, "Susu, what happened? Couldn't you find the places? They're both on the first floor. Did I give you the map?"

I tossed the card key onto the table and said irritably, "George, I didn't go anywhere. I don't want to go anywhere. I only want Kristeene and you, nothing else. As for the party tonight, is it okay if I don't go?"

He reminded me to lower my voice because Kristeene was asleep in her room.

I asked, "Who needs to know if you have a girlfriend or a fiancée? Our love is for us alone. Why do you want to expose me to the public eye?"

George replied, "Susu, you make me proud of you. Your presence will overshadow many. Are you afraid of strangers?"

I said, "Why should it matter to me whether they're overshadowed or not? I don't want to adorn myself with jewels like a showcase. And I don't want to mingle with people of false politeness."

George laughed, and I playfully covered his mouth, saying, "Why are you laughing? Aren't you afraid of waking up Kristeene?"

He said, "My dear, you came to America for higher education. You have to meet people someday. You can't always hide like a child."

I replied, "My major is education, not business. I was a teacher for two years in China. If I want to get my degree, I won't waste my time and energy on parties."

He explained, "Do you think that work in education is so clean? Where there is competition, there is deceit and vying for interests. But, of course, there are public rules. Everything is not so direful as you think. If you really don't want to go, you don't need to go tonight. But when our wedding day comes, you can't hide away like now."

I smiled, "Wedding? I just thought that our trial of living together would

想返身回去啊！买衣服，做头发，花钱买个不愉快，究竟为了啥？为了一个和我毫无关系的酒会？柯丽丝嗅出了我的不愉快，为什么乔治嗅不出来？

我什么地方都没有去，独自在走廊上，从这一头走到底，从那一头倒回来。走过来走过去，最后坐在电梯对面的一张椅子上。我想起了在乔治五十岁生日的时候遇到的那些达官显贵，想起了南西矫揉造作的礼貌，问自己，将来的我就是那个样子，你愿意吗？愿意吗？我不要做笛克荪太太，我要做素素。

取出了钥匙牌，按照上面的指示开门，插进去几次，门上面的那个绿点都不亮。绿点不亮，门就打不开。心里好烦好烦，越是烦越是打不开门。我便“咚咚咚”地敲了门。乔治来开门，一脸的惊讶。他说，素素，怎么啦？

找不到地方吗？都在一楼，不是给了你地图？

我把钥匙牌往桌上一扔，气呼呼地说，乔治，我哪里都没有去，哪里都不想去。我只要你和柯丽丝，别的都不要，晚上的酒会，不去不行吗？

他暗示我说话的声音轻一点，柯丽丝在里面睡觉。

我说，谁需要知道你有女朋友和未婚妻？我们恋爱，是为了我们自己。你为什么要把我拉到公众的眼皮底下？

他说，素素，你让我骄傲，你的出席将让很多人逊色。你是不是害怕陌生人？

我说，他们逊色不逊色，和我有什么关系？我不喜欢珠光宝气，不喜欢和戴假面具的人混在一起。

乔治哈哈大笑，我用手去捂他的嘴，说，笑什么笑呵？不怕把柯丽丝吵醒？

他说，亲爱的，你来美国念大学，将来总要走上社会。怎么像孩子一样？

我说，我学的是教育，不是商学。我在中国已经当了两年教师。如果在美国读出了学位，我不会把时间和精力消耗在宴会上。

他说，教育就那么干净吗？有竞争的地方，就有尔虞我诈和利益权衡，但是，也有公共规则。不如你想像的那么可怕。如果你实在不愿意去，今晚就不去了。但是，到了我们结婚的时候，可不能像今天这样躲起来，嗯？

我笑了，说道，结婚？我刚才还以为我们同居失败了呢！

他走过来搂着我，说，素素宝贝，如果因为生意而影响了我们的感情，我宁可把生意卖了。

end in nothing."

George hugged me, saying, "Susu, my sweetheart, if my business affects our love, I'd better sell it."

I asked, "Will you go alone?"

"Yes, I'll go alone." He went to the desk and sat down. He wrote something on a notepad and then looked up, saying, "But today is Kristeene's birthday. How can we leave her here?"

I said, "Isn't this a cocktail party? What does a cocktail party have to do with Kristeene's birthday? Haven't you said that adult parties are not suitable for children?"

"Yes," he acknowledged, "But Kristeene is also my pride. I hope that everyone in my office can see her."

I pondered for a moment: if he took Kristeene with him, how could he entertain his business friends? If he couldn't ignore his friends, who would look after Kristeene? So I said, "Then I'll go."

George sat back in the chair and closed his eyes. Whenever he did this, with a slight frown, I knew he was trying to calm his emotions. He often used this gesture to hide his feelings.

I told him, "Now I'll go for hair styling and buy some clothes. You can rest for a while."

"Come to me," he said, opening his arms, his eyes filled with tenderness. He embraced me and said, "Sweetheart, if you don't go, half of me will still be here. But you are right. Since you are not used to social parties and don't want to go, I must respect your decision. Forget the star thing. You can decide what you want to do, what clothes you want to buy. I must thank you for sharing the party with me tonight."

I said, "You must promise me one thing."

"What's that?"

"Don't be foolish and try to woo me at the party. I won't accept it."

George nodded and said, "I promise."

我说，晚上你自己去？

他说，是的，我自己去。他走到写字台旁，坐了下来，在便笺上写了几个字。抬起脸来说，但是，今天是柯丽丝的生日，怎么能把她留在家里？

我说，不是酒会吗？柯丽丝和酒会有什么关系？不是说成人的宴会，对孩子不合适吗？

是呵，他说。但是，柯丽丝也是我的骄傲，我希望大家见见她。

我想了想，他把柯丽丝带去，如何应酬生意上的朋友？顾了生意，谁来照顾柯丽丝？

我说：那么，我就去吧！

乔治往椅背上一靠，闭上了眼睛。每当他拧紧了眉头，闭上眼睛的时候，我知道他心潮起伏。他总是用这个方式来掩饰自己的心情。

我说，现在我就下去做头发，买衣服，你休息一会儿。

过来。他说。过来，素素。他张开了双臂，眼睛里溢满了温情。他拥抱着我说，宝贝，如果你不去，今晚，我的心将有一半留在这里。但是，你说得很对，不习惯生意上的应酬，不愿意去，我应该尊重你。忘记当明星的事情吧，你愿意怎么做，穿什么衣服，都由你自己决定。我要谢谢你，和我分享今晚的酒会。

我说，你要答应我一件事。

什么事？

不要傻呼呼地在宴会上向我求婚，我不会答应你的。

乔治点点头，说道，我保证。

Chapter 25

The man who drove us to the party was called Dennis, in a black suit. He was of middle height, stout, broad-shouldered, with dark skin and curly black hair. Dennis's face seemed familiar to me, but I couldn't remember where I had seen him. George sat in the front seat, and Kristeene and I in the back seat. I asked, "Dennis, do you resemble some movie star?" I saw Dennis smile from the rearview mirror, showing his white, neat teeth.

I said, "It seems that I saw you somewhere before. Let me think."

George said, "Susu, Dennis is one of our household. He is the son of Betty."

Oh, that was on the day of George's birthday party that I had seen him. That happened because his hair had been especially bright, which had given me a deep impression. I said, "Did you remember, Dennis, you came to the kitchen to help at lunch time?"

Dennis only smiled. He was a quiet young man.

George said, "Dennis is the pilot of my private plane. We will fly home tomorrow."

I asked, "A small plane? Is it safe? George, whenever you fly back and forth, is it always Dennis who pilots the plane?"

Dennis still smiled. George said, "Yes. It's safe, no problem."

The car suddenly slowed down and stopped after a jerk. Kristeene in her child chair waved her hand excitedly. She shouted from time to time, "Look, daddy. Look, Susu." Outside the car window, many cars moved toward a big hotel. The policemen stood here and there like black posts, directing the traffic.

I remembered the first time that when Anna had told me that guests would have come, I had been excited, hoping to see the scene with many American people. But the result had been like the broth with only a thin layer of butter floating on it: ostentatious on the surface. Once was enough to turn my stomach. But, look at the people and cars in the street, flowing towards the hotel like rising tide. Why were they so excited, never tired of this? What I didn't understand was how George could swim in such a broth all the year round. What happiness could he have in it?

After a struggle in the traffic, following the other cars, Dennis halted before the hotel at last. When we got out of our car, he drove it away. The cocktail

第二十五章

接我们去酒会的司机叫丹尼，穿一身黑色的西装。中等个子，很结实，肩膀厚厚的，幽黑的皮肤，一头卷曲的黑头发。我觉得丹尼很脸熟，想不起来在哪里见过他？乔治坐在前面，我和柯丽丝在后座。我问道，丹尼，你是否和哪个电影演员很像？我从后视镜里看到丹尼笑了，露出一口雪白整齐的牙齿。

我说，好像见过你，让我想一想。

乔治说，素素，丹尼是自家人，蓓蒂的儿子。

噢！那就是在乔治生日的那天，见过他。对了对了，因为他的头发特别漂亮，给我印像很深。丹尼，你记得吗，在厨房里，在吃午餐的时候，你在那里帮忙。丹尼仍旧笑笑。真是个文静的年轻人。

乔治说，丹尼是我的飞机驾驶员，明天，我们坐飞机回家。

我说，小飞机吗？安全不安全？乔治，你飞来飞去，都是丹尼开的吗？

丹尼还是笑笑。

乔治说，是的，很安全，没有问题。

汽车突然慢了下来，动一动，停一停。柯丽丝在儿童坐椅上兴奋得指手画脚，时不时喊道，爹地，看呀，素素，看呀……。窗外，许多汽车都在朝一栋大楼开去。警察东一个，西一个，像一条条黑棍子一样，站立在路旁指挥。这个场面让我想到了第一次听安娜说家里有客人来，着实令我兴奋了一番，希望见到美国人的大场面。结果呢，就像看到了肉汤上面飘浮的那层油，貌似华丽，虚情假意。我有了一次就倒足了胃口。可是，瞧这马路上的车和人，好像潮水一样往这里涌。他们为什么兴致勃勃，乐此不疲？更不明白的是乔治，长年累月地泡在油汤里，有什么乐趣？好不容易，尾随在其他车辆的后面，丹尼开到楼前，我们下了车，他便开车走了。

酒会举办在底楼，里面灯火辉煌。刚走到门口的时候，亮得眼睛不能适应。他搀着柯丽丝的一只手，我拉着另一只手，小姑娘在

party was on the first floor. It was so bright inside. On entering the building, I couldn't open my eyes for the sudden brilliance.

George held one of Kristeene's hand and I the other. The little girl leaped along all the way between us with a broad smile on her face. All I saw at the first sight was men in black and women in colors.

"Men in black and women in colors? What is meant by it?" George turned his face to me and asked. I had said it to myself, but out aloud.

I replied, "In nature, the male animals are prettier than the female, but why are humans the contrary?"

"Because of the rising social status of women?"

"Is that so?" I said, "It is natural for women to dress colorfully, but when men put on colored clothes, green caps and red shoes, they become clowns. Are people used to seeing women like this?"

George stood mute for a little while and said to me, "Susu, you always have weird things to say."

I said, "George, why not get some clowns to enliven the atmosphere?"

George laughed and said, "Susu, you are like your philosophy professor. Do you want to turn the cocktail party into a McDonald's gathering? Susu, you like wild things."

Just as I was about to plead for my philosopher professor, someone was calling George. A clownish face appeared from behind a half-circular desk beside a door at the end of the corridor.

"Hello, Mr. Dickson!"

"Hello, Juliet." George said, "Ah, look at you, so slim, so pretty." He approached her and kissed on her forehead. The makeup powder on her face fell bit by bit as her smile made her face wrinkle.

"This is--?" Pointing at me, she asked, after she handed George a hanging card with his name printed on it.

"She's Susu, S—U—S—U--." George spelt for her.

"And she's your--?"

"My--? No, no. She's my daughter, Kristeene's, best friend."

"Of course, of course." The woman smiled, glancing at me once more and typing in my name on the machine. I said smilingly, "Hello, Juliet." I intentionally showed George that I was afraid of strangers.

A while later, my card came out. She handed it to me.

Kristeene wore a sky-blue dress. Now she clung to George's leg and now she held onto my dress. She moved between us, talking incessantly, but no one could understand her. I put on a dark blue long dress with a high collar. The hair-maker did my hair into a knot on the top of my head, which made me look like an old woman. I knew that George didn't like the color of my dress and the style of my hair. But he didn't show any sign of dissatisfaction.

On entering the hotel, George changed his demeanor and the way of talking. He put his back straight and walked as if he got a spring under each of his feet. And his gait combined with the movement of his shoulders made him look charming and spontaneous. When he shook hands with or beckoned to

中间连蹦带跳，笑逐颜开地跟着我们走。一眼望过去，都是黑男人花女人。

黑男人花女人？什么意思？乔治转过脸来问我。原来我自言自语地把话说了出来。

我说，自然界的雄性动物都比雌性的美丽，为什么人类恰恰相反？

他说，女性提高了地位？

是吗？我说，女人穿得花枝招展，理所当然。男人穿上了花衣服，绿帽子，红鞋子，就变成了小丑。是不是女人见丑不丑，习以为常？

乔治怔了一下，指着我说，素素，你的歪门邪道可不少。

我说，乔治，为什么不安排几个小丑来活跃一下气氛？

乔治呵呵笑着说，像你的哲学教授那样，酒会开成麦道劳快餐店？素素，你真喜欢胡闹。

我刚想为哲学教授辩护，忽听见有人在招呼乔治。走廊的终点有个进口处，半圆形的柜台后面露出了一张大花脸。

笛可苏先生，你好！你好！

好，好，茱利亚。乔治说，啊，瞧你，越来越苗条，越来越漂亮了。他凑过去，吻了她的前额。女人脸上的粉随着笑容皱折了起来，纷纷往下掉。

这位是……？茱利亚给了乔治一个挂牌，上面印着他的名字，然后指着我问道。

她是素素，S-U-S-U。乔治拼给她听。

是你的……？

我的？不是，不是，她是柯丽丝的好朋友。你知道，柯丽丝是我的女儿。

当然，当然。小姐笑了，再朝我看了一眼，往机器里输入了我的名字。我笑着说，茱莉亚你好！我故意向乔治显示，素素才不怕陌生人呢！

一会儿，我的挂牌出来了。她递给了我。

柯丽丝穿一件天蓝色的连衣裙，一会儿抱着乔治的腿，一会儿拉我的裙子，在我们之间串来串去，叽叽喳喳的，不知道在说些什么。我穿一件高领的深蓝连衣长裙，让美容师把披肩的头发拢到头顶，盘成一个结，看上去像个老太婆。我知道乔治不喜欢衣服的颜色和我的发型。但是，他没有流露出任何的不满。

一进大楼的门，乔治的谈吐举止马上变成了另一个样子。他的背挺得笔直，脚底下好像多了点弹性。走路的时候，肩膀的移动配

people, he was very much like what Nancy did: looking so warm and polite outside, but controlled within. The cocktail party was really like a stage for the performance of everybody.

The party hall was as big as the size of a swimming pool, packed with people standing everywhere. George carried Kristeene in one arm and held my hand in the other. He introduced first Kristeene and then me to every guest, saying that I was the friend of Kristeene. All the guests extolled Kristeene and shook hands with me. I had an intuition that all the eyes behind my back centered on me like bright searchlights. I felt uneasy.

I said to George, "I really become a star now. Do you notice the eyes of people?"

He said, "Yes, I did. What's wrong with that?"

I said, "Why introduce me to them?"

He said, "If I didn't introduce you, the bright star, would your brightness fade away without being noticed?"

After a second thought, I knew that he was in a difficult situation. It was I who didn't want to be announced as the fiancée of the president. So now he had to say that I was Kristeene's friend. Was he wrong? Except being Kristeene's friend, what else could he say about me? Who knows if it was just the obscure introduction that caused the people's probing interest? If he had introduced me as his girlfriend or even fiancée, the situation would be better for us. Thus thinking, I plucked up my courage and said to George, "You can say I'm your girlfriend lest people make wild guesses." He looked at me and smiled. Just at that moment, I knew that I fell into his trap and ran on his rails again. I knew that elatedness showed in his eyes.

Someone came to ask George to make a speech on the dais. I said, "I'll take Kristeene." He said, "Doesn't matter. We can go together." Then he took my arm. I pulled my arm out of his hand and said, "Go with you on the dais? I won't."

He said, "Are you not my girlfriend?" So speaking, he turned his face away from me and smiled furtively. I had almost an impulse to fist him, punishing him for showing his presidential prestige to me. But I could not do it in the presence of so many people around.

"Then, I'll go up there with Kristeene." He said.

I was so angry that my eyes would have belched fire. "Don't take the child as a doll. Leave her to me." I said this with strong feelings word for word as if the words spurted out through the gap between my teeth.

George was so calm as though he didn't hear it. But he let me take over Kristeene. He kissed her and went alone to the dais.

When Kristeene saw her father on the dais, she wanted to go there, too. I said, "Kristeene, let's have something to eat. You are hungry, aren't you? There's so much delicious food there. Let's go."

I carried Kristeene to the other end of the hall. All the way down there, I seemed to pass a belt with a lot of eyes focused on me like the machine gun bullets. I pretended to be happy, nodding and nodding, smiling and smiling.

合，挺潇洒挺有魅力的。他和人握手，点头打招呼，都和南西一模一样，看上去很热情，内心很收敛。酒会真像一个演戏的舞台！

哇，好大的厅，就像一个抽干了水的游泳池，人们在里面像插蜡烛一样，挤得满满的。乔治介绍柯丽丝给各位客人，一手抱着孩子，一手拉着我。一路跟在他的旁边，他介绍了柯丽丝，再介绍我，说我是柯丽丝的朋友。

客人们把柯丽丝赞美一番，和我一一握手。顿时，各种目光，像光芒四射的探照灯一样，在我的背后，扫来扫去，非常不舒服。

我对乔治说，我真的成了明星啦。你看见人们的目光了吗？

他说，看到了，有什么不好吗？

我说，为什么要介绍我？

他说，不介绍你，光芒就会自动消失吗？

我想了想，觉得他也挺为难的。是我不要做总裁的未婚妻，现在他说我是柯丽丝的朋友，错在哪里？除了柯丽丝的朋友，他还能做什么介绍呢？也许正是这个不明不白的介绍引起了人们的兴趣。如果介绍我是他的女朋友或者未婚妻，我们的难堪或许要少一些？这样一想，我鼓起了勇气，对乔治说，就说我是你的女朋友吧，免得被人家乱猜。他朝我看了看，抿着嘴笑了。就在那一瞬间，我知道自己又上当了，又进入了他的轨道。看他眼睛里，装着多少得意呵！有人过来，请乔治到台上去讲话。我说，把柯丽丝给我。他说，没关系，我们一起上去。说完，挽上了我的手臂。我甩了甩手，说道，和你一起上台？我不去！他说，你不是我的女朋友吗？说完了，别过脸去，偷偷地笑。我真想给他一拳头，惩罚一下他当总裁的威风。可惜人太多，不好意思。

那么，我和柯丽丝一起去。他说。

我愤怒得两眼冒火，一个字一个字地从牙缝里蹦出来：不要把孩子当玩偶，请把柯丽丝给我留下！

乔治好像没有听见似的，脸上风平浪静。但是，不再坚持，亲了亲柯丽丝，独自走到台上去了。

柯丽丝看到父亲到了台上，吵着也要去。我说，柯丽丝，我们去吃饭吧！你饿了，是不是？很多好吃的东西哎，来，我们走！

我抱起了柯丽丝就走，一口气走到大厅的另一头。这一路，就像穿过枪林弹雨一样，被人们看了个够。我装得 很开心的样子，点头再点头，微笑再微笑，几十米路好像万里长征一样长。最后面的墙壁旁，一张张长桌子上堆满了吃的东西。服务员过来，问我要喝什么酒？

我摇摇手，谢了谢他。把柯丽丝放下，想找个椅子让她坐，然

For some ten meters I seemed to have covered miles.

After a bit of a trek, I finally made it to the end of the hall, where they had tables loaded with a feast of fancy food and drinks. A friendly attendant offered up an assortment of alcohol, but I declined. I was on the hunt for a chair for Kristeene, but it seemed like they were playing hide and seek.

Behind me, the crowd was all ears for George, craning their necks like curious birds. Kristeene, barely tall enough for the table, gave me the nudge to hoist her up so she could pick her food. A helpful attendant plated up her picks.

Laughter bubbled up from the crowd behind me. Then out of nowhere, Kristeene pipes up with, "Thank every friend."

Puzzled, I asked, "What are you saying, Kristeene?"

She comes back with, "Daddy said 'Thank every friend.'" I peeked back to find George deep in his own show. The kid, in a surprising twist, was doing a mini-imitation. Luckily, we were far enough away from the crowd to dodge any possible embarrassment.

Before the official wrap-up of the party, Kristeene and I made our exit to crash back at our digs. Dennis, our wheelman, led the way back. Along the ride, I pelted him with questions about the little plane. Finally, Dennis, with a voice that had a timeless quality, spilled that his dad, a stand-up guy, had passed away a few years back.

Kristeene knocked out on the way back. Dennis gently carried her to her room. The suite was back in order, with our sofa bed back to its original setup. Kristeene was sprawled out on the big bed, flanked by a fortress of pillows to keep her from falling.

I asked Dennis to talk, but he was eager to go back and pick up George. "When's this party over?" I asked. Dennis just shook his head. I prodded a bit more, "Did you see Kristeene's mom when you chauffeured George?" Dennis nodded, showing he knew how to keep a tight lid on unnecessary words.

As he was heading out, he let slip that Laura was resting in the city, not six feet under. "Did George say anything about this?" I asked, noting how he preferred the word "sleep" over "bury". Laura was in a forever slumber.

George hadn't spilled a word about this city's backstory. Not sure how to respond to Dennis's revelations, I offered, "Laura was incredible. She loved George."

Dennis gave a nod, "Yeah, Laura was head over heels for him."

Seeing Dennis off, I mulled over our chat. His deep respect and empathy for Laura, the bittersweet tale of their unfulfilled love, and his heartfelt affection for George and Kristeene, it all shone through in his eyes. With just a few words, he'd given me a ton to chew on. In my head, Laura's story was initially a two-person show. But now, Dennis had entered the picture as a figure in the shadows. Maybe even his mom Betty had played a part. I pictured after George lost Laura, Betty, Dennis, and the crew had been there to help him through that toughest stretch. That's probably why George called them family. Maybe it was this shared history that led them to honor and look out for me,

后喂她吃饭。环顾四周，竟然一张椅子都没有！

背后的那群人，一个个像鸭子一样伸长了脖子，站在那里听乔治演讲。

柯丽丝还没有桌子高，我抱起她，让她自己挑东西，挑中的食品，请服务员装在盘子里。

身后，不时传来一阵阵笑声。忽然，柯丽丝大声地说了一句“谢谢每一位朋友”。

柯丽丝，你说什么呀？

她说，爹地说，感谢每一位朋友。

我回头一看，乔治正聚精会神地在表演呢！小丫头连演讲也要模仿，她把“谢谢”说得很重，讲得比她父亲还要认真，真是出人意料！幸亏我们离人群较远，没有闹出笑话来。

我和柯丽丝在酒会结束之前先回家了，是丹尼开的车。路上，我问了不少关于小飞机的事情。丹尼终于说话了。他的声音浑厚圆润，富有古典的韵味。我从他那里得知，丹尼的父亲是黑人，早几年去世了。

柯丽丝在回来的车上睡着了。丹尼抱她到了客房。客房已经被收拾干净，我们的床恢复了沙发的原状。柯丽丝睡在卧室的大床上，四周放了许多枕头，造了一个围城，怕她晚上滚下来。

我请丹尼坐一会儿。他说，要赶去接乔治回来。我问，酒会要开到几点钟？丹尼摇摇头。我说，你给乔治开车开飞机，见过柯丽丝的妈妈吗？丹尼点点头。他的嘴很紧，没有多余的话。

临走的时候，丹尼说，劳瑞就被埋在这个城市，乔治没有告诉你吗？他没有说“埋”，他说“睡”。他说对了，劳瑞是睡着了，再没有醒来。那个时候，柯丽丝刚刚来到人世。

乔治没有告诉我任何关于这个城市的事情，我不知道应该如何答复丹尼，便说，劳瑞是好人，她很爱乔治。

丹尼说，是的，劳瑞很爱他。

我把丹尼送走。套房在走廊的尽头，我们走了很长一段路，一路沉默走到电梯口。

在我走回来的时候，仿佛觉得丹尼已经告诉了我一箩筐的故事。他对劳瑞的尊重和同情，对这场凄美爱情的惋惜，以及对乔治和柯丽丝的热爱，都透露在他的宇眉之间。他越少说话越让我用心去品味。劳瑞的故事，原来在印像中只有两个人，现在多了丹尼，也许还有他的妈妈蓓蒂。我想像着在乔治失去劳瑞，悲痛欲绝的时候，蓓蒂和丹尼及后楼的一些朋友一定帮助乔治度过了最困难的一段人生。所以乔治称他们自家人。是不是因为这个原因，他们欣赏

recognizing my devotion to Kristeene.

In the bedroom, I sank into a mound of pillows, eyes fixed on Kristeene from head to toe. Since the first time I laid eyes on her in Anna's minivan till now, Kristeene had blossomed in so many ways. Back then, she could only offer a smile, no words to share or ways to express herself. Except for mealtime, she seemed to live in a world of slumber. But in these few months, she'd grown taller and could now wander on her own, even sprint and leap with the best of them. Not only was she a chatterbox every day, mimicking the grown-ups, but she'd also picked up on when to say "Yes" and when to firmly say "No". "Congratulations to you, Kristeene. Susu is proud of you."

Thinking back, when George and Anna had their clashes, George had mentioned that Kristeene was a bit of a lost soul. I hadn't fully grasped it then. Now it dawned on me—Kristeene entered the world without a mother. Anna had to grapple with the reality of accepting a child born from another woman with her husband.

The very first time Kristeene saw me, she took to me like we'd been pals for ages. It nearly made Anna green with envy. Did it spark her maternal instincts? Kristeene leaned on me, trusted me, so much so that I wondered if I could live up to the role of a mother for her. This whole trip, in name it was for her birthday, but it was really a setting for her father and me to find our way to love. At the start, I could give her all my love, but now, I had to split it between her and her father. This city we landed in, it was also where her mother rested eternally. Should we have made plans for her to visit her mother's grave, leave some flowers in her memory? Instead, we went to that party. I felt a pang of sadness. Regret welled up. My tears flowed down.

"Kristeene, sweetheart, can you forgive me?"

I shuffled to the bathroom to scrub off the makeup. This suite had two baths. The ladies' room had a vanity desk, mirrors spanning the entire wall. They could fold so I could get a look from all angles. The gents' was more basic. Both had tiny color TVs and phones. All fancy stuff, but none of it really got me excited.

Bone-tired, I wanted to yank out the bed from the couch, but I was stumped. After a few futile tries, I just plopped on the sofa, waiting for George's return. When I shut my eyes, a parade of elegant women from the cocktail party danced in my head. Any one of them could work a social scene better than I ever could. Why had George picked me? He was fresh out of a divorce, single, sophisticated, loaded, and a true gentleman. Were there really no other women vying for his attention? Tonight's party was like a crash course in the ways of the world. How could I even dream of being on par with these American women? I was just a small-town girl.

I lost track of time, dozing off on the sofa. In my slumber, I felt someone gently lifting me. Who was it? I tried to push them away, but my limbs wouldn't cooperate. I blinked open my eyes and there I was, stretched out on the sofa bed. George hovered, lying on his side, a soft glow from the lamp behind him.

我照顾柯丽丝，对我很尊重很亲热？

进了卧室，我趴在柯丽丝的“围墙”上，把她从头看到脚。从第一次在安娜的面包车上和她相遇到今天，柯丽丝已经有了很大的变化。那个时候，她只会笑，不会说话，不知道如何表达自己，除了吃就是睡。几个月来，她的个子长高了，已经能够自己走路，自己跑跳。每天要说许多话，除了模仿成人以外，还知道选择Yes和No。

祝贺你，柯丽丝，素素为你骄傲。

记得乔治和安娜吵架的时候，曾经说柯丽丝是个可怜的孩子。当时我并不明白。现在知道了，因为这个孩子一来到人间就没有了妈妈。安娜接受了一个自己丈夫和别人生养的孩子，是多么不容易啊！

柯丽丝第一天见到我，就和我无比亲热，几乎让安娜产生妒忌，是不是她下意识里感受到了母亲的感情？她对我是那么地依赖，那么地信任，我能承担得起吗？

我想到这一路旅游，名义上是为了庆祝她的生日，实际上，我和她父亲在谈情说爱。本来，我把所有的爱都给了她，现在，心中有了乔治，我要两面兼顾。我们到了这个城市，到了她妈妈安息的地方，应该安排孩子去见见她的妈妈，在坟上添添土拔拔草。可是，我们去了那个鬼酒会。我不由地一阵难过，心中很愧咎，不禁眼泪汪汪。

我去洗手间卸妆洗澡。套房有两个厕所，女用的，有个很大的梳妆台，一面墙都是镜子，两端还有能折过来，看到后背和侧面。男用的，简单一些。但是，两个洗手间里面都有彩色的小屏幕电视，还有电话。这些被称为高级的享受，对我没有一点吸引力。

突然觉得很累了，想把沙发拉开来，却不知道开关和窍门。试来试去，都不行。于是，便靠在上面等乔治回来。闭上眼睛，却看到了酒会上美女如织。随便拉一个和我比，都比我热情鲜活。乔治为什么偏偏选中我？他刚刚离婚，单身，成熟，富有，风度翩翩，难道没有女人的追求？今晚，总算见了世面，我哪里是美国女人的竞争对手？

我是多么土气啊！不知什么时候，我在沙发上睡着了。睡眠中，被人抱了起来。那个人是谁？看不清他的脸。我把他推开，可是，手脚都不听使唤。我揉揉眼睛，发现自己已经睡在沙发床上，乔治正侧身躺在旁边看我。他的背后亮着柔和的灯光。

乔治，我伸一条手臂给他，又闭上了眼睛。我说，对不起，我怎么睡着了？梦见有人把我抢走了。

"George," I murmured, reaching out to him and closing my eyes again, "I'm sorry I dozed off. I had this dream that someone whisked me away."

He pulled me close, "No apologies needed. I got back late."

I sighed, "You don't really fancy my hair and dress from tonight, do you?"

"Susu, you don't need all the frills. You're a born star. Everyone couldn't take their eyes off you."

I frowned, "There were so many stunning women. I can't even hold a candle to them."

"What's got you feeling this way? Did someone upset you?"

"No, no one hurt my feelings. George, it's just that... I don't feel like I fit—"

"Fit for a cocktail party?"

"No. When I saw you surrounded by all those people, up there on the stage, laughing and chatting, I felt like... I'm not fit to be your wife."

George scowled and turned his back on me, leaving me wide awake. What had I said in my half-slumber? Had I insinuated dissatisfaction, whether from him or me? He'd put so much effort into our relationship already. If I harbored discontent, what could he do about it? Suddenly, regret gnawed at me. I realized I'd made a string of missteps. I regretted not wearing a more dazzling dress for the party, regretted the spat with George earlier in the day, and regretted pushing his buttons.

I inched closer to him, clinging to him tightly, and whispered, "You're still awake, George? Susu admits she was wrong and apologizes."

He turned to face me, tucking a loose strand of hair away from my face, "Everyone congratulated me, shared in my joy. So you should be happy, too. Do you really think they bought it when I introduced you as Kristeene's friend? They're not that naive. The love in our eyes doesn't go unnoticed. Susu, don't torment yourself. Love is meant to be cherished. Why hide it?"

"I love you, George, but I'm scared to love," I confessed.

"Why are you scared?"

"I don't always heed your advice and I often get on your nerves."

George grinned, playfully touching the tip of my nose, "Darling, that's what endears you to me. You've got a unique personality and a mind of your own. You're not one to back down easily. Women like you aren't all that common, you know?"

I didn't bring up Laura, leaving that topic untouched.

他搂着我说，对不起的应该是我，回来那么晚。

我说，你不喜欢我今晚的发式和衣服，是不是？

素素，你不需要靠衣服打扮，你是天生的明星。大家的眼睛都盯着你看。

我说，很多很多漂亮的女人，我不能和她们比。

怎么啦？有谁伤害了你吗？

没有谁伤害我。乔治，觉得自己不配。

他说，不配去参加酒会？

不，看到那么多人围着你转，看到你在台上谈笑风生，我觉得你不应该选我做太太。

乔治沉下了脸，瞪了我一眼，背过身去，不理我了。

这下子，我完全清醒了。我胡里胡涂地说了些什么呀？是在说他不满意我，还是我不满意他？他已经够努力了，如果我还不满意，他能做什么？突然我感到非常后悔，觉得自己做错了许多事情。后悔自己没有穿漂亮的衣服去酒会，后悔自己白天和乔治吵架，后悔现在惹乔治生气。

我一点一点地靠近他，用身体贴上去，贴得很紧，轻轻地说，睡着了吗，乔治？素素错了，向你道歉。

他回过身来，撩起遮在我脸上的头发，认真地说，大家都在祝贺我，为我高兴。你也应该高兴么！你以为我介绍你是柯丽丝的朋友，他们真的相信了？谁有那么傻？我们的爱都在眼睛里，谁也瞒不了。素素，不要和自己过不去。爱情多么美好，为什么要躲躲闪闪呢？

我说，乔治我是爱的你呀，爱得害怕。

他说，为什么要害怕呢？

我很不听话，惹你生气。

乔治笑了，点着我的鼻尖说，亲爱的，这就是我最喜欢你的地方呀！你有个性，有独立见解，不轻易放弃，这样的女人并不多，你知道吗？……

我没有提劳瑞的事情。

Chapter 26

During breakfast the next day, I turned to George and asked, "What's the plan for today?"

He looked up from his newspaper, "Nothing much, just some leisure time. We could hit the seaside, do some shopping, take a leisurely stroll, and savor some delightful food."

I ventured further, "Would you like to pay a visit to Laura? Or perhaps, let Laura see Kristeene?"

The newspaper slipped from his hand in surprise at my first question. Upon hearing the second, he couldn't remain seated and retreated to the balcony, coffee cup in hand.

Had Dennis not mentioned that Laura's resting place was right here in the city, if I hadn't pointed out how close we were, George would never have considered visiting her. As he rose, a fleeting trace of sorrow flickered in his eyes. The balcony was adorned with a glass-topped table and cushioned chairs, crowned by a grand umbrella. George took a seat, facing the sea, his coffee cup cradled against his chest, clutching it like he held his very heart.

I joined him, leaning against his shoulder, and whispered, "My love, shall we go visit Laura?"

He appeared lost in his own thoughts. I settled into a chair beside him, observing him, the sky, and the sea. Beneath the vast, clear heavens, autumn winds swept away the clouds of sorrow, casting their reflections in George's eyes. Resting my chin on my hand, I gazed out at the boundless sea, still and serene. The winds over the water roared. White-crested waves surged a few meters high, then cascaded into sprays, in an eternal dance.

"George, you want to visit her, but you're apprehensive, aren't you?" I ventured.

"Laura departed a month after Kristeene was born. Today marks the second anniversary of her passing. Initially, I planned to come here alone."

"Let's go together. I hold love for Kristeene and also for Laura, who gave her life."

"Susu," he spoke my name.

"Yes, George?" I responded, but silence followed. He gazed into the dis-

第二十六章

第二天在吃早餐的时候，我问乔治，我们还有什么安排？他说，没有了，轻松一下，等会儿我们去海边玩，逛逛街，买点东西，享受美食。

我说，你不想去看看劳瑞？也不想让劳瑞看看柯丽丝？

他正在看报纸，托在手里的报纸一下子掉到了膝盖上。他坐不住了，捧着咖啡杯去了阳台。

如果不是丹尼告诉我劳瑞的坟墓就在这里，也就是说，如果我不点穿劳瑞和我们如此接近，乔治本来没有拜访劳瑞的打算。他站起来的时候，眼神很忧愁很凄凉。

套房的阳台上，有一张玻璃圆桌和几张软椅，圆桌的中央是一把很大的遮阳伞。乔治面海而坐，一直把咖啡杯捧在胸前。他把杯子捧得很紧，好像杯子里装的不是咖啡，而是他那颗破碎的心。

我走过去，趴在他的肩膀上，轻轻地说，亲爱的，我们去看看劳瑞，好吗？他好像没有听见。我在他旁边的椅子上坐下，看看他，看看天，再看看海。晴空万里，秋风把愁云都吹走了，吹到了海里，映入乔治的眼睛。我支着脸，对着大海发呆。海风呼啸着，白花花的浪涛，窜得几米高，狠狠地摔下来，支离破碎。一次又一次地重复，不罢休不回头。

我说，你是想去看她的，又怕去看她，对不对，乔治？

他说，劳瑞是在柯丽丝满月以后走的。下个月的今天就是劳瑞的忌日。原来想独自来一次。

我说，我们一起去。我爱柯丽丝，也爱给了她生命的劳瑞。

素素。他叫着我的名字。

乔治。我答道。等了好久，没有回答。他望着前方的大海，半开着眼睛，给人魂不附体的感觉。

我说，你怎么不说话？

他还是那样，如雕塑一般。

tance, eyes half-lidded, a distant look in his eyes.

"Why aren't you speaking?" I inquired.

He remained still, like a statue.

"George, is your past returning to you?"

He closed his eyes.

Seeing his furrowed brows and pained expression, my heart ached. I recalled his words on the train, how he believed he'd left his past behind because he loved me, because he yearned for a fresh start. Yet, the regret and guilt over Laura still lingered deep within him. I remembered how he'd exuded joy at the party last night. Was it an attempt to shield himself from reality?

"George, I have my own sorrowful past that I'd rather not revisit," I confessed.

He peered at me through half-closed eyes.

"But with your presence in my heart, my old wounds are mending. George, do you believe love is a kind of strength? That it bestows courage? Who can evade life's trials? I only hope that the hardships we face don't go in vain, but transform into treasures. Our meeting and love are intertwined with our pasts. Without my past, Susu wouldn't be the Susu you see today, and George wouldn't be the George I see now. Right?"

He nodded slowly, savoring my words. Setting the coffee cup on the table, he looked out at the sea.

I said, "Don't fear that I can't share your sorrow and agony. I am willing to share and will help you to heal your wound like you healed mine."

His eyes glistened with tears, a tender smile gracing his lips.

I asked, "Do you want to listen to my story?"

He nodded, two teardrops trailing down his cheeks. "Susu, come here, sit on my lap."

I nestled against his shoulder and began recounting my tale.

"I was born in years of famine. Both my parents were intellectuals. My father taught at the university, and my mother was a physician. They had two children. My brother is five years older than me."

George interjected, "Why was there a period of famine? Were you destitute? How could it be that a professor and a doctor had no money?"

"We had no money," I explained. "And even if we did, there was nothing to buy. The government faced severe issues, and production ground to a halt. My mother had no milk for the baby. We were only provided two bottles of milk a day by the local government. I was nourished and grew on rice soup and something akin to paste."

George couldn't hold back his tears. He enveloped me from behind, his body and arms trembling.

I continued, "From the time I began to understand, our family was sent to the countryside."

George choked out, "Sent to the countryside? Why were you sent there?

我说，乔治，是不是过去在向你走来？

他闭上了眼睛。

看着他紧锁的眉头和痛苦的脸，我很心疼。我想起了在列车上，他说和过去作了了结。那是因为爱上了我，有了新生活的希望。但是，对劳瑞的歉疚和负罪感，依然留在心底。我想起了他在昨天晚上的酒会上神采飞扬，难道仅仅是为了麻醉自己？

我说，乔治，我也有很悲哀的过去不敢回首。

他醒了，把脸转向我。

是的。我说，我从来不谈，想都不愿意去回想。

他看着我，眼睛比原来张开了些。

但是，自从我心中有了你，过去的伤痛渐渐地在愈合在收口。乔治，你不觉得爱是一种力量吗？爱能给人勇气吗？人活在世上，哪一个能逃离磨难？只希望磨难不要付诸东流，而成为人生的宝贵财富。我们相遇相爱，都和你我的过去分不开。如果没有过去的经历，你看到的就不是今天的素素，我看到的也不是今天的乔治，对不对？

他点了一下头，点得很慢，好像在品味着我的话。他把咖啡杯放到了玻璃桌上。

我说，不要忧虑我不能分担你的痛苦。我不仅愿意分担，而且愿意帮助你愈合。就像你愈合了我的伤口一样。他的眼睛里出现了泪光，嘴角露出了微笑。

我说，要听我过去的故事吗？让我给你一个完整的素素，好吗？

他点点头，滚出了两行眼泪，说，素素，过来，让我抱着你。

我靠在他的肩膀上，说起了我的故事。

我说，我出生在一个饥饿的年代，父母亲都是知识分子。父亲在大学里教书，母亲是内科医生。他们有两个孩子，哥哥比我大五岁。

乔治问，为什么是饥饿的年代？很穷吗？医生和教授怎么会没有钱？

没有钱。我重复说，有了钱也买不到东西。国家出了问题，生产不出东西。妈妈没有奶，婴儿每天有两瓶牛奶的定量供应，我是喝米汤和面糊长大的。

乔治哭了。他从背后拥着我，手臂和身体都在抽动。

我说，在我懂事的时候，我们全家被赶到了乡下。

乔治抽泣着问道，赶到了乡下？为什么要赶你们？乡下好不好？

Was it better in the countryside?"

"As both my parents were intellectuals, they were mandated to work in the countryside, much like the Jews forced from their homes. People in the countryside were impoverished. They had no income, barely enough to eat. So, my parents and brother toiled in the fields. I took on the role of cook at home. Ovens in the countryside were made of bricks. Back then, I was as tall as the oven, so I'd have to stand on a stool to cook. I often pilfered some of the food intended for my brother because my mother favored him and gave him more. Schools were shuttered then. I could only read what my father fashioned for me as a makeshift textbook. We had no running water and had to rely on the well. Buckets were used to draw water. Clothes were washed in the river. There were no gas or lights, just like the house of the philosophy professor in the east—barren. Of course, it wasn't quite as romantic as the professor's abode. In winter, we laid hay on our beds for warmth, or we couldn't sleep in the cold. The house was plastered with mud and stayed cool in summer, but when it rained, the inside was nearly flooded. Don't cry, George, that was many years ago."

George's sobs echoed, his voice quivering. "Susu, why couldn't I have known you twenty years earlier—so I could have saved you from such hardship?"

I turned to him, wiping away his tears, and said with a smile, "We know each other now. You love me, and you've already saved me."

"Your back?" He inquired, starting to massage my back.

"Yes," I said, "It was hurt then. I had to get water from the well for cooking. I was so skinny."

"We have to find the best doctor to heal your back."

"It's okay," I said. "I'll be fine if the bed is not too soft."

George said, "From now on, you mustn't carry Kristeene, or it will hurt your back. Let her walk. She grows heavier and heavier every day."

Just then, Kristeene was calling my name. I let go of George and wanted to go inside to have a look. But George wouldn't let me go. He said, "You sit here. I'll go to check on her."

He carried Kristeene over, and the three of us sat together.

George's eyes were red. Kristeene looked at him in surprise as if she realized that something had happened. She clung to me. I said, "Kristeene, the Pacific, look, this is the Pacific."

George said, "Kristeene, do you know what is beyond the Pacific? Susu's homeland. Susu's mother, father, and brother. Many of Susu's friends are all there. When you grow up, we'll go there together on a visit, okay?"

Kristeene looked at me, rolling her big eyes, as if saying, 'Is that so?'

I said, "Daddy is right. There's Susu's homeland."

George said, "Kristeene, shall we go to see your mother this afternoon?

我说，因为父母是知识分子，必须到乡下去，就像犹太人被赶出家园一样。乡下很穷，吃不饱，没有收入。父母和哥哥都要下农田干活，我在家里给他们做饭。农村里的炉灶是砖块砌成的，我和炉灶一样高，做饭的时候，脚下要垫一个小凳子。我常常抢哥哥的那份饭吃。因为妈妈不公平，给他装的比我多。当时没有学校，都关门了。我念父亲做的课本。我们没有自来水，用井水，一桶一桶提上来。衣服在河里洗。没有煤气和电灯，就像哲学教授东面的那个房子，里面什么都没有，当然，也没有教授的浪漫诗意。冬天，我们在床上铺很多稻草，否则冻得不能睡。泥巴糊成的房子，夏天很凉快，只怕刮风下雨，一

下雨，家里到处都是水。不要哭，乔治，都是好多年以前的事情了。

乔治哭得泣不成声。素素，……为什么不能……早认识你二十年，……让我把你救出来？

我回身给他擦眼泪，笑着说，我们不是认识了吗？你爱我，已经把我救了出来。

他说，你的背……？他一边说，一边在我的背后按摩。

是的，我说，就是在哪个时候压坏的，我要去挑井水，当时我瘦得皮包骨头。

他说，我们找最好的医生，把你的背治好。

我没事。我说，床硬一点，就没事了。

他说，从此以后，不准你抱柯丽丝，让她自己走。她越来越重了，否则要伤到你的背。正在这时候，柯丽丝在里面叫我的名字。我放开了乔治，想进去看看，被乔治抱住了腰。他说，你坐着，我去。

他把柯丽丝抱了过来，我们三人坐在一起。

乔治的眼睛通红。柯丽丝惊讶地看看他，以为发生了什么事情，扑到我的怀里。

我说，柯丽丝，太平洋，看，这是太平洋。

乔治说，柯丽丝，你知道太平洋那一边是什么吗？那里是素素的家乡。素素的妈妈，爸爸和哥哥，素素的许多朋友都在那里。等柯丽丝长大了，我们一起去那里玩，好吗？

柯丽丝看看我，大眼睛转了一圈，好像在说，是这样吗？

我说，爹地说得对，那里是素素的家乡。

乔治说，柯丽丝，今天下午，我们去见你的妈妈好吗？她睡在这个城市的地底下。

柯丽丝再朝我看看，大眼睛里都是问号，好像在说，你不是我

She's sleeping underground in this city."

Kristeene looked at me again, her big eyes full of question marks, as if asking, 'Are you not my mother?'

I smiled and kissed her cheeks. "Kristeene, daddy is right. Your mother is here. She's sleeping, sleeping forever."

The little girl shook her head, resting her face on my shoulder and saying that she wouldn't go.

I said, "Kristeene, Susu won't leave you. We'll go together."

After lunch, Dennis came to knock on our door. The car went to the suburbs and stopped at a picturesque place. We all got off. Dennis carried Kristeene on his shoulders. We went in together. The graveyard was a stretch of land. It looked like it was expanding to the horizon. The green lawns were like a soft blanket that covered the dead. The tall kapok trees, almost reaching the sky, were lined up like sentinels to guard those resting underground.

I held George's hand, feeling that his hand was trembling. I said, "George, cheer up. We came to meet an old friend." He smiled at me, saying, "Laura will be at rest as long as Kristeene grows up well."

Dennis walked faster than we. Reaching the center of the graveyard, he halted. I asked George if we arrived. He nodded.

The grave sight was so beautiful and colorful! All around the tombstone grew various flowers, shrubs, and trees. Needless to say, I was a bit surprised at how decorated everything was.

'Laura Ford Dickson' was on the tombstone. George had given her his family name. Looking down, I read the next line: '1963—1989.' She was younger than I.

Dennis let Kristeene down. The little girl ran among the trees, looking like a beautiful butterfly. George and Dennis bowed their heads before the grave. I pulled Kristeene to my side and whispered in her ears, "Kristeene, here is the home of your mother. She is Laura Ford Dickson." I lifted her arm to feel the tombstone while saying, "Remember, your mother's lying here."

Kristeene repeated, "Laura Ford Dickson's lying here."

Watching Kristeene, I had a lot to say to Laura. But I thought that it was better to wait for George to speak first. There was no sound in the graveyard. The silence would have made one's ears lose the listening ability. Sometimes silence speaks louder than any sound. I heard a sound I couldn't hear at usual times. I heard the sprouts shooting out of the soil. I heard the insects flapping their wings. I heard the flower buds blossoming gently. I heard the breezes cradling the fallen leaves. I couldn't help but feel like I was almost in heaven.

George didn't say anything all the time. Since we came to the front of Laura's grave, he hadn't uttered a word. What was he thinking? Had he just said that Laura should be at rest as long as Kristeene would grow up well? He should know that Laura would be at rest as long as he had someone to love him.

的妈妈吗？

我笑了，亲亲她的脸蛋，说道，柯丽丝，爹地是对的，你的母亲在这里，她睡着了，永远地睡着了。

小姑娘摇摇头，把脸搁在我的肩膀上，说她不要去。

我说，柯丽丝，素素不会离开你，我们一起去。

丹尼在午饭以后来敲了门。汽车开到了城外，停在一个风景如画的地方。下了车，丹尼把柯丽丝扛在肩膀上，我们一起往里走。那是一片很大的墓地，放眼望去，几乎看不到边际。绿油油的草地如柔软的毯子复盖在这些故人的身上。耸入云天的木棉树，排列得像哨兵一样整齐，好像一道连接天地的屏障，让地底下的人们安心休息。

我拉着乔治的手，只觉得他的手在颤抖。我说，乔治，开心一点，我们来会老朋友。

他对我笑了笑，说道，只要柯丽丝成长得好，劳瑞就放心了。

丹尼比我们走得快，走到墓地的中心时，他停了下来。我问乔治，就在那里吗？他点了点头。

哇，好漂亮，万紫千红，墓碑的周围种着各种灌木花树。

劳瑞．福特．笛克荪

乔治把家姓给了她。

1963年---1989年

她比我年轻。丹尼把柯丽丝放了下来，小姑娘在花树中来回地奔跑，就像一只美丽的蝴蝶。乔治和丹尼都低着头，站在墓碑前。我把柯丽丝拉到身边，蹲下来在她的耳旁轻轻地说，柯丽丝，这里是你母亲的HOME，她叫劳瑞．福特．笛克荪。我提起她的手臂，往前去抚摸墓碑，说道，记住了，你的母亲就在这里睡着了。柯丽丝重复道，劳瑞．福特．笛克荪在这里睡着了。说完，又飞走了。

看着柯丽丝的背影，我有许多话要对劳瑞说。我想，还是等等吧，让乔治先说。

墓地里没有一点杂音，静得让耳朵失去听力。真是此时无声胜有声啊！我听见了平时听不到的声音。我听见了芽尖破土而出，听见了昆虫扇动翅膀，听见花苞开蕾舒放，听见了轻风驾叶摇荡，……。啊，如果真的有天堂，那么，站在这里，就像踏上了一片彩云，来到了上帝的花园。

乔治一直不说话。自从我们来到了劳瑞的墓前，他没有说过一个字。他在想什么呢？刚才他不是说，只要柯丽丝成长得好，劳瑞就应该放心了吗？他还应该知道，只要乔治有人爱，劳瑞也应该放心了啊！

At that time, the taciturn Dennis began to speak. "Dear Laura, before you breathed your last, you hinted to me that you had some health problem. You said that you were totally exhausted and afraid that you would not wake up some day and no one would look after Kristeene you left behind. How should I know then that you wanted to go? Laura, after you left us, George has been heart-heart, but Kristeene has been taken good care of. Yesterday, it was her second birthday. It means that you left us for two years. Today, Kristeene's coming with us to visit you. Look at her, is she a happy girl? This is because Kristeene has a new mother. Laura, may your soul be at rest!"

I said, "Dear Laura, though we didn't see each other, George often told me your story. So in my heart, I feel that we are like old friends, because we love the same man and the same child. Laura, your child Kristeene is an angel God sent to us. She brings me endless happiness. Your beloved George is my protector of life. His love makes me gratified and grateful every day. Be at rest! I will take care of them."

When I finished, George, taking one of my hands, suddenly went down on one knee. He knelt before me and kissed my hand over and over again, saying, "Susu, Susu, will you marry me? Are you willing to be my bride?"

I knelt down, too, leaning my head on his shoulder, with tears down my cheeks. I didn't know what to say.

Dennis urged, "Speak, Susu, speak."

"Ah," I said, "Yes; George. I will be your bride."

George put a ring on my finger. Kristeene ran to us and flung herself on us. Dennis crouched and hugged us together.

At that time, I believed in God. I believed that everything was arranged by God and everything was taken care of by God. I seemed to see Laura's soul slowly soaring into the sky. She was entirely freed.

没想到沉默寡言的丹尼却在这时开了口。他说，亲爱的劳瑞，你临走前，多次暗示我，说你的健康出了问题。你说，你觉得非常累非常累，最怕哪一天醒不过来，留下了柯丽丝没有人照顾。我哪里知道你已经打算走了？劳瑞，在你离开我们以后，乔治心胆俱碎，但是，没有让柯丽丝受到一点伤害。昨天，柯丽丝两岁了，你也走了快两年。今天，柯丽丝和我们一起来看你。你看她，是不是一个快乐幸福的孩子？这是因为柯丽丝有了新的妈妈。劳瑞，你可以放心地睡了。

我说，亲爱的劳瑞，我们虽然没有见过面，但是，乔治告诉了我你的故事。在我的心里，我们就像老朋友一样，因为我们爱着同一个男人和同一个孩子。劳瑞，你的孩子柯丽丝是上帝派来的天使，给我带来无穷的欢乐。你的爱人乔治，是我生命的保护人。他的爱，让我天天满足，天天感恩。你放心地去吧，我一定把他们照顾好。

刚说完，乔治拉住了我的一只手，突然跪下了一条腿。他跪在我的面前，把我的手吻了又吻。他说，素素，素素，嫁给我，好吗？做我的新娘，你愿意吗？

我也跪了下去，把头靠在他的肩膀上，眼泪直流，不知道应该说什么好。

丹尼说，素素，说呀，说呀！

噢，我说，Yes， I do。

乔治把一个戒指套上了我的手指。

柯丽丝跑了过来，扑在我们身上，丹尼也蹲了下来，和我们拥抱在一起。就在这个时候，我相信了上帝。我相信一切都是由上帝安排的，一切都由上帝来照顾。我好像看到了劳瑞的灵魂冉冉地向空中飘去。她彻底地自由了。

Chapter 27

So, I went on the trip home with George's ring on my finger.

We took the helicopter. It rose straight, without a curve like going over a bridge. It went up so suddenly that I held my breath, being afraid that it would hit something in the sky. Although Dennis had warned me beforehand of its abrupt vertical taking off, yet I was so nervous and horrified that my face turned white. Kristeene was scared at the beginning. With a wry face, she even seemed to be unable to make up her mind if she would cry or not. I immediately turned my attention to her, oblivious of my own fright.

There were three rows of seats in the copter. Dennis and George occupied front seats. Kristeene and I sat in the middle seats. Our luggage was put on the back seats. In the noise of the copter, conversation was difficult. I used my fingers in a form like a fluttering bird, saying loudly, "Kristeene, the little birdie flying." I writhed my wrist, waved my arm and let her see my hand. I couldn't stand up and dance even if I intended, because the safety belt tied across my belly. I counted "One, two, three, four." I pointed to four of us and waved my hand up and down, right and left, saying, "Kristeene, we are little birds, flying, flying. We are flying in the air." Understanding or not, she looked at me, with her eyes following my fingers. I held her hand and let it fly with mine. Our hands moved from low to high while we writhed our wrists. Kristeene did it beautifully.

I didn't notice that George turned to watch us all the time. Only when I sat back on the seat did I see him looming before my eyes. He smiled and threw me a kiss. I returned one to him and let Kristeene blow a kiss to him, too. Kristeene smiled and shouted, "Daddy, daddy, birdie, birdie." I kissed her and said, "Kristeene, you are a brave birdie." She said, "Daddy, Kristeene, a brave birdie." Then she moved her hand around, which made George and me laugh.

When Kristeene was speaking, the helicopter reached a certain altitude and began to fly smoothly forward. The city beneath us looked like a model one. We could command a full view of it. It now lost all its majesty and grandeur. I thought of the theory of the philosophy professor. He had said, "Human eyes sometimes play magic on us. They change things and we believe that those are real things. There is no objective standard between reality and falsehood. They depend on each other for standard."

In the gentle rocking of the copter, I already shut my eyes for a rest. The words of the philosophy professor emerged in my mind when I was daydreaming. There were two movies running in my brain, one of black and white, the other colored. My black and white image and my colored image were some-

第二十七章

我带着乔治的戒指，走上了回家的旅程。

坐直升飞机，原地往上升，没有弧度，腾空得突然，如撞天一般，真是捏了一把汗。虽然，丹尼事先作了解释，我还是紧张得变了色。柯丽丝从一开始就惊恐万分，一幅哭丧的脸孔，好像连该不该哭都拿不定主意。我顾不上自己，赶快安慰小姑娘。

飞机里有三排位置，丹尼和乔治坐前面。我和柯丽丝坐中间，后座放我们的行李。飞机轰隆隆地响，说话很累。我一边用手做跳舞的兰花指头，大声说道，小鸟飞飞，柯丽丝。我转动手腕，舞动手臂，叫她看着我的手。腹部系着安全带，要跳舞也跳不起来。我数着一，二，三，四，前后左右，上上下下地比划着，一边说，柯丽丝，我们就是小鸟，飞呵，飞呵，我们飞到了空中。她似懂非懂地看着我，目光跟着我的手指走。我拉着她的手，和我同步飞。由低往高飞，一边飞，一边转动手腕。柯丽丝做得很漂亮。我竖起了两个大拇指。

我没注意到乔治回头一直在看我们。当我松了一口气，背靠在座位上的时候，才察觉到他就在眼前，笑眯眯地给了我一个飞吻。我回了他，并让柯丽丝也吹一个吻给他。柯丽丝笑了，爹地，爹地，小鸟，小鸟，叫个不停。我亲着她说，柯丽丝，你是最勇敢的小鸟。她说，爹地，柯丽丝是最勇敢的小鸟。随即又把手臂舞动起来，惹得我和乔治大笑。

柯丽丝说话的时候，飞机已经升到一定的高度，开始平稳地朝前飞。此刻，城市如玩具模型一样，尽收眼底，完全失去了原本的雄伟和壮观。这让我想起了哲学教授的理论。他说，人的眼睛（经验）有时候变换把戏捉弄我们，自己还信以为真。真和假实在没有太客观的标准，而是互相依赖的难兄难弟。

我合上了眼睛在轻微的摇晃中休息。

times interwoven and sometimes lapped. I walked alone on the road of love. It started when I was twenty years old. How I longed to love! I hated that time was numb and went too slow. When I saw the couple next door caressing each other, I often asked myself how long I should wait to reach twenty-five. (It was the legal age at that time for a girl to marry in China, and thirty for a man.) And how would I look at twenty-five? As lovely as now, or turned into an old woman? Would anyone still love me at twenty-five? As a result, I didn't reach twenty-five when I began to love someone. Love won't wait. Love comes at due time and no one can push it away. And love can make time fly.

My first love could not be publicly known. I acted like a spy. I must conceal it from my parents and friends. I had to play two-faced and tell lies against my own will. We hid here and there. We went where no one would go, under the bridge, by the heart walls or in the ruins, as long as we could get together. At first, when our eyes met, I blushed scarlet like a cooked lobster. When we sauntered together and our hands touched involuntarily, I would be startled and quickly pull back my hand. But my heart, once being shot out like an arrow, could not be retrieved.

The first time when he held my hand, I wished that he would never let it go. The first time when he held me in his arms, I wished that I would fall asleep like that and never wake up. The more we kept it a secret, the happier we felt when together. The happier we felt, the more we were desperate to meet. Soon we broke the bound until we saw the spot of blood on where we were making love. We were both scared out of our wits, silent and motionless. At that moment, the sweet love suddenly became ugly. We were like two betrayed soldiers facing the surrounding troops approaching us. Two pairs of terrified eyes, one looking toward the sky, one looking at the ground. We both knew that it was too serious for us. There was no other way for us to do but to keep it an eternal secret, to let it remain forever in the bottom of our hearts. To the outsiders, we shut our mouths tight and never admitted that we had an unusual relationship. To ourselves, we became more intimate. Our reason was that we would sooner or later get married. As we got a reason, we acted more freely. The taken-for-granted reason was like oil added to our fire.

So a man and a woman rolled on the floor, forgetful of everything in the world. On the carpet of the train, the black-and-white Chinese changed into the colored American. . .

The feeling in the copter was just like that on the train: my feet shaken, hands shaken, even the seat was shaken. Now I was back in that familiar train compartment, seated across to a man. He said, "Don't leave, Susu, don't leave." He said, "Because we love each other." He embraced me and asked, "Can I kiss you?"

It was a summer night when it was pouring cats and dogs. We were hiding behind a huge tree. Perceiving that I was shivering with cold, he shared with me his body warmth.

My colored self said, "The love won't do when it's the result of teaching. So I must consider if his love is worth mine."

My monochrome self said, "Never go back home. Let's die here." We were like sexually hungry ghosts, wanting more and more, and swallowing the whole of it as if we could never have enough. At last I found out that I was pregnant. It was like a thunderbolt out of the blue. I was scared to death. Love

脑海里放映着两部电影，一个屏幕是黑白的，另一个是彩色的。黑白的我和彩色的我交织着，一会儿离得很远，一会儿重叠起来，播放着我的爱情之旅。

走向二十的岁月，多么想恋爱呵，只嫌时间走得太慢，太麻木太不仁。看到隔壁邻居小夫妻俩亲亲热热，常常问自己，还要等多久才能长到二十五岁？二十五岁的我又将是什么模样？也像今天这么漂亮可爱，还是变成了小老太婆？二十五岁的我还有人喜欢吗？结果，没有等到二十五岁，已经偷偷地爱上了。爱情是不能等的，说来就来，推之不去。爱情让时间飞起来。我的初恋是秘密的，天天像做间谍一样，瞒着父母和所有的朋友，吹牛撒谎做两面派。我们躲到东藏到西，只要没有人的地方，我们就在那里出现。桥底下，断墙旁，废墟里，我们都去。只要两个人能够单独地在一起。开始是眼对眼，目光如电，碰上了，满脸通红。走路的时候，不经意地触及到他的手，吓得马上缩回来。可是，一颗心就像射出去的箭一样，再也收不回来。

第一次被他捏着手，就希望他永远不要再松开。第一次倒在他的怀里，希望就这样睡着了，永远不要醒过来。越秘密爱得越欢畅，越欢畅越不顾一切，很快突破了界限。直到看见那滩血，两个人都吓得惊惶失措，无以言对。这个时候，美好的爱情突然间变得面貌可憎。我们像被出卖了一样，面对着正在向我们包抄而来的千军万马。两双恐惧的眼睛，一双望着天，一双望着地，谁都知道担当不起。没有其他的途径，只能永远地秘密下去，让它留在两个人的心底里。对外，我们守口如瓶，绝不承认不“正常”的关系。对内，我们更加亲密，理由是，反正早晚要结婚的。心一宽，好像火上加了油，更加肆无忌惮。一男一女在地上滚到东滚到西，完全忘记了天南地北。

火车的地毯上。黑白的中国人换成了彩色的美国人。坐飞机的感觉和坐火车一模一样。脚在动，手在动，座位也在动。我回到了那个熟悉的包间，坐在一个男人的对面。他说，不要走，素素，不要走。因为我们相爱。他把我搂在怀里，问我吻一下是否可以？

倾盆大雨的夏夜，我们躲在一棵大树的后面，见我冷得发抖，他和我分享他的体温。彩色的我说，教育出来的爱情不算数，我要考虑考虑。

黑色的我说，不要再回家，让我们死在这里。我们像饿死鬼一样，要了还要，囫囵吞枣，好像永远吃不饱。我发现自己怀孕了，

betrayed us again. I must get abortion since I am not yet twenty-five. How cruel! I had no choice. We took a long-distance bus running over the rugged mountainous roads for hours. It was there, the gray-tiled brick house, the far-off countryside clinic, where I went, trembling with fear. We would spend the least money to get the abortion done. I lay on that simple operating table and he was also terrified with a whitened face.

Ah, the whitened face of George and the back of a woman. He feared a life together without marriage.

Pregnant again. Abortion again. When we were in love, we had no means, nor were we ready to get married. But when we reached the age to marry, we often quarreled. The situation was that when we were not together, we thought of each other, but when we were together, we blamed each other for everything. Our love mildewed and went stale. All that happened, the quarrels and hurts, originated in that we had entered the forbidden area, eaten the forbidden fruit. Whose fault was it? Who was responsible for it? Who else to blame except ourselves? Thus he left me forever. I stared at his back with my anxious eyes

In life, there are boundaries we dare not cross, much like a moth drawn to the flame. Love, the riskiest of them all. Yet we leaped, and our love met its end. Still, it was the same love, once filled with poignant sorrow, now aglow with happiness and sweetness. As for my initial love, maybe without the constraints, things might have taken a different turn. The landscape has shifted for the youth, offering a myriad of paths – love, cohabitation, changing partners, solitude, matrimony, or divorce. It seems every road leads to Rome for them. Yet, without the past to guide me, could my present self ever have taken shape?

I emerged from that abyss. When he left, he already had another paramour. She must have surpassed me, but why did he abandon me? What had I done wrong? I had secured admission to a university. Why, then, did he no longer desire me? We had been akin to husband and wife.

As the old Chinese adage goes, one day in heaven, ten years on Earth. Daily existence resembles a train ride – days slip away, carriages roll past. We traverse tunnels, cross rivers, loop and wind, but always on those winding tracks. Love, on the other hand, is akin to this helicopter, soaring ever higher, unbridled. Did we truly dwell in paradise? We'd met for mere days, or perhaps months at most, and we'd fallen in love. Now, we've transitioned from love to wearing George's engagement ring. Is the myth in this paradise something we can believe, or should we remain skeptical?

Upon opening my eyes, I beheld a brilliance emanating from my diamond ring. The once transparent gem had transformed into a resplendent, multicolored floral mosaic beneath the sunlight. Was it the sun's caress that made the unyielding diamond appear so soft, so aglow? Ah, this exquisite ring – gazing at it, no words were needed.

After a brush with mortality, the tension between us waned. I forgave him. People divorce after years of union. Why should I not release him? To forgive him was to absolve myself. At least, we'd loved each other fervently. Why hadn't we cherished those moments?

George had spoken, "It's better to divorce, or it would have burdened her and encumbered me, too."

晴天霹雳，吓死了。爱情再一次地出卖了我们。因为不到二十五岁，必须打胎。残忍啊，没有选择的余地。我们乘坐的长途汽车颠簸在山路上，开好了几个小时。就在那里，那个灰顶白墙的瓦房，遥远的乡村打胎诊所，

我们胆颤心惊地进去了，化最少的钱把事情了结，我躺在那个简易的手术台上，他在旁边吓得脸色苍白。再怀孕，再打胎。在相爱的时候，我们没有条件也没有准备结婚。到了结婚的年龄，我们三天两头吵架。分开了互相思念，聚到一起，互相埋怨。爱情已经发霉变质。所有的争吵和伤害都起源于我们闯入了禁区。谁之过？谁来负责任？除了谴责我们自己？……

他离开我走了。我瞪大了一双焦灼的眼睛。如果说，人生有许多禁区，一旦踏进去，就像飞蛾扑火自取灭亡，那么，最禁不住的就是爱情。我们扑过去了，所以我们毁灭。同样是爱情，过去是那么的胆颤心惊，现在是如此的欢乐甜蜜。

我是从地狱里爬出来的。他离开我的时候，已经另外有了女人。这个女人一定比我好。否则，他为什么抛弃我？但是，我不好在哪里？我已经考上了大学，他为什么不要我了呀！我们和夫妻有什么不一样啊？……

俗话说，天上一日，人间十年。日常的生活就像火车，过一天，就是一节车厢。我们钻山洞，越河流，千回百转，离不开逶迤的铁道线。而爱情，就像这飞机，扶摇直上几千里，无遮无掩，自由自在。难道我们真的活在天堂里？只有几天几个月，从相遇到相爱，从相爱到带上了乔治的订婚戒？天堂里的神话可靠吗？我究竟应不应该相信它？睁开眼睛，只见到光芒四射，透明的钻石在阳光下变成了一朵流彩飞溢的宝石花。是阳光让坚硬的钻石柔软生辉？还是我们的爱情感动了阳光？漂亮的戒指啊，你想告诉我什么？

死去活来以后，爱情反而变得轻松了。我原谅了他。结婚多年都可以离婚，为什么不让他走？原谅他，等于原谅了我自己。我们毕竟刻骨铭心地爱过，难道不值得珍惜？

乔治说，看来还是离了好。否则，拖累了她，也拖累了我自己。

爱情是容易的，只要两情相悦。婚姻是危险的，不再相信天久地长。热衷于恋爱，我好像卸下了所有的负担。而今却带上了乔治的这枚戒指，我准备好了吗？

柯丽丝喝了点牛奶，迷迷糊糊地睡去了。乔治伸来一个手臂，

Love, when both parties are enamored, flows effortlessly. Marriage, however, is a treacherous path, with few believing it leads to eternal bliss. Upon parting, I felt as if a weight had been lifted. Yet now, I wore George's ring. Was I truly prepared?

Kristeene sipped her milk and drifted into slumber. George extended his arm for me to grasp. I leaned in, letting his hand rest upon my face. He caressed me tenderly, fingers grazing through my hair, palm tracing over my eyes, cheeks, and jaw, moving with a gentle grace. How love intoxicates, making one feel secure!

Returning from the graveyard, George seemed reborn. Ecstasy radiated from his eyes. He alternated between strides and leaps, with Kristeene in joyful pursuit. He scooped her up, tossing her skyward, only to catch her again, as if playing with a cherished ball.

Come nightfall, we ventured to the bar for a drink, dancing upon the floor. He remarked, "I never truly savored life in its entirety, only fragments of it. Now, you fill the gaps."

I replied, "What I dread most is your silence, as if an obstacle has sundered us."

He assured, "No more. We've cleared the traffic. You can scold me, even strike me, if you wish."

I chuckled, "I find your playfulness most endearing."

"Then brace yourself, and don't shed a tear when I act on the child."

"Why would I weep?" He quipped, "Oh, my sides ache with laughter." Then he made a comical face, and I playfully punched him.

The copter sailed through an expanse of cloud, each billow gilded by sunlight, resembling a grandiose palace.

Did the ring act as a threshold? Had I been pounding on the door of matrimony, making all that racket? Life was replete with events and hues. Would serenity await beyond that threshold?

The copter began its descent. Dennis engaged in communication with the ground crew. I glanced at my watch. A journey that once demanded two days by train now took little more than half a day by air.

Stepping off the copter, George remarked, "Susu, I worried initially that you might be afraid. Yet you proved to be an adept air traveler."

I replied, "I was fearful at first, but when concern for Kristeene took over, I ceased to worry for myself."

"I witnessed it all." George threw his arm around my shoulders.

Dennis unfurled the stroller and placed the half-slumbering Kristeene within.

I said, "Kristeene, my brave little birdie, we're home now."

Kristeene blinked her large eyes and pointed to the copter, exclaiming, "A big bird," then to herself, "A little bird."

Dennis and George erupted into hearty laughter.

要我接住。我向前倾身，让他的手贴在自己的脸上。他轻轻地缓缓地移动着，手指插入我的头发，他的掌心掠过我的眼睛，面颊和下巴，移动得如同温柔的舞姿一般。爱的感觉，多么安全多么令人陶醉！

从墓地回来以后，他好像经过了洗礼一般，眼睛里有了喜悦的光芒。他边走边跳，惹得柯丽丝在后面追。他把孩子抱起来，抛到空中，像在玩皮球一样高兴。晚上，我们一起去酒吧喝酒，一起下舞池跳舞。他说，活了半辈子从来没有活完整。那欠缺的部份终于被你填满了。我说，最怕你不说话，不理睬我，好像有什么东西堵在我们中间。他说，没有了，通了，通了，要打要骂随便你。

我大笑，说道，最喜欢你的孩子气。

他说，准备着吧！到时候不要哇哇叫。

叫什么呀？

笑得肚子痛，痛死了呀！说完，他做怪脸，我给了他一拳。……

飞机在云间穿来穿去，阳光拥抱白云，周围好像金碧辉煌的宫殿一般。戒指就是一扇门吗？以前的我是不是一直在婚姻的门外吵吵闹闹，门的里面却是安宁和平？

飞机往下降了，丹尼正在和地面的对话。我看了看手表，火车上两天两夜的路程，上了天，只开半天多一点！

下飞机的时候，乔治说，素素，开始，我还担心你害怕呢！你好像老乘客一样。

我说，我也害怕的，因为担心柯丽丝，自己就不怕了。

我都看到了。乔治搂着我的肩膀说。

丹尼把柯丽丝的小车打开，让半睡半醒的柯丽丝坐了进去。

我说，柯丽丝，勇敢的小鸟，我们到家啦！

柯丽丝眨着大眼睛，指着飞机说，它是大鸟，我是小鸟。

丹尼和乔治都哈哈笑了起来。

Chapter 28

As our car pulled into the gate, I spotted a gathering of people near the main house. Among them, I recognized Betty and some of the helpers from George's birthday bash, eagerly welcoming us. They crowded around, offering their assistance. The entire house had a freshly cleaned scent, lingering detergent in the air. The wooden railing gleamed, polished to a shine. Our luggage was conspicuously absent, likely already taken upstairs. I assumed George had instructed them to distribute our belongings to their respective rooms. Betty showered Kristeene with kisses, repeating "Sweetheart" incessantly.

I couldn't help but notice the joyous faces, akin to Chinese families preparing for the Spring Festival or some other festive occasion. Was it because we'd returned from our trip, having been away for a week? Unlikely. Since I'd taken up residence in this "castle," this was only the second time everyone had gathered. Paid help came weekly to tidy the house and attend to our laundry. The gardener made his monthly visit. Americans cherished their personal space, seldom dropping by for casual chats with George. So this festivity must be for me, undoubtedly because I now wore George's ring. News traveled at lightning speed.

A middle-aged woman arrived, bearing a tray of neatly cut fruits. She placed it on the coffee table in the living room. She stood at a medium height, donning a green pullover, faded jeans, and a blue-and-red-striped apron. Her slightly plump figure gave away her age, likely over fifty, with features suggesting a Mexican heritage. Kristeene had a hankering for watermelon. Betty inquired, "Sweetheart, would you like some salad first?" Then, addressing George and Dennis, she added, "Everything's set in the kitchen."

As customary, her silvery hair was swept back, radiating a bright sheen. This time, there was a newfound confidence in her gaze and a touch more authority in her tone, as though everyone were bound to heed her directives.

They made their way to the kitchen, but I took Kristeene to the living room. It was second nature for me to tend to her before attending to my own needs. As I settled Kristeene on the sofa, the middle-aged woman entered, carrying a high chair and an apron for Kristeene.

"Susu, let me feed her."

"What's your name?" I asked.

第二十八章

我的估计显然是不足的。

汽车开进大门的时候，老远就看到主楼的门口站着一排人。靠近时，认出了蓓蒂和曾经照过面的，在乔治生日时出现的那些帮手。他们对我们很热情，一涌而上来帮忙。

大楼里刚刚清扫干净，空气中残留着清洁剂的化学味道，楼梯的木扶手上了腊，亮得耀眼。我们的行李一眨眼不见了，都被提到楼上，乔治关照他们送入各人的房间。蓓蒂抱着柯丽丝亲了又亲，宝贝宝贝地叫不停。

我注意了这些人的神情，脸上喜气洋洋，好像中国人准备过春节或者喜事临门的样子。是因为我们出了远门，一个星期没有见面的关系吗？好像不是。我在城堡住到现在，这么多人全体出席，这是第二次。每星期有人来打扫一次卫生和洗衣服。花匠好像是每个月才工作一次。美国人保留自己的生活空间，从来没有什么客人到家里来和乔治聊 家常。难道说，喜事就是我呀！因为我带上了乔治的戒指。消息传得真快啊！

一个中年妇女端着一大盘切好的水果走过来，放在客厅的咖啡桌上。她中等个子，上穿绿色的绒套衫，下着洗得发白的牛仔裤，腰上系着蓝红条子的围裙。她那稍微发胖的体型来判断，她的年纪大概出了五十了吧，有点像墨西哥人。柯丽丝吵着要吃西瓜。蓓蒂说，宝贝，先吃点色拉吧！转身对乔治和丹尼说，都弄好了，在厨房里。

蓓蒂像往常一样，银色的头发拢到后面，梳得十分光亮。她的眼睛里多了一点自信，说话的口气也较以前显得有权威，好像大家都在听她指挥。

他们都去了厨房，我拉着柯丽丝的手留在客厅。我已经习惯了先把柯丽丝照顾好，再管自己的事情。刚把她抱上沙发，那个中年妇女抱着柯丽丝的高椅子和围兜，跨着大步走过来。

素素，让我来喂。

"Helen."

"Helen, have you had lunch?"

"We have. Just waiting for your return."

"Thank you. I'll handle it."

Just then, Betty's voice called out, drawing nearer.

"Susu, sweetheart, why don't you join us for lunch?"

"I'll come after Kristeene's done," I replied.

Betty insisted, "Here we have Helen and me. Don't worry about Kristeene." She appeared at my side, gently guiding me away. I stole a glance at Kristeene. Helen was deftly offering her a slice of watermelon. Her cheeks puffed up, lips tinged with red. Betty enveloped my shoulder with one arm, clasping my left hand in hers, guiding me along.

From the living room to the hallway, and through the hallway to the kitchen – I'd lost count of how many times I tread this path in a day. Yet today, it all felt peculiar. It was as if I was not entirely myself, as if I'd relinquished control.

While propelling me forward, Betty mused, "Thank goodness George has finally settled down."

A smile involuntarily played on my lips.

"George is a kind man, very gentle, but he's always troubled. None of us know how to ease his burdens. You're the angel sent by God to help him."

Inwardly, I thought, "No wonder she's holding on so tightly. She must have feared the angel might flutter away." I chuckled, and Betty joined in.

In the kitchen, George and Dennis sat across from each other at the round table. Dennis had taken my usual seat, leaving me to settle by George's side, which was usually Kristeene's spot. Just as I was about to sit down, George extended his hand, smiling, "Home, sweet home. Are you content now?"

"Happy," I answered without thinking, but my eyes welled up. He cherished being home. Only a few days earlier, he'd mentioned how liberating it felt to be away. Now, his smile reached his eyes and arched his brows. It moved me; he loved this place. I lowered my head quickly, taking my time with the napkin, hoping to conceal my misty eyes.

"Susu, which salad dressing would you prefer?" Betty's voice came from behind.

"Eh, blue cheese," I replied, opting for that distinct, slightly pungent cheese similar to the aged bean curd in China - salty yet delicious.

"Blue cheese dressing?" Betty confirmed. Dennis stood up and fetched my salad. The plate was adorned with vibrant leaves - red, yellow, white, and green, all coated in dressing and a dusting of dry cheese, akin to a frothy woolen coat. Atop the salad, nestled small morsels of chicken breast and crisp bread.

"So much?" I remarked.

George chuckled, "Aren't you hungry? We're famished."

"You can help yourself from my plate, George."

我说，你叫啥？

海伦。

海伦，你吃午餐了吗？

早吃了，在等你们回来呢！

我说，谢谢你，我来吧！

正在这时候，我听见了蓓蒂在喊我，声音越来越近。

素素甜心，你怎么不来吃午餐？

我应道，等柯丽丝吃完了，我就来。

蓓蒂说，这里有海伦和我，你不要操心了。音落人到，蓓蒂拉上我就走。我回头看看柯丽丝，嘴里已经被海伦喂了一小块西瓜，脸腮鼓鼓的，嘴唇都被染红了。

蓓蒂一手环住我的右肩，另一手捏住我的左手，连拥带携地夹着我。

从客厅到走廊，从走廊到厨房，这条路，我每天不知道要来回走多少遍，今天却变得陌生，觉得自己不完整，好像失去了控制。

蓓蒂一边走一边说，感谢上帝，乔治终于安定了下来。

我笑笑。

她说，乔治是个好男人，很善良的人。但是，他一直不愉快。大家都不知道应该如何帮助他。你就是上帝派来帮助他的小天使啊！

我心里想，难怪她把我夹得那么紧，是怕我飞走了不是？我忍不住笑出声来。蓓蒂和我一起笑。厨房的圆桌子旁，乔治和丹尼面对面坐着。丹尼占去了我平时的座位，我只能坐到乔治的旁边，那是柯丽丝的位置。我还没有坐下，乔治已经伸过手来拉我，笑咪咪地问道，到家了，高兴吗？

高兴。我顺口答道。答时无心，话一出口，心里一惊，不觉眼圈热了起来。他喜欢回家！几天前，他还感慨于“离家的感觉多么好”，现在的他，乐得眼睛眉毛都在笑。我好感动啊，他爱这个家！赶快低下头去，把膝盖上的餐巾铺铺好，铺了好长时间，不想让他看到我潮湿的眼睛。

素素，你要哪一种沙拉酱？蓓蒂在身后问我。

嗯，Blue Cheese。我答道。那是一种发酵长霉的奶酪，像中国的臭豆腐的，很咸很鲜。

蓓蒂重复道，Blue Cheese Dressing。

丹尼起身把我的沙拉端了过来。盆子里是各种颜色的叶片，红黄白绿，片片裹在沙拉酱和干酪粉中，如穿上来奶白色的毛线衣，生菜上面是切成小块的鸡胸脯肉和一粒粒的干面包。

"Don't give me anything. If you can't finish it, just toss it. You're not in China."

I locked eyes with him and stated, "I grew up in a famine."

Betty chimed in, "Young folks nowadays don't fathom the struggles of the Depression. Back then, no one dared squander a thing."

George, still smiling, interjected, "I'm not against your thriftiness. I only hope you'll eat heartily."

It dawned on me that Americans typically refrained from transferring food between plates. So, I polished off my salad, pleasing everyone.

"See, you were hungry too," George noted.

I turned to Betty, "Thank you, it was delicious."

Betty replied, "I'm glad you enjoyed it. No need to thank me."

As Dennis rose to clear the table, I followed suit. He offered, "Susu, I've got this. You can stay."

I glanced at George. He took my hand, pulling me toward him. I perched on his lap, his arms encircling my waist.

"Have you had enough, my ravenous Chinese girl?" he asked, his tone tender.

I whispered in his ear, "If it brings you joy, I'll eat even more."

Suddenly, the soft footfalls of Kristeene reached our ears, like the patter of a young lamb.

I called out, "Come, Kristeene, it's time for lunch."

She replied, "I ate. Helen fed me."

I said, "Let me check your tummy. Ah, there's a piece of chicken in there. I can feel it."

Kristeene giggled, squirming away, ticklish from my touch.

Now Helen entered the kitchen, joining Betty and Dennis in their tasks.

George took my hand, guiding us to the living room.

The array of fruits on the coffee table beckoned, their scent and freshness irresistible. George snagged a slice of pineapple and inquired about my preference.

I tilted my head, asking, "Why did news travel so swiftly?"

He feigned innocence, "What news?"

I countered, "Do you think I'm oblivious? Just a short while ago, there were no visitors in the daytime. Now it's bustling like a market."

He responded with a smirk, "Perhaps it's because of the ring on your finger. Why are you wearing it?" He chuckled.

"You're right," I conceded. "I almost feel like the American president. This ring is my oval office."

"The American president?" George's brows lifted in curiosity. "What do you mean?"

I found myself contemplating the American president and the political system. From the moment we left the train until lunchtime, barely over an

这么多？我说。

乔治说，你不饿吗？我们都饿坏了。

乔治，给你一些。

不要给我，吃不下就倒掉，这里不是中国。

我瞪了他一眼，说道，我是在饥饿中长大的。

蓓蒂接我的话说，年轻人都不知道经济萧条的日子，那个时候，谁敢浪费？

乔治笑着说，我哪里反对你珍惜？是希望你多吃一点。

他提醒了我，美国人是不喜欢把菜夹来夹去的。

我把沙拉全吃完了，皆大欢喜。

乔治说，瞧，你也饿了么！

我转过头去说，蓓蒂，谢谢你，很好吃。

蓓蒂说，好吃就好不要谢。

丹尼站起来收拾桌子，我也站了起来。他说，素素，我来，我来，你坐。

我朝乔治看看，他拉我过去，坐在他的膝盖上，双手环着我，问道：饥饿的中国女孩，吃饱了吗？我在他耳朵旁悄悄地说，你开心，我就多吃一点。

这时，听到了柯丽丝的脚步声，笃笃笃地响，像头小羊一样。

我说，来，柯丽丝，吃午饭吧！

她说，吃了，海伦喂的。

我说，让我摸摸你的肚皮。噢，确实有鸡肉在里面呢，摸到了。

柯丽丝怕痒，笑着一溜烟似地跑开了。

海伦也过来了，和丹尼，蓓蒂他们一起干活。

乔治拉着我的手去了客厅。

咖啡桌上的水果，芳香诱人，鲜丽欲滴。乔治吃了一块菠萝，问我要吃什么？

我歪着头问，消息为什么传得那么快？

他装糊涂，说道，什么消息？

我说，你以为我是笨蛋？以前这里白天没有其他人，现在热闹得像赶集一样。

他一本正经地说，也许是因为你手上的那枚戒指。谁叫你带戒指了呢？说完“嘿嘿”笑了两声。

你说对了。我说，我有一种当上了总统的感觉。这枚戒指意味着椭圆形的办公室。

当总统？乔竖起了眉毛，问道，什么意思？

hour had passed, yet I'd already fallen into a routine, a system that seemed ingrained. This system consisted of an array of different rituals and procedures. Everyone had their designated role for specific routines. Each day seemed to mirror the one before. While the people within this system might change, much like presidents stepping in and out of office, the routines and procedures remained constant. In this "castle," my position had shifted, offering me a taste of something new. But to everyone else, it was simply their duty to attend to the lady of the house.

I turned to George and voiced my thoughts. "George, I'm not accustomed to being waited on, but I understand the situation and the reasoning behind it."

George burst into hearty laughter, gasping for air, and tears welled in his eyes. He exclaimed, "You—Susu—you're a born politician. You could run for office. There are plenty of women politicians in America who were housewives before." He chuckled as he listed off a few congresswomen.

I inquired, "George, can I step down if I don't fancy this kind of life?"

He was still chuckling as he replied, "No, no. You'd have to go through a performance evaluation first." Then, his laughter faded, and his expression grew more serious. My heart sank; I realized I'd taken the joke too far.

He asked, "You truly don't enjoy being catered to, do you? Susu, it's not a matter of who waits on whom. It's about dividing the tasks. You're handling different responsibilities. Consider that, is it not fair?"

"You're right, division of labor. A clear explanation," I conceded, but I couldn't help but regret being overly particular about my new life. George never minded our differences. If he had, there were plenty of flaws he could have pointed out, like my imperfect English, the noises I made while eating, my occasional temper, and my amateurishness in lovemaking. If he mentioned wanting to step down, how would I feel? I'd be furious.

"Is the pineapple tasty?" I asked. "I'll give it a try."

George handed me a piece, remarking, "Madam President, now we must address some practical matters. We need a bed."

"A bed? Not a problem," I assured him. "The bed on the third floor is quite comfortable. Shall we head there?"

He replied, "In that case, my bed shouldn't be an issue, as it's the same brand and model."

"Really?" I asked, wide-eyed.

Our conversation tapered off when it came to the bed. When reminded of it, both of us exchanged glances filled with a certain spark. We'd shared a roof for months, but never a bed in the same room in this house. He gazed at me with affectionate eyes, motionless like a statue. I saw my reflection in his cerulean irises. He wrapped his arms around my waist and gently pulled me onto his lap. "Anywhere will do, as long as we're not sleeping on the floor," he murmured.

我真的联想到了美国的总统和政治体系。从下车到结束午餐，一个多小时，我遭遇了一个难以打破的运转体系。这个体系由不同的程序组成，各就各位，各司其职，打发着每天的日子。人在体系内是可以变换的，就像美国的总统上台下台，各种程序固定不变。我在城堡里只是换了一个位置而已。这种变动，对于我很新鲜，对于其他人来说，服侍女主人，是应该和必然的。

我把自己的想法告诉了他。我说，乔治，不太习惯被人伺候。但是，想通了其中的道理。

乔治大笑，笑得气喘吁吁，眼泪都流出来了。他说，你……素素……你是一个天生的政治家。你应该去参加竞选，美国有不少女政治家原来是家庭主妇。他一边笑一边点了好几个参眾女议员的姓名。

我说，乔治，如果我不喜欢这样的生活，可不可以辞职？他还在笑，说道，不行，不行，必须经过程序的审查。说完，他怔了一下，收住了笑容。他的脸像速冻了似地冷了下来，问道，真的不喜欢被人伺候吗？素素，这不是伺候，是分工，不同的分工，你再想一想，对不对？

对，不同的分工，很好的解释。我说。心里不免一阵后悔，不该对新生活那么挑剔。

乔治从来不把我们之间的不同当回事儿。如果要数落的话，我的破英文，吃饭的时候有响声，倔强的脾气，包括在床上男欢女爱时的不够专业，毛病多着呢！如果他说要“辞职”，我会怎么想？不跳三丈高吗？

菠萝好吃吗？我说，我也来尝一下。

乔治递给我一块，一边说，总统先生，我们需要解决实际问题。我们需要一张床。

床？没有问题。我说，三楼的床很好。你就到三楼来吧！

他说，这么说，我的床也没有问题？都是一个牌子，一样的工艺结构。

真的吗？我瞪大了眼睛问。

我们的谈话，因为床的出现而中止了。提到床，我和他的眼睛都不约而同地出现了火苗。我们在同一个屋檐下生活了好几个月，却从来没有睡在同一个房间同一张床上。他深情脉脉地瞅着我，看呆了一样。我在他的蓝眼睛看到了自己。他搂着我的腰，一把携我到他的怀里，说道，到那里都行，只要不睡地板。

我说，我习惯了睡三楼。

他说，那么，我们就睡三楼。

"I'm used to sleeping on the third floor," I replied.

"Alright, we'll sleep on the third floor," he agreed.

"I imagine our first night together must have been a bit challenging for you," I ventured.

His tone softened, "That night left me with nothing but joy. I forgot everything else."

I closed my eyes and whispered, "I've known many men, but none like you. You make me happy and content."

"My dear, are you content? I feel like I haven't done enough."

"Enough talk," I urged. "You'll make me addicted to you." With that, I reclined, most of my weight resting on his lap.

I hadn't even finished swallowing the pineapple when George pressed his lips to mine. Suddenly, a fire ignited within me. My heart, my blood, my very breath, all aflame. My body felt like a joyful explosion, bursting forth with a resounding bang. I couldn't recall when I'd been carried by him to the third floor. We lay side by side, my head next to his. As I regained my senses, I saw him looking at me, one arm propped up on the pillow.

Feeling a bit peculiar, I asked, "What? Why the secrecy?"

He replied, "You made quite the passionate sound."

I let out a surprised cry and turned over, cheeks flushed, my back to him.

"Susu, are you happy? Would you be willing to die for it?" he inquired.

I covered my face. In truth, I couldn't quite remember what had transpired. I only remembered feeling myself dissolve into pure bliss. Did this constitute a form of self-exile and self-discovery?

His hand grazed my side, gently tracing my chest. My heart pounded like the beat of a drum. In an instant, a flash of light seemed to burst forth, propelling my soul from my body. I felt as though I were riding a steed, galloping wildly. Abruptly, I turned toward George, offering my chest to his mouth. Gripping the bedstead tightly, I cried out to him relentlessly. I wanted to surrender my entire self to him. I shouted, "George, everything is yours, yours, yours!"

"Ah, Susu!" he exclaimed, closing his eyes, burying his face in my bosom as if he wished to dig a hole and dive in. He became fervent, a tempest of sensations. His body clung to mine, every inch of skin pressed against me, as though he wanted to meld us together. In that moment, I harbored a fervent desire. I declared, "George, I want a child! Let me bear your child!"

He responded, "Of course, I want a child of ours too, perhaps many of them. Susu, I want a whole brood of children."

These words, spoken in the throes of passion, ignited a fiery blaze in our home, incinerating any reservations I had about my newfound life.

我说，想到第一夜，真委屈你了。

他轻轻地说，第一夜，只留下欢乐，其他都忘掉了。

我合上了眼睛，喃喃地说，我接触过许多男人，没有一个像你那样让我满足和快乐。

亲爱的，你满足了吗？我觉得自己做得不够好。

不要说了，你让我上瘾。说到这里，我已经横躺下来，大半个身体叠在他的大腿上。

嘴里的菠萝还没有咽下去，乔治的唇已经贴上来。霎那间，火焰窜了起来。我的心脏我的血液我的呼吸都在燃烧，身体变成了快乐的炸弹，轰隆隆地爆得粉碎。

不知道何时被他抱到了三楼，我们头靠头地睡着。等我恢复了常态，看见他一条手臂支在枕头上对着我笑。

我觉得有点奇怪，问道，怎么啦，神秘兮兮的样子？

他说，你叫床了。

啊！我大叫一声，害羞地转了个身，以背对着他。

素素，快活吗？死了也愿意，是不是？

我故意蒙上了脸。不记得刚才发生了什么，只觉得自己消失了，在快乐中毁灭了。难道这就是所谓的自我放逐和拯救？

他的手从背后插过来，抚摸我的胸部。我的心“梆梆梆”像打锣一样敲打着。突然，一道亮光把我弹出体外，我好像骑上了一匹野马，疯狂地奔驰。我猛地转向乔治，把乳房对准了他的嘴巴，双手板着床架，不停地喊他。我要给他，整个身体都给他。我大喊，乔治，都是你的，是你的，是你的！

啊，素素。他闭着眼睛，把脸埋在我的胸口，好像要掘一个洞钻进去一样。他变得野蛮起来，用力地撞我。他的身体贴上了我每一寸的肌肤，好像要把我碾碎。

就在这个时候，我萌生了一个非常强烈的愿望。我喊道，乔治，我想要孩子！让我怀孕，让我怀上你的孩子！

当然，素素，我想要我们的孩子，一群孩子。素素，我要一群孩子。

这些在欲火中说的疯话，一直在这栋房子里燃烧，燃烧……。当我想怀上他的孩子的时候，我把自己彻底地交出去了。

Chapter 29

After our trip, George settled back into his routine, heading to the office during the day and returning home promptly in the evening. If he considered throwing a party, he'd seek my input. I'd join gatherings mainly with Asian attendees, mostly to support George's business ventures. Most of the time, he attended these events alone. This made me the lady of this "castle." I delved into books, overseeing Kristeene's early education, while Betty and Helen managed the household chores.

Everything flowed smoothly, except for one thing that weighed on me: I had promised to call Charlie upon our return, but I never did.

Since our engagement, George and I have openly discussed our past loves. He shared a lot about his experiences with sex workers, from how they treated people to their experiences in bed, expressing genuine compassion and respect for them. I, too, recounted my first love, my views on love and marriage, and most importantly, about Charlie. Though the love between Charlie and me wasn't long-lasting, it was distinct from my previous experiences. He always left room for me, never pushing me into something I wasn't ready for. At times, I felt a pang of regret for him, and at others, a deep appreciation. Especially after our engagement, any lingering sense that he hadn't considered me enough had dissipated. On the contrary, I felt his deep respect for me. I valued the friendship I shared with Charlie.

Whenever I mentioned Charlie, George would remind me that we should invite him out for dinner and catch up. One weekend, I compiled a list of people we planned to invite to our wedding. I had few friends in America, so Charlie's name was at the top of the list. I resolved to call him and suggest meeting up for a chat.

Charlie asked me a barrage of questions on the phone—why he hadn't heard from me, if I'd enjoyed our trip, and where we'd been. I told him, "I owe you dinner, Charlie. Pick a restaurant, and we can catch up there." As luck would have it, he chose the same Chinese restaurant where we'd dined before. I told him, "I know how to get there. You don't need to pick me up."

After applying a touch of makeup, I slipped into a high-collared blue dress. I descended to the living room and turned around before George, inquiring, "Is this outfit alright?"

第二十九章

旅游回来，乔治白天去公司上班，晚上准时回家。有宴请的时候，来征求我的意见。我只愿意出席有亚洲伙伴的宴会，主要是为了帮助乔治的生意。大部份的宴请他一个人去。我就这样当起了这个城堡的女主人。我看许多书籍，负责柯丽丝的早期教育。家务由蓓蒂和海伦来照顾。

一切都很顺利，只有一件事常常令我心烦。我答应查里，回来以后打电话去，一直没有打。我们订婚以后，我和乔治都没有回避过去的恋情。他说了许多关于妓女的事情，从待人接物到床上经验，对她们深表同情和尊重。我也说了我的初恋，对待爱情和婚姻的态度，尤其说到了查里。我和查里恋爱的时间并不长，但是，和以前的恋爱很不一样。他总是留给我许多空间，从不勉强我做不愿意的事情。有时候，我觉得对不起他，有时候又很欣赏他。尤其在订婚以后，原来觉得他顾我不够的感觉消失了，反而感受到了他对我的尊重。我很珍惜和查里的感情。

每次谈到查里，乔治总是提醒我，应该约查里吃一次饭，好好谈谈心。

我正在排一份参加婚礼的名单。我的美国朋友不多，把查里排在第一位。那天我下了个决心，拿起电话，约他出来谈一次。

查里在电话里问了许多问题。诸如为什么没有消息？旅游快乐吗？去了哪里？等等。

我说，欠你一顿饭，查里，你选饭店，到那里再谈。他正巧选了我们去过的那家中国餐馆。我说，我知道怎么走，你不用来接我。

那天下午，我梳妆打扮了一番，穿上了那件高领导藏青连衣裙，走到楼下客厅里，在乔治的面前转了个圈，问道：这样出去可以了吗？

He sat there, engrossed in his newspaper. Removing his glasses, he remarked, "Let your hair down. Perfect. You look elegant and poised."

I smiled and teased, "I can't dress too provocatively to meet an old flame, can I?"

He responded, "You look just fine, beautiful."

As I was about to leave, I felt a twinge of restlessness. I couldn't resist asking him, "George, do you feel alright about me meeting Charlie alone?"

George smiled and assured, "Your friend is my friend. Why wouldn't I be alright with it?"

I admitted, "Actually, I was asking myself. Would I be alright if you were meeting an old flame?"

"So, you don't trust me?" he quipped.

"I trust you. Or maybe I don't trust in my own charm, huh?" I replied.

He playfully raised his fist in agreement. "Good point."

"But," I pressed on, "I have a question. I've always wondered. Would you be willing to tell me?"

"What is it?"

"When you've established yourself in your business circle, do women chase after you?"

"Ah, you're conducting an investigation, aren't you?" George chuckled. He rose from the sofa, placing his glasses on the newspaper, and approached the long glass door. The outside world was bathed in brightness, with fallen leaves blanketing the lawns, resembling aged printed sheets.

Listening to his laughter, I could infer the answer was affirmative. Nowadays, women seemed quite forward, unbothered by a man's marital status. But love works both ways. I wanted to hear it directly from George.

He mused, "If I say yes, will it startle you?"

"But if you say no, I won't believe you," I retorted. He came closer, peering into my face intently, and admitted, "Yes. Women do often pursue me."

"Oh, I'm positively green with envy," I playfully quipped, leaning back as if feigning a swoon.

George held me, making sure I didn't actually topple over. He asserted, "But none of them hold a candle to you."

"Why is that?"

"Because they lack self-respect."

"So, I'm the top woman in your heart, and you're the finest man in mine, and we're not worried about any third wheels?" I queried.

"Exactly," George affirmed. "One genuine connection outweighs a sea of admirers."

I grinned and teased, "Save the details for later. I must be on my way."

He embraced me, whispering softly, "Could you extend my apologies to Charlie?"

"Apologies?" I chuckled. "Are you suggesting you swept me away from

他正坐在那里看报纸，摘下了眼镜，看一眼便说，把头发放下来很好，很文静很清纯。

我笑了，说道，不能穿得很性感去会旧情人，是不是？

他说，就这样，很好，很漂亮。

我要走了。但是，不知什么原因，心里有些忐忑不安，走到门口又退回来。

忘了什么东西？乔治问。

乔治，我一个人去会查里，你放心吗？

他笑了笑说，你的朋友就是我的朋友，为什么要不放心呢？

我说，其实我在问自己呢！如果你去会一个旧情人，我放心吗？

他说，你不放心我吗？

我说，应该放心你的。否则就是不相信自己的魅力，对不对？

他赞同地挥了挥拳头，说，有道理。

不过，我说，有一个问题，一直想打听，你愿意告诉我吗？

什么问题？

你在外面呼风唤雨，有女人追你吗？

啊，调查敌情。他哈哈大笑，从沙发上起身，把眼镜放在报纸上面，走到了落地窗的玻璃前。外面很亮，草坪被落叶覆盖，像一条陈旧的印花被单。

听他那个笑声，我已经猜着了八九，答案是肯定的。现在的女人都很开放，谁管你是订婚还是结婚呢！但是，爱情是两个巴掌不打不响。我要听乔治怎么说。

他说，如果我说有。不会把你吓着了吧！

我说，如果你说没有，我才不相信你呢！

他走到我身旁，真诚地看着我，说，是的，常常有女人追求我。

啊，我好妒忌哎！说完，身体往后一仰，假装要昏倒的样子。

乔治托住了我的腰，说道，可惜她们都比不上你。

为什么？

因为她们不看重自己。

我笑嘻嘻地说，等我回来，你要告诉我详细的故事。现在没有时间，我得走了。

他拥抱了我，轻轻地说，能代我向查里说一声对不起吗？

对不起？我说，我是你抢来的吗？

him?"

"You were once his girlfriend. I respect that," George explained.

"Alright, I'll make sure to do that."

"Enjoy yourself. I'll handle things at home," he assured.

As I stepped outside, a chill greeted me. The wind was brisk, sending my high-collared blue dress fluttering like a flag, its fabric snapping in the breeze. My hair rebelled, dancing chaotically in the tempest. I hastened back to the third floor and donned a white woolen coat.

Charlie arrived first. Spotting me from a distance, he rushed over and hugged me tightly. I caught a whiff of his familiar cologne. With his arm linked in mine, he guided me along, remarking, "Susu, you're as beautiful as ever."

I commented, "The wind's quite forceful today."

The restaurant was bustling on weekends. Charlie scouted for a table, and I sought out my Chinese friend. He was on duty that day, and he was quite astute. As he directed us to an unoccupied table, he inquired, "Married?" His gaze repeatedly shifted to the ring on my finger.

I glanced at Charlie, uncertain if he understood the Chinese gentleman's words. It seemed unlikely, as he was engrossed in the menu, and my friend spoke in his dialect. He pressed on, "Very good. Married so young, wasting no time."

He must have assumed that the ring was given to me by Charlie. He even compared Charlie to George.

I said, "I'll call you to invite you and your wife to our wedding."

My friend beamed, "Susu, you're quite clever."

Charlie chimed in, "I'm ready, sir. Susu, what would you like to order?"

"Dinner's on me. You go ahead and choose first."

So Charlie selected steamed codfish, mixed vegetables, and savory boiled duck.

I smiled and teased, "Are you sure you're not a secret Chinese expert, living as an American?"

My friend interjected, "Then you'll have no differences in your married life later." He said it in English, but Charlie didn't seek clarification.

I ordered fried radish cake and spring rolls, thinking to myself, "Right. Charlie understands Chinese culture. If we live together, there's no language barrier."

Charlie cooled his tea with a gentle breath and took a sip. I awaited the moment for him to ask questions, to share my engagement news. However, he seemed to have forgotten entirely and made no inquiries.

We chatted about Chinese cuisine. I recounted how I mixed hot tofu with sweet-and-sour pork, serving it to one of George's friends who praised it. He smiled, but continued to sip his tea.

乔治说，你曾经是他的女朋友。我很尊敬他。

好吧。我说。

他说，好好玩，家里有我呢！

天气开始冷了，出门便感到了风的力量。藏青高领连衣裙被吹得像旗帜一样，呼腊腊地飘。我的头发更像发脾气似地，无规则地甩来甩去。我赶紧跑上三楼，套了一件白色的毛线大衣。

查里比我先到，老远地看见我，快步走过来，一把抱住。我闻到了他的体味，那种熟悉的香水味。他挽着我一边走一边说，素素，你还是那么美。

我说，好大的风啊！

周末的饭店里很热闹。查里找座位，我找我的中国朋友。果然，他在上班。中国朋友的眼睛真厉害，领我们坐下以后，便问道，结婚了吗？目光朝我手上的戒指扫了几次。

我朝查里瞄了一眼，不知他听懂了没有？好像没有，他正全神贯注地翻菜谱。他只懂中国的官方语言，朋友说的是家乡话。朋友继续说，很不错啊，年轻，没有拖泥带水。

他以为我的戒指是查里给的，而且把查里和乔治做了对比。

我说，我给你打电话，邀请你和太太来参加婚礼。

朋友说，素素，你真有本事啊。

查里说，先生，我准备好了。素素要点什么菜？

今天我请客，你先点。

查里点了清蒸鳕鱼，罗汉斋和盐水鸭子。

我笑着说，你是美国人吗？怎么长了一个中国的胃？

朋友插话道，这样，你们今后的生活就没有什么矛盾了。他说英文。查里竟然不予澄清。

我对朋友说，还要一客萝卜丝饼和春卷。心里想，是啊，查里了解中国文化，如果我们在一起生活，语言几乎没有障碍。

查里吹了吹茶盅里的热气，呷了一口茶。

我等着他来问我，然后，准备把订婚的事情告诉他。可是他好像忘掉了一样，什么问题都没有。

我们谈了一些中国烹饪。我告诉他，我把麻婆豆腐和甜酸肉混在一起，招待乔治的朋友，受到了夸奖。他笑了，什么都没说，再呷一口茶。

我突然想起了第一次学生Party上他把我扛在肩膀上的事情，这个谜至今没有解开。便问了他。

Since he remained silent, I had to think of something to say. Suddenly, I remembered my first party, when he had hoisted me onto his shoulder. This was a riddle I hadn't unraveled yet. So, I inquired.

He blew on the tea, took a sip, and blew and drank again. After a prolonged silence, he said, "There's a well-known Chinese saying: a step amiss may involve endless remorse. Many women in human history were either killed by themselves or by others because of a misstep. You seem like a classically virtuous woman. So, I had to ensure you were safe."

I smiled and remarked, "Then why did you entirely forget this well-known saying?"

"I don't know," he shrugged, looking uneasy. "I really don't know." He fixed his gaze on the teacup.

I asked, "Was it love at first sight? You didn't want anyone else to have me, did you, Charlie?"

He stammered, "No. Yes. You captivated me. But—" He struggled to continue.

"Charlie, have you ever thought about marriage and children?" I inquired.

He lifted his eyes to meet mine, asking, "What do you mean?"

I glanced at him. "Just a question."

He admitted, "This is the most perplexing, contradictory dilemma for me. I'm at a loss."

Turning towards me, he caressed my hand resting on the table. His fingers nearly brushed against my ring, but he seemed oblivious.

"The issue is, I'm drawn to Oriental women, but they all believe love must be validated through marriage. Yet, I lack confidence in marriage. Considering the high divorce rates, who dares to take that step? Susu, do you ever feel that when people make vows at a wedding, they're deceiving themselves?"

"Yes," I nodded. "I used to think that way too. Marriage seems like the end of love. It's easy to love, it's joyful. But marriage is a weighty responsibility. It carries too many obligations."

"Susu, I see you like this: you're independent and self-assured. You're not an average Oriental woman," Charlie remarked.

As the dishes arrived, I realized my appetite was quite hearty. Every dish was delightful, and I reveled in the experience. I felt every muscle relax, as if I'd been released from some kind of restraint. I wondered if this conversation was helping me further understand Charlie's perspective, or if it was a confirmation that I'd made the right choice.

As I sat there with Charlie, I couldn't help but notice how adept he was with chopsticks, spitting out fish bones like a true Chinese. George, in comparison, was less practiced. It was intriguing to see how this man, fluent in Chinese with knowledge of its history, philosophy, and even familiar sayings, could still grapple with Oriental perspectives. Yet, George, who knew very little about the East, was eager to marry a Chinese woman. Life, it seemed,

他吹了喝，喝了吹。沉默了半晌才说，中国有一句著名的哲言：一失足成千古恨。历史上有不少女子因失足而自杀被杀。你看上去很古典，就拉你一把。

我笑了笑说，那么，后来你怎么把这个著名的哲言忘得一干二净？

我不知道。他耸了耸了一下肩膀，皱紧了眉，一付很烦躁的样子。我不知道，真的不知道。说完，眼睛看着杯里的茶水。

我说，是不是一见钟情？你不想让别人占有我，查里？

No，他说，Yes，你很吸引我。但是，……他语无伦次。

我说，查里，你考虑过结婚生孩子吗？

他看着我问，你是什么意思？

我斜睨了他一眼说，问问而已。

他说，这就是我最困惑最矛盾最无法解决的难题。他侧过身来，抚摸我放在桌上的手。他的手几乎是从我的戒指上擦过去的，居然没有一点感觉。

他说，难题是，我欣赏东方女性。但是，她们都认为，恋爱必须用婚姻来证明。而我，对婚姻毫无信心。你看看，那么高的离婚率，谁敢结婚？素素，你不觉得人们说结婚宣誓的时候，其实在欺骗自己？

是啊，我说，以前也是这么想的，婚姻好像已经走上了末路。爱情很容易，很快乐，婚姻太沉重，有太多的责任。

他说，素素，我就是这样看你的。你很独立，很有自信，不是一般的东方女子。

这时，菜上来了。我突然胃口大开，吃得很香很高兴。不知道是因为这席谈话让我进一步了解了查里的观念，还是因为证实自己做出了正确的选择，我好像被松了绑一样舒适自在。

查里用筷，吐鱼刺，都很中国化，乔治在这方面远不如他。有意思的是，这个会说中国话，对中国的历史哲学谙熟无比，甚至能讲出著名哲理的男人，却困惑于东方的观念。

而我的乔治，对东方一窍不通，却要娶一个中国女人做老婆。人生真是无模式可寻啊！如果没有遇到乔治，我可能赞同查里的生活方式，两人同居？也许一辈子，也许到爱情消失？现在和乔治在一起，很安全，很甜蜜，觉得自己很像女人，很愿意当母亲。

朋友送来了账单，被我抢到手里。我故意在签字的时候，把手臂伸到查里面前。我相信他看到了我的戒指，那么大一颗钻石，闪

had no fixed pattern. Had I not met George, perhaps I might have agreed with Charlie's approach to life – living together without marriage, perhaps indefinitely, or until love faded. Now, living with George, I felt secure, cherished, and truly like a woman, ready and willing to become a mother.

When my friend handed me the bill, I deliberately extended my hand in front of Charlie. I was certain he must have seen my ring. How could he have missed it? Such a sizable diamond, sparkling with such radiance. The only explanation was that he didn't place much importance on it, because he didn't desire marriage, and so, such a ring held no sway in his heart.

Outside the restaurant, Charlie raised the collar of his coat and asked with seriousness, "Susu, do we part ways like this?"

I genuinely didn't know how to respond. I had come to conclude our relationship, but all we'd done was share a meal, and nothing had been said about our parting. I glanced at him and saw his eyes glistening with melancholy tears. At that moment, the gusty wind nearly knocked me off balance, causing me to turn around. He swiftly stepped forward to steady me. Was he afraid I might be swept away by the wind, or was he simply reluctant to let me go? I couldn't say. Still, I found solace in being held in his arms. This would be the last time he would embrace me. I clung to his arms, unwilling to let go.

It was an early winter afternoon. The strong wind swirled around us, enveloping us tighter and tighter.

"Charlie, I'm engaged," I finally confessed.

"I know," he murmured, still holding me from behind, his jaw resting on my shoulder. He spoke in a low voice, "Did you say it now to spare me the pain?"

"Charlie, Charlie," I repeated his name. His face pressed against my ear, cold like an ice pack.

I inquired, "Did you find out before or after dinner?"

"From your conversation with the waiter. You invited him to your wedding," he explained.

"Ah, you understand our dialect?"

"I know a little, the basics."

"Then why did you say I'm an independent woman?"

"You are an independent woman. Choosing in marriage is not the same as acting by tradition. Today, it takes great courage to choose marriage. Your husband is an exceptional man."

"He wants to apologize to you."

"You mean George?"

"Yes. How did you know?"

"I sense that he loves you. Tell him that Charlie said it's of no consequence. I hope he will love Susu forever."

My eyes welled with tears. I told myself, "I can't let my tears fall at this moment, nor can I blink. I must force them to stay in." I said, "He will, Char-

着耀眼的光芒，怎么可能视而不见？唯一的解释是，他不把戒指当一回事，因为他不要结婚，戒指在他的心目中没有地位。

出了饭店的大门，查里把外套的领子竖了起来，脸色凝重地问，素素，我们就这样分手了？我真不知道应该如何答复他，为了终结关系而来，吃了一顿饭，却什么都没有说。抬头看他，看到了一泓忧郁的泪水在他的眼睛里打转。正在这时，脚一软，身体被风吹得转了个圈。他跨步上来抱住我。他是怕我被风刮倒还是不舍得分开？我不得而知。但是，被他拥在怀里的感觉还是那美美好。这是他最后一次拥抱我了呀！我夹住了他的手臂，不让他走。

这个初冬的午后，狂风是为我们而起舞的，绕着我和查里卷了一圈又一圈，把我们越卷越紧。

查里，我订婚了。

知道了。他说，依旧抱着我依旧在我的背后。他的下巴搁在我的肩膀上，悄声问，为什么要等到分手再说？怕我受不了吗？

查里，查里。我叫着他的名字。他的脸贴在我的耳朵上，像冰袋一样冷。

我问：从哪里知道的呢？吃饭前还是吃饭后？

他说，你和招待的对话，你邀请他参加婚礼。

呵，原来你听懂了我们的家乡话？

简单的，我懂一些。

那么，为什么还说我是独立的女性?

你确是独立的女性。选择婚姻和被传统收编不是一个概念。在今天，选择婚姻需要很大的勇气。你的未婚夫也很了不起。

我说，他要向你说声对不起。

是乔治？

嗯。你怎么知道？

我感觉到他爱着你。告诉他，查里说没关系，希望他好好爱素素。

我的眼睛红了。我对自己说，不能在这个时候掉眼泪，不能眨眼睛，强行让泪水留在眼眶里。我说，他会的，查里。他很爱我，我也很爱他。没有说完，泪如泉涌，叭答叭答地掉在查里的手臂上。

那就好。他从口袋来掏出来手绢，抹去我的眼泪，说道，祝福你，不要忘了邀请我。

不会忘记的，不会忘记的，查里，你真好。

lie. He loves me deeply, and I love him too." The tears fell before I could finish. They landed on Charlie's arm.

"That's good." He retrieved a handkerchief from his pocket and gently wiped away my tears, saying, "May God bless you. Don't forget to invite me."

"I won't. I won't forget, Charlie. You're a good man," I cried.

He gazed at the sky, tears shimmering in his eyes.

I let him go first. I wrapped my shoulders in my own arms, with my neck hidden in my high collar, watching him recede into the distance. Just as he was about to step into his car, I sprinted towards him, calling his name.

"Charlie – Charlie – wait for me!"

He heard and turned around. He opened his arms, tears staining his face.

I threw myself into his embrace while saying, "Charlie, I'm a flawed woman, not deserving of your love. I'm a coward. Charlie, please forgive me."

He said, "Susu, don't think that way. I'm the one who's the coward, not you."

"I'm a pragmatic woman. I chose a wealthy man."

"No, Susu, why torment yourself? I'm genuinely happy for you. Do you believe me?"

He cradled my face in his hands and gave me one last kiss. Then he turned and got into his car, driving away.

The street in front of the restaurant stretched out straight and true. The powerful wind sent dust swirling into the sky. The dust was caught up by his departing car, blurring my view. Thus, Charlie had entered my life quietly and now departed just as quietly.

我哭了起来。

他望着苍天，眼睛里闪着泪光。

我让他开车先走。自己缩着脖子抱着肩膀，默默地看着他越走越远。就在他要坐入汽车的那一霎那，我不顾一切地奔过去，一边跑一边喊着他的名字。

查里！……查里！……等等我。

他听见了。他转过身来。他向我敞开了胸怀。他的脸上挂着泪。

我一头扑过去，一边哭一边说，查里，我是个坏女人，是不值得你爱的。我是个胆小鬼。查里，原谅我。……

他说，素素，不要这样想。胆小的是我，不是你。

我说，就把我当作一个俗气的女人吧！我选择了一个很有钱的男人。

不，素素，为什么要折磨自己？我真的为你高兴，真的，你不相信我吗？

他捧起了我的脸，最后一次亲了亲，转身进了汽车，“呼”地一声开走了。

饭店门口的路笔直如线，狂风把他车后的尘土掀起来，搅得昏天黑地，模糊了我的视线。就这样，查里悄悄地走进了我的生活，不声不响地走了出去。

Chapter 30

As I drove aimlessly on the highway, my mind was in turmoil. I kept going until my car's gas indicator warned of dwindling fuel. I had to exit, but I was lost, unsure of where to turn. Ahead, I saw a forest, and without much thought, I turned onto a small road and drove in. Dust billowed behind my car as I parked beneath a grand old pine tree, its trunk tall and sturdy, bearing the marks of age like wrinkles on a wise elder. Pine needles blanketed the ground, filling the gaps between the exposed roots. It was utterly still, no wind, no signs of human presence. The tree's canopy filtered the sunlight, casting dappled shadows on the ground. It felt like fate had led me here, seeking refuge. A squirrel darted down the tree trunk, bounding across the pine needles, rustling the otherwise serene air. It paused by my car, rising on its hind legs, gazing at me. Those tiny eyes seemed to ask, "What are you doing here? Is this red turtle of a car a spaceship from another world?" I wished I had something to offer the squirrel. I searched around, but found nothing edible. It observed me for a moment before scampering away. I felt a pang of sadness for not being able to help it. How I wished to assist, on this early winter afternoon! Where would it find sustenance?

Who would keep Charlie company this weekend afternoon and evening? How much loneliness and emptiness could his white Nissan contain? Generally, when we didn't frequently meet, Charlie paid it no mind, because he held me in his heart. But today, he learned that I was leaving him, never to return. Could he bear the solitude? He'd always been patient with me. It seemed like he was always waiting for a day when we'd draw nearer. But what he received was our separation. Why didn't he fight for it? I wasn't married yet, no signature on any document. If he had called out to me, saying something like, "Do you truly want to be a housewife? Don't you want to achieve something in some kind of enterprise?" Unraveling the conflict in my heart should have been easy for a philosopher like him. Why didn't he make a move? Besides, he possessed many other advantages that George didn't.

What if he had acted this way? Would he have maintained his ground? Would he have won back my respect, my heart? If he had, he wouldn't be Charlie. He would never meddle with my choice. He believed in me, in my ability to take responsibility for myself. His faith in me reflected his self-respect. Some men may appear strong outwardly, but lack confidence in themselves. Charlie, however, held his head high with dignity and pride. He was

第三十章

我没有马上回家，开着车没有目的地跑。上了高速公路，开啊，开啊，开到汽油出了红灯，才下了出口。我不知道要上哪里去，脑子里一片混乱。看到前面有一片树林，便下了岔路，开了进去。车后尘土飞扬。

车子停在一棵古老的松树下，树干笔挺，布满皱纹，好像一个精神矍铄的老人。松针满地，像稻草一样蓬松松地铺在露出地面的树根之间。很安静，没有风，没有行人，斑斑驳驳的树影落在草地上，把阳光挤了出去。这么巧，我正需要一个世外桃源。

树上窜溜下来一只小松鼠，在松针上一跳一跳，点拨着宁静的空气。它在我的车旁停了下来，竖直了身体朝我看。这个小脑袋，这双小眼睛，此刻你在想什么？是不是这红色的乌龟车，好像外星飞来的宇宙飞船？我想给小松鼠一个见面礼。在车内左右前后扫荡了一边，什么吃的东西都没有。它看了我一会儿，一溜烟走了。

我心里想着查里，这个周末的下午和晚上，谁去陪伴他？白色的丰田车装得下多少孤独和失落？平时我们不常见面，他可以不在乎，因为我在他的心里。今天，我走了，不会回来了。他耐得住寂寞的吗？他一直对我很宽容。他好像一直在等着那一天，我们都做好了准备的那一天，双方可以走得更近一些。可是，他等来的却是我们的分离。他为什么不争一争啊？我还没有结婚，没有签字呢！如果他对我吼一吼，诸如，你甘心当家庭主妇吗？你不想在事业有所造就吗？把不能两全的矛盾挑开，应该是哲学家的本事。他为什么不反击呢？再说，他还有许多把乔治比下去的优势。如果他这样做了，又怎样呢？赢回他的领地？赢得我的尊敬，赢回我的心？如果他这样做了，他就不是查里了。他是决不会来干涉我的选择的，他是相信我的，相信我是对自己负责任的。相信了我也就是看重了他自己啊！有的男人表面上很强悍，恰恰没有自信。而他有一颗自尊和骄傲的心。他是准备了为自己的爱情方式付代价的。这不是他的第一次失败。他根本不想妥协和改变。

啊，小松鼠回来了，捧着一个棕红色的松果！我真为它高兴

willing to pay any price for embracing his philosophy and style of love. This wasn't his first setback. He'd never back down or change.

The little squirrel returned, clutching a red nut in its tiny paws. I was happy for it. It had found sustenance for itself. "My dear squirrel, don't tell me my concern is unnecessary, and my sorrow is in vain." What a fool I was! I would have everything I needed. Everything was set in motion. Goodbye, my dear squirrel!

I slowly reversed my car out of the forest and merged back onto the highway. The wind was still fierce, and caught between its strength and the high speed, my car occasionally shuddered. Other vehicles on the highway sped by like vibrant meteors under the brilliant sun. George must have been worried about me at home. I took the next exit and pulled into a gas station. Once the tank was filled, I called George on my cell phone.

"George, I don't know where I am right now. I'll ask the attendant here to tell you, alright?" I found a young man working at the station and had him speak to George. After a while, he handed the phone back to me. George's voice came through, "Susu dear, how did you end up so far away? Where's Charlie?"

As I arrived home, the dark of night had already set in. George, holding Kristeene's hand, greeted me at the door. My face, streaked with remnants of washed-away makeup and wearied from the long drive, seemed to startle him.

He embraced me, saying, "Sweetheart, you're back at last."

"I'm back, George," I replied. "Did you have dinner?"

"Kristeene did, but I was waiting for you."

"You can eat now. I'm not hungry." I crouched to kiss Kristeene and said, "Susu wants to take a shower." Then, I headed towards the staircase. George called out, "Susu, what happened?"

"Nothing," I replied, continuing up the stairs. But after a few steps, I halted, leaning on the railings. I turned to George, saying, "I have a lot to tell you. I have many strange ideas. But you should go eat first."

After my shower, I donned my sleeping gown and entered the bedroom, where the scent of onions filled the air. An oval plate sat beneath the milky lamp on the bedside table, bearing browned chicken legs, creamed mushrooms, and Italian macaroni. George informed me, "I've already called for Helen to come look after Kristeene. Today is her day off, after all."

He sat on the bedroom sofa, saying, "I've already had dinner." He didn't mention, "It's your dinner," as though it were his duty to provide my meal. I'd initially planned to say so much, but now, my words seemed to have vanished. His gestures, which always touched me deeply, had a way of leaving me speechless.

As I combed my hair, I explained, "I had a big lunch. I'm not hungry now."

He asked, "How was Charlie?"

"He's the same as always, not too humble, not too proud. But when we parted, at the last moment, he seemed sad and teary."

"Did you apologize to him on my behalf?"

"I did. But he said you have more courage than he does, and he hopes you'll love me forever."

啊！可爱的小松鼠啊，你是不是要告诉我，我的担心是多余的，我的伤感是不必要的。我多么傻啊！什么都会有的，都是被安排好的。再见了，可爱的小松鼠！

我的车慢慢地从树林里退出来，上了高速公路。风依旧很大，车速和风力在路上较量，车身动不动摇晃一下。车道上的汽车在明媚的阳光下如五颜六色的流星一般，划过去划过来。乔治一定在家里等急了吧！下了第一个出口，我便进了加油站，加足了油，给乔治打了电话。

我说，乔治，我不知道自己开到哪里，我让这里的人告诉你好吗？我找了加油站的小青年，请他听电话。不一会儿，小青年把电话传给了我。乔治在电话里说，素素，亲爱的，你怎么跑那么老远啊？查里呢？

我说，他吃完饭就走了。

他说，我让这位先生给你画个图，如果你没有把握的话，就等在加油站，我来接你。

不用了。我说，我能找回来。

就这样，我按照图纸上了路。真的离家好远啊。开了好久好久，还没有到家。距离也是一种心情吗？为什么刚才开过来的时候，不觉得遥远？

天黑了。听见汽车的声音，乔治搀着柯丽丝来到了楼门口。我脸上的化妆被泪水洗得残缺不全，加上开车的疲劳，从车里出来的时候，让乔治吃了一惊。他一把拥着我说，宝贝，你终于回来了。

回来了，乔治。我说，你们吃饭了吗？

柯丽丝吃了。我在等你呢！

你去吃吧，我不饿。我蹲下身去亲了亲柯丽丝，说道，素素要去洗个澡。说完就往楼梯走。乔治在背后喊，素素，出了什么事吗？

没事。我继续朝楼上走。走了几步，停了下来。我靠在楼梯的扶手上，对乔治说，我有许多话要对你说，许多奇怪的想法，你先吃晚饭吧！

我穿着睡衣出来的时候，闻到了卧室里一房间的洋葱香。床边柜乳白色的灯光下，有一个椭圆形的餐盘，里面放着金色的鸡腿，奶油蘑菇和红色的意大利面条。乔治说，已经通知海伦过来照看柯丽丝。本来今天海伦休息。他坐在卧室的沙发上，说，我已经吃了。

他没有说那是你的晚餐，好像他给我端上来是应该的。原来一肚子的话，到了这个时候，不知道哪里去了。就是这种感动，常常让我失去了对自己的控制。我一面梳头发，一面说，中午吃好多，不饿。

他说，查里好吗？

"Of course, I will. But how did you get lost? And so far from home?"

"So? How did I get lost?" I pondered. In those few hours, my emotions had surged and roiled like a ship on stormy seas. Now, standing before him, because of dinner, because of my gratitude, the words I'd initially planned to say had melted away like ice. But I felt a suffocating weight, like sinking to the ocean's depths. If I didn't struggle, I wouldn't break the surface. Suddenly, I felt an urge. I tossed the comb on the bed and shouted, "You ask me how I got lost. I got lost the moment I left home."

George looked at me, surprised. "I don't understand, Susu."

"You asked me why I got lost. It's because I went to see Charlie. That's why I got lost. I shouldn't have gone. You let me go. George, why did you let me go alone to meet my old lover? Are you that confident? Are you really that confident?"

I spilled those ambiguous words out in one breath, caring little whether he comprehended them. It was as if I'd finally shed weight off my back. I felt immensely better. I had spoken my truth. I didn't want to pretend anymore. I told him I was a worldly person, reluctant to let go of my old love. I wasn't as good as he thought.

He shifted on the sofa, his shadow dancing on the white wall as if there were two figures gazing at me. He bit his lower lip, contemplating. Then he said, "Susu, what if I hadn't encouraged you to go? Wouldn't you still cherish your memories of him?" His innocent eyes widened, fixed on me.

He was right. I treasured my memories of Charlie. I didn't need to deceive myself.

He continued, "Time has a way of sifting out impurities. Humans tend to select happy memories to comfort themselves. I understand you. Just like Laura and me, when we were together, we often quarreled. But once she was gone forever, she left me with all the joyful memories."

As George held me in his arms, I confessed, "Laura's gone and won't be a threat to us, but Charlie is alive. Do you fear that I will go back to him some day?"

He responded calmly, "Can I retain you if you really want to go back to him?"

Tears welled in my eyes as I continued, "Though I don't want to go back to him, I still have feelings for him. George, love is selfish. Why are you so generous? The more generous you are, the more guilty I feel. Do you know that?"

"Susu, come sit here. Let me hug you," he said, pulling me close. He comforted me as if I were a child, patting my back gently. "It's okay. It's not a bad thing to have feelings. It's better to face them and choose whom you love than to hide your feelings and live with regret. Susu, you can only have one husband, but the right to choose is in your hands."

"I love you, George," I whispered.

"I love you, too," he replied. "Thank God, I have a Chinese girl looking after me."

I teased him, "Why are you so nice to me? You dote on me, which might turn me into a bad woman. Be careful."

不错。他还是老样子，不卑不亢，很沉稳。分手的时候，挺伤心的。

你代我说对不起了吗？

说了。他说，你比他有勇气，希望你好好爱我。

你怎么迷路了呢？跑得好远啊！

是啊，我怎么迷路了呢？我自言自语。我的情绪在几个小时里左右摇晃，忽高忽低。现在，我站在他的面前，因为这份晚餐，因为这份感动，本来想要说的话都像冰一样被消溶了，不见了，没有了。心中真沉闷啊，好像落到了海底，不挣扎一下就浮不出海面。突然，我得到了一种爆发力，我把梳子往床说一扔，冲着他说，你还问我呢，怎么会迷路？我从家里出去的时候就迷路了。

他惊诧地说，我不明白你的意思，素素。

因为我去见了查里。我迷失了，我是不应该去的。是你让我去的呀！乔治，你为什么要让我独自去会旧情人？是你的自信吗？你真的那么自信吗？

我一口气说了这些不明不白的话，不管他听不听得懂，我好像扔掉了包袱一样，心里好受了许多。我终于说出来了，我不必作任何伪装，我告诉他，我是个俗人，我留恋旧情，我没有他想像的那么好。

他的身体弹了一下，往后一仰。雪白的墙壁上，他的身影和他一起动，好像有两个人同时看着我。他咬着唇想了一会儿，说道，素素，如果我不鼓动你去，又怎么样呢？你就不怀念他了吗？

他张大了一双无辜的眼睛，目不转睛地看着我。

他说对了，我怀念查里。我不需要骗自己。

他说，时间过滤杂质，人总是本能地选择美好的回忆来宽慰自己。我很理解你，就像我和劳瑞一样，我们在一起的时候，曾经吵架不断，但是，一旦她永远地离开了我，留给我的都是美好的记忆。

我说，劳瑞已经过世，不给我们造成威胁。查里活着，你不怕我退回到他那里去吗？

如果你真要回去，我挡得住吗？他说得很平静。

我不要回去，但是，我对他还是有感情的呀！说完，我哭了起来，一边哭一边说，乔治，爱情是自私的，你为什么要那么慷慨？你越慷慨，我越觉得自己有罪，你知道吗？

素素，来，坐过来，让我抱着你。

他抱着我，靠在沙发上，像哄孩子一样，拍着我的背。他说，It’s okay. 人有感情没有什么不好，与其闷在心里，凝结成一种遗憾，永远地伴随你，不如让你去面对，看你究竟选择谁。素素，你只能有一个丈夫，选择权在你自己手里。

我是爱你的呀！

He chuckled, saying, "How bad could you possibly become? I'll watch and see how far you'll go."

Blushing, I admitted, "Since you're so nice to me, I don't dare to be bad."

George smiled and didn't say anything. He was like a book, and each time I read him, I discovered something new.

Changing the subject, I said, "When I saw Charlie, I thought of Anna. You must go see her. You lived together for over ten years. You must have feelings for each other, and so you must forgive each other."

He asked, "Do you really think so?"

"Yes," I affirmed. "Bring Kristeene with you. Anna must think of her, too."

He shared some surprising news, saying, "Here's something that might surprise you." He paused for effect, a mischievous smile playing on his lips.

"Out with it!" I urged.

"This afternoon, Anna came to see Kristeene."

"How coincidental!" I exclaimed. "Did you arrange it? Why did she come when I was away? I've been thinking of her, too."

"She called around noon for financial reasons. I told her about our engagement."

"What did she say?"

George relayed, "She said Susu's a wonderful woman."

"You're making that up. You just want to make me happy," I accused, raising my fist in jest. He intercepted it, laughing.

"No, she really said that. They just wanted to see how we are. They waited for you and only left when you called around five."

"They came together? Did you see her lover?"

"I did."

"See? Not as bad as you thought, huh?" I grew more intrigued.

"Honestly, Susu, I'm still getting used to it, but you're right, we shouldn't discriminate against them."

"I already added her name to my list of friends. I didn't dare tell you, afraid you wouldn't agree. But now it's no problem."

"For the wedding?" George clarified.

"Yes."

"Who said I wouldn't agree? Did I say that? Anna's on my list too."

"Really? I misunderstood you. Put her lover's name down. What's her name?"

Suddenly, I felt ravenously hungry, almost famished.

George informed me, "Her name's Mary."

As he continued his tale of the afternoon, I dug into my dinner, savoring each bite. The meal was truly delightful.

我也爱你啊！他说，我感谢上帝，让一个中国女孩子来看护我。

你为什么要待我那么好？你宠我，当心我变成坏女人。

他哈哈大笑，说道，你能坏到哪里去！坏给我看看。

我低下头，不好意思地说，想到你那么好，我想坏也不敢啦！

他笑笑，没有再说什么。乔治就像一本好书，让我读了又读，每读一次都有新的收获。

我说，见了查里以后，我就想到了安娜，你应该去看看安娜。你们共同生活了十多年，以前也是有感情的，应该互相原谅。

他说，你这么想吗？

是啊，我说，把柯丽丝带去，安娜一定想死她了。

他说，我告诉你一个消息，你不要太吃惊。他抿嘴笑笑，故意停在那里。

说呀！

安娜来了。今天下午来看柯丽丝了。

真有这么巧吗？我跳了起来。是你事先安排的吗？为什么要乘我不在的时候来呢？我很想念安娜的呀！

她是中午来的电话，为财务上的事情。我告诉她我们订婚了。

她怎么说呢？

她说，素素很出色。

你瞎编，哄我！我举起了拳头，正要抡下去，被他一把接住。

她说顺路来看望我们。我以为你马上就要回来的呢！她们等你等到你来了电话，大概近五点才走的。

她们？她们一起来的吗？你看到了她的恋人了吗？

看到了。

怎么样？不如你想像的那么坏吧！我的兴趣越加浓了起来。

说实话，素素，我还是很不习惯的，但是，你说得对，我们不应该歧视她们。

我早就把她排在我的朋友名单里呢！怕你不同意，没敢说。这真是太好了啊！

婚礼名单？

对呀！谁说我不同意？我说过吗？安娜也在我的名单上。

是吗？那是我小看你了。把她的爱人也写上吧！她叫什么？

就在这时候，我突然觉得好饿呀，饿得发慌。

乔治说，她叫玛丽。

我一边吃一边听他讲下午的故事，这顿晚餐，味道好极了。

Chapter 31

The snow was falling gently as I dialed Lisa's number.

"Lisa, it's me, Susu. I wanted to invite you to the wedding," I explained.

She responded with a burst of enthusiasm, "Bravo, Susu! You got him at last!"

That was just like Lisa, always speaking her mind, even if it could be a bit brash at times. She rushed over, eager to hear every detail of how I had won George's heart.

The snow-covered scene was breathtaking. The world was blanketed in white, with snowflakes drifting down gracefully, landing on trees and houses. The snow melted and was swiftly replaced by more falling from the sky. It was a picturesque winter day.

Kristeene, Helen, and I ventured out into the backyard, bundled up in heavy coats, scarves, and hats. We scooped up handfuls of snow, shaping them into balls and playfully tossing them at one another. Our clothes and caps were dusted with delicate snowflakes. Laughter filled the air as we exchanged snowballs. Kristeene stumbled and fell, but she quickly picked herself up without shedding a tear.

I suggested, "Kristeene, tomorrow morning, we can build a snowman. Do you remember the story of the snowman from the book?"

She nodded eagerly, "Yes."

"And can you put eyes and a nose on the snowman?"

"Why wait until tomorrow morning?" Kristeene inquired.

"Because the snow now isn't quite enough."

"How do we put eyes and a nose on the snowman?" she asked.

"We'll use a carrot for the nose and a piece of coal for the eyes. And for the mouth... Helen, what can we use for the mouth? It should be curved, like in a smile."

"Banana! We can use a banana for the mouth," Kristeene chimed in. Then she looked up at me, asking, "Bananas are curved. Can we use them?"

Helen suggested, "We could also cut a thin piece of tree branch and shape it into a curve for the mouth."

I gave Helen a knowing look and said, "Kristeene's quite clever. A banana is curved, which is perfect for the mouth, a big smile."

Just then, a black car pulled up. It was Lisa. I waved excitedly and rushed over to greet her. Helen followed with Kristeene in tow, her little feet creating

第三十一章

给莉莎打电话的时候，外面下着大雪。雪景很雅致。雪花无声无息，从从容容地飘着，贴在地上，树上，房子上。前面的化了，后面的跟着。前面的滑落了，后面的来扶持。有秩有序，前赴后继，织造了一片银白色的天地。

莉莎接电话的时候很吃惊。她以为我已经离开了城堡，因为多次来电话，没有人接。

我要结婚了。

啊……！她惊叫了起来。

邀请你来参加婚礼。

素素，好样的，你到底把他搞到了手！

莉莎就是这个模样，说话没有遮掩，有时锋利得令人难以招架。她兴致勃勃地赶来就是想听听素素如何“俘虏乔治”的故事。

我，柯丽丝和海伦都穿上了羽绒大衣，裹上了围巾，套上了帽子，到院子里玩雪。我们把雪抓起来，捏成一团，扔来扔去。衣服上帽子上绽开了无数雪花，一团团白气夹着笑声在我们之间传来传去。柯丽丝在雪地里摔了跤，一骨碌自己爬起来，白了一身，像小雪人。

我说，柯丽丝，明天早上，我们大概能够做一个雪人。记得书上讲的雪人故事吗？

她点头说，记得。

我说，你能给雪人装眼睛鼻子吗？

为什么要等到明天早上？柯丽丝问道。

因为雪不够多不够厚。

怎样给雪人装眼睛鼻子？

噢，我说，胡萝卜当鼻子，烧烤的煤炭做眼睛，嘴巴么，……海伦，用什么做嘴巴？要弯弯的，微笑的样子。

香蕉，用香蕉做嘴巴。柯丽丝脱口而出，扯着我的衣服说，香蕉弯弯的，香蕉可以吗？

海伦说，我们还可以剪一段细树枝，弯曲了以后当雪人的嘴

a path through the snow. We reached the roadside.

Lisa looked as stunning as ever, wearing gray boots, a matching heavy coat, a brown woolen skirt, and a corresponding jacket. She carried herself with a dignified air, standing tall with her chin slightly raised. But when we embraced, she transformed into a playful child, bouncing with her arms around my neck.

Turning to Kristeene, with one hand still on my shoulder, she said, "I know you're Kristeene, right?"

Kristeene looked up at Lisa and asked, "Yes, how did you know?"

I explained, "This is Lisa, my classmate from school."

"Is this your first visit?" the little girl inquired.

"Yes, Kristeene, it's my first time," Lisa confirmed, stooping down to plant a kiss on her rosy cheek.

"I'll start school next year," Kristeene announced.

"Do you like school?" Lisa asked.

"Susu said a lot of children play with me there," Kristeene replied, her eyes sparkling with excitement.

As we made our way toward the house, Kristeene's questions flowed non-stop, "Why doesn't Susu go to school?"

"Susu wants to stay here and take care of you, Kristeene," Lisa explained.

"Will Susu go with me to school next year?"

I replied, "If Kristeene wants a sister or brother, Susu will stay at home to take care of them." By the time I finished speaking, we were already inside the house, shedding our heavy coats. Helen opened the closet in the hallway and hung them on the hangers. Everyone seemed absorbed in their own thoughts, except for Kristeene.

"I want a sister, not a brother," she declared, wrapping her arms around my leg. She looked up at me and asked, "Susu, where is my sister?"

I took her hand and pressed it against my belly. "Here. Wait until she grows as big as your doll, then you'll be able to see her."

In unison, Lisa and Helen exclaimed, "Susu, you're pregnant?" Helen's coat slipped from her hand and fell to the floor.

"When I took the urine test this morning, it came out positive," I confirmed.

"That's wonderful!" Helen rejoiced.

"Is it true, Susu?" Lisa shouted.

"I'm not sure," I admitted. "Helen, could the test result be wrong?"

"It's highly unlikely," Helen reassured.

"Good." I threw my arms around Lisa and said, "If George finds out, he'll be over the moon."

"My God! My God!" Lisa exclaimed. "Susu, I'm so envious of you, so jealous!" Her excitement was almost deafening. When she finally calmed down, I noticed tears glistening like diamonds on her long eyelashes. At our side, Helen picked up Kristeene and declared with joy, "Kristeene will soon have a sister!" Kristeene echoed her enthusiasm.

"Lisa, how's David? Are you two married?" I inquired.

"Please, Susu, don't bring him up right now. Let me revel in this happy

巴。

我朝海伦眨眨眼睛，说道，柯丽丝真聪明！香蕉弯弯的，太好了，可以做雪人的嘴巴，大嘴巴。

正说着，一辆黑色的汽车开了进来。啊，莉莎！那是莉莎的汽车。我一边扬手一边奔跑过去。海伦抱起了柯丽丝跟在后面跑。脚后雪浪追逐，一直闹到路边。

莉莎还是那么漂亮，穿一双米灰色的高统皮靴和同样颜色的皮风衣，咖啡的呢制长裙和配套的上装。她的举手抬足还是那么高贵，挺胸收腹，下巴微微上翘。但是，当我们拥抱的时候，她完全像个孩子，绕着我的脖子，跳了又跳。她一手搭在我的肩膀上，侧过脸去望着柯丽丝，说道，我知道你叫柯丽丝，对不对？

是的，柯丽丝仰着小脸问，你怎么知道我的名字？

柯丽丝，我说，这是莉莎，素素的同学。

你是第一次来吧！小姑娘问道。

是的，柯莉丝，我是第一次。她弯下腰去亲了亲小女孩苹果一样通红的脸蛋。

明年，我也要上学。

你喜欢上学吗？莉莎问。

素素说，学校里有许多小朋友和我一起玩。

我们向楼里走，一路都是柯丽丝的问题。

素素，你为什么不上学呢？

我说，如果柯莉丝希望有个小妹妹或者小弟弟的话，素素需要继续留家照顾他们。我说这话的时候，已经进了大楼，她们都在脱外套，海伦打开了走廊口存衣室的门，用衣架把它们挂起来。没有人注意到我说了些什么，只有柯丽丝。

我要小妹妹，不要小弟弟。她跑过来，抱住我的腿，昂起了小脸问道，素素，小妹妹在哪里？

我拉她的手贴在腹部上，说道，在这里。等她长到和你的玩具娃娃一样大的时候，你就能见到她了。

莉莎和海伦不约而同地叫了起来：素素，你怀孕啦？海伦手里的滑雪衫掉到了地上。

我说，今天早晨测的小便，是阳性。

那就是了。海伦说。

真的吗，素素？莉莎捂着嘴巴叫起来。

不知道呀！我说，海伦，测试会出错误吗？

很准，很准的。

是吗？我上前抱住莉莎，说道，乔治要是知道了，准发疯呢！

莉莎喊道，我的上帝！我的上帝！素素，我好羡慕你！羡慕死啦！

我的耳朵差点儿被她震聋了。等她停下来，我看到了泪花像钻

moment a bit longer."

"What happened, Lisa?"

"We just couldn't get along. We'd make up and then argue again. It was a never-ending cycle. There were temptations all around us. He had no shortage of admirers, and neither did I. It's better for us to go our separate ways."

"Do you have a new boyfriend?"

"How could I not? A person can go without a family, without children, but not without love, right, Susu?"

"Yes, you can't go without love," I agreed. Seeing the determination in her eyes, I thought, "No man can resist her." A woman might be fragile and crumble after being hurt, struggling to find her footing again. But Lisa was strong, possessing a spirit of self-preservation.

"Bravo, Lisa!" I patted her on the shoulder. "You're absolutely right. Does your boyfriend love you a lot?"

"He does, he does. He seeks companionship above all else. I have no idea how long our relationship will last."

"Don't lose faith so easily," I advised with a smile. "As long as there's love, everything will work out."

Suddenly, Lisa grasped my hand tightly and stared at me with an intensity that made me feel like she was assessing a stranger.

"What's on your mind, Lisa?" I inquired, smiling.

"You—Susu—have you made the pledge?" she asked, her eyes searching mine.

"Yes, we did. Before the judge," I confirmed.

"Were you afraid?" she pressed.

"Why should I be afraid, Lisa?"

"Why?" Her eyes widened in disbelief. "It's not real, it's a falsehood, a deception."

"I believe what we said is all true," I replied calmly.

"No, Susu, you misunderstand me," she said, shaking her head, her golden hair cascading over half of her face. "A vow can't be put to the test, which would render it false."

I was taken aback and leaned back, taking a deep breath.

"No, I didn't see it that way at the time, Lisa."

She explained, "When you make a vow before a judge or a priest, even if it's truly what you mean at the moment, it can only validate the present, not the entire journey of the marriage. It's no assurance that you'll always live happily until old age. It's better to vow that when the time comes, I'll love you and cherish it."

"Wow, Lisa, I had no idea you were a philosopher," I exclaimed.

Lisa burst into laughter suddenly. She unbuttoned her jacket and settled back comfortably on the sofa.

Helen brought us hot coffee and biscuits. She asked, "Is there anything else you'd like, Susu?"

"Nothing else, Helen. Thank you," I replied. "Lisa and I used to be roommates. We haven't seen each other in a long time. She came over to hear my story."

石一样在她长长的眼睫毛上闪烁。

海伦抱起了柯丽丝在旁边高兴地说，柯丽丝有小妹妹啦！

柯丽丝跟着一起喊：小妹妹！小妹妹！

我说，莉莎，戴维德好吗？你们结婚了吗？

哎呀，素素。她叫道，别提了，求求你，让我多高兴一会儿。

怎么啦，莉莎？

吹了。

噢，抱歉，你们那么相爱……

我和他处不长，好了闹，闹了好。周围的诱惑太多，他不缺女人，我不缺男人，还是分手好。

有了新的男朋友？

怎么会没有呢？一个人可以没有家室，没有孩子，但是不能没有爱呀，素素，对不对？

对啊，不能没有爱。我说。看着她那明亮的眼睛和自信的神态，心里想，哪个男人会不喜欢她？女人在受伤以后往往很软弱，有的人就趴下了，爬也爬不起来。莉莎是坚强的，属于自救型。

好样的，莉莎！我拍拍她的肩膀，说道，说得真好，男朋友很喜欢你，是不是？

她说，喜欢，喜欢，找个伴而已。不知道能维持多久？

不要那么没有信心么！我笑着说，只要有爱就好。

莉莎突然拉着我的手，聚精会神地看着我，好像在打量一个陌生人。

我笑着说，怎么啦，莉莎？

你们，……素素，……你们宣誓了吗？

宣誓了。在法官面前。

你害怕吗？

为什么要害怕呢，莉莎？

为什么？她瞪大了疑惑的眼睛，说道，那是假的，是谎言。是欺骗。

我想我们说的都是真话。我沉静地说。

不，素素，你理解错了。她一边说一边摇头，金色的头发遮住了半个脸。她说，这个誓言是经不起证明的，是不堪一击的。

我吃了一惊，身体往后一靠，深深地吸了一口气。

没有，我当时没有这样想，莉莎。

她说，当你们在法官或者牧师面前宣誓的时候，那怕当时是真心实意的，只能证明一时，不能证明整个的婚姻过程。与其保证白头到老，不如宣誓爱一天珍惜一天。你说是不是？

哇！莉莎，真没想到你是个女哲学家！

莉莎仰天大笑，一边把外套的钮扣统统解开，舒畅地靠在沙发上。

Helen smiled and left the room.

"Alright, Susu, tell me your story now," Lisa urged.

I pondered for a moment. "Where did my story leave off when we last talked?"

Lisa thought for a while and said, "You were considering finding a new job because Kristeene's mother had a falling out with her husband."

"Ah, yes," I said with a laugh. "You were there behind the scenes. I was dating Charlie at that time. George swooped in and stole me away from him."

"You mean Mr. Thomas? He's a good man. George is quite the catch."

"He's like a pirate. Once he got me, he decided to become a gentleman and apologized to Charlie."

"What's the truth, Susu? I can't tell if George snatched you away or if you snatched George away," Lisa said, eyes wide with amusement.

"You don't know. Laura passed away, and I didn't need to snatch George away from anyone."

"Really?" Lisa asked. "When George got divorced, there must have been a lot of women vying for his attention. You might not know all the details."

"That's possible," I admitted. "But I had some advantages. At least I could see him every day. As the Chinese saying goes: Whoever's closer to the water can get the moon (reflecting in the water) first."

Lisa collapsed onto the sofa in fits of laughter. "So you're saying: whoever's closer to the water can get the moon first," she mimicked me, repeating the Chinese saying.

"Exactly," I said. "If things had unfolded that way, I'd be a heroine—no, no, a woman pirate. In reality, there's no one else to look after his child but me. That's why he wants to marry me."

Lisa burst into another hearty laugh, her coffee nearly spilling from her hand. She narrowed her eyes in amusement and declared, "Susu, you're a master storyteller."

"Indeed. And here's another scenario: George got me pregnant and now he has to marry me."

"Susu, don't spin tales. One question: do you love him?"

I purposely avoided answering and instead asked, "Can you think of another scenario where a man and a woman get engaged so quickly?"

Lisa replied, "Of course, like love at first sight."

"Love at first sight? That's too simplistic."

海伦给我们送来了热咖啡和小饼干，问道，素素，你还要什么吗？

不要了，海伦，谢谢你。我说，我和莉莎曾经是室友，好久不见了。她来听我的故事呢！

海伦笑着走开了。

对呀，素素，讲你的故事吧！

我说，我和你分手的时候，故事发展到哪里？莉莎想了想，说道，你想另外找工作，因为柯丽丝的妈妈夹在中间。

噢，对了。我大笑。你太落后了，太落后了。我那时候正在和查里谈恋爱。乔治把我抢了过来。

汤玛斯先生吗？他很不错的。乔治本事不小啊！

我说，他像强盗一样，抢到手了以后，便做起了君子，向查里道歉。

到底是怎么回事？素素，是你抢乔治还是乔治抢你？莉莎瞪大了眼睛问。

我说，你不知道，劳瑞已经去世了。没有人和我抢乔治。

真的吗？莉莎问，乔治离婚以后，一定有许多女人打他的主意，你可能不知道细节。

我说，那倒是的，不过，我有优势，近水楼台先得月啊！

莉莎笑得倒在沙发上，说道，看你美的，近水楼台先得月。哈哈，她重复道，近水楼台先得月。

我说，好了，好了，真是这样的话，我成女英雄了，不，不，女强盗。事实是，没有人给乔治带孩子。我给他带，他就娶我做老婆。

莉莎又是一阵大笑，捧在手里的咖啡差点儿溅了出来。她眯上了眼睛说，素素，你是故事大王。

我说，还有一个版本，乔治把我的肚子搞大了，不得不娶我。

素素，你乱编。回答我一个问题，你爱他吗？

我故意不回答她，说道，一男一女在这么短的时间里订婚，还可能有别的版本吗？

莉莎说，当然有啦！比如一见钟情。

一见钟情？我说，太简单了。

Chapter 32

As I was about to call the philosophy professor, Helen handed me a stack of letters. Most of them were addressed to George, but one particular airmail envelope caught my eye, its blue and red edges standing out. It was from my mother.

The evening I had received the engagement ring, I wrote a letter to my parents. George had also penned a letter to them on the second day after our return. He had asked me to translate it into Chinese, but I reassured him, saying, “My parents have a better grasp of English than I do. They’ll be able to read it without a problem.”

My parents responded with their consent to our marriage, wholeheartedly embracing Kristeene as their own granddaughter. They framed the photo we had sent and proudly displayed it on their wall. They expressed gratitude to George for caring for me, their strong-willed, unfortunate daughter. We had invited them to our wedding, but they declined due to my mother’s aversion to flying. Nevertheless, they eagerly anticipated our visit for our honeymoon. The letter was penned by my father, with my mother adding her signature.

Upon reading the letter together, George seemed to overlook the words “headstrong” and “unfortunate.” Instead, he focused on their wholehearted agreement to our marriage. He swept me up in his arms, twirling me around like he had won the lottery.

We hadn’t yet replied to that letter. Why would my mother write again? Was there something urgent?

As I opened the letter, I soon learned that my friend from the restaurant had inadvertently stirred up trouble for me. He had mistaken Charlie for my fiancé. If I hadn’t invited him and his wife to the wedding, he likely wouldn’t have gotten involved, as it wasn’t his affair. However, I felt obliged to invite him since he had picked me up from the airport when I first arrived in America. When he saw Charlie and me together, along with my engagement ring, he assumed the best and happily wrote to report it. The news of the “American son-in-law” spread like wildfire. By the time it reached my mother, it had transformed into a tale vastly different from what we had conveyed. Mother must have shared George’s story with all her friends. Now, which version of the story should she believe? People were saying that the “American son-in-law” was young, handsome, and unattached, yet the photo we sent painted a different picture—a middle-aged man with a child. Doubts and fears filled her mind, especially considering her wild and unruly daughter back at home.

第三十二章

那天傍晚，我正准备给哲学教授打电话，海伦送来了一叠信件。大部份是乔治的，其中有一封蓝红锁边的航空信引起了我的注意。抽出来一看，是妈妈的笔迹！

我在带上了订婚戒指的当天晚上就给大陆写了信。乔治也在到家以后的第二天给我的父母写了信。他让我翻译成中文。我说，父母的英文词汇量比我还要多，阅读绝对没有问题。

父母回信说，同意我和乔治结婚，而且把柯丽丝当作自己的外孙女。我们寄去的照片，已经被装入镜框，挂在墙上。他们感谢乔治照顾他们那个总是自说自话，多灾多难的女儿。我们要求他们来参加婚礼。妈妈因为晕车，怕坐飞机，就不来了，欢迎我们回国度蜜月……回信是爸爸手写的英文，妈妈签了名。

乔治当时没有留意“自说自话”和“多灾多难”的具体含义。他最在乎是否得到他们的同意。当他看到求婚得到了批准时，抱着我乱转，好像中了彩一样。

我们的回信还没有写，妈妈怎么又写了信来？有什么急事吗？

拆开一看，才知道是我那个餐馆工作的中国朋友“惹”的祸。他把查里当做我的未婚夫了。如果不是我邀请他们夫妇来参加婚礼，他可能不会管这种闲事。当初，毕竟是他第一个迎接我，现在又是他亲眼看到了我的婚戒和查理，他是为我高兴才写信回去报告的。这个未来的美国女婿，七传八传，到了妈妈耳朵里，和我们所说的，完全不一样了。妈妈一定也把乔治的故事告诉了周围的朋友。现在，她应该相信谁呢？别人说，洋女婿是英俊的年轻的无牵无挂的，可是我们寄回国的照片却是中年的有孩子的。她心虚了，因为他们的女儿在大陆的时候，就是一个管不住的野姑娘。

妈妈特别容易担心，总是从消极的方面来看问题。她在信里说，当父母的，宁可你找一个年纪大一些的丈夫，将来不会出变故。后面她又说，你是不是被年轻的美国人迷了心窍，做出三心二意对不住乔治的事情？本来只是她自己的猜想，可是下面的文字简直就像真的发生了一样，火辣辣地把我教训了一顿。这些话，我在

My mother was a worrier, tending to view things through a pessimistic lens. She wrote in her letter, "As parents, we'd rather you marry an older husband, someone less likely to change in the future." She continued, "Have you been enchanted by a young American and become so fickle that you've wronged George?" What began as a mere suspicion took on the weight of a fact as she scolded me sternly—a familiar refrain from my days in China. Her words were like the steady ticking of the grandfather clock in our living room, a sound we heard every minute but seldom truly registered. She knew that her words might not bring about any change, but she found comfort in their repetition. It was as if, without the constant refrain, my problem might somehow become hers.

It was a night I would never forget. Just before I left China for America, I awoke at midnight to the sound of my parents arguing. My father remarked, "A problem child in China may not be a problem child in America, because the standard of judgment is not the same." My mother fretted, "We can disregard public standards, but how can we escape the worry about what kind of person our daughter will become?" My father countered, "Can we separate your hopes from public opinion?"

My father was always my steadfast supporter. During my teenage years, I remember most of the textbooks he compiled were Western children's stories and mythologies. He only allowed me to read "A Journey To The West" from the Chinese classical novels. In those days of hardship, these stories were my spiritual sustenance, bringing me immense joy. When he taught me mathematics, he also imparted logical thinking. Often, under the glow of a small oil lamp on moonlit nights, my brother and I would listen intently as my father explained the origins of species, ecological chains, and world geography. When I struggled to grasp a concept, he would sketch it out beneath the lamplight. As soon as I saw the drawing, I'd comprehend his words. It was during this time that I acquired my foundational knowledge of English. When China embraced open policies, he encouraged me to pursue education overseas.

My mother consistently sided with my brother. The main distinction between my parents was that while my father prioritized our education, my mother was more focused on our health and well-being. Perhaps it stemmed from her profession as a doctor, contrasting with my father's role as a professor. My brother and I were vastly different, seemingly not from the same family at all. He was sensible, obedient, careful, and ever-eager to assist others. When universities resumed normal operations after the so-called Cultural Revolution, my brother gained admission to a medical college, while I pursued an education major.

After arriving in America, my mother's worry for me amplified. At times, she'd write to me without my father's knowledge. Her letters would either inquire about my needs or offer instructions on various matters. In her eyes, I never truly grew up. This letter, too, was solely written by her, devoid of my father's signature. He never concerned himself with whether my future spouse would be Chinese or foreign, young or old, and paid little heed to what others might say. My mother, on the other hand, held a special interest in these matters, and it often troubled her.

She mentioned something that filled me with excitement: she had used the money I sent her to install a telephone line at home. I hadn't heard my

中国的时候听了几百遍，从来就像客厅里那个落地钟，叭答叭答地摆来摆去，听而不闻。她是知道的，说了也没有用，但是，她特别喜欢重复，好像不重复，我的问题就变成了她的问题一样。

记得我来美国读书的前夕，有一天晚上，我半夜醒来，听到父母在争论。爸爸说，在中国的“问题孩子”到了美国可能并不坏，因为评判标准不一样。妈妈说，我们可以不在乎社会的评判标准，但是，自己女儿应该成为什样的人，回避得了吗？爸爸说，你的希望和社会标准分得开吗？

爸爸总是帮我的。小时候他编的课本里，大部分是西方童话和神话。中国的古典小说，只给我看“西游记”。在那贫困苦难的日子里，这些故事真像精神粮食，给我带来了许多快乐。他教我数学的时候，把逻辑学的常识一起教了。我和哥哥常常在月夜，点个小油灯，听爸爸讲物种的起源，生物链和世界地理。有时候我听不懂，爸爸就在油灯下画图，看了图，我就懂了。我的英文基础就是在那个时候打下的。中国对外开放以后，爸爸一直鼓励我到国外去接受教育。

妈妈总是帮哥哥。和爸爸不同的是，她更关心哥哥的身体和衣食住行。可能因为她是医生爸爸是教授的关系吧！我和哥哥完全不像是一个家庭出来的人，哥哥很懂事，很听话，很细心，也很愿意帮助人。大学开门以后，他考取了医学院，我读了教育专业。

我来美国读书以后，操心最多的还是妈妈。她有时候瞒着爸爸给我写信，问我需要什么东西，继续教育我应该怎样做人。在她的眼睛里，我永远长不大。今天的信，又是她单独写的，没有爸爸的签名。爸爸是不会在乎女婿是洋是中，年纪轻还是年纪大的，也不会在乎别人怎么说的。妈妈特别在乎这些事，真是自讨苦吃啊！

信中提及了一件事，令我兴奋无比，那就是，用我寄去的钱给家里装上了电话。我已经这么久没有听到父母的声音了呀！看到这个消息，我不由自主地把客厅里的电话抓了过来，放在腿上。两只手在电话上摸来摸去，我恨不得马上拨电话回去。我看了几次手表，心里在呼唤，乔治，你为什么还不回来？

抱着电话，呆呆地坐在沙发上。八仙桌，长板凳，老家的白墙壁，水泥地，我的小房间，就像从中国搬来了一样。还有那房门关进开出的凉风，那黑夜中拨开的一个空洞，亮着我小日光灯青白的灯光。

乔治终于回来了。我跳了起来，三步并作两步走，差点而被电话线拌倒在地。本来我应该说怀孕的事儿。可是，丢到了九霄云外。

乔治，妈妈来信，家里装上了电话！

妈妈信里怎么说？乔治问我。

parents' voices in such a long time. As I read the news, I instinctively grabbed the phone from the living room and cradled it in my lap. I ran my hands over it, much like one might pet a beloved animal. I was eager to make an overseas call, glancing at my watch several times and silently willing George to return.

Sitting on the sofa, I held the phone close, envisioning my childhood home with its square table, benches, white walls, cement floor, and my small bedroom—all seemingly transported here from China. I could almost feel the chill of the wind as the door swung open and closed. In my mind's eye, I saw a sliver of light piercing the night through my small fluorescent lamp.

Finally, George returned home. I leapt up from the sofa and rushed to him, nearly tripping over the phone cord. Initially, I had wanted to share the news of my pregnancy, but it slipped my mind entirely.

"George, Ma mentioned in her letter that they have a phone at home now," I exclaimed.

"What did Ma say in her letter?" George inquired.

I was so focused on making the call that I couldn't recall the exact contents of my mother's letter. After translating it for him, George chuckled and remarked, "A misunderstanding caused Ma so much worry. Go ahead, Susu, make the call."

Dinner was forgotten. George encouraged me to call, still clad in his work attire.

"Do you want to speak with them?" I asked.

He sighed in frustration. "What can I say? I can't speak Chinese."

"You can speak English," I assured him. "No problem."

Kristeene rushed towards us like a little bird, calling out, "Daddy, daddy!" George scooped her up in his arms and said, "We're going to call China."

"Who's China?" Kristeene asked.

"China is a country, west of the Pacific. Remember when we played by the seaside? China is beyond the sea," George explained.

"Beyond the sea is Susu's home," Kristeene stated.

"Exactly," George affirmed. "We're going to call Susu's parents."

"Who are Susu's parents?" Kristeene inquired. We both burst into laughter.

"Susu's parents are your grandpa and grandma," I told her.

"Can I talk to them?" she asked.

"Of course," George replied. "What do you want to say?"

Kristeene blinked her large eyes, pondered for a moment, then said, "I'm Kristeene, two years old. My daddy is George. My mom is Susu."

Hearing Kristeene call me "mom," I was so moved that my tears threatened to spill. It was the first time she had called me that, and it came straight from her heart. I turned away, not wanting Kristeene to see my tears.

George chimed in, saying, "That's right. Your daddy is George. Your mom is Susu. Anything else?"

"Um, let me think," Kristeene pondered. "I want to say... Susu, what should I say?"

George lifted her up and brought her over to me. Confused, Kristeene asked, "Daddy, why is Susu crying?"

George mused, "Let me see. Oh, Susu's crying." He turned to Kristeene. "Susu is happy. They're happy tears. You can ask Susu."

我只想着打电话，把妈妈的话都忘了说。乔治听我翻译了以后，大笑，说道，一个误解就把你妈妈愁成这样？赶快，素素，打电话，打电话。

我们晚饭都顾不上吃，乔治衣服都来不及换，就催着我拨电话。

我说，你准备和他们讲话吗？

他苦恼地说，我不会讲中文怎么办？讲美国话。我说，不会有什么大问题吧！

柯莉丝像小鸟一样飞奔过来，一边喊着“爹地爹地”。乔治抱起她，说道，我们要和中国打电话啦！

柯丽丝问道，谁是中国？

乔治说，中国是一个地方，在太平洋的西面。记得吗，我们曾经在海边玩？海的那一边就是中国。

柯丽丝说，海的那一面是素素的家。

对啦！乔治说，我们和素素的家长打电话。

谁是素素的家长？柯丽丝问道。我们都笑了。

素素的家长就是你的外公外婆。

我可以和他们讲话吗？她问。

当然可以。乔治说，你想说什么呢？

柯丽丝眨着大眼睛，想了想，说道，我叫柯丽丝，两岁，我的父亲叫乔治，我的妈咪叫素素。

听到柯丽丝叫我妈咪，我感动得直想哭。这是她第一次用话语叫我妈咪，是出自内心的呀！我背过身，不想让柯丽丝看到我的眼泪。

乔治说，对啊，你的爹地叫乔治，你的妈咪叫素素。还有呢？

嗯，我想想。柯丽丝说，我还想说，……素素，我应该说什么好呢？

乔治抱着她走近我。柯丽丝不解地说，爹地，素素为什么哭了？

乔治说，我看看，噢，素素真的哭了。他对柯丽丝说，素素是高兴，高兴得哭了。不信你问问她。

柯丽丝说，是这样吗，素素？

我点点头，说道，是的，柯丽丝，素素是高兴了才哭的。因为我们要和中国打电话。

和你的家长打电话。柯丽丝纠正我说。

对，对！我说，和我的家长打电话。

电话拨通了。那“滴铃铃”的声音就像一条细细的丝线，把我的心牵了过去。妈妈在电话里说了一声“喂”，我的眼睛就红了。声音真清楚啊，就像在身旁一样。

Kristeene inquired, "Is that true, Susu?"

I nodded, affirming, "Yes, Kristeene. Susu is just too happy. They're happy tears because we want to call China."

"To call your parents, right?" Kristeene corrected me.

"That's right, that's right," I agreed. "To call my parents."

I dialed the number. The ringing echoed like a thin thread, tugging at my heart from across the ocean. My mother's voice greeted me with a warm "Hello!" My eyes welled up with tears. Her voice was so clear, it felt like she was right beside me.

"Ma, it's me," I choked out, tears streaming down my face without even saying my name.

George took the receiver and mimicked me, saying, "Ma." Then he greeted her in English, "How are you, Ma? It's George. We got your letter and called you right away." He then handed the receiver to Kristeene.

Kristeene was ecstatic and chatted away on the phone for quite a while. She was never afraid of strangers. She answered yes or no to whatever questions my parents asked her. Then she shared her own stories, like building a snowman, watching cartoons on TV, drawing, and reading. Her sentences were incomplete, or consisted of separate words. If someone was familiar with her, they could guess what she was saying. So, I wasn't sure how much my parents could understand.

I gave a brief explanation of why Charlie and I had dined in the restaurant. My mother responded that she already knew. She didn't want to dwell on that topic any longer. She must have realized she was mistaken and didn't want my father to find out she had been writing to us all on her own.

When my father came on the line, I started crying again. Sobbing, I told him, "Pa, I'm so grateful to you. You were right. I feel like a fish in water here. I'm very happy."

My father said, "It's good to hear that. Let me talk to George."

George took the receiver, listening respectfully, like a soldier in the army receiving orders from a commander. He only said yes, never no. He and my father conversed in English. They talked for a long time.

Watching George listen so intently, I couldn't help but smile. This man, a VIP in social circles, was perspiring as he spoke to my father. I handed him a few tissues and picked up a magazine to fan him. I marveled at how modern science had brought my parents' voices so close. Their words painted vivid images of them in my mind. They felt as if they were right beside me.

George hung up the phone, but his face still held a look of tension. I smiled, enjoying the moment. "It seems that even you can be made to feel tense by someone," I teased. He glanced at me, his face still tense.

"It's not a big deal," I reassured him. "They're my parents. What do you have to be afraid of?"

He replied, "You were quite the naughty little girl, it seems. You never mentioned that to me."

Blushing, I asked, "Did they say I used to bully my brother?"

He nodded, a playful glint in his eyes. "So you do have a bit of a record. Come on, confess. How did you bully your brother?"

I realized I had been tricked and exclaimed, "You're a sneaky one, aren't you?"

“妈，是我，……”，没来得及报名字，我”哇”地一声哭了起来。

乔治接过电话，学我叫了声“妈妈”，然后用英语问候，你好，妈妈，我是乔治。我们收到你的来信，马上给你们打电话。说了没几句，把电话传给了柯丽丝。柯丽丝眉飞色舞，在电话上说了好久。她本来就不怕陌生，父母问她的问题，都用Yes和No来回答，然后，她讲自己的故事。比如，堆雪人啦，卡通电视啦，画画啦，读书啦，妈咪不让吃很多巧克力，爹地用关禁闭惩罚她，等等。她的表示常常不是完整的句子，而是一些零碎的单词，熟悉她，能猜出其中的意思。我 不知道父母究竟听懂了多少？

我把和查里到中国饭店的事情解释了一遍。妈妈说，知道了。她不希望谈这个话题，可能是觉得自己理亏，更可能是不想能让爸爸知道给我们写信的事。

爸爸来接电话的时候，我又哭了，一边哭一边说，爸爸，我多么感激你啊！你说的话都对，我在这里如鱼得水，很开心很幸福。

爸爸说，开心就好。让我和乔治说说话。

乔治握着电话。恭恭敬敬地好想像军队里的士兵接受首长训话一样。他和父亲说英文，两人谈了很久。

看着他那个认真的样子，我不由地笑了起来。这个曾经在大场面上叱咤风雨的人物啊，被父亲的电话搞得满头满脸都是汗。我抽了几张面纸给他，拿起一本杂志给他扇风。我一边扇，一边想，科技真伟大，一个电话，突然缩短了我和中国的距离，声音载着父母的身影，好像他们就在我的身边。

乔治说完了，挂了电话，还留着一张紧张的面孔。我忍俊不禁，幸灾乐祸地说，上帝到底创造了制服你的人

啊！他朝我看看，还是紧绷着脸。

哎哟，什么了不得的事情，我说。他们是我的父母，你怕什么啦？

他说，你小时候是个非常调皮的孩子，你可是从来没有告诉我。

我脸一红，说道，他们说我欺负我哥了，是不是？

他说，原来你是有前科的。老实交待，怎么欺负你哥哥的？

这时，我大呼上当了。我说，你真坏啊，引蛇出洞！

乔治大笑，说道，你以为你是个坏蛋？

我说，那么，爸爸说我什么了，让你那么紧张。

他说，你很倔，主意很大，叫我要有思想准备。

我笑道，乔治上当了，找一个不可救药的女人。

他说，如果你没有那么坏，我恐怕还看不中呢！

我唱道，两个坏蛋，两个坏蛋，跑得快，跑得快。

George laughed. "And you think you're a bad egg?"

I smirked. "What did my father say about me that made you so tense?"

He explained, "He mentioned that you're headstrong and often stick to your desires. He advised me to be prepared for it."

I grinned. "Well, George, it looks like you've found yourself a 'bad' woman with no cure."

George responded, "If you weren't a bit 'bad,' I wouldn't have taken you."

I playfully sang, "Two bad eggs, two bad eggs, running fast, running fast."

Kristeene, sitting in the corner of the sofa, looked up from her pictures and stood on the sofa, jumping. George inquired, "What song are you singing?"

"The Song of Bad Eggs," I replied. "Two bad eggs, you and me."

George leaned back, looking at the ceiling, and burst into laughter.

I joked, "Good, good. You're revived. I was starting to think your parents raised you to have a wooden head."

After dinner, George suggested, "Should we invite your Chinese friends, the couple, to our house so they can see how we live with their own eyes? That way, they can send the right messages back to China."

I agreed. "That sounds like a good idea. I'll call them."

The evening passed in a whirlwind of activity. I was occupied every moment, as the Chinese saying goes. When we finally said goodnight to Kristeene, who lay in bed, she hooked her arms around my neck and whispered, "Can my little sister in your belly sleep with me tonight?"

I gently declined, "Not now, sweetheart. She's too small. You can't have her yet."

George overheard and asked loudly, "What did you say, Kristeene?"

"Mom said my little sister in her belly. I can feel it," Kristeene replied.

George was taken aback. He looked at me, then at Kristeene, wide-eyed, but speechless. He leaned over us, his face full of nerves, and asked anxiously, "You're not kidding, right?"

With a smile, I assured him, "I was so busy with the calls, I forgot to tell you. Yes, George, I'm with child."

"My God," he exclaimed, embracing me tightly and carrying me up to the third floor. He gently set me down on the bed and showered my belly with kisses. He knelt beside the bed, smiling through joyful tears. He murmured, "Is this real? Is this real? My child, my child... you've come so quickly. I'm not ready for you yet." He turned to look at me, tears still in his eyes. "Susu, my darling, how can I ever thank you? I'm fifty now. You're really going to be my child."

I ran my fingers through his disheveled hair and wiped away his tears with the back of my hand. I called his name, overflowing with gratitude and love.

In that moment, I felt the profound happiness of expecting a child, a woman's happiness. Out of our love, George and I were creating a new life.

柯丽丝原来盘在沙发的角落里看画报，听到我唱歌，便站在沙发上乱跳。

乔治说，你唱什么歌？

坏蛋歌。两个坏蛋。你和我。

他仰面朝天地大笑。

我说，好了，好了，你总算活过来了，我真怕你被父母教训成木头人了呢！

晚餐的时候，乔治说，要不要请你的中国夫妇朋友来家里玩一次？干脆让他们仔细地看看，感受一下我们的生活，向中国发送正确的情报？

好哇，我说，我打电话问一下。

饭后，我和中国朋友约好了来访问的时间，打电话通知了哲学教授，并请他把我要结婚的消息转告同学。

一个晚上就这样过去了。一直在忙，没有喘息的机会。我们在和柯丽丝道晚安的时候，小姑娘躺在床上，搂着我的脖子悄悄地说，你肚子里的小妹妹能否借我用一用？让她和我一起睡？

我说，不行啊，柯丽丝，妹妹太小，现在还不能借给你。

你说什么，柯丽丝？乔治大声问道。

妈咪说，小妹妹在她的肚子里，我摸着了呢！

这个消息对于乔治来说，实在太意外了。他张开了嘴巴，瞪大了眼睛，半晌说不出一个字。他躬着背弯着腰，把脸转来转去，朝我看看，再看看柯丽丝，战战兢兢地问：你们不是在开玩笑吧！

我笑着说，忙着打电话，忘了告诉你。是的，乔治，我怀孕了。

我的上帝啊！他大喊一声，把我拦腰抱起来，一口气上了三楼。他把我放在床上，扑在我的腹部亲了又亲，亲了再亲。他跪在床沿边，一边掉眼泪，一边微笑。他说，这是真的吗？这是真的吗？孩子啊，我没有准备，你来得那么快，我一点没有准备啊。

他侧过脸来，泪眼汪汪地看着我。他说，素素，我的宝贝，我应该如何感谢你？我已经五十岁了呀，你真的怀上了我的孩子！

我用手指整理他凌乱的头发，用手背抹去他脸上的泪水。我喊着他的名字，感动得没有了言词。

这个时候，我才真正感到了怀孕的幸福，做女人的幸福。因为爱，我和乔治创造了新的生命！

Chapter 33

The days leading up to our wedding were a flurry of preparations and excitement.

One day, George handed me a cream-colored envelope with a wide smile. Intrigued, I opened it to find a beautifully designed wedding invitation. The background featured a colorless castle with intricate details, and a cartoon depiction of the bride and groom. The bride resembled an angel with transparent wings, dressed in a red, long Chinese-styled gown. The angel's face was mine, while the groom was portrayed as Chaplin, complete with a little beard and a cane. It was a delightful surprise, and I almost couldn't contain my laughter.

George explained, "Do you like it? We can still make changes. It's just a sample, and I designed it."

I couldn't help but praise, "It's very good. Extraordinary, fantastic."

He continued, "I've found an ideal location for the wedding. It's a small island with a secluded church. We can rent a boat to ferry the guests."

I questioned, "Why make things so complicated?"

"Because it's a treasured moment," he said with a smile. "After the wedding, we'll have our one-week honeymoon on board a ship."

I was intrigued. "Where are we going?"

He playfully replied, "I'll leave that for you to guess."

With my college on vacation, my classmates learned of my impending wedding from the philosophy professor and called to congratulate me. They wanted to know the exact date.

George decided, "We'll have the wedding when the snow is gone, and spring revives the world. It will be noted on the invitation."

Thanksgiving marked the start of the holiday season, and George and Dennis frequently joined us for dinner. Visitors came by, and Betty, busier than ever, took charge of the kitchen. The house was filled with the aroma of freshly baked bread, and people bustled about, bringing life and energy to

第三十三章

婚礼，婚礼，这些日子，除了正常的生活，我们就在筹备婚礼。

那天，乔治笑嘻嘻地从公文包了取出了一个奶黄色的信封，递给我。我好奇地打开一看，原来是婚礼请柬！真高雅啊！凹凸无色的城堡轮廓作背景，配上了新娘新郎的卡通图画。哈！女的像天使，插着透明的翅膀，黑发红旗袍，印着我的脸。男的像卓别林，留着小胡子，夹着文明棍，是乔治！我笑得差点儿断了气。

他问，喜欢吗。还能改，这是样卡，我设计的。

很好！我说，不同一般，很有趣。

他说，我找到了理想的场所办婚礼。在一个小岛，非常幽静的教堂，租船把客人接过去。

我说，何必搞那么复杂啊？

因为珍贵。他说，婚礼以后，我们将在船上度一周的蜜月。

去哪儿？哪儿？

他笑着说，给你一个悬念。

学校放假了。同学们从哲学教授处得到我要结婚的消息，纷纷打电话来祝贺，打听什么时候办婚礼？

乔治说，等雪停了，冬天过了，万物复苏的时候，就是我们结婚的日子。日期将写在请柬上。

美国从感恩节开始就拉开了度假的帷幕，乔治和丹尼经常回家吃晚饭。有时候，还有客人来访问。蓓蒂也来得比以前勤多了。海伦以照顾柯丽丝为主，也帮着做一些家务。蓓蒂忙碌在厨房里。冰箱里堆满了食品，空气中充满洋葱和面包的香味。我回想起刚来这里工作的时候，只有安娜和柯丽丝，整栋楼冷冷清清没有炊烟。后来，安娜走了换成乔治，我搬进来住，基本是我和柯丽丝的两人世界。现在，从早到晚，在厨房书房客厅和走廊上，进进出出，人来人往，看到一张张笑脸，这才像个家呀！

外面连续几天大雪，好一个热闹的冬天！

唯一不称心的，就是我的妊娠反映越来越明显，动不动恶心，呕吐，两眼泪汪汪。这时，我才想起，明年春天办婚礼，我正大腹便便。

乔治说，大肚子也能当新娘，有什么关系？

every corner. It truly felt like a bustling household.

We were greeted with several days of continuous snow, adding to the excitement of the winter.

The only source of concern for me was my increasingly obvious pregnancy symptoms. I experienced frequent bouts of vomiting, tears streaming down my face. At one point, I couldn't help but worry about attending the wedding with a prominent baby bump. George reassured me, "It doesn't matter. A bride can be pregnant. Why not?"

I hesitated, "Perhaps it's better to have the wedding either before or after the child is born. A heavily pregnant bride might seem a bit... untraditional."

George's concern for my well-being was evident as he said, "It's so chilly now. I can't have you getting into any incidents."

I reassured him, "To be honest, it might be better to invite friends over for a celebration at home. Let's not take the wedding too seriously. I'm not too fussed about how it goes."

"You don't care?" George looked at me skeptically.

"I really don't. I've had my fill of it."

"But we can't skip the wedding."

"You seem to care more than I do. We'll have one, sooner or later."

I recalled a lesson from the philosophy professor, who had emphasized that weddings and funerals were for others, not the individuals involved. He even mused about having his funeral before he passed, so he could hear the most beautiful eulogy in the world.

George chuckled and declared himself "somebody" after hearing this.

I shared a funny anecdote about asking the professor what he'd wear to our wedding, to which he jokingly replied, "Perhaps, I will put on nothing."

George burst into laughter, exclaiming, "No wonder you like him so much."

Since our engagement, George had become more carefree and joyful. Laughter now echoed through the house, and he engaged in playful antics, displaying a mischievous side. He even attempted to learn some Chinese in preparation for our dinner with the Chinese couple.

While George was fluent in several languages, he struggled with the tones in Chinese. His attempts at "How are you?" and "Welcome" had me on the verge of laughter. Despite my exasperation, he was genuinely proud of his pronunciation.

George explained, "They're coming to our house as guests. If the host can speak their mother tongue, they'll feel at home, right?"

I realized the significance of this and agreed to teach him again, starting with their Chinese names. However, his pronunciation turned my friend's

我说，要么早一点办了，要么等孩子出生以后。大肚子新娘多难看。

乔治说，现在天冻地裂，绝不能让你出意外。

我说，其实，请朋友来家里玩玩，不要把婚礼看得太严肃。我是不在乎的。

你不在乎吗？乔治怀疑地看着我。

真的不在乎，我已经得到太多了。

婚礼是不能不办的。

你比我在乎得多。我说，办一个吧！早晚得办一个。

我想起了哲学教授曾经在课堂里讲，婚礼和葬礼都是为别人办的，不是为自己。他说，人可以逃避婚礼，但逃不了死亡。他希望自己的追悼会开在断气以前，听完了世界上最美丽的赞词再离开人间。

乔治听后笑了，说他确实是个不同寻常的角色。

我说，给他打电话的时候，问他，如果参加我的婚礼，你将穿什么衣服？他说，也许什么都不穿。

乔治“哈哈哈”大笑，说道，难怪你这么喜欢他。

乔治的笑声越来越多，越笑越放肆，有时候，整栋楼都能听见。深沉老练，文质彬彬的乔治，在笑声中消失了。他和我打打闹闹，和柯丽丝抢玩具，从厨房里偷东西吃，简直顽皮得像孩子一样。这栋古老的房子，越来越在他的笑声中变得年轻。

圣诞节前的一个周末，我的中国朋友夫妇应邀来我家吃晚饭。乔治临时抱佛脚，想学几句中国话。

我以前教过他说“你好”，“欢迎”。他对四声毫无感觉，每个字到了他那里都成了第四声。他把“你好”说成“逆耗”，把“欢迎”说成“混硬”。笑死我不算，他还自以为说得很好，差点儿把我这中文老师活活气死。乔治说德文，法文，西班牙文，都非常流畅，他哪里知道中文与其它语言的区别？如果我听不懂他的中文，还有谁能听懂呢？

我说，乔治，他们生活在美国，能用英语和你交流，就不要说中文了吧！

不，他说，你不了解人的心理。他们到我们家来作客，如果主人能说几句他们的家乡话，意味着宾至如归，对不对？

他说得如此认真，我不教他也说不过去。我想起，我们刚来美国，大概也是这样的吧！对于我们的洋泾帮，美国人是不是像我一样，又好气又好笑，又不能不为我们的认真而感动。学习外国话不容易，接受外国人更不容易。美国接受了那么多不同种族和肤色的外国人，是何等宽阔的胸怀！我想，如果他坚持要学，我再教他一次试试，也许能有进步。

我说，你从哪里学起呢？

他说，从他们的中国名字学起，可以吗？

好吧！我说，男的叫“王达”。你能说“王达”吗？

王达被他说成了“What（王）”“Duck（鸭子）”。结果我的

name, Wang Da, into "What Duck." I couldn't contain my laughter and had to step outside.

George followed, concerned about the cold, and urged me to come back in. He looked so serious, I couldn't help but continue laughing.

He gently lifted me and guided me back inside, asking, "Did I say it wrong? Why didn't you correct me? Why did you go to the backyard?"

Through my laughter, I managed to explain, "You pronounced it wrong. It's not 'What Duck.' Let's not continue. Can't you just call him Mr. Wang?"

George inquired, "What's his real name then?"

"It's Wang Da."

He repeated, "Wung Dai."

I pleaded, "Let's stop. I can't stop laughing, I have no strength left."

George chuckled and asked, "Why are you laughing so much? Are you going on strike?"

I implored, "George, I'm exhausted. Can I rest for a while, please?"

When our Chinese friends arrived, George greeted them in his casual attire, which might have seemed a bit unusual for a host. I imagined that if I were a guest arriving at this grand "castle" and saw him at the door, I might have mistaken him for a worker. However, once I introduced George as my husband, he approached Mrs. Wang and gave her a warm hug, causing her to blush in surprise. Thankfully, he refrained from speaking Chinese, sparing himself any potential embarrassment with mispronunciations.

As we sat in the living room, George engaged in a conversation about Chinese cuisine, discussing soy sauce, sugar, tea, and mushoo pork. Mrs. Wang smiled and observed every detail around her, while Mr. Wang remained silent, his eyes darting around like he was sending a telegraph.

I could almost picture the telegraph in his mind: What's going on? When Susu was with this man, she said they weren't married. Will they apply for her green card? She didn't have a diamond ring then. When she was with that man, did she mention a wedding? The American man didn't deny it, and now Susu has the ring. Are there two weddings in this story?

Just then, Kristeene woke up, and Helen brought her downstairs. Kristeene had already started calling me "Mom" or "Mom Susu." She mentioned wanting to play the piano and climbed onto George's lap. She was full of energy in front of our guests, seeking all the attention. When I asked if she remembered our dinner at the restaurant, she shook her head.

I couldn't help but wonder if Mr. Wang's interpretation of events was getting even more complicated with Kristeene's sudden appearance. It reminded me of the American press and the two political parties, always seeing things from their own perspectives. Now, I understood that under different logics,

朋友变成了“什么鸭子”。

我差一点笑疯了，拔腿就跑，跑到了后院，抱着一颗大树，捏紧了拳头，一边笑。一边使劲地捶。

乔治跟了出来，喊道，外面这么冷，赶快进来！我回头，看到他那认真的样子，又忍不住大笑。

他跨着大步走来，一把抱起我，驼在肩膀上，进了客厅。一边说，我说错了吗？你为什么不帮助我纠正？你跑到后院去干什么？

我说，你念错了，不是“What Duck”。不要学了。你就不能喊他“王先生”吗？

他一本正经地问，那他究竟叫什么名字？

我说，王，达 。

他说，噢，叫“忘，大”。

我说，别学了，别学了，我笑不动了。

你为什么要笑？他说，还要罢工？

乔治，我累了。我求他，让我休息一会儿，好吗？

中国朋友夫妇来访问的时候，乔治穿了一件花格子的薄绒针织衫，下着牛仔裤，脚上是一双高帮旅游鞋。如果我是客人，走进如此豪华的城堡，看见他来开门，很容易误认他是个工作人员。可是，他却在我介绍王太太了以后，上前就是一个拥抱，把人家吓得满脸通红。我暗暗庆幸他忘了说中文，否则“忘大”“枉大”地乱叫，真不知道还要闹出什么样的笑话来。

我说，这是乔治，我的丈夫。

王达往后退了一步，犹犹豫豫地把手伸出来。乔治一把握住，嘴里说，老朋友老朋友，我们在餐馆见过面。我记得你，你不会忘记吧！说完也是一个拥抱。到了这个地步，王达像掉了魂一样，眼珠子在我和乔治之间像机器人一样扫来扫去，好像走错了地方。

我们坐到了客厅里，乔治七搭八搭地说酱油糖茶，木须猪肉等中国菜。王太太满脸笑容，把客厅的各个角落都细细地看来了一遍，嘴里说着一些别人都听不清楚的话。王达闭口不言，不停地眨眼睛，好像在给谁发电报。我想像着他的那份电报：这是怎么回事呢？和这个男人在一起的时候，素素不是说，没有结婚，他们给办绿卡吗？那个时候，手上并没有钻石戒指啊！和年轻男人在一起的时候，素素不是说，要办婚礼吗？那个美国人并没有否认啊！素素是带着钻戒的，难道这里 介入了两场婚姻吗？这些问题还没有得到解答，乔治却超越式地把我怀孕的事情捅了出来。

夫妻俩的惊奇的目光霎时都集中到了我的身上。一连串的问号，都写在他们的脸上。

王达有了新的版本：这会儿，那个年轻的美国男人成了情人。素素在怀上了乔治的孩子以后，继续与情人约会。

柯丽丝醒了，被海伦抱到了楼下。柯丽丝已经改口叫我妈咪或者妈咪素素。她一会儿说要弹钢琴，一会儿爬到乔治身上，在客人面前很不安分，只怕我们不注意她。

我问她是否还记得在中国餐馆吃饭？她摇摇头。

the same truth could transform from black to white, from night to day.

I said to Kristeene, "Alright, my dear, let's enjoy a classic Chinese children's song." I played it on the piano, singing along:

"Seek and seek, I find a good friend, Salute and shake hands, you are my good friend. Seek and seek, I find a good friend, Salute and shake hands, you are my good friend."

Kristeene's joy knew no bounds whenever music graced her ears. She stomped her tiny feet and tapped her heels, arms swaying with the rhythm. Her hands floated in the air like a carefree bird in flight. Mrs. Wang, captivated by this little whirlwind, couldn't resist joining in. They saluted and shook hands, laughter and claps filling the room.

As if waking from a dream, Wang Da turned to George, remarking, "This is a cherished childhood tune - 'Find a Good Friend.'" It finally clicked for George, who rose with a salute and a handshake, leaving Wang Da chuckling.

This impromptu dance served as an introduction to George's playful nature and Kristeene's innocent charm. The evening progressed with lively conversation. Betty had prepared succulent prime steak ribs, marinated with a medley of spices and pepper the day prior. After roasting and keeping them warm, the dish emerged - a ten-pound marvel, bronzed and crisp on the outside, tender and blushingly pink within, a true culinary delight.

Wang Da shared that in their two-plus years in America, they had stuck to Chinese cuisine, never venturing beyond. The savory beef was an uncharted territory for them, particularly for Mrs. Wang, cautious of the lingering traces of blood. Wang Da gallantly took on the role of tasting on her behalf, while Betty thoughtfully served Mrs. Wang a bloodless portion. "America offers such a vast array of beef varieties," mused Mrs. Wang, struggling to discern them all. George, ever the gracious host, embarked on an impromptu bovine anatomy lesson. Whether the finer points were fully grasped remained a mystery, but nods of intent attention prevailed.

As the evening drew to a close, George, in his customary kindness, arranged for leftover beef and cake, along with two bottles of white wine, for the couple to take home. Mrs. Wang leaned in and whispered, "Susu, you are blessed to have such a wonderful husband." Warm handshakes and heartfelt embraces sealed the evening, with Mrs. Wang no longer holding back, allowing George to hug and gently kiss her cheek.

半路上杀出来一个柯丽丝，王达的版本是不是更变得扑朔迷离？这可不是道听途说，而是真切切的亲眼目睹啊！

我连想到美国的媒体和两大政党，整天吵吵闹闹的，公说公有理，婆说婆有理。现在我才明白了，同样的事实，在不同的逻辑下，可以黑夜变成白昼。

我说，好吧，妈咪弹一首中国的儿童歌曲给你听。我一边唱一边弹琴。

找呀找呀找朋友，找到一个好朋友，

敬个礼呀，握握手呀，你是我的好朋友。

找呀找呀找朋友，找到一个好朋友，

敬个礼呀，握握手呀，你是我的好朋友。

再见。

柯丽丝听到音乐就要跳舞。她一边蹬着脚尖脚跟，一边舞起手臂，两只小手就像小鸟一样，飞上飞下。王太太爱极了这个孩子，情不自禁地去和柯丽丝跳舞。王太太向小姑娘敬礼握手，两人一边击掌一边跳。

这时，王达像睡醒了似的，缓过神来对乔治说，这是我们儿童年代的流行歌曲，题目叫“找到一个好朋友”。乔治听懂了意思以后，马上站立起来，向王达敬个礼，握握手，惹得王达哈哈大笑。

这场意外的舞蹈，至少让他们了解了乔治的幽默性格和柯丽丝的天真可爱。所以，到了晚餐的时候，王达的话就多了起来。蓓蒂给大家烤了Prime ribs。昨天就用各种香草料和胡椒粉腌了一晚上。今天上午放进烤箱，烤完后闷在里面，一直到晚餐前才加热。近十磅重的大块牛肉，上桌的时候，外面焦黄香脆，里面半生半熟，呈粉红色，鲜嫩如琼膏一般。

王达说，他们来美国两年多，从来没有去西餐馆吃饭，一生没有见过如此美味的牛肉。王太太见到牛肉的血汁不敢吃，王达把太太的那份也吃了。蓓蒂另外切了外层的牛肉给王太太。王太太说，美国的牛排种类太多，永远也搞不清楚。于是，乔治便从牛身体的各个部位说起，一种一种给他们解释。我怀疑他们是否听懂。但是，他们却不停地点头，表示了专心致志的态度。

离开我们家的时候，乔治关照蓓蒂把剩下的牛肉和蛋糕全部让他们带回家。还送了两瓶白葡萄酒。

王太太在我的耳边说，素素，你好福气啊，嫁了这么一个好老公。王达主动和乔治握手拥抱告别。王太太也不怕难为情了，被乔治搂着并在脸上重重地亲了一下。

Chapter 34

George and I agreed that we would have a wedding sooner or later, but something more important came up.

During Christmas, I ended up catching a cold. I would stay up all night coughing, and worst of all, the cough medicine didn't seem to work at all. I was afraid that my constant coughing would disturb George's sleep, so I spent my nights in the guest room. George, being the considerate man that he was, worried that no one would be taking care of me. He was so worried, in fact, that he insisted on laying next to me (even though I tried to convince him otherwise).

My coughing was a problem for a while now. Even back in China, there was a time when I couldn't stop coughing for about three months. In fact, when I went to college, I would attend class with my horrendous cough! Even the professor couldn't bear to witness my miserable condition and would ask my classmates to help me back to my dormitory.

It took months to realize that healing my chronic cough could only occur through natural means, and I learned that medicine was of no use for me. I tried to drink more water while eating less unhealthy foods, hoping that George wouldn't worry too much about me. I only had one wish: to never hurt the baby in my belly.

Now, in the peak of night, I was unable to sleep. As I quietly crept out of bed and toward the bathroom, I noticed that I wasn't feeling… Quite right. When I looked in the mirror, I noticed that my crotch area was red and bloodied. I involuntarily shouted, and before I knew it, George rushed to my side while fighting to keep his eye open.

However, it didn't take long before his eyes widened and he took action. At the speed of light, George wrapped me in a blanket, ran around, and drove me to the emergency room in the middle of the night. His whole body-- lips, teeth, hands-- was trembling, and his voice became soft and inaudible.

I stayed in the hospital for two days and two nights. During this time, George never left my side. The doctor diagnosed me with mild asthma, and assured the two of us that the baby was just fine.

Although the situation was anything but dire, it had a major impact on George. When I woke up the next morning, he had already made the decision to reorganize his whole life. When I asked him about it, he froze and insisted that he was not prepared to tell me his plans right away.

第三十四章

我们说好了早晚要办一个婚礼，没想到发生了更重要的事情。

圣诞节前夕，我不小心着凉咳嗽，咳得通宵不睡，医生开的处方药一点不管用。乔治急得走投无路，不知道应该睡在哪里。我怕影响他的睡眠，要去客房睡。他怕我没人照顾，坚持躺在身边。

这是我的老毛病，在中国也是一咳就停不住，时间长达三个月左右。记得上大学时，一边咳一边去上课，老师不忍目睹我的惨状而停止讲授，请同学扶我回宿舍。后来我发现，那是一个自然愈合的过程，吃药没有用，多喝水少消耗，两三个月，咳嗽就走了。我断断续续地告诉乔治，希望他不要太紧张，太揪心，这个病需要时间。我不停地喝水吃药，不停地上厕所，腹部肌肉被咳得又酸又痛，心里只有一个愿望，千万不要伤着了肚子里的宝贝。结果还是发现裤裆“见红”，抽水马桶里也是一滩血水。当时他在睡梦中，我蹑手蹑脚去厕所，不想吵醒他。关上门，一阵大咳。当我看到鲜血时，不由自主地喊了他的名字。乔治冲进厕所，眼睛都没有完全睁开。一滩血让他顿时变成救美女英雄，不顾一切地为我裹上毯子，连奔带跑到车库，半夜开车送我去看急症。他的嘴唇，牙齿，双手，全身都在颤抖，说话的声音变得模模糊糊，听不清楚。我住了两天医院，整整睡了两天两夜，他一直陪在身边。医生诊断我有轻微的哮喘病，一用激素马上见效。出血止住了，孩子没问题。这件事给乔治很大冲击，等我醒来，他已经做出重新规划生活的决定。

他没有准备立刻把计划告诉我。直到圣诞节后的那个周末，吃

Until that fateful weekend, after he gave his post-dinner good night wishes to Kristeene. That night, he ate his dinner quickly-- too quickly-- and I couldn't help but notice that both his expression and smile seemed strange.

"Mommy isn't feeling too well. Can you read by yourself tonight?" George had asked Kristeene. She glanced at me, a hint of concern in her eyes, but nodded quickly. At her gesture, George went upstairs in a hurry.

I didn't know what to do, but I decided to follow him. Unsure of whether or not he wanted to be alone, I stood at the top of the stairs, waiting for George to speak.

He finally gathered himself and looked at me. "I'm going to light the fire now, my dear. Come sit with me." He said, turning around to face the fireplace.

I took a moment to really look at the furnace. We had placed a large piece of lambskin on the floor. The wool was dense and soft, making it very comfortable to lie on. Lighting the fireplace felt like a strange occasion, as normally, we only lit it when guests came over.

George squatted down, put some mixture of sawdust and wax on the iron shelf, stuffed some old newspapers underneath, and with the sound of a fleeting "whoosh", the flames came up. It reminded me of how something as primal as making fire has been given a romantic meaning by modern people, something that our ancestors could not have imagined.

George added some wood to the fire, closed the glass door, and finally sat down beside me. I shifted to make room for him to lie down and opted to rest my head on his shoulder. None of us spoke as we glanced at the tongues of fire licking up and down.

It started to get warm. George noticed this and swiftly stood up. "Let me turn down the wind control switch," he said. Just as he leaned forward to touch the switch, a document fell out of his back pocket.

The document was folding in half. I picked it up, spread it out, and read it, only to find that it was a plan to sell the trading company that George was so involved in.

'He wants to sell the business?' I thought to myself, confused.

When George was finished, he turned to me. He stayed calm as he noticed the document in my hand, seeming to wait for me to ask him about it.

The more I thought about it, the less I was surprised. Since we had gotten engaged, George's heart moved closer to home. Just as I had given up my studies, he was willing to give up his career.

"Are you really willing to give it up? The company is a cornucopia with decades of your hard work poured into it," I finally broke the silence.

George paused and pursed his lips. "Susu, what kind of life do you want when we have a child? I don't want anything but a stable life," he said calmly. "What else could we possibly want? We have everything we need. A castle with a bunch of servants, a collection of cars, airplanes, and more... We have a wealthy life that I couldn't have even dreamed of when I was a child," he finished softly.

"I see what you're saying," I replied. "There's nothing else that we want."

"Should we want what we don't have?" He asked. I knew it was rhetorical, but let him continue. "What don't we have?" George glanced at the large

完晚饭，他与柯丽丝道了晚安，说要到客厅去坐一会儿。我们平时都是到三楼看一会儿书，说说话，然后上床。那顿晚餐，他吃得很快，表情有点异常，微笑不自然。

他问女儿，妈咪有点不舒服，今晚你能自己看书吗？柯丽丝看看我，眼神中藏着一丝忧虑，不过点头点得很快，一溜烟上楼了。

我站在楼梯口，等他说话。是他要自去客厅还是要我陪着？

亲爱的，我去点炉火，你来坐一会儿吧！他回过头来说。壁炉前面的地上铺了一大块羊羔绒皮，有长沙发的尺寸。羊毛绵密柔软，躺在上面很舒服。我们平时很少烧木材，只有来客人时，才把壁炉点起来。他蹲下，在铁架子上放了些木屑和蜡块的混合物，旧报纸塞在底下，"呼"的一下，火焰往上冒。原始的取火方式被现代人赋予浪漫的意义，古人怎么也料想不及。

乔治把木桩加进火堆，关上壁炉的玻璃门，便在我旁边坐下来。我挪了挪身体，腾出地方让他躺下，我的头枕在他的肩膀上。望着东舔西蹿的火舌，我们都没有说话。空气干哄哄的，开始热起来。乔治起身说，我把控风开关调小一点。就在他倾身去摸那个开关时，上衣口袋里掉出一份文件。文件一折为二，我拣起来，摊开一看，是出售贸易公司的计划。他要把生意卖掉？我怀疑地瞅着他。他的神情却因为我手里拿着那份文件，而变得坦然一些。他好像在等我问他，不急着做出解释。其实，我倒不觉得惊奇，他的心越来越多地放在家里，就像我放弃学业一样，他在放弃自己的事业。

你舍得？公司是一个聚宝盆啊，有你几十年的心血。

他没有直接回答，反问我，素素，等你生下孩子，你要什么样的生活？

我什么都不要，只要生活安定。

我们还要什么？该有的，我们都有了。

是啊，我们住在城堡里，有一群佣人。我们不仅收藏汽车，还有飞机，我做梦都没有想到的富裕生活。我们什么都不要。

他说，我们没有的，该不该要？

什么是我们没有的呢？

chunks of wood that were burning to ashes in the furnace. "It's like… These logs. What else do we need before they burn out completely?"

"Why did you sell the company?" I asked.

He gently took the document from my hands and smiled, his eyes becoming clear and tender. My shoulders instinctively relaxed; it was nice to see him smile so genuinely again. "I want to raise a group of children with you."

"There's no need to sell the company, though."

"But I want to stay at home," he responded.

"And help me take care of the kids?"

"Yes."

"Do you want to retire early?"

George paused, the smile still lingering on his face. "I do," he said softly. "In fact, Susu, we should move. Why don't we?"

"Move? Move where? Are you going to sell this castle, too?" I asked. I couldn't wrap around his change in attitude. However, he nodded again at my questions. "Why leave? Don't you have so many memories here?"

"Let our children be born in the embrace of nature," George replied.

To be honest, I had never really thought about where our children should be born. "But aren't castles nice? Plus, this castle had a garden-- wasn't that nature?" I asked curiously.

"I just think the castle is too big and life is a bit too luxurious," George quipped. "Why don't we look at some houses in the next few days, and if you like any, we'll move. How about that?"

I agreed, and soon enough, the time came to look at some new properties. However, I wasn't expecting us to house-hunt hundreds of feet in the air.

To my surprise, our little property-hunting adventure was led by Danny, who flew the plane. At our first destination, we were all granted a lovely view from above, bearing witness to hundreds of acres of land, mountains, water, stables, flat greenery, and dense forests. I was in awe, but somehow, George didn't seem phased.

As we landed, I thought about the previous conversation I had with George. Moving seemed to have been a dream for him, but I didn't understand the motivation behind it.

As we stepped foot off the plane, I took some time to intake the scenery. Every time I walked toward the nature in front of me, I realized that nothing was obstructing my sight. It felt like you could see beyond the horizon.

I shouted George's name into the empty valley, taking note of the beautiful resonant echoes the topography granted us. It was like a beautiful billowing symphony, as sweet as it could possibly be.

At my shout, George hollered my name back. His voice was so soul-stirring that it moved me to tears. We quickly hugged each other, neither of us wanting to leave or return to the castle that we previously called home.

I felt as though I had matured from a naive child to an adult, simultaneously taking part in George's simple yet meaningful dream. It turned out that his dream was also mine; I wanted our children to be born in the embrace of nature. It took about four months for George to sell his company and his castle, and by then, I was already walking with a hand on my swollen belly.

火炉里大块大块的木头正在烧成灰烬。他说，我们就像这些木头，在烧完之前，还有什么遗憾的事情？

你卖掉公司是为了什么？

他接过文件，笑了笑。那是真实的微笑，如释重负的表情浮上他的嘴角。眼神在笑意中变得清澈温柔。他说，我要一群孩子。

那也没有必要卖掉公司。我说，你想留在家里。帮我带孩子？我们有保姆。

他说，不一样的。

你想提前退休？

是，我们搬家吧，素素！

搬家？搬到哪里去？你想把城堡也卖掉吗？

他点点头。

为什么要离开祖传的城堡？

乔治说，让我们的孩子出生在大自然的怀抱中。

城堡难道不好吗？城堡也有花园，不是大自然吗？

他沉默了一会儿，等待我把所有的疑问都说完。炉火在缓缓地暗下来。我们俩都不说话。

等你咳嗽好一点，我带你去看一个地方。说完，他站起来，拉着我的手说，去休息吧。

我没有想到，这个地方是要坐飞机去的，是从空中鸟瞰大地，在几百亩土地的上空绕圈子。有山有水，有马厩有牛棚，有平坦的绿地，有茂密的森林。

乔治说，你喜欢吗？如果我们住在这里？

我没有回答。他好像也不在乎我的意见。过几天，又去了另一个地方，乔治都没有看中。

每一次外出，每一次走向宽旷无际的大自然，视线无阻无挡，延伸到天地相接的地平线，我喜欢对着空谷喊一声“乔治 ----”，顿时回声四起，好像滚滚声浪返回过来好像一支乐队的演奏，悦耳动听。

素素！乔治也喊，声声回肠荡气，感动得我热泪盈眶。我们拥抱着不想离开，不想回家。几个礼拜，我好像从幼稚的孩子一步一

George took his fancy on a hilly property beside a lake. The land wasn't extraordinarily big, stretching out for about one-hundred and twenty acres, but the house was lovely and was built on top of a hill. The sun, which constantly reflected off of the huge glass windows, felt like our next-door neighbor. At night, the moon and stars were easily visible, and the hill was so high that we could practically feel soft clouds under our feet.

Living on top of the mountain's hill was like entering heaven. Previously, it had been the property of a pair of retired construction experts. The main building was quite small with two floors. The lower floor was a public area while three bedrooms could be found upstairs. To my surprise, there was a solar installation on the roof and a sustainable water well outside.

Halfway up the hill was a small independent house. It doubled as both a library and a swimming pool. At the bottom of the hill lay a swimming pool, tennis court, and parking lot, as well as more than a dozen mountaineering vehicles. A winding mountain road wrapped around the top of the mountain, surrounded by various wildlife, grasslands, vegetable gardens, ponds, and orchards. A small guest house with two bedrooms lay at the foot of the mountain, containing many appliances needed for a kitchen, bathroom, and laundry machines. We considered this house suitable for Betty and Helen.

On the west side of the hillside, there was a cave. After opening the code-controlled iron door, you would find a large wine cellar that runs one hundred meters deep. After walking about fifty meters, there's an elevator that leads directly to the main building at the very top of the hill.

The previous owners of the property gave us all of the books and videos they had collected over the decades, and also gave away the remaining wine to local buyers. Their names were Peter and Mimi, and both were silver-haired yet energetic.

George and I hit it off with the elderly couple quite well. We drank their homemade beer, and sat in the sunshine only to talk for hours. Mimi told us that the property was designed to have a group of children and let them grow up in an environment curated by God. Unfortunately, after decades of marriage, Mimi and Peter didn't have a single child. Peter said that architecture is an art, but the price of art is the destruction of nature. The couple brought their shame into this hillside and wanted to atone for their sins with meticulous care.

At their story, George and I both found ourselves tearing up. We told them to let us carry their burdens, as we wanted to raise a group of children here. At our words, Mimi glanced down at my protruding belly and her eyes carried a hint of red, seeming to catch a glimpse of hope. She bent down, slightly trembling, put her ear on my stomach, and started crying.

"If you have a boy," she started. "Teach him how to ride a horse. If you have a girl, teach her how to grow vegetables. Let them learn to respect different lives and dedicate love from an early age."

I nodded.

After the elderly couple sold their property, they drove their RV on the last journey of their lives to bid a special farewell to the world. Soon after, we received two letters and some photos from them. The letter stated that they

步地成熟，一步一步地回归，一步一步地走进乔治的梦境。原来，这也是我的梦啊！

从出售他的公司到卖掉城堡，大约花了四个月的时间。我已经捧着肚子在走路了。乔治终于看中了湖边的的一片山坡，地并不很大，一百二十亩左右，房子造在山顶上。太阳好似隔壁邻居一样，在巨大的玻璃窗上爬上爬下。月亮和星斗好像镶在天花板上，我们脚下是柔软的云朵。住在山顶犹如进入天堂般一般，美得无以伦比。

那是一对退休建筑专家的房产。主楼很小，共两层，下层是公用场所，楼上有三个卧室。屋顶有太阳能装置，用的是水井。半山腰有一栋独立的小房子，里面无遮无拦，是图书馆兼电影院。山脚下是游泳池，网球场和停车场，还有十几辆登山运动车，一条弯弯曲曲的山道如纽带一般，绕到山顶。树林，草原，马厩，菜圃，池塘，果园，好像天生的兄弟姐妹，和睦相处。山脚下还有一栋两间睡房的小客房，里面厨房，厕所，洗衣机应有尽有，最合适给蓓蒂和海伦住。山坡的西面有一个山洞，打开密码控制的铁门后，是一个纵深一百米的大酒窖。再走五十米左右，有个电梯，直通山顶的主楼。他们把几十年收藏到书籍和影片都送给我们，也把剩余的好酒一同赠送给买主。

老先生叫彼得，老太太叫咪咪，满头银发，精神矍铄，和我们一见如故。我们喝着他们自制的啤酒，坐在客厅的阳光里，一聊就是几个小时。

咪咪说，整个设计就是为了有一群孩子，让他们在上帝设计的环境中长大。可惜，结婚几十年，我们一个孩子都没有。

彼得说，建筑专业本身就是艺术，但是，艺术的代价是对大自然的破坏。他们把惭愧带进这片山坡，以精心的照料来赎罪。

我和乔治都听得泪流满面。不约而同地说，我们要生养一群孩子，让我们来实现你们的愿望。

咪咪看看我突起的肚子，眼睛红了，好像看到希望一样。她微微颤颤地弯下腰，耳朵贴在我的肚子上，竟然流出了眼泪。她说，如果你们有了男孩，要教会他骑马。有了女孩，要教她种菜。让他

both felt like "wandering children" who were heading toward their mothers' arms.

Two years later, we received the tragic notification that they had both passed. At this time, we were also caught up with the birth of our first child, deemed "Little George". George thought that Little George was an accident or a gift from God. However, I unexpectedly became pregnant again shortly after giving birth. Because of this, I gave birth to two boys in two years, and the second child was named Bruce. Three years later, little Amy was born, and Kristeene had become a big sister to two younger brothers and a younger sister.

们从小懂得尊重不同的生命，懂得把爱奉献出来。

他们卖了房子以后，开着房车走上了人生最后的路程，向世界做特殊的告别。我们曾经收到两封信和一些照片。信中说，他们像流浪的孩子正在走向母亲的怀抱。两年后，我们收到一个通知，得知他们双双过世。

我们赶上了第一个孩子出生在这栋房子里，取名小乔治。乔治以为小乔治是意外，是上天给我们的礼物。没想到刚断奶，我又怀孕了，两年里生了两个男孩，第二个孩子叫布鲁斯。三年后，艾蜜问世，柯丽丝成了两个弟弟和一个妹妹的大姐姐。

Chapter 35

From then on, George became our family's "taxi driver", having the responsibility of picking up and dropping off the children in both the mornings and evenings. He would also take the whole family into the city on weekends to visit museums, buy daily necessities, or attend markets to sell his agricultural products.

Meanwhile, I played as the family counselor. When I came back home from school, I was half-concentrated in the library and would do my homework first. Then, I would return home and play ball, swim, and do farm work with the children.

Every morning, assuming the weather was good, our family would walk down the mountain trail together. After sending the children down the hill, George would then drive them to school. I would then bring Amy back to the top of the hill via the elevator in the west cave. Betty and Helen both lived at the bottom of the mountain and helped with household chores, and we hired two daytime employees to help out during the busy season.

Meanwhile, Danny now works as a flight instructor for an airline and has a family. On the other hand, I'm still always in touch with Charlie and Lisa. Charlie now lives with a beautiful Malaysian girl. Lisa is still single and works as a supervisor at a computer company. Wang Da, Zhang Jie, and Wang Cheng returned to China to start their own businesses after studying, all of them focusing on international trade in food and agriculture.

Living with George has its ups and downs. We have many differences and disagreements, spanning from political views to details in living. We are especially different when it comes to taste! In fact, it's often difficult for any of us to compromise. The children adapted quickly and like Chinese food very much. George, on the other hand? Not so much.

We also struggle a little with language barriers. I can understand English and George can understand some Chinese, but there have been many times when we will experience little miscommunications. Luckily, the United States is rather diverse and does not seek uniformity, so it's easier to work through these issues.

Our family eats Chinese food twice a week and western food three times a week. The other two times are flexible. Sometimes, we eat in restaurants in the city, and other times, we let the children cook regardless of whether the dish comes out tasty or not.

However, despite these differences, I wouldn't trade this life for anything in the world. In fact, life becomes rich and colorful because of differences!

第三十五章

从此，乔治成了我家的出租司机，早晚接送孩子，周末载着全家进城，或者游览博物馆，或者购买一些生活必需品，或者参加集市，出售自己的农产品。我是家庭辅导员。放学回来，集中在半腰上的图书馆，先做回家作业。然后，打球，游泳，干农活。每天清晨，只要天气好，我们全家在山道上走路。送孩子们到山下，乔治开他们去学校。我带艾蜜坐电梯回到山顶。

蓓蒂和海伦住在山脚下，帮助料理家事，我们还请了两名墨西哥短工来往于繁忙季节。丹尼在一家航空公司当飞行指导，已经成家立业。我和查理和莉莎始终保持着联系。查理与一个美丽的马来西亚姑娘同居。莉莎仍旧独身，在一家电脑公司当主管。王达和张洁完成学业后回国创业，做食品方面的国际贸易。

嫁给乔治，从政治观念到生活细节，有太多的差异和分歧，简直数不胜数。尤其在口味上，我们谁都难以让步。孩子们反而比他容易适应，非常喜欢中国菜。不仅食品，语言上，他们也能听懂一些中国话。好在美国是开放社会，不求一致。我们一周吃两次中餐，三次西餐，另外两次灵活，有时候在城里的餐馆吃，有时候让孩子来掌厨，不论好坏，都要吃下去。。

那是一个夏季的清晨，我们全家在山道上散步。艾蜜坐在童车里，其他孩子都跟着我们走。半夜一场雨，清洗了大地，万物生辉，山谷中横空架起两条彩虹。路边盛开的野花，错落有致，五彩缤纷。我摘了几朵，放在艾蜜手里。柯丽斯也采，揣在怀里，积少成多，回家插入花瓶。

我对乔治说，这个夏天好事不断啊！

哪些好事，妈咪？柯丽丝蹦蹦跳跳地问道。

爹地六十周岁的生日。

One summer morning, as we walked on the mountain path, Amy sat in the stroller while the other children trailed behind us. It had rained the previous night, sweeping away the dirt and making everything glimmer under the current sunlight. Two rainbows appeared in the valley, and wildflowers bloomed alongside the road, making the scene even more magical. I picked a few flowers and placed them in Amy's hand. Kristeene picked some too, kept them tightly bound in her hand, and when she got home, she arranged them in a beautiful vase.

"Good things are happening this summer, aren't they?" I quipped to George, sighing contentedly.

"What good things, Mommy?" Kristeene asked with her big, round eyes.

"Daddy's sixtieth birthday is coming up," I mentioned.

"Sixty years old?!" Kristeene gasped in disbelief. "Daddy, are you really sixty years old?"

"Sixty is a really big number!" Bruce exclaimed, counting on his fingers.

"Daddy is old," George explained with a chuckle. "If I hadn't met your mother, you wouldn't have this dad."

Amy peeked up shyly. "Happy birthday to you," she muttered quietly. George laughed and thanked her, stroking Amy's hair.

"Mommy, my birthday is in the summer too," Kristeene mentioned.

"Yes, and you will be ten years old!" I replied. At my words, George mentioned that this year was also the tenth anniversary of me coming to the United States.

"Sixty years old, ten years old, tenth anniversary..." Bruce trailed off, still using his hands to count all of the upcoming events.

"Wait, wedding anniversary?" Kristeene said softly. Out of a sudden, all of the children seemed to perk up as they glanced at each other and at their parents.'

"What does it mean to get married?" The children asked in unison.

George and I couldn't help but laugh a little. However, after a brief pause, George came up with an answer. "Getting married is when a man and a woman prepare to start a family and become parents."

"Mom, can I marry you?" Little George asked innocently!

"I wanna marry Daddy!" Amy exclaimed.

Then, Kristeene piped in. "When can I get married?"

The children all started talking and asked questions excitedly. "Don't worry, don't worry," I said casually. "Don't worry about it until you're all older."

George smiled. "This conversation reminds me of something. Now, I want to show you all something when we get home."

"What is he talking about, Mommy?" Little George asked, tugging at my sleeve.

I shrugged. "I have no idea," I said.

"Can you give us a clue?" Kristeene asked her father. George shook his head playfully, saying that he couldn't in the name of confidentiality.

When we got home, the children eagerly sat upright, as if they were in a school classroom. They watched as their father took out a box. My eyes widened slightly. Those were our wedding invitations.

The children rushed forward, pointing to the elaborately-drawn clowns and angels on each invitation. They stared at me, then at their father, and

六十岁？柯丽丝说，爹地，你有六十岁吗？

布鲁斯一边走，一边数着自己的手指头，一边自言自语地说，六十岁，是个很大的数字啊！

乔治说，爸爸老了，要不是遇到你们的妈妈，你们就没有这个爸爸啦。

艾蜜轻声轻语地说，Happy Birthday to You（祝你生日快乐）！

谢谢，宝贝！乔治揉着艾蜜的头发说。

柯丽斯说，妈咪，我的生日也在夏天。

是啊，你今年十岁了。

乔治说，今年也是妈咪来美国十周年。

布鲁斯说，六十岁，十岁，十周年。

我说，在中国，十年要大庆。

还有呢，乔治说，我们结婚十周年。

结婚是什么意思？孩子们异口同声地问。乔治想了想说，结婚就是一个男人和一个女人，准备成立家庭，准备做爸爸妈妈。

小乔治问，妈妈，我可以和你结婚吗？

艾蜜说，我要和爸爸结婚。

柯丽丝问道：我什么时候才能结婚呢？

孩子们七嘴八舌，争先恐后地问。

乔治说，一个男人和一个女人，不能多不能少。回家后我要给你们看一样东西。

妈咪，什么东西？小乔治拉拉我的衣角，轻轻地问。

我不知道。

爹地，给我们一点线索好吗？柯丽丝说。

保密。乔治摇摇头。

到了家，孩子们正襟危坐，好像在教室里上课一样，一脸期待和盼望的神态。乔治拿出一个盒子。一看到盒子，我就明白了，那是我们的婚礼请柬。孩子们一哄而上，指着卡片上的小丑和天使，一会儿看看我，一会儿看看爸爸，一连串的问题。这时，只见柯丽丝一根手指挡在唇前，“嘘”------，她说，我知道，这是爹地和妈咪的婚礼请柬，本来要开盛大的派对，因为你，你，你，她指着弟弟妹妹说道，没有开成。

你怎么知道？乔治打断问。

蓓蒂告诉我的。

started asking questions rapid-fire style.

Finally, Kristeene put a finger in front of her lips. "Shh," she said. "This is Mommy and Daddy's wedding invitation! There was going to be a grand party, but…" She paused. "They couldn't because of you, you, and you," she pouted, pointing to each of her younger siblings.

"Wait, how do you know that?" George asked his daughter incredulously.

"Betty told me!"

"What else did Betty say?" Her father inquired.

"She said that the wedding would have to happen sooner or later. I heard there was going to be a party, and the atmosphere would be lively again."

"Do it today!" Bruce blurted out.

"Okay, I don't think that's possible," George admitted, chuckling. All the children booed at his response. George sighed. "Okay, why don't we celebrate a few good things together? As a family?" The children nodded.

"That's a good idea," I said in support. "Kristeene, you can be the supervisor. You can choose anyone as your assistant," I proposed. At my words, all three of Kristeene's little siblings raised their hands in excitement, trying to convince her to choose one of them.

"All right!" George exclaimed. "Starting today, you will spend a week arranging celebrations in the library. During the preparation period, no one else is allowed in there."

"Yay!" The children shouted in unison, all of them jumping in excitement.

That night, I placed the wedding invitations into envelopes. Many of them still had the names and addresses of the guests written on them!

I gingerly placed the last invitation on a frame and hung it on our shared bedroom wall. George stood at the window and looked at me silently. The dark night sky was behind him, with twinkling stars that complemented the silvery moonlight. I walked up to him and touched his cheek, analyzing the wrinkles at the corners of his eyes that traveled to his silver beard. George was old yet innocent and simple, similar to a big child. He smiled all day long.

I was also old. I was entering my middle-aged life, accompanied by an American man and a group of mixed children, repeating simple and ordinary days every day.

"Susu, are you happy?" George asked suddenly.

"Happy?" I was stunned. I was busy every day for the sake of our children and our family. "I can't say yet! But what about you, George? You're not like me. You lost your career, sold your castle, and now live in the mountains… Are you happy?" I asked.

"I am, Susu. This is the best time of my life." George's voice was soft and genuine. "I want to thank you, an angel sent by God, for making my life this perfect."

"...I do too," I responded. "When a couple loves each other and grows old together… Isn't that happiness?"

George nodded. We smiled and hugged each other, relishing in the mundanity of our perfect lives.

The End

蓓蒂还说什么？

她说，这个婚礼早晚要办的。

听说要开派对，气氛热闹起来。

今天就办。布鲁斯抓抓脑袋，脱口而出。

好！好！大家起哄。

这样好吗？乔治说，我们把几件好事办在一起庆祝，怎么样？

我说，柯丽丝，你当主管，可以选择任何人做你的助手。

另外三个孩子都把手举得老高，愿意当助手。

好吧！乔治说，从今天开始，你们用一个星期的时间，在图书馆安排庆祝活动。准备期间，别人都不准进去。

好！孩子们齐声高呼，欢奔乱跳。

那天晚上，我把婚礼请柬装进了一个个信封，不少信封上还写了客人的名字和地址呢！最后一张我装在一个镜框里，挂在卧室的墙上。

乔治站在窗前，默默地看着我。他的背后是深蓝色的夜空，星光闪烁，与银白的月色交相辉映。我走到他身边，抚摸他的脸颊，从眼角的皱纹到灰白的胡子。乔治老了，老得天真，老得单纯，好像一个大孩子，整天满面笑容。我也老了，年轻的素素正步入中年，伴着一个美国老头和一群混血的孩子，每天重复着简单平凡的日子。

素素，你觉得幸福吗？

幸福？我愣了一下，心里想，每天忙忙碌碌，为了孩子，为了这个家。要说我个人是否幸福，我还一时说不上来呢！

乔治，你幸福吗？你不是和我一样，丢掉了事业，卖掉了城堡，住进深山老林，你觉得幸福吗？

我愿意，素素。这是我一生中最美好的时光。我要感谢你啊，上帝派来的天使，你让我的生命获得完美。

我也愿意。夫妻相亲相爱，白头到老，不就是幸福吗？

我们相拥而笑。

（全书完）

About the English Editor:

Emili Hart is a current student at Washington State University who is pursuing her Professional Science Writing Certificate. She is extremely passionate for writing and has won awards for the subject, such as winning first place for the Washington State HOSA Happenings competition in high school (a medical newsletter-creation competition). While medical and nonfiction writing is Emili's specialty, she highly enjoys more creative endeavors such as creative writing and short stories. In her free time, you may find Emili on the piano, creating small trinkets and jewelry, and of course, writing more.

作者简介：

融融，1987年留学美国，她是新闻记者，小说家，专栏作家，出版长篇小说，散文集，游记，短篇小说集多部。美国西北华文笔会创始人。

About the Author:

Rong Rong came to the United States from Shanghai China in 1987 to study. She is a journalist, novelist, columnist, has published many novels, essay collections, travel notes, and short story collections. She is the founder of The American Northwest Chinese Writers Association.

Made in the USA
Middletown, DE
01 May 2025

75003611R00197